Nigel Lampard was a Lieutenant-Colonel in the British Army and after thirty-nine years of active service he retired in 1999. Trained as an ammunition and explosives expert, he travelled the world and was appointed an Order of the British Empire for services to his country. As a second career he helped British Forces personnel with their transition to civilian life, and finally retired in 2007, when he and his wife Jane moved to Leigh-on-Sea in Essex. Married for over forty years, they have two sons and four grandchildren.

Nigel started writing after a tour in Berlin in the early 1980s – he fell in love with what was then a walled and divided city. After leaving Berlin, the only way he could continue this love was to write about it. By the time he completed the draft for his first novel he was already in love with writing.

Also by Nigel Lampard

Pooh Bridge
Subliminal
The Loser Has To Fall
In Denial
Obsession

Naked Slaughter

Nigel Lampard

A Bardel Publication

Published by Bardel 2015
© Nigel Lampard 2008

Second Edition - Naked Slaughter

Cover designed by Bardel
Image provided by www.123RF.com

I would like to dedicate this novel to the residents of Upper Slaughter in Gloucestershire, England. I have visited their village on numerous occasions, but my very first visit sowed the seeds for the novel.

I stopped by the ford and the stone footbridge over the River Eye and looked up Church Lane. In my mind I saw Michael Griffiths going to post a letter for his mother and I saw Sarah and Phillip Preston looking longingly at Primrose Cottage.

To protect the anonymity of the residents of the village I have added some artistic licence by creating Primrose Cottage, Clifton House and other homes from my imagination, and Cress Coppice and its surrounding area has become Copper's Ridge.

The residents and visitors to the village are assured that all characters in this novel are fictitious.

Prologue

Michael waited.

They would be going out soon.

They always went out on a Friday evening. He didn't know where they were going but that didn't matter as long as wherever they were going kept them away for at least an hour.

That was all he needed, just an hour.

But if their previous nights out were anything to go by they would be gone for over three hours.

He checked his watch. It was ten minutes after eight.

Waiting wasn't a problem.

It wouldn't be long now.

He wondered if they would go through their normal routine. Everyone he watched had their routines: the couple he was watching were no different. Well, they were different but in other ways – very different and Michael knew just how different they were.

Through the window he saw her appear.

She was smiling and oblivious to the irritation she was causing her husband. He was still pacing to and fro across the living room as he had done for at least the last ten minutes. He always paced up and down while he was waiting, his frustration obvious. She was always late so why didn't he just delay his own readiness?

He would have said eight o'clock and she would be ready ten minutes later. Perhaps she did it deliberately to annoy him. Maybe he should have said they would leave at ten to eight when he actually meant eight and then he wouldn't have found it necessary to pace up and down.

They left by the back door.

They always did.

Then as usual, she suddenly remembered something and went back into the house. Also as usual, her husband lit a cigarette, blowing the smoke in a stream as he looked towards the darkening sky, his irritation becoming anger. It was always the same. He was ready ten minutes early and she was ready ten minutes late.

Michael waited.

She re-appeared, still smiling as she passed her husband in the doorway. Perhaps the smile confirmed she knew exactly what she was doing: perhaps it was her way of silently saying that she was always in control.

Michael had seen that smile before.

Neither husband nor wife had spoken. Everything was done in silence. There was no need for words when it was all a matter of routine.

They had their secrets. Or they thought they were their secrets.

They might look like any other couple when they were shopping, or out for a meal or even on the odd occasion when they went to the village church, but Michael knew their secrets too.

So they were their secrets but they were also his. He knew what they did when they were alone. He had often watched them and they never drew the curtains or dropped the blinds at the back of the house.

Their house was totally private at the back, wasn't it?

Michael gave them no reason to think otherwise. Their small garden backed onto woods so there was no need.

After she re-appeared for the second time they left in silence but not before her husband put the door key under the same stone on the back door step.

Michael smiled.

Just as there might not be a need for them to draw the curtains there also was no need to worry about where they hid the key.

For Michael they were just being considerate.

He waited another five minutes just in case they had forgotten something else. Sometimes she returned. A car engine started followed by a screech of tyres as it was driven away. That man, the husband, was angry.

After the five minutes were up, Michael went to the back door. He let himself in with his own key, took off his shoes just inside the door and listened. A clock was ticking and the fridge was making its usual buzzing noise but other than that, there was nothing.

He walked across the kitchen towards the hall, smiling again when he remembered visiting a number of other houses where the hall light was left on. It was supposed to be for security but for him it was very considerate of the people he visited without their knowledge.

Looking into the living room he saw that they were recording something on the video and the television was on standby.

Avoiding the third step, which he knew creaked, he went slowly up the stairs to their bedroom. He didn't know why he avoided the third step because no one was here but him to hear the creak.

He had been to this house on three previous occasions, and as with his previous visits, he wouldn't disturb or take anything – only touch.

Touching women's clothes gave him a real thrill and it made him feel quite powerful. He liked to smell the perfume they used.

In his mind, nothing he did was peculiar.

He opened the drawer he knew contained her underwear and put his hand inside, feeling the silkiness.

He smiled.

There was at least an hour.

They would never know.

Chapter One

Upper Slaughter was different.

From the moment Phillip turned the car off the main road towards the village Sarah felt they were entering another world, another age. She was too excited to speak and Phillip said nothing either, but she knew within minutes that the decision to live in Upper Slaughter was immediate and mutual.

With no more than a hundred or so houses, according to the travel brochure, Upper Slaughter was small enough to be called a hamlet. But with a church and a rather grand looking hotel, Sarah thought it was a village – a small village but nonetheless a village.

She pointed out to Phillip that the presence of the hotel, which went by the rather grand name *Lords of the Manor*, lifted the tone of the village, and accordingly the prices of property. She hadn't noticed a pub or a shop or a post-office but at the top of the village and just as they entered it from the west and before the small walled village green, she spotted an antiquated post-box set in a stone wall, and then not far away down Church Lane was an equally old-fashioned telephone box.

Just a few yards from this telephone box she saw a cottage. "Stop, Phillip, stop!" she shouted.

"Yes, I've seen it too," he said putting on the brakes.

The cottage was set at almost right angles to the lane with its front windows looking down a long and steep grassy slope towards a ford that was adjacent to a small stone footbridge. Two very large houses stood beyond the narrow river – which the map told them was called The River Eye –

11

and to the left was an equally grand looking dwelling. After leaving the ford the road curved away to the right towards some smaller but very attractive houses and cottages.

She looked at Phillip and he nodded, still saying nothing. He reversed the car back up Church Lane and parked by the village green. Hand in hand they walked back down the lane to the cottage.

An ornate wooden nameplate said *Primrose Cottage*. Sarah smiled as she saw that the short path leading to the front door was bordered on each side by masses of bright yellow primroses.

But it wasn't the flowers that set her heart pounding, it was a small *For Sale* sign fastened to one of the gateposts and it looked as though the previous owners had already moved out.

They stood hand in hand at Primrose Cottage for what must have been five minutes as they looked down towards the ford. They watched the smoke curling slowly skywards from the chimneys of the houses and cottages beyond. They also listened to the rooks cawing in the copse away to their left, and they sighed together in their mutual contentment.

A young man wearing a hooded top and carrying a letter in his hand walked up the lane towards them. They smiled at him and Sarah said, 'Hello'. He appeared very shy as he only responded with a slight nod of his head and without looking directly at them. Quickening his pace, he hurried away up the lane towards the post box they had seen.

After a few minutes and in silence, Sarah and Phillip walked back to their car.

"We're being watched," Phillip said as he peered in the rear-view mirror.

Sarah turned round and saw an old man leaning on a garden gate a few feet from the road, chewing on something and taking particular interest in their car. He could have been anything from sixty to eighty years old, she thought. His face looked weather beaten and his clothes seemed to match the age of the antiquated phone and post boxes they had seen. In his right hand he held a smouldering pipe.

"They probably don't get many townies around here," she suggested, passing Phillip a plastic cup of steaming coffee.

"Thanks." Phillip took a sip of the coffee. "Maybe not during the week and in early April, but I bet the tourists flock here during the summer."

"Are you trying to find a reason not to like it?" she asked, a slight smile giving away the fact that she was pulling his leg.

"Not at all," he replied with a shake of his head. "I must admit I do like what I see. It's … so peaceful."

"And the cottage?"

She stared through the windscreen, willing him to give her the reply she wanted.

He shrugged. "Hmm. It has a certain appeal, I suppose." He glanced sideways to see his wife's reaction, hiding his smile with the back of his hand.

As he sat drinking his coffee, Phillip Preston thought for the thousandth time how lucky he was to be married to Sarah. Only one thing was missing: they were both desperate to start a family but after ten years of marriage Sarah had not fallen pregnant.

With a sudden leap of hope in his chest he thought this delightful new environment might even change that.

With a secret smile he remembered their chance meeting – Sarah tripping inelegantly while rushing to the Crown Court in Gloucester from the chambers in which she worked as a legal secretary, and the sheer chance that he happened to be there to pick up the files she dropped. As he piled the files back into her arms he suggested on an impulse and because he liked what he saw, that they meet for a drink that evening. Although embarrassed by her clumsiness she accepted without hesitation and they were married two years later.

"What do you mean – a certain appeal? You loved it," Sarah said without fear of contradiction.

Phillip was still watching the old man in the rear-view mirror. "He's unnerving me," he said.

"Who is?"

"That man who's watching us."

She turned round again and looked back at the man.

"We're probably providing his daily entertainment. Anyway stop evading my question. The cottage?"

"I didn't realise you'd asked me a question. I thought you were making a statement."

He opened the car door and tipped the remains of his coffee onto the gravel. Sarah slapped him playfully on the shoulder.

"Come on, Phillip, tell me. You did like it, didn't you?"

"It's attractive, in a nice position, in an idyllic village, but the practicalities might present a few disadvantages."

"What practicalities and what disadvantages? We're no more than forty-five minutes from Gloucester and we're still young enough not to need a doctor within easy reach. All right, I admit there isn't a shop or a pub, well not that we've seen yet but we can do our shopping anywhere we like. And there's the hotel." She folded her arms defensively. "So what are these … disadvantages?"

Phillip traced the edge of the leather steering wheel with his index finger. "It might need thousands spending on it. Looking at the rest of the village, they seem to be living in the dark ages."

"That's part of its attraction," Sarah said. "If it needs thousands spending on it, we've *got* thousands to spend on it. I know it's different from what we're in at the moment but we need a change, Phillip." She stopped and lowered her voice. "We need a change and who knows what that change might bring."

He reached for her hand and stroked it gently.

"I was only joking, love. I'll give the agents a ring tomorrow and arrange a viewing."

She twisted round and faced him. "And you'd be doing that for us and not just for me?"

"I'd be doing it for us and for what it might bring us."

He leant over the handbrake and brushed his lips against Sarah's before turning the key in the ignition.

Gregory Woolmer watched the expensive looking black car leave the village green, the tyres kicking up gravel as it accelerated out onto the road.

He walked slowly back to his end-of-terrace cottage. His wife Grace was stirring a blackened pot on top of the range next to the kitchen window.

"What you been lookin' at?" she asked without turning round. Stupid question he thought as she must have known only too well that as usual he'd been watching people.

Gregory stood and watched people for hours. He didn't really have anything else to do.

He sat down at the table just inside the door. "A coupla outsiders," he said, picking up the matches to light his pipe.

"Lookin', was they?"

"Too closely. They's lookin' at Primrose Cottage. I don't think we're seen the last o' them two."

"Why're they any differen' to them others?" Grace asked, tapping the wooden spoon on the side of the pot, a smile on her face. "An' I wish you wouldn't smoke that damn thing in me kitchen."

Ignoring his wife's mild rebuke Gregory puffed even harder on his pipe. "I got a feelin' 'bout 'em. They's differen' to 'others," he said. "I smells trouble."

Sarah stood at the front bedroom window looking down towards the ford, still amazed that everything had happened so quickly.

They had viewed Primrose Cottage four days after finding it, put in an offer that same day which was accepted without the need for negotiation. As an offer had already been accepted on their own house there were no delays and here they were two months later as though they'd been here forever.

Unexpectedly Sarah had felt uneasy when viewing the cottage. She didn't say anything to Phillip because he would not have understood. Walking from room to room with Henry, the estate agent, Phillip had marvelled at its cleanliness and its readiness for occupation.

Overcome by her husband's enthusiasm, Sarah tried to hide her surprise. The previous owners, about whom Henry was somewhat evasive, were apparently a middle-aged couple, no children or pets as far as he knew and they were now living abroad. Primrose Cottage was therefore ready to move into straightaway.

Whoever the mysterious previous owners were, Sarah thought their taste was excellent. She loved the dark wooden beams and each room was stylishly decorated. The curtains and carpets contrasted well with the cream walls and the kitchen, family bathroom and en-suite bathroom to the main bedroom at the back of the cottage had all been refurbished.

The final touch was the small conservatory that led off the drawing room – not Sarah's or Phillip's description because they preferred *living room* – which gave easy access to a small but well-stocked rear garden.

"That'll do as my study," Phillip commented as he left the fourth bedroom. Sarah had already moved to the front of the cottage so his decision fell on deaf ears. Slightly miffed at being ignored, he joined Henry and Sarah in what he heard Sarah announce would be the guest bedroom.

"Is there a garage?" he asked as they stood at the window in the main bedroom.

"A converted barn," Henry explained, "over there behind those trees. Big enough for a good-sized car and a runabout, and there's a workshop above it."

"I suppose the only thing that's missing is a swimming pool and a Jacuzzi," Phillip suggested, as he slipped his arm round Sarah's slim waist.

"As you can see," Henry said, pointing down to the garden. "It's quite private and I'm sure planning permission for a pool wouldn't be a problem."

Phillip exchanged glances with Sarah and rolled his eyes. In his youthful naivety it was obvious Henry thought Phillip was being serious.

"What I can't believe is the asking price," he said. "I know it's probably a strange thing to say but it's considerably below what I'd have expected. Why hasn't it been snapped up ages ago?"

Sarah turned from the deep windowsill and waited for Henry's reply. She'd been on the point of asking the same question. She watched Henry as he thought through his answer.

"Well," he said slowly, "there've been other interested parties but we think the lack of facilities in the village has put some people off and others had young children. It's not really the place for young children."

"What on earth makes you say that?" Sarah shot at him. "I'd have thought it was perfect."

Henry looked embarrassed. "Well that's what I've been told. This isn't one of my properties, but Samantha is away on holiday and ... and I was the only one available today."

"So," Phillip said, shaking his head slightly as he tried to tell Sarah not to say anything, "if we were to offer, say three and a quarter, what do you think our chances would be?"

"Is that a formal offer, sir?" Henry asked hesitantly.

This time Phillip looked at Sarah for confirmation and she nodded.

"Yes, that's a formal offer."

"I'll leave you to look around a bit more and I'll go into the garden and call the office," Henry said.

17

Sarah shivered. It was a warm day outside but the cottage, although it had oil-fired central heating, was quite chilly. But it wasn't that sort of shiver. It was more of a premonition sort of shiver.

She dismissed the thought as quickly as it arrived.

"Well?" she asked tentatively, reaching for Phillip's hand.

He looked down at her. "I'm not sure where we're going to get the balance from but my offer was serious."

"You like it?"

"I love it, Sarah."

"I do too, but only if you're sure. It won't need the thousands spending on it we thought might be necessary."

Phillip bent down and held her face between his hands.

"We're going to be very happy here and when I say *we* I mean more than just you and me." He kissed her gently.

Her eyes began to water. She held onto Phillip's hand and looked up at him. "Don't be too hopeful. It might not happen," she said.

He knelt down in front of her. "If we can't get our act together in a place like this then it was never meant to be," he whispered, running his hand up her thigh, over her hip and onto her breast. "We'll have to talk about the alternatives again but before we do that, we'll simply have to enjoy trying."

Under Phillip's touch she so much wanted to feel her pulse quicken but as was now so often the case she actually wanted to be left alone. She just wished they could find the magic that was once there.

She had read articles in magazines about the way the thrill of discovering each other can fade and new ways had to be found to keep the excitement in a marriage.

Phillip's needs were now very different to hers, so she thought her feelings or lack of them were perhaps one-sided. She hoped Primrose Cottage would help: maybe the change would bring other changes that she so desperately needed.

Just then she heard Henry coming up the stairs.

18

"He's back," she told Phillip, brushing his hand away.

Henry coughed before he entered the room and Sarah and Phillip smiled at each other. "Mr Temple says he thinks your offer is good enough to put to the vendors."

"Then tell your Mr Temple to do exactly that," Phillip said.

Sarah smiled her approval but as she turned to look out of the window she shivered again. She wasn't a negative person but even though they were surrounded by exactly what they had been looking for, she felt as though something awful was going to happen.

A premonition or was she just being silly?

Sarah stood at the main bedroom window staring at the garden, a mug of black coffee in her hands as she pondered over the conflicting thoughts she had now that they had actually moved into the cottage.

She had deliberately left much of what needed to be done until Phillip returned to work. But at the back of her mind was the unexplained and uneasy feeling she had experienced when first viewing the cottage.

For some reason the feeling was still there.

The cottage itself was not to blame because it was most welcoming. Their first few nights had been restful and the tranquillity of Upper Slaughter had introduced different night sounds into their lives.

She believed she was a caring, hardworking and conscientious sort of person and being blessed with a pretty face and good figure had their advantages. She was convinced she would make a good mother, as she believed she was a good wife to Phillip.

He was so sure the change in their circumstances was going to bring them luck, but his positive attitude wasn't mirrored by her own beliefs. There was no medical evidence to support how she felt but she still blamed herself for not falling pregnant.

It had to be her.

19

Her body and mind were ready but for some reason nothing was happening. She actually believed their chances of starting the family they so wanted were still as remote as they were from the outset.

Taking a deep breath, she tried to dismiss the feelings and doubts that always forced their way into her mind.

She must get on.

Draining the last of the coffee, she headed for the shower.

Phillip was sitting in a stream of traffic on his way into Gloucester docks.

He had allowed an extra half hour for the trip from Upper Slaughter but he assumed correctly that it would make little difference to the slow crawl into the city.

Normally he would have become fractious along with many of those around him but as the engine idled and he waited for yet another set of lights to change, he was smiling to himself.

He couldn't believe the change in Sarah.

Whereas she always saw the bright side of everything, trusting that something good would always come out of something bad, he adopted the attitude that if you expected the worst then things could only get better.

There were times though, before they moved and totally contrary to how she normally was, when Sarah experienced bouts of depression which she refused to discuss.

But he knew the cause.

Whenever they discussed why they had been unable to have children she always blamed herself. She felt she was letting them both down. He was the one who remained resolute.

It was obvious before they moved that she had become more and more resigned to the fact that she would never fall pregnant.

He remained enthusiastic but even her attitude towards their sex life in general had waned.

But now early signs were encouraging, suggesting that the move to Upper Slaughter would introduce more zest into their lives, and his hopes would be realised.

As he edged slowly forward following the ubiquitous white van, the smile returned to his face. Sarah had changed already. She was now more vibrant, more enthusiastic and was ready to throw all her energy into setting up their new home.

He was more than happy to leave her on her own as he was sure he would only be in the way. They needed a change and finding Upper Slaughter and Primrose Cottage was from the outset an absolute godsend.

He felt the engine bump into third gear as the traffic began to pick up speed for the first time in about two miles. He accepted he wasn't a religious man but he thanked God once again for sending Sarah to him. He absolutely worshipped the ground she walked on, so when she felt low he felt utterly useless.

At thirty-two Sarah was three years younger than him but she looked as though she was in her mid-twenties whereas he looked older than his thirty-five years. He often looked at the photograph on the mantelpiece of them together on holiday soon after they met, and another taken just a year before they moved to Upper Slaughter.

He remembered her saying when she unpacked the photographs that in the first one they looked like husband and wife but in the second like father and daughter but had added that she preferred her men to be mature.

Always feeling proud when they were out together, he loved the envy he saw in other men's eyes. His love for her had grown and grown but it wasn't only their relationship that had thrived – his antiques business was also going from strength to strength and diversification was more than on the cards as he was now extending into exports and imports.

Having discussed his intentions with his father before embarking on the changes he proposed, he now spent two weeks abroad every three months, giving Sarah some time on her own, which he knew she enjoyed.

Renewing their relationship on his return from the away-trips was perhaps one of the highlights in both their lives. He was due to go to Singapore and Hong Kong in three weeks' time.

Sitting down at last behind his desk Phillip picked up the cup of coffee Jennifer had brought in moments earlier.

The extra time it had taken to get to work had allowed him to think a lot more and he decided he was going enjoy commuting between Upper Slaughter and Gloucester.

He would soon find a particular junction where each morning he would switch from home to work mode and then in the evening the reverse would apply.

All the first signs were positive, so perhaps Upper Slaughter would work its magic. He smiled and reached for the morning's mail.

Chapter Two

Sarah had just got dressed into her work clothes – a pair of lightweight joggers and a paint-splattered old light-blue sweatshirt – and tied back her hair with a rubber band when the front door bell rang for the first time.

Standing under the rose-covered pergola was an austere looking woman whose age Sarah guessed was probably mid to late fifties. The woman had swept-back dark greying hair and although the temperature was in the low seventies she was wearing a polo neck sweater, fawn jodhpurs and brown scuffed Chelsea boots.

"You must be Sarah Preston," the woman said, thrusting out her hand. "I'm Hilary Bond-Smithers. Welcome to Upper Slaughter."

Sarah took the proffered hand that gripped hers so tightly. "Yes, I'm Sarah Preston and thank you for the welcome."

"My pleasure, my dear," Hilary Bond-Smithers said in a matronly tone, handing Sarah a small package. "I thought I'd pop by to give you a little welcoming present and to see if you've settled in."

"Well, thank you, and ... would you like to come in?" Sarah asked hesitantly. "Please excuse the way I'm dressed. I was about to do some decorating."

"Not a problem, my dear but I can't stay long," Hilary said as she brushed past Sarah into the hallway. "Where do you want me? In the kitchen?" Without waiting for a reply, she headed down the hall.

"Yes, that would be fine," Sarah said, her eyebrows raised in amusement as she followed her guest.

"Lovely little cottage, isn't it?" Hilary observed after taking in the various bits and pieces round the kitchen. "And such a quaint garden," she added, peering out of the window.

"Coffee?" Sarah asked reluctantly, putting the package she had been given on the table beside her.

"The Tuckers spent a small fortune on it, you know. They loved their garden," Hilary said, making herself comfortable at the table. "A coffee would be lovely, my dear. Black please, no sugar."

Sarah was beginning to feel a little annoyed. She hadn't been called *my dear* since her childhood and saw no reason to put up with it now. She didn't know who Hilary Bond-Smithers was or where she was from. She decided to find out.

"Where do you live, Mrs Bond-Smithers?" she asked, searching among the jars on the side for the coffee and feeling silly trying to be polite when Mrs Bond-Smithers had been so condescending.

"Hilary, please. We don't stand on ceremony in Upper Slaughter." She smiled sweetly. "Where do I live?" she repeated making it sound as though Sarah ought to have already known. "We live down the hill on the other side of the river – in Clifton House."

"Oh, which one is that?" Sarah enquired obviously adding insult to injury.

"From the ford," Hilary said as though talking to a child. "The one on the far left."

Sarah's back was to Hilary so she allowed herself another wry smile. Apart from the hotel Clifton House was probably the biggest building in the village. The kettle clicked off so she poured water into the mugs.

"Sorry it's instant and in mugs but we're still unpacking." She put the mugs on the table and sat down.

"No need to apologise, my dear. It takes time to sort oneself out after a move." It was a mild rebuke but one that Sarah was willing to let pass for the time being.

"Clifton House looks beautiful. Have you lived there long?"

"All my life. It's been in the family for five generations." Hilary looked at the design on the mug, a pink pig selected by Sarah deliberately. "So what do you think of our little village?"

"It appears idyllic," Sarah said, sitting down on the other side of the table. "We fell in love with it the moment we drove into the village."

"A bit like Marmite," Hilary said. "It affects people in different ways. Some hate it on sight whereas others feel the opposite. The Tuckers loved it."

"The Tuckers?"

"The previous owners of this cottage. They loved it."

"So why did they move? The estate agent said they were living abroad."

Hilary's eyes never left Sarah's. "He was being diplomatic or showing his ignorance," she said somewhat secretively. "It was a little more complicated than that but I'm surprised you didn't read about it in the papers. It was in most of the nationals."

Sarah shrugged but had a feeling she wasn't going to like what she was about to be told. "We didn't see anything or if we did we didn't connect it to Upper Slaughter."

Hilary broke eye contact as she looked down into the mug in front of her. "You're not squeamish, are you?"

"It depends," Sarah said, "but if it's something to do with this cottage then I'm bound to find out sooner or later so sooner would be better." She was going to add that it would be better if it came from the horse's mouth but decided that might be construed as being a little pointed.

"I'd have thought the estate agent would have told you," Hilary said, then paused but only for a couple of seconds. "Betty Tucker committed suicide and her husband Bill didn't want to stay here afterwards. He went to live with his daughter in Australia."

"What happened?" Sarah asked.

25

"Are you sure you want to know?"

"Better now than later."

"All right then. The Tuckers were in their late fifties. He'd taken early retirement from British Telecom or whatever they call it now, and they moved here about five years ago. They had their other daughter living with them. Abigail was such a sweet, pretty gel, always full of life. She and my daughter Belinda became firm friends. They did everything together – riding, tennis and things. Almost exactly eighteen months ago, Belinda and Abigail went for a ride early in the evening. It was threatening to rain and a storm was forecast, but they went anyway. We weren't worried because they were both experienced riders." Hilary fiddled with her mug as she spoke. "The gels were up on Copper's Ridge –"

"Copper's Ridge?"

Hilary pointed over her shoulder. "It's the high ridge that runs at the back of the village, called Copper's Ridge because there's an old copper mine on the other side of the hill. Anyway the gels were up on the ridge when suddenly there was a clap of thunder and the horses took fright. Belinda, thank God, managed to control The Minstrel but Abigail was on Bluey and he was always a bit boisterous. Abigail lost control and was thrown. As she fell she hit her head on a rock by the trackside. The poor child was in a coma for weeks. Unfortunately she died. She was only nineteen and such a lovely, lovely gel."

"That's awful," Sarah said.

Hilary looked up. "Yes it was. Belinda has never got over it, losing such a close friend and so tragically."

"And Mrs Tucker?"

Hilary shook her head. "It was too much for Betty. Abigail was their younger daughter, an afterthought and both she and Bill doted on her. They had their other daughter Rebecca, the one in Australia and a son named Allan, but he was the black sheep of the family and as far as I know he's still not in touch with his father. Even Abigail's death didn't bring them back together. Could I have another coffee, my dear?"

"Of course," Sarah said getting up from the table. Suddenly she didn't mind being called *my dear*; she didn't mind what she was called.

"Betty changed overnight," Hilary continued as Sarah made fresh mugs of coffee. "She became depressed and reclusive. Everybody in the village rallied to help but nothing we tried to do seemed to do any good. For the six months before she took her own life we hardly ever saw her. If she was alone in the cottage she didn't answer the door if anybody called and Bill, he guarded her like loyal dog. He wouldn't let anybody near her."

Sarah put the mugs on the table and resumed her seat.

"And then one morning about six months ago a police car came to the cottage. Bill had reported Betty missing. Evidently he hadn't felt very well so he'd taken a sleeping pill before going to bed early. He woke up the following morning and Betty wasn't anywhere in the cottage. He checked all her clothes and nothing was missing. He searched every inch of the village but didn't find her so he called the police." Hilary sat back in her chair and sighed. "They discovered her up on Copper's Ridge. After Bill had fallen asleep she'd walked the mile and a half in her nightdress and slippers. They found her hanging from a tree at almost the exact spot where Abigail had fallen from Bluey. It was awful." Hilary's eyes watered and she reached for her bag. "Sorry, my dear, I still get upset just thinking about it," she said extracting a large white handkerchief and dabbing her eyes.

"How terrible," Sarah said as she too felt herself filling up.

Hilary nodded. "It was. That poor woman – she must have been living in hell after the accident."

"I can understand why her husband decided to move."

"Yes, he'd lost his younger daughter and his wife. He was devoted to them both."

27

"What a tragedy," Sarah said softly, wondering if that was the reason she had felt uneasy when viewing the cottage.

"Upper Slaughter has had its fair share of tragedies, my dear. It may seem idyllic but over the years nearly every family living here has had one misfortune or another."

"I see."

"But don't let me put you off, my dear. Nothing has happened since losing Betty. We all hope the jinx has moved on to somewhere else."

Hilary Bond-Smithers stayed another hour and in that time Sarah found that although normally a private person, she willingly told Hilary all about herself, her family and of course, Phillip.

Her visitor was particularly interested in Phillip's Antique business, adding without actually explaining why, that his expertise would be to the village's advantage.

After Hilary left, Sarah contemplated ringing Phillip straightaway to tell him about the Tuckers but then decided it could wait until the evening.

Just as she got back to her decorating the doorbell rang again. Phillip's departure for work that morning seemed to be the signal for the village to descend on her.

This time it was a younger, very attractive vivacious woman at the door. Sarah took to her straightaway. She had brought with her a fair-sized cathedral candle as a welcoming present accompanied by a genuine smile which communicated warmth. Sarah remembered Hilary Bond-Smithers' present was still unopened.

Her visitor introduced herself as Elspeth Warrington. She told Sarah she lived at the top of Church Lane near the village green in a row of terraced cottages. Sarah assumed correctly the cottages being referred to were the same ones the old man who had watched them the first time they visited Upper Slaughter was from.

Elspeth accepted Sarah's invitation to have a coffee and Sarah had a strong feeling that they were going to become firm friends.

Explaining that the other rooms weren't really ready yet for visitors' scrutiny, Sarah guided Elspeth to the seat recently vacated by Hilary Bond-Smithers.

"I waited until Hilary had gone," Elspeth said, sipping her coffee.

Elspeth had swept back her long blonde hair from her face and tied it with a pretty blue bow. Her eyes were as blue as the bow and her face didn't have a touch of make-up on it, which endeared her to Sarah even more. She was taller than Sarah and had a fuller figure.

Sarah thought she was the kind of woman who might be considered by other women as being an immediate threat, but to the contrary she felt there were the makings of a very good friendship.

She didn't make friends readily but on this occasion she was willing to make an exception and hoped she would be given the opportunity.

"I must admit I was spying," Elspeth said. "I was about to come and see you when I spotted Hilary walking up from the palace, so I thought I'd wait."

"The palace?" Sarah was amused by the description.

"Oh, yes," Elspeth replied, a wicked grin on her face and a glint in her eyes. "Everybody refers to Clifton House as *The Palace*. Lord and Lady Bond-Smithers do tend to treat the rest of us as their subjects."

"Lord and Lady? She didn't say –"

"I was only joking but if they had their way that's exactly what they'd be."

"I suppose I should be honoured."

"Good heavens, no. Every newcomer, not that there are many, gets a visit from Lady Hilary. I bet she didn't bring you anything though."

"Well actually she did, it's over there."

"In that case you really are honoured. It's just that she normally doesn't. Little gifts are something she expects when you're invited to *The Palace* for a cocktail party or garden party – even dinner if you're really acceptable. Having said that though, they do throw some super parties."

"She was telling me about the Tuckers," Sarah said as she took a sip of her coffee. It was her fourth mug in the space of a couple of hours and normally she only had one at breakfast. The caffeine was beginning to affect her, giving her a slightly jumpy feeling.

"Yes, that was terribly sad in more ways than one."

Sarah sensed Elspeth's reluctance to talk about the accident but then she went on. "It happened after we'd been in the village for just a few months. I knew Abigail quite well. Living so close helped but I think we clicked because we had similar interests and were of the same generation give or take a few years, well – nearly ten actually." Elspeth smiled again as she looked about her and then back at Sarah. "Do you allow people to smoke in your house?"

"God yes but only on the condition you blow in my direction," Sarah said as she searched in a box near the cooker for an ashtray. "I gave up a couple of years ago but quite enjoy being a passive smoker."

"Are you sure?" Elspeth asked, extracting a crumpled packet of cigarettes from her jeans pocket. She lit one and inhaled deeply. "That's better. I know I ought to give up but whenever John nags me it makes me more determined to carry on."

"John?" Sarah said, wanting to know more about her new friend.

"Oh yes John, sorry. He's what society calls nowadays my partner. I don't think the rest of the village approve and especially not her ladyship down the lane, but sod the lot of them." Elspeth suddenly looked concerned. "You don't disapprove, do you?"

"Why on earth should I?"

Elspeth looked down at Sarah's wedding and engagement rings. "Well, you're married."

"That doesn't make me a prude or judgemental. How long have you lived together?"

"It'll be four years this October. We had a flat in London but moved out here with John's job."

"What does he do?"

"He's a lawyer – a solicitor in a Bristol law firm. It's quite a long way to commute but as soon as we saw this place we fell for it."

"So did Phillip and I."

"It's beautiful, isn't it? It has its downsides though but perhaps it would be best if we leave those until later." Elspeth smiled. "I don't want to put you off after you've been here for such a short while."

Sarah started to giggle.

"What are you laughing at?" Elspeth said, her face breaking into a full smile. "What have I said?"

"No, nothing," Sarah replied with a wave of her hand. "It's not something you've said, it's what I'm going to tell Phillip this evening."

"What do you mean?"

"He was home all last week and we didn't see anybody other than the odd person when we went out for a walk, but the day he goes back to work I start to have visitors. He may take it personally," Sarah added, still giggling.

"No, I don't think so," Elspeth said. "From what I've seen he didn't seem the sort to do that."

"From what you've seen?"

"Oh, don't think your presence hasn't been noted, especially after walking round the village. The jungle drums will have been beating on every corner."

"But nobody seemed to know –"

"They knew all right. No," Elspeth added, reaching over and putting her hand on Sarah's arm. "Phillip mustn't be offended. It's an unwritten rule of the village that newcomers are given a week to settle in and then the world descends. I wasn't the first and I'm afraid I won't be the last. They'll want to see what you're like and what you've got before they meet in each other's houses to discuss you."

"Including you?" For a reason Sarah couldn't readily hit upon, she wanted Elspeth to say no. She wasn't disappointed.

"No, not me. John and I are still *outsiders* as you and Phillip will be for at least the first sixty years."

"You're joking!"

"Yes, but the timeframe is only slightly exaggerated." She stubbed out her cigarette. "Tell me about Phillip."

For the second time that morning Sarah found herself telling a complete stranger about what Phillip did and where he worked. With Hilary Bond-Smithers she felt she had said too much, but Elspeth was different.

She went on to tell Elspeth about herself and how as each day passed, she was loathing more and more her job as a legal secretary. Although she enjoyed the work, the people she worked with were so pompous and patronising.

"It's a coincidence that you and John are both working in the legal profession. But I can assure you, Sarah, there's nothing pompous or patronising about John. He's a teddy bear, all cuddly and soft. Why don't you try something new?" she suggested as she drank the last of her coffee

"Another? Or would you like something stronger? I think I know where the box containing the alcohol is."

"Shall we? I try not to drink at lunch times but as this is a special occasion ..."

"Why not? Wine or something stronger?"

"Wine would be lovely and red if you've got it."

"I drink little else," Sarah said getting up and going into the pantry for a bottle.

Once they were settled with two large glasses of red wine, Sarah went back to Elspeth's question. "Something new," she said, "is definitely on the cards. Phillip doesn't know but I've almost decided to hand in my notice."

"What will you do?"

"Don't know yet. My priority is to get this place sorted out first. What do you do?"

"Me? I write. I write children's short stories which means I can work from home."

"How marvellous," Sarah said. "Have you had many published?"

"Enough to allow me to pay for the weekly shop." She smiled. "No, it's a little more than that but I'm afraid I'm not another JK Rowling. It keeps me out of mischief unfortunately, but I enjoy doing it."

"I wish I could do something creative like that. It must be lovely to be in control of when and where you work."

"I don't regard it as work. It's a diversion but if it brings in a pound or two I can't complain."

"A diversion? A diversion from what?"

Elspeth shrugged. "From doing anything else, I suppose. John earns quite enough to keep me in the style to which I've become accustomed," she said, giggling. "And the cottage doesn't take a lot of looking after."

"Which one is it?"

"You know the four terraced cottages adjacent to the green?" Sarah nodded. "We live in the one on the left as you look at them. It's got a small frontage but it's quite deep and more than adequate for just the two of us."

"I know where you mean. The first day we came to look at the village we parked by the green and an elderly man from one of the other cottages was leaning on his gate watching us."

"That would be Old Greg, Gregory Woolmer. He's nearly ninety. He lives three down and at the other end from us with his wife, Grace. They've been in the village all their lives. He calls all newcomers *outsiders*, that's why I used the word earlier on. You and Phillip are *outsiders*, John and I are *outsiders* and anybody who can't talk about relatives who lived here two hundred years ago is also an *outsider*."

"So Hilary isn't an *outsider*?"

"Good Lord no, and nor are fifty percent of the village. It's a bit of a divide but we all get by in one way or another. We also have the odd character or two, Old Greg for example."

"What do you mean?"

"You'll see," Elspeth said, reaching for the bottle of wine and topping up both their glasses. "You'll see," she said again, but this time without the hint of a smile on her face.

Chapter Three

In the following two weeks – both of which Sarah took as unpaid holiday – she toiled nearly every hour Phillip was away at work.

Because the cottage was so *them* when they moved in, if she thought the easy life was preferable there was actually almost nothing left for her to do.

But she needed to stamp her own personality on every area of Primrose Cottage. Every nook and cranny was there to be investigated. So the cottage began to take shape and each night she went to bed satisfied with what she had achieved. As she drifted off to sleep she would plan the following day's work.

The friendship with Elspeth she hoped would grow did exactly that and the reason why so much was achieved in the cottage was because Elspeth was such a willing helper.

They enjoyed being together and Sarah accepted alternative suggestions from Elspeth of where things should go and whether a colour needed changing.

Phillip was more than happy to arrive home, put his feet up and admire what she had achieved that day. On a couple of occasions they were invited back to Elspeth and John's for supper. The four of them got on well.

Sarah, as Elspeth had implied, liked John immediately. He was tall – an inch or so taller than Phillip – but whereas Phillip was muscular and lean, John was as cuddly as Elspeth had described him. A mop of unruly wavy hair topped a podgy face, and if Sarah were being polite, a large body.

If she wasn't being polite she would say he was approaching obesity. However, a tremendous personality complemented a wicked sense of humour.

Regardless of his size John and Phillip discovered that they were similar standard squash players and agreed they should meet at least once a week to sweat out the pressures of their respective occupations.

A few weeks after moving to Upper Slaughter Sarah was happier with herself and more relaxed. She had thought the story about the Tuckers would unnerve her but it didn't. If anything the discovery gave her a satisfactory explanation for her initial unease, but as she didn't believe in ghosts she moved on very quickly.

She was also pleased she and Phillip were finding new friends so easily, so she was determined to put the cottage in order and also sort out her own life.

If she allowed her mind to run freely there was still something more than just their sex life that was troubling her, but she wasn't sure what it was. She wasn't always open and honest with Phillip about her feelings and that must stop.

They married because they loved each other and because they wanted to spend the rest of their lives together. If something was worrying her then she was obliged to share that worry, especially if it involved the man she loved.

It wasn't just that they both desperately wanted a family, it was more than that. She was a lot happier than she had been before the move and she was also more relaxed but there was still something ... something she couldn't put her finger on.

Before she could share her concerns with Phillip she needed to know what it was she was looking for, or what was worrying her. Until she found the root cause of what was troubling her there was little point in confiding in him.

Sarah soon met other members of the village community: there were the *outsiders* as Elspeth described them, and then there were the others who tended to keep more to themselves

– those whose history in the village went further back than the Doomsday Book, or so she was told. She was aware when she and Elspeth walked round the village that once again she – now they – were being watched.

Having taken two weeks paid and two weeks unpaid holiday it was on the Friday before Sarah was due back to work that the invitation arrived. She and Elspeth were hanging a shower curtain when an envelope was pushed through the letterbox.

Elspeth decided it was time for a coffee break and when they reached the bottom of the stairs they both noticed the envelope lying on the front door mat.

Sitting at the kitchen table with mugs of coffee, Elspeth puffing on what she deemed to be a well-earned cigarette, Sarah opened the envelope and took out the enclosed card. It was white embossed with gold letters. She read the wording out loud:

"*Hilary and Jeremy Bond-Smithers request the company of Sarah and Phillip Preston,*" she read slowly, "*at a Cocktail Party to be held in Clifton House on Saturday 30th September 2000 at 6 o'clock.*" She glanced at the bottom left hand corner where it said, "*RSVP,*" and then in the other corner, *"Dress: lounge suits."*

Sarah looked up to see Elspeth smiling.

"I hope you've got a party frock," Elspeth said, stubbing out her cigarette.

"Well, yes but I'm not sure Phillip will want to go. It's more my mother's scene. Phillip went to a couple of cocktail parties soon after we were married and his reaction was ... how shall I put it? Not complimentary to say the least. I remember him referring to those attending as being stuffed shirts, pretentious and haughty. No, I don't think Phillip will be at all happy."

"That's a pity," Elspeth said, "because I've been to a couple of their parties. Although I would agree with Phillip's opinion, they are also highly entertaining. When you throw in copious quantities of free booze and food what can be lost? It's the ideal time to pick up on the gossip, like who's having an affair with who and who would like to have an affair with who." Elspeth grinned. "I'm sure there should have been a few *whoms* in there somewhere, but you know what I mean. And there am I professing to be a writer."

"But we don't know anybody."

"You know us and if we're not good enough what a superb opportunity to meet some of the more pretentious people who live in the area."

Sarah laughed and shook her head. "Of course you and John are good enough. We were so lucky you lived here already but it would be exciting, wouldn't it?"

"In more ways than you can currently imagine. You just wait until some of the supposed gentry feast their eyes on you. I suggest you wear a pair of iron knickers."

"They don't, do they?"

"Oh yes, they do. When I got home after the last one my bum was black and blue."

"But why did you let them?"

"It's only a bit of harmless fun. It's like the old days when the aristocracy felt they owned their servants and could do anything to them they liked." Elspeth lit another cigarette.

"But surely you were a guest as much as they were."

Elspeth sniggered. "A token among tokens," she said.

"But is that all that happens, a bit of bum pinching?"

"With me it is, I'm not sure what others get up to."

"If I tell Phillip he definitely won't go. He might finish up hitting somebody."

"Then don't tell him."

"Will you be there?"

"I'll see if there's an invitation when I get home, I'll be a bit annoyed if there isn't. Groping apart though, they really are good fun." Elspeth drained her glass before putting out her half-smoked cigarette. "Come on, we'd better get on if you want to be finished before Phillip gets home."

"You're too good to me," Sarah said, following Elspeth out of the kitchen.

"Rubbish." Elspeth stopped and turned round. "Oh, and if you want a real laugh make sure that you wear something that's as low at the front as is decent."

Sarah smiled. "I've got nothing to show so there's little point."

Elspeth reached forward and pulled away the front of Sarah's paint-splattered T-shirt, her fingers briefly touching the top of Sarah's breast.

"That's a matter of opinion," she said

Looking at her new friend, Sarah felt a quiver of excitement but didn't know why.

Phillip arrived home soon after six o'clock.

As he was drinking his usual early evening whisky and lemonade Sarah told him about the invitation. He looked at her over the rim of the glass with an amused expression on his face. "That'll be fun," he said.

She tried to detect sarcasm in his voice, but couldn't. "Do you mean that?"

He shrugged. "Why wouldn't I? I suppose it'll be a good introduction to the real village community."

He undid his tie as he watched Sarah.

"But you hated those parties we went to with mummy," Sarah said as she reached for the bottle of red wine on the kitchen dresser and poured herself a glass.

"I wouldn't say hated but they were rather contrived. Anyway we were guests of your mum's, giving her some support."

"What's the difference?"

"The Bond-Smithers have asked us in our own right and I doubt whether there'll be a load of old military codgers present, sharing their war stories."

"And you tell me female logic is hard to understand. I told Elspeth it would be the last place you'd want to be," she said as she sipped her wine.

"Well on this occasion you got it wrong, didn't you? And talking of Elspeth I presume she's the one who left that ashtray full of dog-ends."

Sarah glanced at the ashtray.

On previous days she always emptied the ashtray before Phillip arrived home and made sure she sprayed the kitchen to get rid of any residual smells. They were both ex-smokers but whereas she tolerated people who hadn't kicked the habit, Phillip hated to be in the vicinity of anyone who had been smoking let alone were smoking.

"I wouldn't say it was full. She's been very good to me – no to us – and if letting her have the odd cigarette or two is the price we pay then that's the least I can do."

"Maybe," Phillip said.

"Have you had a bad day or something?"

"No, not exactly. A couple of sales I thought were guaranteed fell through but nothing that can't be recovered."

"You seem a little on edge."

He shrugged again. "Do I? Sorry."

She reached across the table and put her hand on his. "You are happy to be here, aren't you?"

"What, in this cottage or in the village?"

"Both."

"I'll get used to it."

She had experienced the Friday evening blues before.

Asking how he felt about the cottage was necessary because Sarah wanted reassurance. In the last couple of hours she was aware that she had felt unsettled herself. But on this occasion she didn't have to question what was behind this growing feeling, she knew the reason why.

It was Elspeth.

She was so happy when they were together, chatting away about everything and nothing but she found that when Elspeth left the cottage she felt miserable and lonely until Phillip arrived home.

On this particular Friday evening she felt even more unsettled because she didn't understand the way her whole body had tingled when Elspeth touched her: it wasn't deliberate but she had still touched her.

Tingle was the only word she could think of but it was more than that; it was as though every nerve ending in her body was suddenly alive. It was the way she remembered feeling when Phillip touched her for the first time.

Like Elspeth, Sarah was also a tactile woman, but there was never anything intimate about it. Yet when Elspeth brushed her fingertips across her breast plus the way she said "that's a matter of opinion' it made Sarah feel excited but anxious.

Excited because of the sensation Elspeth's touch generated in her and anxious because she knew she shouldn't have felt any such thing.

When he got home she wanted Phillip to be in a good mood. She wanted him to *want* her. It wasn't only because she knew she was the one who had to work on their sex life, but now ... well, for whatever reason she was ready for him.

However, as he had no idea what was troubling her, he slipped straight into his Friday evening routine. They would make love later she was sure but she needed him now. If she asked him outright without an explanation he wouldn't understand.

They never made love the moment he got home on a Friday evening, so why should it even cross his mind?

Sarah realised that she could have instigated what she wanted but Phillip's mood dictated otherwise.

"So, what plans do we have for the weekend?" she asked. "The cottage is almost sorted and what still needs doing can wait. It's back to work for me on Monday."

"My priority is to have a bath first and then get changed," Phillip said, standing up and moving towards the door where he stopped and turned round. "Do you fancy going out to eat tonight? There's that Italian place in Stow we said we'd try once we were relatively settled."

"Well, yes," she replied, a little surprised. "I got some chops out of the freezer for this evening but they'll keep until tomorrow. Yes, that would be nice." She was pleased to see Phillip's face relax.

"What about asking Elspeth and John, see if they'd like to join us?" he said.

She hesitated for a moment, taken aback by the fact that she felt thrilled by the thought. "Well, I suppose we could."

"You don't sound very enthusiastic," he said, beginning to move towards the stairs.

"Yes, yes, I am, that's a good idea. Will you ring them or shall I?"

"You know Elspeth better than I know either of them. You ring."

"Okay," she said, hoping her nervousness wasn't showing.

"Great, and when you've finished," he said, already half way up the stairs, "you have my permission to join me in the bath."

Sarah allowed a smile to play on her lips.

There hadn't been a need to ask after all. For some reason he had sensed her mood. That was one of the reasons she loved him.

"It's your turn for the taps," she shouted after him.

"Not with what I've got planned for you," Phillip replied.

Chapter Four

Michael Griffiths watched Sarah and Phillip Preston walking slowly up the lane towards the village green. He guessed where they were going because he had seen them walking to the cottages by the green before. But this time he was ready for more than just watching.

Observing the Prestons moving into Primrose Cottage had been fun. Over the years he had also enjoyed watching other outsiders moving into his village.

It was his territory so they moved in under his terms, although as his terms were never discussed they had little choice.

But this time things were different.

He knew where all the outsiders lived. At one time or another he had watched them, especially the ones who really interested him. None of them knew they were being watched as he believed he was too clever to be seen. No, that wasn't strictly true: he *knew* he was too clever.

As he watched the Prestons walking up the lane this particular evening he was in the bushes by the pathway that led to the church. His dark combat clothing blended in well with the leaves and branches. He always blackened his face just like the soldiers did on the television.

Putting his hand in his jacket pocket he felt for the key, and smiled.

They had been silly, as so many others had been equally silly.

It was so easy to borrow the back door key for a few seconds so he could make an impression in some Plasticine.

Six days ago and reasonably early on the Saturday morning, the Prestons had gone for a walk and they left through the back door.

Michael had seen where they hid the key.

That was when he borrowed his eventual means of entry to their cottage. It was a risk but one that was worth taking because it was a risk he had taken many times before.

Manufacturing the replica key wasn't a problem. The key was a bit rough at the edges but he was sure it would work. He had keys to a lot of the outsiders' houses and had used them all. None of the others knew he had been in their houses. He looked, touched and noted, but he never took anything, although the temptation was always there.

He was always excited when he was about to have a look at the inside of a house or cottage for the first time, but on this occasion he felt more apprehensive than excited because the situation was different.

Having watched the Preston woman far more than any of the others he had watched, he had his reasons for being apprehensive. There was something very special about her. She was so delicate, almost childlike and he knew she would be the one: the one he always believed would come into his life at some stage though he didn't know when.

But he must be patient, his patience would pay off in the end.

The man she lived with was unknown to Michael, but he didn't like him. Imagining her being with that man as he did things to her was almost too much. It was unfair but he would be patient.

For over seven years Michael had had no physical contact with another human being let alone a female. What happened back then was something he would never forget.

He referred to it as his *awakening* but there had been nothing since. His frustrations were managed when he was on his own but he always knew that one day his awakening would become reality.

The incident happened when he was young and inexperienced and the girls involved were equally young but also silly and immature.

From that day on and when he was lost in his own fantasies, the women he imagined he was with were always older than him.

That was why he liked the Preston woman. He knew she was older than him – he guessed she might be ten years older – but she looked young and fragile.

Watching her legs as she walked brought a smile to his face. She was nearly out of sight now, walking hand in hand with that man.

The skirt she was wearing wasn't a short skirt. She was not the sort of woman who enjoyed flaunting herself in front of men.

Her calf muscles relaxed and tightened as she walked and he could hear the clip-clop of her heels on the road. He could feel himself reacting as he watched her, imagining what she was really like, and groaning inwardly as he tried to make the feeling go away.

When they were out of sight he would wait the usual five minutes then he would find out a little more about her.

He smiled nervously. His apprehension grew alongside the excitement.

A month earlier, he had watched their cottage when they were moving in.

Always in his secret hiding place by seven o'clock in the morning, he took some bread and water with him in case he felt hungry or thirsty. There was plenty of time before he needed to go to work.

He was a patient man – thinking of himself as a man in every respect because of the way Mrs Preston affected him, and despite what others said about him. So physically, he knew he was a man. Other people in the village and at work thought he was simple, but he knew he was far from being stupid.

People laughing and pointing had become part of his life. But when he went to post the letter for his mother and he saw Mrs Preston for the first time, she didn't laugh or point; she smiled at him instead.

She smiled and she looked at him and he saw her eyes were smiling too – not laughing, they were smiling. She was special.

From the hiding place he went to nearly every morning he was able to see the man she lived with get his car out of the garage before driving to work.

On one occasion he got as close to the garage as he dared just so that he could see her husband better.

He knew they were married because they both wore wedding rings and he wondered what sort of man she liked.

Although he didn't like the man, Michael was pleased to see that her husband was similar to himself physically. He was about the same height, maybe a little taller but not as slim.

After watching the cottage a few times, Michael knew the Prestons' bedroom window looked out over the back garden towards the church and the woods where he had his secret hiding place.

When he watched he always waited patiently.

The first few times he saw her at the bedroom window after her husband had gone to work, she always had a towel wrapped round her body.

He saw her fingers first and his pulse began to race in anticipation. But then, when she pulled back the curtains, she was wearing a pink towel. Yes, he was disappointed but he was close enough to see that her hair was still wet and glistening. He was sharing a private moment with her.

She had probably just had a shower or a bath. He didn't mind which it was but he decided quite early on that she would prefer a shower to a bath. Imagining her in the shower occupied his mind quite a lot: he imagined her doing lots of things but not with that man. He didn't want to think of her with that man, but sometimes he couldn't stop himself.

On his fifth visit to the woods behind the cottage he saw what he longed to see.

It was a warm morning.

If he were patient he knew it would happen eventually, and then there would have been another step forward towards what he believed was his destiny.

It was her destiny too.

The back of the cottage was very private: it wasn't overlooked by anybody else other than by him. Wherever he hid to watch the outsiders was his territory, nobody else's: they were his private places.

On this particular morning, he watched her husband go off to work as usual and then he moved round to the other side of the garage so that he could see the bedroom window.

Distracted as he undid the top of his army water bottle for a drink, he almost missed her. But then he looked up and there she was.

He couldn't believe his eyes.

Previously she hadn't stayed very long at the window. She normally drew the curtains, opened the window and disappeared. But this time, and maybe because it was a warm sunny morning, she stayed at the open window for longer and she wasn't wearing a pink towel.

His mouth dropped open when he realised what was happening. He was looking at her breasts. He could see her dark nipples. Bending forwards she put her forearms on the windowsill and she was smiling. She took a couple of deep breaths then stood back as she stretched her arms upwards. Her stomach was flat, her skin firm across her ribs and tummy and he could see her navel.

He thought she looked unbelievably beautiful.

Suddenly with one last deep breath she was gone.

He imagined her walking naked across the bedroom. He hadn't been aware of the feeling as he watched her but as soon as she disappeared his need was evident. Slipping his hand down the front of his trousers he closed his eyes and imagined again what he had seen, but this time she was looking down at him from the bedroom window as she beckoned him towards her.

She wanted him and she was inviting him into her bedroom.

Michael Griffiths didn't remember much about his early childhood but what he did remember was vividly etched in his mind.

He had lived in Upper Slaughter all his life. His older brother and sister both left home before his tenth birthday and he lived now with his divorced mother in the last house on the left before the junction with the minor road that led out of the village to the north towards Lower Swell and Stow in the Wold.

When he started school in the C of E Primary School in Lower Swell, he didn't understand when he overheard a teacher saying to another one that little Michael Griffiths had learning difficulties. The following year, when he was seven, he was moved to what he had heard was a *special* school in Evesham though he told his mother there was nothing special about it.

He was always good at overhearing what people said but he was confused when he heard someone say he might be *autistic* and he might have *Asperger's Syndrome*. He loved his class teacher and he was pleased when she told his mother that he was extremely inventive and imaginative and what he lacked academically he more than compensated for with his hands.

"He's artistic," she said, "and seems to have innate skills enabling him to turn his hands to anything: woodwork, metalwork, even basketry and weaving, though he's also surprisingly good at English."

Her words made him glow all over. When he was being practical he was at his happiest so when he left school at sixteen his teacher told his mother in front of him that his practical abilities were his future.

He still spoke very little but when he did speak he always tried to be polite. His English was grammatically correct and often surprisingly articulate but when anybody tried to extend even the simplest of conversations into a discussion, he always clammed up and withdrew into a world that nobody else understood ... or wanted to know.

One of his happiest memories was when his father left his mother, a year before Michael was due to leave school. There were times when he wished his father was dead. He used to lie awake at night and pray for a life without his father, because if his father wasn't there the beatings wouldn't be there either. His mother showed little interest in Michael, leaving him alone in his room to make his models.

But his father used to beat him and more often than not for no apparent reason. The physical scars stayed with Michael for only a few months but the mental scars never went away.

Nobody was more pleased than Michael when his father walked out forever.

When he left school Michael started work at a carpenter's shop in Evesham. He was good at his job and particularly enjoyed working on the lathe. He didn't have any friends so he got most of his satisfaction from his hobby.

Before his father walked out Michael started to make ships and planes out of matchsticks, but one day he embarked on his most adventurous project to date – he decided to make a scale model of the village church.

It was when he went to the churchyard in order to estimate the angles and measurements of the intricate stonework, that he encountered girls for the first time.

This was what he called his *awakening*.

At fifteen and like all boys of his age, girls had become a source of both intrigue and confusion. But regardless of his inquisitiveness Michael tried to keep himself to himself because the girls in the village ridiculed him and when he tried to give as good as he got, he always became tongue-tied and made a mess of things.

By this time his brother and sister had been long gone and his father wouldn't have helped him with a simple arithmetic problem let alone tell him about the changes adolescence brings. His mother simply gave him no thought at all.

He had bought some magazines which he kept hidden in his bedside cupboard. Looking at pictures of nude women and reading about things he didn't understand caused more confusion. He knew how to cope with the frustration the pictures generated but he didn't understand what he was doing.

On this particular day in the churchyard Michael stumbled on a couple of the village girls who were at the back of the graveyard sitting behind a large headstone. He saw them before they saw him so he tried to sneak away but wasn't quick enough.

"There's Michael," said the girl he knew was called Wendy.

He thought that both girls were laughing at him but he couldn't take his eyes off them. Their jeans were undone and the girl he thought was called Sharon had her hand down the front of her jeans and was moving it about as she looked at him. "Hello, Michael," she said. "You bin spyin' on us?"

"No," he replied quickly. "I came –"

"I bet you did," Wendy said, nudging her friend.

He wanted to tell them why he was there but he thought they would laugh at him even more. "I'm ... I'm sorry," was all he could think of saying.

"Why're you sorry, Michael? You ain't done nuffin to be sorry about." As she spoke Wendy lifted the hem of her T-shirt, revealing her pierced navel. "D'ya like lookin', Michael?"

"Looking ... looking at what?" he asked innocently, his eyes not leaving the girl's bare midriff.

"Us," Sharon added as her hand still moved under the front of her jeans.

"I ... didn't –"

"Come a bit closer, Michael," Wendy said. "You'll be able to see better."

Both girls' backs were against another smaller headstone and he thought it was wrong that they should be sitting on someone's resting place, doing what they were doing – whatever that might be.

Wendy crossed her arms and pulled her T-shirt over her head. She wasn't wearing a bra. When he was a lot younger he had seen his sister Chrissie naked in the bathroom – enough as the keyhole allowed – but he had never seen a girl's breasts this close before, not in real life. The pictures in the magazines were different, but he didn't know why. The feeling in his trousers was no different though, because it was always the same. There was nothing he could do about it, not then, but he might later when he closed his eyes and imagined what Wendy had looked like.

Both girls were watching him. "D'you like 'em, Michael?" Wendy asked.

He nodded, his mouth open.

"Wha' about mine?"

Sharon took her hand out of her jeans so that she could undo the buttons on her shirt. Michael looked from one girl's chest to the other, the feeling in his trousers more intense and more uncomfortable. Sharon's breasts were bigger than Wendy's. Michael preferred Wendy's because they seemed more in proportion with the rest of her.

"Would you like to touch 'em, Michael?" The girls exchanged looks and giggled.

"No, I must –"

"Don't be a prat, come a bit closer and you can touch "em."

He moved a few feet closer.

The girls giggled again.

"Crouch down," Sharon told him, "so no one can see you."

He did as Sharon asked.

Sharon reached for his hand, guiding his fingers towards her breast. He didn't know what to expect but he found touching the girl was pleasant as her skin was soft and smooth. Wendy took his other hand and put it on her breast.

"There," she said, "bet when you left 'ome you didn't fink you'd be doin' this, did ya?"

"No ... no," he said, though he was beginning to feel that crouching down was more uncomfortable than standing.

Sharon took his fingers and moved them against her nipple. Wendy saw what her friend was doing and did the same. Their eyes opened wide with amusement when they looked at the expression on Michael's face.

"Do you like that, Michael?"

He nodded, his tongue moistening his lips.

"Wha' about down "ere?" Wendy took his hand so that she could guide it over her pierced navel towards the top of her jeans, pushing his fingers under her pants.

As soon as he felt the silkiness of the girl's pubic hair he jerked his hand free, almost falling backwards as he did so.

The girls laughed.

"I've ... got ... got to go," he said.

"Not before we see a bit more o' you," Sharon told him, swinging forward onto her knees and pushing her hand between his legs. "He's rock hard," she said, looking over her shoulder at Wendy.

He wanted to run away and get out of the churchyard as quickly as he could but he couldn't move. He just looked down as Sharon undid his belt before pulling down the zip on his jeans. Wendy was on her knees as well, looking up at him and when Sharon's fingers encircled him he wanted to scream.

Nobody had ever touched him there before. He played with himself often enough but nobody else had ever touched him there, not even his mother.

He felt his jeans being pushed down over his hips. Again he wanted to scream and run but it was as though somebody had staked him to the ground. He was on his knees and the girls were crouched in front of him, their hands on him.

"E's bigger than I fort 'e'd be," Wendy said.

As was usual the sensation seemed to start somewhere deep in his stomach and slowly it grew and grew. But he had never experienced such a marvellous feeling before, even when he did it to himself. He tried to pull away from the girls but as the sensation became too much he couldn't help thrusting forwards.

"You messy bugger," one of the girls said.

"It's all over me," the other one said. "You could 'ave bloody warned us."

He didn't know what he should have warned them about. He couldn't have cared less at that particular moment. The sensation was intense and he reached down with his hand, putting it where the girls had held him.

"You bastard," one said, "look at me fuckin' shirt."

"I'm goin', you comin' Sharon?"

"You're dead fuckin' right I am. He's a loony."

His eyes were still closed and when he opened them a couple of minutes later there was no sign of the girls, no sign that they had ever been there. He was still on his knees, his jeans open.

He left the churchyard having done only half of what he had set out to do. He couldn't concentrate any more. He walked through the village in a daze, not fully understanding what he had seen and what he had done, but more importantly they had done to him. He had never experienced anything like it before. By the time he reached the front door of his mother's house he had already decided he was going to experience it many, many more times.

Michael knew where both girls lived. Surely if they were willing to do it to him once and without him asking, they would be willing to do it again.

A few days later, after he went back to the church to complete the calculations he needed, Michael started on the finishing touches to the matchstick model of the church. He was willing to devote a lot more time and energy to his project because while he worked on it he remembered what had happened, and while he remembered he smiled.

He couldn't remember being so happy.

After a further two weeks the model was almost finished. He spent hours in his bedroom cutting the heads off the matchsticks and gluing the sticks into place. He spent nearly half the money he earned on the matches, but it was what he wanted to do. His mother couldn't have cared less. As long as he kept out of her way she was happy.

As he glued the final matchsticks to the top of the small spire he couldn't remember what the weather vane looked like, so he sneaked out of the house and walked through the village to the church. As he was passing the village green he saw Wendy and Sharon coming up Church Lane from the ford. They were going to have to pass each other.

He hesitated.

He had not seen the girls since that afternoon in the churchyard and he felt embarrassed. The girls saw him at almost the same moment and they slowed, whispering to each other.

He walked slowly towards them, his head bowed. But when they were closer he plucked up courage and lifting his head he smiled. The girls stopped and just stared at him.

"Hello," he said, his eyes drifting to their chests. When they didn't reply he looked at their faces. They were clutching each other and just looking at him.

"Hello," he said again.

Wendy pulled at Sharon's arm but she carried on looking at him. "Fuck off and don' you ever come near us again," Sharon spat at him and after another tug from Wendy they walked past the green without looking back.

Michael stood in the middle of the lane, watching them as tears came to his eyes.

That evening while in his bedroom he heard his father arrive home. Almost immediately he heard him shouting at his mother but he felt safe as long as he kept quiet and didn't go downstairs. He closed his ears to the noise, concentrating as he began to carve the weather vane out of a couple of matchsticks already glued together.

He was standing back to admire what he'd achieved when his father burst into the room. Michael tried to get as far away from his father as he could, pushing himself against the wall by his bed and shaking with fright as he anticipated the beating he knew he was going to get, although for what reason he had no idea.

With his hands on his hips his father stood and stared at him, a crazy look in his eyes. "It's your fucking fault," his father growled. "If you'd been normal your mother and I might have stood a chance. It's all your fucking fault."

Michael couldn't work out what was his fault and what his father meant about him standing a chance with his mother. He couldn't remember doing anything wrong. Had they found out about what he had done with Wendy and Sharon in the churchyard? His mum and dad weren't religious, so why should they care? He had thought about nothing else while he was putting the finishing touches to his model. He couldn't understand why one minute they were letting him touch them as they were touching him, when the next time he saw them they told him to fuck off. Now his father was using the same word.

Why were they all getting at him?

"You're a fucking whacko," his father shouted, stepping closer. "All you fucking think about are your fucking matches." He walked up to the model of the church and stared at it. For a moment Michael thought his father was going to say something good about it. "What's this?" his father sneered at him.

"It's ... it's the church," Michael said, his voice catching in his throat, his whole body still shaking.

55

"I can see it's a fucking church. What fucking use is it?"

"What –?"

"Why can't you be like other boys of your fucking age? Why aren't you out there playing football or getting into trouble, and if fucking miracles do happen, getting your fucking end away like any normal lad?"

"I –"

"Because you're a fucking idiot, a fucking numbskull, that's why." His father brought his fist down on the model of the church, smashing it into pieces. "Now perhaps you'll do something fucking useful."

With that his father stormed out of the bedroom, slamming the door.

Michael stayed on his bed and stared at the damage to his prize possession. He was so proud of what he'd achieved. He would have preferred a beating to this. He would have preferred to have the scars and bruises. It didn't matter what anybody else thought, he was still proud of what he had done.

After a while he slowly got off his bed. The shaking had stopped but the tears streamed down his face as he picked up the bits of the church that were lying on the floor. He felt a rage building up inside him. When it became so intense that he couldn't control himself any longer he picked up the rest of the church and threw it against the bedroom wall.

The five minutes were almost up.

Nobody returned to the cottage so he smiled in anticipation of what he was going to find.

He would soon be seeing what Mrs Preston was really like.

It was almost time.

After his experience with Wendy and Sharon, he didn't go near another girl. He wanted to because he wanted to relive the experience but he was too scared. He did think a lot about what happened but only when he was in his private world.

56

He had decided he didn't need anybody else, not yet, not for a while. Whenever he got off the bus on his way home from work and he walked back towards the village, he would enter that private world. He gave up making models out of matchsticks after his father destroyed the church. He didn't want anything else he made destroyed. After that dreadful evening he never saw his father again. His brother and sister visited but they hardly spoke to him. They used to go into a huddle with their mother and talk in whispers. Whenever Michael entered the room they would stop talking, only to start again once he left. He tried to listen at the door, but all he could hear were mumblings. The secret world he made for himself to replace all his unhappiness and uncertainties was far better than huddling in his bedroom trying to make something out of nothing.

He only went home to eat and sleep but he didn't sleep at home all the time. Soon after starting work when he was out walking on Copper's Ridge he found a place in the woods where nobody else ever went.

Copper's Ridge was to become his refuge and only he and the wild animals knew about it.

In the woods he built himself a den.

He constructed the den out of a deep natural hollow in the ground, scraping the walls to make them straight and using the loose earth to flatten the floor.

This was where he stored the things he didn't want to keep in the house, especially the combat clothing he bought in the second hand shop in Evesham. He kept it in a plastic bag so it didn't get damp. It wouldn't have mattered if it rained because he made the den waterproof and over the two years since he first started building it he also added bits here and bits there. From only a few yards away the den was invisible, and a couple of times early on when it was getting dark, even he hadn't been able to find it.

He now knew every tree, every bush, every fallen branch and every tuft of grass in the woods. He knew where the rabbits, the foxes and the badgers lived.

Finding his den with his eyes closed was now not a problem.

He kept a supply of food and water in the den and off to one side he dug a simple toilet. He even built a small cesspit well away from the den using lengths of builders' pipe to connect it to the toilet. Neither pipe nor pit was detectable from the outside. He kept the inside of the den very tidy. Using all his woodworking skills, he made a bed, a chair and a table out of branches and planks he took from the outhouse at home, tying the pieces of wood together with twine and wire. He made some shelves that he wedged into the earthen walls, supporting them with simple brackets. Being no more than twelve by fifteen feet it wasn't a big den, but it was where he preferred to be when he was not at work.

The den was his and it was where he could be himself.

At the same time he bought the combat clothing, he also bought other ex-military items he thought would be useful. He added to them from time to time, things like kerosene lamps, a heater and a camping stove. On one side of the den he made a sort of window at ground level that he covered with a flap of canvas on the inside. From the window he could just see the top of the village church well over a mile and a half away.

He was always very careful and made sure he kept a lookout for any movement close to where he was working. But he needn't have worried because other than the farmers in their fields and sometimes people walking past over fifty yards away he was never disturbed.

Except that is for the night Mrs Tucker came up to Copper's Ridge.

On that fateful evening dusk was drawing in.

After changing into his jeans and sweatshirt Michael left his den. On reaching the edge of the wood he stopped as he always stopped. To his surprise he saw Mrs Tucker sitting under the old oak tree with her head in her hands. He recognised her straightaway because she had spoken to him once or twice and in a nice way. She didn't appear to be aware that she was being watched. She was sobbing and was dressed very strangely. It looked as though she was wearing her nightdress and slippers.

Because he liked Mrs Tucker, Michael wanted to help her but he didn't want to give away the fact that Copper's Ridge was where he went to be in his own world. He watched her patiently. She remained sitting under the tree for nearly an hour and all the time he could hear her crying. Eventually she stood up, reached into a bag and took out a thin rope. She tied a loop in one end of the rope and threw the other end over a branch about ten feet above her head. She then fastened the loose end round another low branch.

It was a clear night with a full moon.

His night vision was very good and he thought hers must be too because without faltering she hauled a thick log over to where she had been sitting. He watched in amazement not believing somebody as small as Mrs Tucker could be so strong. After looking across the fields towards the village for a few moments, she climbed onto the log. Reaching up for the rope she became unsteady, missing it the first time but with her second attempt she was successful. She lost her balance again but eventually managed to stand a little unsteadily on the log, holding the rope.

Wondering from the outset what she was doing, it then became rather obvious.

He wanted to scream at her to stop.

He knew about her losing her daughter in the accident up on Copper's Ridge but had been with his mother visiting an aunt in Blackpool at the time. He had worried in case somebody went into the woods and found his den because it was still very much in the early stages of building and was not so well hidden then.

But he needn't have worried.

All his senses screamed as Mrs Tucker placed the loop over her head. She had to stand on tiptoe because the rope wasn't quite long enough. Clasping her hands together as she wobbled on the log, he thought she looked as though she was praying. But suddenly she tried to take the rope from around her neck. She had changed her mind but this time she did lose her balance. She fell forward but the rope stopped her.

Her feet were just a few inches from the ground.

He would remember forever the gurgling noise Mrs Tucker made.

Her fingers were caught between the rope and her neck, meaning the more she struggled the more noise she made and the tighter the rope became.

But soon the noise stopped and Mrs Tucker went limp as she swayed slowly from side to side, the only sound coming from the friction between the rope and the branch.

He waited for a few minutes, wanting to help her but still not knowing what he should do. Oh God, why wasn't he helping her? At last he got up from where he was hiding and ran over to the tree. Mrs Tucker's feet were still only a few inches from the grass beneath her. He took out a small torch he always carried and shone it in her face.

He jumped back when he saw her contorted features: her tongue was hanging out of her mouth and her eyes were wide open and bulging. It was as though Mrs Tucker was staring straight at him, pleading with him for his help.

She was dead.

His breathing became restricted and his head was playing tricks with him. He had known what Mrs Tucker intended doing but had done nothing to help her. Saving had been an option.

What had stopped him?

Being so close to his den should not have been a concern: he had witnessed Mrs Tucker committing suicide and he could have stopped her. If he were normal, would he have helped her? Was that it? Did his own self-doubt stop him from helping Mrs Tucker?

He believed she had changed her mind. She had gone up to Copper's Ridge to end it all but she had changed her mind. And he could have saved her.

If he were normal he would have saved her.

He turned and ran all the way back to village, tears streaming down his face not caring if anybody saw him.

He would never forget the horror of what he had seen up on Copper's Ridge but more importantly, he hated himself for not doing anything.

Living with the fact that he could have saved Mrs Tucker's life, would stay with him forever.

Reaching the stone wall by the Prestons' garage, Michael waited a further few minutes before running the short distance across the cobbled patio to the back door.

He prayed that the key would fit.

He took it out of his pocket and dropped it, shuddering as the noise it made on the stone slabs was amplified a thousand times. He swiftly picked it up and inserted it in the lock.

The key turned without any resistance.

He knew the house was not alarmed. He had set off an alarm once before and the experience scared him so much that he was determined he would never make the same mistake again.

Stepping into the Prestons' kitchen he stopped to listen. All he could hear, as in so many of the other houses he visited, was a clock ticking somewhere in the cottage but still he waited, taking in what he could see in the kitchen.

Sometimes Michael wondered what had made him begin his visits to outsiders' houses. About three months after starting work on his den, when he became bored with threading branches and reeds, he used to take one of his secret routes back to the village and watch people instead. He was amazed by what they did when they thought they were on their own. There were stories to tell but unfortunately, there was no one to tell them to. The village was riddled with his secret pathways and the places from which he watched the others.

He saw things that nobody would believe. He saw things that even he didn't believe or sometimes understand. But some of the things he saw made him feel better.

He knew people thought he was stupid, a whacko, an idiot – that's what his father had called him – but if they knew what went on under their very noses, they wouldn't say those things about him. He never did anything wrong other than when he watched Mrs Tucker accidentally kill herself. That had been very wrong.

What other people did, though, was sometimes wrong.

He saw Mrs Higgenbottom from Willow Cottage drown her cat in the river. She stroked the cat's head and even kissed it before looking round to make sure there was nobody about. Then she pushed the cat under the water.

The cat fought back and covered Mrs Higgenbottom with water. He wanted to rush over and push her into the water so that the cat could be saved. He would take it to his den, feed it and look after it, and name the cat Mrs Tucker.

Finally, the cat gave up struggling and Mrs Higgenbottom watched as its dead body floated away down the river.

He saw Mr Bateson who lived just beyond the ford to the right, and the Kelly's daughter from over by the hotel, meet in the field behind the top wood. Mr Bateson was married with three small children and Fiona Kelly worked in the hotel as a receptionist. She was probably half Mr Bateson's age and half his size too. They went into the long grass but Michael still saw her bare back and bottom when she was on top of Mr Bateson, moving about as though she was riding a horse.

All Michael ever did was watch and listen.

Later that day he saw Mr Bateson going off in his car with his wife and children. As they reached the green Fiona Kelly was walking the other way with a letter in her hand. He saw Mrs Bateson wave to Fiona and she waved back. Michael thought that was a bit strange.

And then there was the young couple who went to church sometimes and prayed to God. He wondered if God knew that they watched films in which people did things to each other, things that Michael never imagined people were capable of doing. When they watched a film, he also watched it with them through the back window.

He visited their house quite often. They never drew the curtains at the back, so watching the films with them and then what they did afterwards was easy.

Michael wondered if everybody was the same.

Did everybody have such secrets?

Mr Drayton, who lived down the Lower Swell road towards Parsons Hill Farm, had secrets too. His garage was full of boxes. From the pictures on the boxes Michael knew that they contained TVs, videos, DVD players and all sorts of other electrical things.

Why did Mr Drayton need so many electrical things?

Michael saw a white van go to the garage in the middle of the night and more boxes were off-loaded. At other times a blue van would arrive and the boxes would be re-loaded. He was confused by that as well but he guessed they were doing something wrong.

Whenever they were loading or unloading, the men and sometimes a woman always made sure nobody was watching them, and guilt was written all over their faces. Just like Mrs Higgenbottom had looked when she drowned her cat.

One evening after he'd been watching the village people for a few months, he went to an outsider's house not far from his own. It was a bit of a risk but as things turned out, very worth it.

This time he was quite close to the front of their house.

Seeing nothing of interest other than Mrs Singleton washing up in the kitchen he decided to leave. But just then her husband arrived home. The man was in such a hurry to get into the house he left his keys in the front door. Michael watched for a few minutes before thinking it would be fun to pinch the keys and see what the man would do. He sneaked round the edge of the garden up to the front door and it was so easy.

When after ten minutes the man didn't come out looking for the keys Michael took them home and looked at each key. Going into a drawer where he kept his old modelling bits and pieces he found the Plasticine he used when he used to make his models. He took impressions of what he thought was the back door key and as an afterthought, of the ignition key to the Audi the man drove.

He didn't know anything about cars other than their makes and models and he could not drive one, but it gave him a thrill to know he could steal the car if he wanted to.

Afterwards he went straight back to the house so that he could drop the keys at the front door. He had smiled to himself when thirty minutes later the man came out of the house only half dressed, looking for the keys. His smile broadened as the man looked around but didn't see him hiding only a few feet away.

During his lunch hour a few days later Michael took the piece of Plasticine to a key cutting shop in Evesham where he tried to explain he had lost his key and could they make him a new one. The man in the shop didn't believe him and threatened to call the police, so Michael went to a hardware store and bought a small vice, hacksaw and files.

It was easy, so easy.

It took three attempts to get his first key right but ten days after he borrowed the keys he let himself into the Singletons' house while they were away for the weekend. He spent an hour wandering from room to room looking in drawers and wardrobes. He found some things he didn't recognise or understand.

Within a couple of months he visited another six houses and cottages belonging to outsiders.

He also watched Wendy and Sharon, not believing he would ever forgive them for what they did to him after that time in the graveyard. He was sure he would get his revenge one day but he was willing to wait. He knew he ought to be grateful to the girls for what they did to him, but there was no need to treat him the way they did only a few days after letting him touch them.

But that was all seven years ago.

He often lay awake at night wondering what it would be like to kiss a girl properly or even just hold her hand. If he could pluck up the courage he would like to talk to a girl as well, but she would have to be a very special sort of girl to want to listen and talk to him. Sometimes he cried himself to sleep and on other occasions he went to sleep smiling because he remembered reading somewhere that there was somebody for everybody, so perhaps this girl really did exist, she was really out there somewhere ...

He just needed to meet her.

And one day by sheer chance he saw her.

If he had been five minutes later he would have missed her. His mother gave him a letter to post and he was walking up Church Lane from the ford towards the post box when he saw her. She was with a man and they were standing at Primrose Cottage looking down the lane towards the ford. She smiled and said hello but he was too shy to reply so he just nodded.

There was something very special about her.

In those few seconds he took on board every detail about her. He could describe every inch of her face, he could tell anybody how tall she was, what colour shoes she wore, how slim she was and what her smile was like when she said hello on that very first day. That smile told him all he needed to know because when she smiled at him it felt as though she had never smiled at anybody else – as though her smile was only for him.

From that moment he decided she would be the one.

He had found her.

It was worth the wait because she was special.

She was with someone but he had no idea what the man's face was like, what shoes he wore or how tall he was. All he knew was that the woman – no she was a girl – the girl he dreamed about was now living very close to him in Upper Slaughter.

It would take time.

But he could wait.

He would be patient and one day it would happen.

Chapter Five

Elspeth and John waved goodbye to Sarah and Phillip.

It was nearly midnight and they were ready for bed. Asking the others in for coffee when they got back from the restaurant was the friendly thing to do but Elspeth thought John had looked tired all evening and he didn't enter into the conversation as he normally did. They stayed longer at the table than they would have liked and after they got back it was a good hour before Phillip suggested he and Sarah ought to go home.

After clearing the mugs away Elspeth joined John in the kitchen.

"Did you enjoy the meal?" she asked him as she put the mugs in the sink.

John was pouring himself another brandy. "It was as good as many other Italian meals we've enjoyed, but nothing special." He turned and faced her, lifting the glass to his lips. "And you?"

"Yes," she said. "I enjoyed it. You were very quiet though."

"It's been a long week," he said. He very rarely discussed his work. Elspeth knew he was a stickler for client confidentiality so over the years she got used to dismissive statements when she asked him about his day. She respected him for not revealing more than he did.

"I think I've worked harder this week than ever before," Elspeth said as she washed up the mugs.

"I sincerely hope Sarah appreciates what you're doing for her."

"Of course she does but I'm not doing it for her appreciation. I know what it's like moving into a place like that. I wish there'd been somebody for us when we moved." She was going to add that she also wished John had been a little more useful when they moved in, but considering the mood he was in she decided that although she was being light-hearted it might just cause an argument.

She reached for the teacloth and picked up one of the mugs. "Did you notice anything strange about Sarah this evening?"

"Sarah? No, not really. You said I was quiet. I suppose she was a little quiet as well, for her anyway."

"That's what I thought. She seemed distant, that's all. We've been getting on very well this week so I don't think it's anything I might have said or done."

"She seemed pleased enough that we've also been invited to the palace, but there's no reason why she wouldn't be pleased," John said, draining his glass.

Elspeth screwed up her eyes. "No, she was genuinely pleased but maybe you're on the right track. I told her about the bottom-pinchers. I think she may have taken me a little more literally and seriously than I intended."

"I wouldn't mind pinching her –"

Elspeth let a smile creep onto her lips.

John had done the driving and she thought that maybe the lack of alcohol hadn't helped his mood. But now the brandy was obviously beginning to take effect. "You put your hands anywhere near her bottom and you'll have me to deal with!"

"What? As well, you mean? At the same time?"

"And what precisely are you suggesting?" she asked him.

"A man can dream, can't he?"

He put the glass on the side and walked across the kitchen. He put his hands on Elspeth's hips and smiled.

"I think the two of you together would satisfy a good fantasy," he said, still smiling.

"Oh, do you?" she said, pushing her hips forward. "I presume you'd be including yourself in this fantasy?"

"I might be, but then again I've always thought a bit of voyeurism didn't do a man any harm." He leaned forward and kissed Elspeth on the lips.

She reacted then pulled away. She didn't like it that he tasted of brandy. "I think Phillip might object."

"I doubt it," John said.

Elspeth tilted her head back so that she could focus on his face. "You're serious, aren't you?"

"The thought has a certain appeal, yes."

"And would I have any say in this?"

"If you needed to, but it might be better if you just let such things happen. You never know – you might enjoy it."

"John!"

Elspeth wanted to be shocked, really shocked, but what was more shocking was the fact that the thought did have a certain appeal. She had found herself watching Sarah as they went about their chores in Primrose Cottage. She had seen the intensity on Sarah's face as she concentrated. She had watched her move from room to room and waited for the look of sheer delight on her face when something finished up exactly as she wanted.

She had liked Sarah from the moment she set eyes on her and her feelings seemed to intensify by the day. Now that she thought about it she would admit – but only to herself – that her work was suffering and she was only too aware that her editor and publisher had set any number of deadlines for her next book. She reckoned she was at least two chapters behind schedule. She could always blame writers' block, the same excuse she used to create the time she wanted to spend with Sarah.

If JK Rowling could have writers' block then so could she.

John's suggestion, albeit wishful thinking, took her back over twenty years to her final year in school and to a relationship she had pushed to the back of her mind. But she had to admit that since meeting Sarah this brief affair had been on her mind more and more.

When she was seventeen, she did have a 'thing' with another girl. At the time she put it down to her hormones sorting themselves out: too much oestrogen or too little; she never knew which. Anyway it only lasted a couple of months but she did admit to herself that it was a thought provoking experience and could explain why she was without a really steady boyfriend until she met John. She just thought the right man had never come along, but then again she had never really gone looking.

Her thoughts were interrupted.

"But that's just a fantasy," John said as he took hold of her hand. "There's nothing like the real thing."

"Have you locked up?" she asked.

"Stop being so bloody romantic."

"It's important."

"Not as important as what I'll be thinking about in about ten minutes' time."

"That long," she said, smiling.

Michael watched the Prestons walk back down the lane to Primrose Cottage.

He had left the cottage an hour and half earlier which gave him enough time to go home and cook himself a simple meal. He didn't have to change because he knew his mother was out and when she was out on a Friday night it was unlikely that she would be back before the morning. On the way home he used one of his many secret routes so that he would not be seen in his combat clothing.

He smiled.

This was a special evening, a very special evening.

He didn't have to use his imagination anymore because a few hours earlier he had seen what he wanted to see. He remembered to wear gloves, not thick ones because thick gloves would have stopped him feeling things properly. He bought the gloves from a chemist shop in Evesham.

Wearing the gloves was a strange but enjoyable experience – so enjoyable he was still wearing them as he watched the Prestons walking slowly down Church Lane.

He would never throw the gloves away because they had touched her things, her very private things. As he watched he thought back to what he had seen ... and touched ...

After standing inside the kitchen door for a few minutes listening to the clock ticking, he moved slowly towards the door leading to the hall.

There was nothing in the kitchen that interested him. The things in the kitchen belonged to them both and he just wanted to see and touch and smell her things. He did think the kitchen was very different from the one at home. The kitchen at home was always in a mess but this one was very clean and tidy.

It would be, he thought. She would make sure everything was in order, that everything was as it should be.

The hall light was on.

He smiled.

He switched off his small torch.

At the bottom of the stairs he waited and listened.

The clock he heard ticking was a few feet away by the door that he guessed gave access to the front room. They would have a dining room as well because they were posh. When he thought of them as posh he didn't mean to be critical: he just knew they were different. There were a lot of people in the village who were different; those like him and his mother lived down one end and the posh ones lived everywhere else and most of them were outsiders. There were a few of the posh lot who had lived in the village for a long time, the Bond-Smithers for example. They were not outsiders but they did have a silly name.

When Michael was a young boy he remembered his mother and father referring to the people who lived in the big

71

house as the Smithers. Even that was a silly name. People at the other end of the village, near them, were called the Smiths.

He crept slowly up the stairs, testing each step to make sure it didn't creak. At the top of the stairs he switched on his torch again and shone it at the five doors that faced him.

All the doors were closed.

He tried to remember which window the Preston woman had appeared at when he saw her naked. Moving through the hall and up the stairs was disorientating, which annoyed him. If he could find his way through Copper's Ridge woods in the dark, constantly turning left and then right, sometimes turning back on himself, he ought to be able to find his way round a simple cottage. When going to his den he would always choose a different route so that he didn't trample down an obvious path, so surely he could decide which door he now needed. But a small hall and a simple set of stairs and the excitement of being where he was had resulted in him losing his sense of direction.

Trying the door nearest to him, he shone his torch through the crack. It was the bathroom. He would be going in there later. The bathroom's frosted window was at the front of the cottage so the main bedroom would be opposite. He went to the door on the other side of the landing and opened it. The first thing he was aware of was the smell. He had never smelt anything like it before. It was like the aroma of roses but was stronger, more overpowering.

He was sure this was the right room.

Yes, there was a double bed, a dressing table and a chair, a chest of drawers and on the wall to his right a huge mirror stretching from floor to ceiling. On the wall to his left was another door that could be a cupboard.

He wondered where he should start.

Planning ahead had not been an option because he'd been unaware of what he would find.

He made his way to the chest of drawers and opened the top left-hand drawer. It was full of men's handkerchiefs, pants and things. The urge to tip the drawer and its contents out of the window was strong. After trying the other drawers and found they all contained that man's things, he moved to the bedside table nearest the window.

It had two drawers.

Opening the top one first, he found nothing but a couple of books, some small tins and loose coins.

His things again.

Two minutes had passed already and he had seen nothing of hers. He went round to the other side of the bed, opened the top drawer of the bedside table and smiled.

At last she was here, she was his.

He had found her.

These were her things.

Opening the drawer a little further, he shone his torch towards the back. There were make-up bottles, tubes and some bits of card like the ones he remembered seeing his mother use on her nails. He hated the rasping noise they made. It made his teeth feel funny.

There was what looked like a sleeve of aspirin, the sort you pushed so that the tablet popped out automatically.

He enjoyed doing that.

Crouching down, he twisted his head so that he could see the words on the sleeve. He would buy the same tablets from the chemist so he could imagine he was sharing them with her. The dim light meant he couldn't read the small print but the pills were not like anything he had seen before. He recognised the word *prescription*, and then there was an easy word, *only*. The sleeve looked very old, almost as though she hadn't taken anything from it recently. But then, holding the sleeve closer and with help from the torch, he saw that each slot had three letters next to it – Mon, Tue, Wed, Thu, Fri, Sat and Sun – of course, they were days of the week.

But all the pills were still in their slots.

Was she ill?

Was she supposed to be taking some medicine but not doing as she was told? The pills didn't look like anything he had ever taken. He tried to pronounce the other word he could now see, *Tri-Cyclen*, but gave up.

He thought for a moment.

Did she have to take medicine every day? He closed the drawer, his eyebrows knitted in confusion.

He would not like it if she were ill.

Next he opened the bottom drawer.

Nothing interesting. Just birthday cards and a couple of small books that looked like diaries. He would have liked to read her diaries especially on the day he saw her for the first time.

There was a strange looking thing sticking out from under one of the diaries. It was a sort of dark colour, but he could only see a little of it.

It intrigued him. He moved one of the diaries to get a better look. He used the end of the torch to touch it.

He frowned. He had seen something like it before in the bedside cupboard drawers in other outsiders' houses. He took off one of his gloves and touched it with his finger. It was slightly rubbery. He couldn't remember what this thing he was looking at was called but he remembered seeing the name in one of his magazines.

As he moved the diary back over the object he remembered what it was for. Why did she need one of those when she had that man?

He shrugged: he was confused again.

Putting the glove back on before closing the drawer, he shone the torch at the large mirror. He was a little shocked when he saw himself kneeling by the bed.

Was he really here? Was he really kneeling next to where she slept?

He shone the torch over the mirror seeing for the first time that there was a join running from floor to ceiling. He stood up and touched the join. Curling his finger round the edge of the join he pulled. The mirror slid smoothly revealing an array of shelves and drawers on one side and on the other a row of her clothes on hangers.

On the shelves he saw pullovers and T-shirts in the colours he had seen her in. He bent forward and smelt them. They had a clean and perfumed smell. He opened one of the drawers below the shelves and smiled.

This was what he was looking for.

An Aladdin's cave of pants and bras. Some things that looked like belts with bits hanging down and other things that didn't seem to be any more than bits of string.

Something started happening between his legs.

He took off one of his gloves and reached into the drawer. Some of her underwear felt very silky. When he touched the bras the feeling in his trousers increased. He knew what he wanted to do but he mustn't. He would do it later.

Could he risk taking something?

He had never taken anything from anyone before, but she was different.

This visit was very special.

No, she would miss whatever he took.

But she could have mislaid it.

Surely he could risk taking just one thing. Perhaps the things at the back of the drawer were things she didn't wear very often and wouldn't miss straightaway.

He pulled the drawer out further.

At the very back he saw a pair of red pants tucked away in one corner. He quickly put them in his pocket as though he was being watched. It was more than he could have wished for.

She wouldn't miss just one pair. He moved the other pants at the back to conceal the gap and closed the drawer.

Knowing what was in his pocket made him want to leave the cottage as soon as possible, not because he knew what he would be doing as soon as he could but because he felt like a thief. Until then all he had ever done was look and touch.

He was not doing anything wrong.

He hadn't broken anything.

But now he was a thief.

The temptation had been too great.

He started to leave the room but stopped at the door. Should he put the pants back? No, he needed them. And anyway, it was too late. Putting the pants back in exactly the same position he had found them wouldn't be possible.

It would be better to keep them.

After closing the door behind him, he looked at the bathroom door. He wanted to go in there but now he needed to get out of the cottage as fast as possible.

For the first time he was a thief.

Sarah was pleased to be home.

Phillip opened the front door and the light flooded the path leading to the gate. The evening had gone well but it was just a little too challenging. She was sure Elspeth sensed something was wrong, but by not asking what it was in front of the men suggested she had probably guessed the truth already. As she'd be back to work on Monday Sarah hoped by the time she and Elspeth were next alone she would have forgotten all about it.

Or was it too serious to forget?

Phillip closed the door behind her.

She shivered as she looked around. She was experiencing exactly the same feeling she had felt when they first viewed the cottage, and once or twice since. It made her feel very uneasy. She dropped her wrap on the hall chair and hurried to the kitchen expecting there to be signs of an intruder. She flipped on the light-switch, quickly checking to see if everything was in its place.

It was.

She turned the back door handle. It was locked. The locks had been changed soon after they moved in.

"What are you doing?" Phillip asked as he walked into the kitchen.

She turned round, not knowing if she ought to tell him how she felt. "I was checking the door," she said.

He reached for the brandy bottle. "I could see that, but why? Night cap?" he asked, holding out the bottle.

"Just a small one, please," she said, moving away from the door and feeling a little foolish. "We always check the doors," she said, moving across the kitchen towards him.

He handed her the glass. "Shall we take these upstairs?"

She could see in his eyes that he was being defensive.

She was well aware that when she drank too much she could become argumentative – Phillip's word not hers. She became more assertive but as he was not confrontational, he always seemed to think she was being aggressive. The amount of alcohol she had drunk this evening didn't dictate her mood, it was generated by her confusion.

"Why not," she said.

She checked the kitchen again before switching off the light and following Phillip up the stairs, stopping again on the landing to sniff the air. The feeling was even stronger: somebody definitely had been in the cottage.

Phillip was putting the bedside lights on so she took a moment to open the bathroom door. She went over to the window and checked it. No, that was silly. If somebody wanted to break into the cottage it would be from the back not the front. The single streetlight by the cottage was not good but was bright enough to act as a deterrent. She crossed the landing, went into the bedroom and immediately checked the en-suite shower room.

"What are you doing now?" Phillip asked, looking at her from the doorway.

She shook her head. "Nothing. I was just thinking."

"What about?" he asked. He was already undressed.

"Nothing," she said, feeling as though she needed to say something.

"Nothing! When you say *nothing* you normally mean *everything.*" He smiled at her. "Come on, it's late," he added as he got into bed.

"I haven't cleaned my teeth yet."

About fifteen minutes later Phillip rolled onto his back and sighed deeply. "I don't know what's the matter, Sarah, but it's like making love to a block of ice."

"I'm sorry. I'm just not in the mood."

"That's pretty obvious."

On the other occasions when she wasn't in the mood, she always managed to summon up enough enthusiasm so that he was none the wiser. But tonight ... tonight was different. She was going to have to tell him. She flipped on her bedside light, threw back the covers and knelt at Phillip's side. He put a hand on her thigh but she gave him a look that told him she wanted to be serious.

"What is it?" he asked.

She put her index finger on his chest and lowered her eyes. "You promise not to laugh?"

"Something was getting to you while we were out and now something's been bugging you since we got in. If it's something I've said or done for God's sake tell me. Then maybe we can get on with the job in hand – or not, if the expression on your face at this precise moment is anything to go by."

"You do promise?"

"Of course I do."

Sarah ran her finger down to his stomach, her eyes still lowered. She certainly hadn't wanted to discuss how she felt while they were out but what she had sensed since getting home was different. "I think while we were out tonight we were burgled," she said quietly.

He put his hand over his mouth. "I'm sorry, Sarah, but you're kneeling stark naked in front of me. We've been back in the house at least twenty minutes, and now you tell me you think we've been burgled. May I ask what makes you think that?"

"A feeling," she said as she closed her eyes, her finger making little circles on his stomach. She knew how stupid

78

she must sound but if she was unable to discuss these feelings with him, who else was there? She had promised herself things would change so she must be open and honest with him ... about most things.

"A feeling?" Phillip said. "I've seen nothing and I might have noticed if we'd been burgled."

"I don't mean burgled. I mean that while we were out somebody else has been in the cottage, been in here, in this room." She opened her eyes and looked at him. "I mean it Phillip, I know."

"But how do you know?" he said, sitting up and putting his hands on her shoulders.

She shook her head slowly as her eyes began to water.

"I don't know how I know. I just know. The air has been disturbed, there's a smell, there's a feeling." A tear ran down her cheek and she lifted her hand to wipe it away.

"You're serious, aren't you?" he said as he moved his hands slowly down her arms. He swung his legs off the bed. "Look I'll go and check every room and then perhaps you'll feel a bit better."

"You won't find anything," she told him.

"I'll check anyway."

She watched him over her shoulder as he left the room. It was a little incongruous that her husband should conduct a security check of the cottage without even bothering to put his pants on. He was making fun of her but he didn't realise it. She sat on the side of the bed and looked at her reflection in the mirror.

She shivered.

On impulse she got off the bed and opened her wardrobe. Checking every hanger from left to right, she quickly concluded that nothing was missing. She opened her underwear drawer half way and once again, nothing was missing. She glanced at all the shelves, but as far as she could see, nothing had been disturbed.

But she was sure somebody had been in the house and if nothing was missing why else would they break in.

But nobody *had* broken in.

She could hear Phillip going from room to room, checking every window. He would find nothing. He could check the entire cottage, even the small cellar under the two front rooms and he would find nothing.

When he came back into the room she was sitting on the bed, her knees drawn up to her chin.

"Absolutely nothing," he said closing the bedroom door. "Nothing's been moved and nothing's missing. You're not convinced are you?" he suggested, sitting on the edge of the bed.

Still she looked at him.

"What makes you so sure, Sarah?"

"I just know."

Phillip couldn't make it out.

The change in Sarah since they moved to Upper Slaughter was wonderful in so many ways, but the positive changes were marred by her less discernible mood swings. When they were in Evesham her moods had been predictable. He could always tell the moment he walked into the house whether she was happy with her day or not. Before moving he had noticed that the good days were becoming less and less, but they were still there every now and again. He wanted her to stop work, well not stop, but at least do something she looked forward to doing. If there had been a career for her to follow then he wouldn't have interfered but it was almost as though she was going to work waiting for something else to happen.

But since they moved to Upper Slaughter she appeared to be a lot happier. She seemed to have a real purpose in life. He knew she was as upset as he was because the family they so dearly wanted was still eluding them. She so wanted to be a wife and a mother because the two in her mind were inextricably linked. They would be a proper family then.

Perhaps that was what it was all about.

Perhaps she had expected to fall pregnant straightaway because of the changes in their lifestyle and environment.

About a year ago they discussed the possibility of IVF treatment, but she quickly dismissed the idea. He could even remember her exact words – "If we're going to have a family it'll be by purely natural means. If I become pregnant that would be fantastic, but if it's not meant to be we'll have to accept it. I'm not going to become an object of research. It's going to be natural or not at all."

No matter how much he tried to argue that IVF treatment merely enhanced the natural process, he did not get anywhere. She was adamant.

He had hoped her happiness since the move would overcome whatever was stopping them having a family. He hoped it would make her relax more. But she had got herself into bit of a state. This silly business about a possible intruder had never happened before. Whatever was stopping her falling pregnant had to have something to do with her – not him. He didn't feel bitter about it but it had to be her. He'd had all the checks and the analysis showed that there was nothing wrong.

However, tests had shown there was nothing wrong with Sarah either.

The cottage looked absolutely splendid.

Each day he arrived home, he marvelled at what she had achieved. She seemed inspired. Their house in Evesham was no different to all the other executive houses on the estate, so they were limited with what they could have done with it. On the other hand, the cottage had a character of its own and Sarah, with Elspeth's help, had made every wall, every corner into something special.

But something was still wrong, very wrong.

She would tell him when she was ready.

Her knees remained drawn up under her chin, her expression morose. He wanted to get inside her head and help if he could. He would never believe just how lucky he was finding someone like her. She seemed so fragile on the outside but he knew how strong she really was. Looking at her now he loved the contoured lines of her curved back. He cherished the silky smoothness of her skin, the tantalising way her breasts were pressed against her thighs. Her small hands and feet looked as delicate as the rest of her. She oozed sensuality and he could feel the desire building up in him again. But something was really troubling her and he would have to find out what it was.

He reached across the bed and slowly ran the backs of his fingers across her thigh. Sarah twisted her head and looked at him.

"Would you just hold me, Phillip?"

"Of course I will," he said, stretching out next to her.

She straightened her legs before slowly sliding down onto her back.

"No, I mean just hold me. Nothing else, just hold me."

He took her in his arms. "What's wrong?" he asked, kissing the top of her head.

"I'm scared," she whispered. "So very scared."

When Michael watched as the lights were switched one by one in the rooms and he saw that man checking the windows before drawing the curtains, he frowned.

Moments later each light was switched off again.

He was confused.

Had he made a mistake? Did they know he had been in their cottage? But maybe that man checked the windows every night before drawing the curtains. Was he worrying unnecessarily?

Feeling for the pants in his picket he wondered if they had been a risk too far.

Chapter Six

Michael went to bed just after one o'clock.

As he expected, his mother wasn't home so there was no need for him to go back to his den. He put his combat jacket and trousers under his bed as he was confident he would have time in the morning to hide them. It wasn't his normal routine but this was not a normal occasion.

He was euphoric: he had visited her cottage for the first time, his smile covered his face a she put Mrs Preston's red pants under his pillow. The following day he would keep them with him in his pocket and take them to his den later. But for tonight, because he was alone in the house, he would sleep with her pants next to his face. They were so soft and silky, and they smelt of her perfume.

Michael shuddered in anticipation.

His first time would be with her.

It wasn't wishful thinking because it was now a matter of fact.

There was nobody else, not for the first time.

She would show him what to do and how to do it.

Michael lay back in bed and thought about the times he walked from the bus to work and then back again in the evening. He saw some of the girls flaunting themselves. They wore their jeans so tight and so low that their bare midriffs were an open invitation to touch, just like Wendy had let him touch her. He thought some of the girls he saw ought to look at themselves in a mirror because what they were showing everybody wasn't very pretty. Some of the girls bulged out of the tops of their jeans and at the front, the sides and the back. They were disgusting.

Others wore short skirts that showed their legs almost to their hips, and tops that exposed their breasts for everybody to see. He wondered why they did it. Was it some sort of ritual he didn't understand?

Mrs Preston wasn't like that. She would never flaunt herself.

The girls he saw in the town were different to her. There wasn't any need for Mrs Preston – he wished he knew her first name – to flaunt herself. When he saw her at the bedroom window, she wasn't flaunting herself. She didn't know he was there: if she had she would not have let him see her the way she did.

Not yet.

Michael could see her now. He loved it: whenever he wanted to, he could picture what he had seen. Unlike Sharon and Wendy, Mrs Preston's breasts were small – no he would use the word *petite*. He liked that word but he couldn't remember how he knew it meant small. Was it French? Anyway, her breasts were petite like the rest of her. But that wasn't why she didn't parade herself in front of everybody. She was a private person.

But he now had part of her.

The red pants were in his hand.

He sat up and looked at his reflection in the mirror on the wall.

She *was* a private person but only with other people, that man would see her, see all of her … and touch her, as she would touch him.

Letting that man do it to her was not something he Michael wanted to imagine.

She would speak to that man; they would have conversations during which she would tell him everything: her secrets and her worries, when she was happy and when she was sad. That man would talk to her, he wouldn't become tongue-tied and he wouldn't dry up when he couldn't say the right words.

Michael looked at his reflection in the mirror: tears came to his eyes and the image blurred. Nobody else ought to be allowed to touch her and nobody else should share her private thoughts.

She was sacred – was that the right word? – she was meant only for him.

She didn't really want to let that man touch her and do it to her, she did it because they were married. What was it he heard in the church that time his mother had taken him to a boring wedding?

The bride who had been half the size of the man – a bit like Mr Bateman and the Kelly girl – had promised to *honour* and *obey*. He remembered shaking his head not understanding why she had to *honour* and *obey* the man she was marrying but the man didn't have to do the same. That was why Mrs Preston would do it, because Mrs Preston had promised to *honour* and *obey* her husband. She had promised and she wouldn't break a promise once made.

She was so small and delicate, so ... petite.

He would be gentle with her.

Would she touch him the way Wendy and Sharon had touched him? No, Mrs Preston would touch him in a different way. She would touch him so that he felt ... he didn't know how he would feel but he knew it would be different and wonderful.

Wendy and Sharon were the same as the girls he saw in the town. They had exposed themselves to him, they had encouraged him, they had done dirty things to him. That is not what he wanted. He wanted it to be gentle and kind, not filthy and nasty.

His eyes were still watering.

A tear ran down his cheek so he lifted the pants to his face and wiped the tear away.

That man did not deserve to have somebody like her next to him.

He knew he could not and would not treat Mrs Preston the same way that man treated her. When he saw them walking up Church Lane and back again, they were holding hands. She was only doing it to please that man. If he had been walking beside her he would have put his arm round her, to protect her.

He smiled through his tears.

Maybe before he did anything with Mrs Preston he ought to get rid of that man. That would be fun. She would thank him because it would be what she wanted. She wouldn't want to *honour* and *obey*. Yes, that is probably what he ought to do: kill the man and then she would be his.

He shook his head but the smile remained, killing somebody would be something new to him. He had never killed anybody before.

Of course he hadn't because the need had never existed before: not knowing how to do it didn't help. But he had seen death: Mrs Tucker killed herself in front of him but that was different. Mrs Higgenbottom had drowned her cat, but that was also different.

So he was right, he had never killed before.

Wait … no, that wasn't strictly true.

Early on after starting to build the den, he had put out some rabbit traps, although he didn't know why. Maybe he wanted to catch some food. To his surprise he trapped a fully grown male but one look at the lolling tongue, the big open eyes and the feel of the soft fur in his hands, made him cry like a baby. He took the still warm but surprisingly heavy little body to the far edge of the wood to bury it. He made a small cross for the grave. He stood over the little mound of earth and bowed his head, his hands clasped together as he said he was sorry.

But that man was different.

The little rabbit hadn't done any harm to anybody but that man was abusing another lovely creature: he deserved to be punished so he deserved to die.

The girls he saw in town flaunting themselves were asking for trouble, and Michael was sure they got everything they deserved but Mrs Preston did not.

There would be no grave for that man, no little cross and certainly he would never say he was sorry.

But how would he do it?

That would give him something to think about each night before he went to sleep because he never doubted what he would dream about. He had dreamt about her every night since the afternoon he had first seen her, since the afternoon she looked at him and said Hello.

Michael lay down on his bed, clutching Sarah Preston's red pants in his hand.

He felt tired now.

As he drifted off to sleep there was a smile on his face. The tears had stopped.

Elspeth woke suddenly.

For a second or two she was totally disorientated but then she wondered what had woken her. She expected to hear the pitter-patter of rain or even a crack of thunder; the clouds had looked very threatening earlier on.

But there was nothing.

Was it John? John was breathing evenly next to her. He always had a good night's sleep after they made love: making love seemed to act as a soporific tonic or drug ... she couldn't decide which would be the right description.

No, it wasn't John. So what was it?

She looked up at the beamed ceiling trying to get some inspiration from the patterns and shadows generated by the moonlight streaming in through the window, now that the threat of a storm had passed. She was sure she had been dreaming. Dreams normally woke her up. They were often bizarre and she would wake up to make sure her fantasies were not in fact reality. But she was sure it hadn't been some implausible mental process that had woken her. It was something far more tangible. After spending three weeks helping Sarah sort out Primrose Cottage she had fallen behind with her writing schedule, so perhaps it was her conscience.

Then her brain told her to go back a thought or two.

She had been dreaming about Sarah, that was it.

She screwed up her eyes trying to drag from her memory what had happened with Sarah in her dream to make her wake up. Why would dreaming about Sarah wake her up? It was the fantasies that normally woke her up. Sarah was not a fantasy, she was real, a person, a living thing. Elspeth closed her hands into tight fists under the bedclothes, straining and willing herself to think.

And then it came to her, not in a flash but sort of oozing out of her mind as though it wasn't what she really wanted to see.

She saw rejection: in her dream she had been rejected.

Beads of perspiration broke out on her forehead and the hairs on the back of her neck began to prickle. Why would she dream of rejection?

Regardless, going back to sleep was now an impossibility so she carefully got out of bed without disturbing John, retrieved her dressing gown from the back of the bedroom door and went downstairs to the kitchen to make herself a cup of tea.

Sitting at the kitchen table, she tried again to recall the dream.

Yes. They were in Sarah's cottage painting one of the walls in the sitting room a very garish colour, purple she thought.

Why purple she didn't know.

She hated purple.

They were laughing together because bizarrely they were dressed ready for the cocktail party at the palace in a couple of weeks' time. The purple paint was splattering on their dresses and it was all very amusing. She was asking Sarah to pass her a paint roller and she dropped it onto her shoes. Her shoes were covered in the purple paint and it was also on the carpet.

They laughed again.

88

As they both bent down to pick up the roller their hands touched. Standing up, still laughing, they were only inches apart and on impulse Elspeth leant forward and kissed Sarah on the lips.

"What are you doing?" Sarah asked, no longer smiling, her eyes fiery.

"Kissing you."

"Why?"

"Because I think I've fallen in love with you."

Sarah laughed again but this time is was derisory. "What do you mean you've fallen in love with me?" She lifted the roller in front of her to form a barrier between them.

"I want us to be together. I want to live with you."

"Well you can't. What do you think I am?"

"I need you."

"You need your head looking at."

As she spoke, Sarah ran the roller down Elspeth's face, from her hairline to her neck.

It was the feeling of the paint smarting in her eyes that had woken her.

Elspeth couldn't remember ever recalling a dream so vividly. She often tried to analyse her dreams – she thought it would be useful for her writing – but previously she was only able to recollect roughly what the dreams were about.

This dream was vivid in her mind.

As she sipped the hot tea, she remembered once again the relationship she had during her last year at school. She was sure it had been just a passing phase. It worried her at the time, but then she dismissed it. Nothing happened in the interim years to add to her concerns. Of course she thought about it every now and then, but just as part of her personal, very personal, life. She never felt the need to discuss it with anybody.

All girls go through that sort of phase, don't they?

So why did she dream of telling Sarah she loved her? No, not *loved her* but *in love* with her. Of course she loved Sarah because that was how good friends felt about each other, but *in love*? That meant she wanted Sarah physically as well as emotionally.

She smiled.

Of course!

It must be a combination of what John had been fantasising about before they went to bed and the relationship from school which flitted into her mind but flitted out again just as quickly.

That was it.

Of course it wasn't because she was in love with Sarah. As she thought, she loved her as one woman can love another woman because they are simply very good friends.

She frowned.

But could the real truth be staring her in the face?

While they worked together and she watched Sarah moving about the cottage, did she ever feel anything for her other than friendship? Did she feel the urge to take her exquisite little friend in her arms and kiss her as she had in the dream? Had she ever wanted to put her hands under Sara's T-shirt and run them all over her body? Had she ever ...

She hesitated. She hesitated because the answer was yes, yes she had. Of course she had.

Why hadn't she admitted that to herself straightaway?

Just because she hadn't felt like this about another woman for all these years didn't mean she had to deny her real feelings now.

So was she really *in love* with Sarah? Had she been *in love* with the girl at school too? Was it the real, real truth that scared her? Was she denying that it was the truth?

Had she suppressed her true feelings for all these years?

Her eyes filled with tears. She didn't understand. It couldn't be how she really felt.

She made herself another cup of tea and ten minutes later went back upstairs and crawled into bed next to John, still choked up with tears.

Michael was awake, lying in bed staring at the ceiling with his hands behind his head and he was still thinking of that man.

His mind was in such a whirl, sleep would not come to him..

There were some very unpleasant thoughts. He was thinking of all of the ways he could kill that man, smiling when he imagined a particularly gruesome method but because it involved lot of blood he dismissed it immediately ... he hated the sight of blood.

Admitting that he didn't hate Mrs Preston's husband was not easy. How could he hate him when he didn't even know him? His ghoulish thoughts would have been the same regardless of who Mrs Preston was with. It didn't matter who it might be.

But caution was important.

If that man were to meet with a tragic accident, Michael must not do anything that might cause the finger of suspicion to be pointed at him.

He couldn't remember ever seeing a policeman in Upper Slaughter, not since Mrs Tucker had killed herself. His mother had told him that was what it said in the paper – Mrs Tucker had committed suicide – but he knew Mrs Tucker had changed her mind and it had been an accident.

The police put tape round the tree and the area where they found her body but not for long. Michael watched from inside the woods. Nobody had known he was there.

Although he thought he was too clever and would never be discovered in his den, killing somebody was different.

There would be clues. There were always clues.

Were policemen in real life as clever as the ones on TV?

No matter how hard he tried to cover things up there would always be clues. That is what the people on the television said. He didn't understand a lot of what he heard but it seemed that the police always found the murderer because he – it was usually a man – always made a mistake.

So he must be careful. He must make it look like an accident. There must not be any clues.

Still smiling he turned off the bedside light. He would enjoy planning that man's death.

For a few minutes he listened to the noises of the night before closing his eyes and drifting off to sleep. The red pants were next to his cheek.

Sarah woke up with a start, the dream still vivid in her mind's eye.

If asked she would normally have been able to tell Phillip what she was going to dream about before she went to sleep. He said once that there was no way of disproving her theory because afterwards she could say whatever she liked about her dream.

"Why would I do something like that?" she had said.

But this time, even though Phillip had conducted a thorough search of the cottage and found nothing missing and no sign of forced entry, Sarah remained convinced that somebody had been there while they were out.

She could smell whoever it was.

It was not a smell that was immediately discernible from the other smells in the cottage, but by separating the smells in her mind she knew there was one that wasn't there when they went out. The smell was at its strongest in the bedroom.

She could smell it now as she lay awake, watching the reflection on the ceiling of the branches moving on the trees outside. She had no idea what time it was. Lifting herself onto her elbows she looked at the illuminated clock on Phillip's bedside table. It was just after three. She closed her eyes as she shook her head. She was being stupid. Of course there were no smells: they were just in her imagination. She had wanted to satisfy herself that there was something different because she was so convinced there had been an intruder.

She pulled her knees up under the duvet and rested her head on them. Perhaps the house was haunted. Perhaps

Hilary Bond-Smithers hadn't told her everything; she had implied there was more to tell. Sarah wondered whether if she was told that a particular house in the village was haunted, she would tell someone who moved in exactly what she knew about it. She didn't know but she didn't think so. It would depend on whether the stories were harmful or not. There were good ghosts and bad ghosts, or so she had been told. Anyway such stories become grossly embellished with time. Not that Sarah had heard many ghost stories, especially not when living on an Evesham housing estate. But one evening when she was in her early teens she heard her mother and father talking about ghosts and she lay awake all night with the light on.

The story, now nearly twenty years old, was immediately recallable. They were living in army quarters in a place called Deepcut, near Aldershot, in a longish cul-de-sac that led away from the Officers' Mess. A World War 1 army officer who smoked a pipe supposedly haunted the Officers' Mess. The officer was often seen in full battle uniform leaning against the wall in a corridor smoking a pipe, as though he was leaning against a trench wall. Even when he couldn't be seen, in certain areas of the Mess the faint aroma of his pipe tobacco lingered.

She screwed up her eyes.

The smell of pipe tobacco.

Perhaps that was why she associated smells with things that might be out of the ordinary. The story had stuck in her subconscious.

The Officers' Mess was knocked down to make way for a bigger more modern building, and the story went on to say that as a result the World War One officer became homeless and so he wandered round the army quarters rapping on doors looking for a new home. People heard his hob-nailed boots on their paths, heard him knocking on the doors but when the doors were opened there was nobody there – except the aroma from his pipe.

Perhaps it was because when her mother saw how wide Sarah's eyes became as she listened to the story, she laughed it off by saying that she had never seen the officer, nor smelt his pipe tobacco, and it was probably children playing games by knocking on doors and running away. But her father, who wasn't as perceptive as her mother, had said: "What? At four o'clock in the morning?"

Sarah smiled to herself as she thought about her mother and father. Her mother had been to the cottage a couple of times and liked what she saw. She hadn't been for a weekend yet because Sarah wanted the cottage to be completely organised before she had anybody to stay over. Probably in a couple of weeks' time, maybe the weekend after the cocktail party. She wished her father could have come too. He would have liked Primrose Cottage and especially Upper Slaughter.

Phillip's parents Peter and Margaret had also been to visit but she didn't get the same vibes from them, especially his mother. She said very little but Sarah could tell. She also knew that Margaret was as disappointed about her daughter-in-law not having become pregnant as she and Phillip were. But it was pretty obvious on whom she placed the blame. Phillip's father just wandered around the garden puffing on his pipe oblivious of the little overtones and undertones that always came her way from Margaret. She had never said anything about this to Phillip because she knew it would cause a row.

Still with her knees up under the duvet she continued to stare into space for what seemed like hours. Thoughts normally reserved for such private moments whirled round in her mind. She felt very alone.

She shivered when she felt Phillip's fingers running slowly down her back as he lightly traced each vertebra.

"Can't you sleep?" he asked, his voice soft and sluggish.

She shook her head. "No."

His fingers went the base of her spine and trailed across her bottom to the underside of her thigh, over her knee then onto the top of her leg and back towards her hip. She could feel his gentleness having the usual effect on her: it always did initially but it was what he did next that would be routine. She hoped that this time he would do something different, something that would excite her. She appreciated that she could also initiate change – she could move his hands, his fingers and lips to where she wanted them to be – but where sex was concerned he always wanted to be in control and she no longer had the enthusiasm to do anything about it. She couldn't remember the last time they made love at four o'clock in the morning. Perhaps the unusual time would make a difference.

He moved a little closer to her so that he could put his hand on her stomach and then upwards towards her breast.

Okay, she thought, she couldn't refuse him.

She was wide-awake and maybe, just maybe, something she longed for might happen.

Straightening her legs, she lay down with her head on the pillows.

And waited.

Phillip smiled as he held himself up on his arms and looked down at her in the gloom. He knew what she was thinking, what she was praying for. Her eyes were closed and her arms were spread sideways across the bed like a crucifix. He kept his eyes open as he began to move slowly, praying for what they both so dearly wanted.

Foreplay had not been necessary. It was obvious what they both wanted most of all.

Sarah pleaded with her body to accept him.

She begged whatever was stopping her from conceiving to give them what they wanted. Would it matter that when she did discover she was pregnant she wouldn't be able to remember the actual conception?

She *needed* to be pregnant: they needed a baby because a baby would give greater strength and reason for their marriage. A baby would change their lives and take them out of the rut she felt they were slowly but inexorably slipping into.

Maybe they were already in it.

Moving to the cottage was a start and she was happy with the changes, but the most precious part of their relationship had to happen. If it didn't she was worried that it could eventually have a long term and dreadful consequence.

She wanted to conceive and she wanted a daughter.

A daughter-father relationship, she believed, was very special and that was what they needed, something very special to wipe out the fearful omen that engulfed her every time they made love.

Phillip was enjoying moving slowly.

He enjoyed making love to Sarah so much that he never wanted it to end. She was so lovely, so very, very lovely.

For the millionth time he thought how lucky he had been to find her. She was everything he ever wanted. Before they met he often tried to picture the female who was out there somewhere waiting for him as he would be waiting for her. When they did meet for the first time – the day she dropped the files at his feet – he knew his dream had come true.

He fell in love straightaway, the moment he gave her the files and looked into her smiling eyes. There was no need for either of them to say anything. And since that day he never for one second doubted his love for her. He thought it impossible for one human being to feel so strongly about another.

She knew he was watching her.

When they had sex she liked to do it with her eyes closed, but he liked to watch. She understood why.

She didn't like being watched because it meant that she had to make an extra effort to fake fulfilment. If he didn't watch then she would just have to make the right noises.

She shouldn't be thinking like that, but she hadn't felt fulfilled for, oh she couldn't remember how long, but it must be years now. He would do what he thought was his best but he always fell short, and afterwards she felt disappointed and unfulfilled.

So was that the problem?

Was conception related to how she felt during and after the sexual act?

Pregnancy would never result if she simply screwed up her eyes and whimpered. She knew she was being unkind but before they were married and for a few years afterwards, she never had a problem. She remembered looking forward to making love with him: she remembered how it once was.

So what had changed? Why was she bored?

When they were making love Phillip was kind, caring and thoughtful. He did everything he believed she needed and wanted so that she could enjoy sex as much as he did, but ... now there was always something missing.

So what *was* the problem?

Did she think that when she conceived everything had to be wonderful? Would she know at the time, would she feel as though it had happened at last? Not even the lack of her own satisfaction ought to stop what they both wanted, what was so natural for so many others. But maybe that was it. Maybe she was expecting too much. Maybe she ought to try to separate her needs: her need to fall pregnant and her need to enjoy sex. Perhaps if she concentrated on one and not the other, it would happen. They had both wanted children straightaway and after three years when nothing happened, maybe her body started to ask *what's the point?*

Rather than being bored maybe she had lost interest because nothing had happened. The very fact that she was thinking that way suggested she was the one with the problem, not Phillip.

But was she?

Each time they started to make love, her body reacted but then it seemed to lose interest. He was caring but that was not enough. It was always the same, there was never anything new.

She was bored. Really bored.

He was still moving slowly: she knew he was waiting for her.

She bent her knees, forced her thighs against his sides, and began to make the noises he would want to hear. Keeping her eyes closed, she tried to dismiss the negative thoughts from her mind and imagine that this was the time it would happen, this was the time ...

But totally unexpectedly she thought of Elspeth.

And she could see her. She could see her face, her smile and her eyes just as she had watched her when they were getting the cottage sorted. At first she had felt a little unsettled by the other woman's close attention but she got used to it and started to enjoy the closeness such a friendship brought with it. She remembered how she felt when Elspeth left after they finished work for the day. She always felt low until Phillip arrived home.

She saw Elspeth's smiling face in front of her now as she leaned towards her. She could feel Elspeth's lips on hers.

She squeezed her eyes more firmly shut, trying to understand what was happening. She could still feel Phillip moving slowly, doing everything he could to please her. She tightened the grip with her thighs and crossed her ankles above his back. In response he lowered his head and kissed her.

But it wasn't his lips on hers – they were Elspeth's, sweet and soft.

What was happening?

They were in a field, a field of long grass and buttercups, lying in the grass, their clothes discarded. It was still Elspeth's lips on hers, not Phillip's. It was Elspeth's warm breath against her skin, not Phillip's. It was Elspeth's hands either side of her face not Phillip's. Elspeth was doing things to her she had never experienced before –

Then somewhere in the distance she heard Phillip groaning as he always groaned. She felt him tense as he always tensed. She tried to pull him deeper, wanting to feel him and not wanting him to leave her. He wasn't waiting for her as he usually did. But it wasn't his body she was pulling against her. It wasn't his groans she could hear.

They were Elspeth's.

It was Elspeth making the noises.

Suddenly the throbbing that had started began to recede.

She felt Phillip lower himself gently onto her as he took her in his arms, his face against her face, the prickle of his stubble against her skin.

She was back in the real world but she was confused. Every nerve in her body was still tingling like it hadn't done for years, in spite of not being fulfilled. Something had gone wrong again, and yet she had felt something different, something more thrilling than she had felt before. So why had it left her full of bewilderment? Why had she thought of Elspeth? Why did thinking of Elspeth give her such fantastic sensations?

She dared not open her eyes. If she did he was bound to see the truth but if she didn't he would doubt the truth. He was still lying on top of her, totally relaxed, his breathing beginning to slow.

"I love you," he whispered in her ear. "That was fantastic."

As she was now tenser than she had been before, she couldn't say anything.

"I hope we didn't wake the neighbours. You've never been like that before. I've never heard you make such noises, as though you were really enjoying it. What happened?"

She opened her eyes and smiled because she had to. "I don't know, maybe it was because it was so unexpected."

"We'll have to set the alarm for four o'clock every morning," he said.

"No," she replied, the first flush of guilt washing over her. "If we plan it then it won't be unexpected."

"True! Let's try to get back to sleep. It's a couple of hours before we have to get up."

"We don't have to get up. It's Saturday," she said, wishing she could relax enough to sleep.

Yes, it was Saturday.

She had agreed to go shopping with Elspeth in Gloucester today and be with her for as many hours as she wanted.

Should she tell her?

Tell her what?

"I knew there was something I wanted say, Elspeth. When Phillip was making love to me at some ridiculous hour this morning, I thought of you and you'll never guess what happened."

No, it would stay with her.

Chapter Seven

Phillip stopped the BMW in front of John and Elspeth's gate and tooted the horn. Old Greg was at his usual perch, pipe in his mouth, surveying everything, taking it all in. Raising his hand as he drove past, he smiled when Old Greg acknowledged him with a slight lifting of his eyebrows.

As he waited for John, Phillip realised he had never had that many close friends. Outside his relationship with Sarah, he considered himself a very private person. He believed a true and close friend was difficult to find: he would be somebody with whom he could confide and know that not a word would be passed on, and in his opinion there were few people he had met who would fit into that category.

With John and Elspeth he was willing to make exceptions. He thought they were extremely lucky that all four of them got on so well because couple-friendships could be a bit one-sided. He enjoyed the times he met John after work for a game of squash and was pleased when he realised they were pretty much the same standard. In the bar afterwards, he found they shared many similar interests.

He was also pleased that Sarah had found a friend, being very aware that her job was getting her down and had been for quite a while. If she announced she was going to stop work completely, he wouldn't be surprised. That wasn't a worry for him; the money she made was hers and anyway he made quite enough for both of them.

There was an important meeting the following Monday with a Hong Kong Chinese woman with whom he was put in touch via a contact. His proposed visit to Hong Kong needed cancelling as a result. He hoped this contact would lead to a little further diversification. Successful diversification would mean more money and more money would mean there was even less reason for Sarah to work if she didn't want to.

However, all of that could wait.

It was Saturday morning and the rest of the weekend was ahead of them. Yes, he always felt a bit down when he got in on a Friday evening – he put it down to loving his work, but come Saturday morning things were different. If last night, or four o'clock this morning was anything to go by he might even be able to do away with the Friday evening blues.

Yes, he was pleased that in Elspeth, Sarah had a good friend and his friendship with John was a bonus: he had a good sense of humour but he was also deep thinking, intelligent and understandably circumspect, which was something else they had in common.

He liked Elspeth: she was gregarious, fun to be with and she called a spade a spade. Her directness was a little off-putting at first but once he was used to it he found himself more often than not egging her on. He loved the way her face lit up in obvious triumph when she won an argument. He guessed that somewhere in her life she had been trodden on in a big way. She was reasserting herself and he didn't mind offering her a helping hand. He decided she had every reason to be confident: she had the looks, the body and the personality but he believed that deep down she was fighting some sort of demon.

He would admit – but only to himself – that he quite fancied Elspeth.

What man wouldn't?

He smiled as he remembered how she had crept into his mind as he was making love to Sarah that morning. At first Sarah had been just lying there, her arms stretched out, her eyes closed, and probably in line with the cliché, thinking of England.

So what if he did imagine it was Elspeth instead of Sarah? At least Elspeth might have been a little more receptive. But then something happened. He hadn't the faintest idea what he did differently but Sarah had certainly never screamed like that before. She normally groaned a little and screwed up her face, but that was all.

He knew there were times when she was faking. What woman didn't fake such things on occasions when she wanted to please her man?

But that morning she had arched her back, clamped her legs to his sides, crossed her ankles and screamed.

That had been for real.

Perhaps the move to Upper Slaughter was the best thing for them after all. If she was more relaxed – and what had happened earlier that morning suggested she was – then who knew what might come from it. She might want to give up work for far more important reasons – lack of enjoyment would be secondary. She had already told him she would never be a working mother.

Over breakfast, he wanted to discuss what happened and ask why she screamed the way she did, but from his assessment of her mood he decided to leave it until later. She was in one of her more reflective moods and Phillip didn't think she was reflecting on what he might have done differently at four o'clock this morning. They would discuss what happened but not until they were both ready.

His mind leapt back to the present as he saw John walking down the path towards the car. He was casually dressed and carrying his bag of squash gear and rackets.

"Morning Phillip," John said, opening the back door of the car and throwing his bag on the rear seat.

"Morning, John."

"Ready for a thrashing?" John said, sighing deeply as he climbed in beside Phillip.

"You sound knackered so I'm not sure who you think is going to thrash who," Phillip said. He turned the key in the ignition and got the usual satisfaction from the deep throb of

103

the engine. Glancing in the rear view mirror he noticed he still had Old Greg's undivided attention.

"I'm not knackered," John said, "but Elspeth kept me at it for ages last night."

"I'm not going to ask *at what*," Phillip said.

"You know, women can be so strange on occasions ..."

Phillip smiled. "Just on occasions?"

"Unpredictable," John said, returning his smile. "Most of the time they seem to regard sex as a duty, but then suddenly and without any explanation they can't get enough of it. It must all be down to their hormones. Is Sarah the same?"

Phillip felt a little uncomfortable with the way the conversation was going. "What do you mean?" he said. Yes, they were all good friends, but even after a few drinks their discussions were never about each other's sex lives.

John glanced sideways at Phillip.

"Well, do you always have to instigate sex with Sarah, or does she sometimes leave you in little doubt what she wants?"

"As you know, John, we're trying for a family and no woman knows better than herself when her body is ready."

"That's not sex, that's procreation." John adjusted the seat so that he was half lying in the car. "What time was our game booked for?"

"Ten," Phillip said, pleased the subject had changed. "I see Old Greg was on watch again."

"When isn't he? I reckon he spends most of his waking hours at that gate. Someone told me, I can't remember who but it must have been a neighbour, evidently he gets no more than three or four hours sleep a night and he has been seen in his back yard smoking his pipe at ridiculous-o'clock."

"I reckon he must know everything and everybody." Phillip said, turning right for the cross-country route to Evesham. They had time and as it was a bright early autumnal morning, the slightly longer trip would be far more enjoyable.

"You'd think so, wouldn't you?"

"Are you saying he doesn't?"

"Have you ever seen him anywhere else in the village? Have you ever seen him anywhere else but at that damned gate?"

Phillip thought for a moment, negotiating the left turning onto the B4088 before answering.

"Can't say I have, but I haven't gone out of my way to look for him. Presumably living so close you've seen him leave the cottage?"

"No. In the nineteen months we've been here we've never seen him anywhere else nor have we ever spoken to him, other than to pass the time of day. And then you only get a grunt in reply."

"Is he married?"

"Oh yes, he's married all right. Her name's Grace and she's a different kettle of fish. She's the social athlete of the village compared to him."

John paused as Phillip slowed the BMW in order to pass a couple of horses going in their direction. Both riders, young girls, waved their crops in acknowledgement.

"I hate it when they do that, it's so bloody superior."

"They're only saying thank you."

"Yes, but in a very condescending way." John added dismissively. "Anyway I was telling you about Grace Woolmer. They're a strange couple, no kids or grandkids as far as I know. She's quite chatty when you get her on her own but as soon as he appears she clams up and scuttles indoors."

"You've talked to her then."

"Only a few times, and not for the past couple of months. When we first moved in she stopped Elspeth one day in the village and they got chatting. Elspeth had been walking round the village looking for inspiration for one of her books. Grace Woolmer was coming the other way and smiled and said hello. Being the inquisitive sort, Elspeth got her talking. She learnt quite a lot about the village and more importantly its inhabitants. I had to smile when you inferred some of the more long-standing villagers were perhaps –"

"Inter-related," Phillip said.

"Sort of, but it's certainly a 'them and us' situation. I didn't get to speak to her for ages but after Abigail Tucker died and her mother committed suicide it was obviously the talk of the village. It sort of gave licence for everybody to speak to everybody for a while. A shared disaster often does that, except for Old Greg of course."

Phillip slowed the car for the turning to Winchcombe.

"Sarah only told me what happened in outline. There wasn't anything more to it other than a grieving mother taking her own life, was there?"

"Not as far as I know but a couple of days after it happened Grace Woolmer was in the front garden and we got chatting about what happened," John said, wincing as he stretched his legs.

Phillip glanced at him. "Problem?" he asked.

"An old rugby injury that gets to me every now and again. Just have to put up with it."

"You're not looking for excuses are you?"

"Don't need them, mate. Anyway, I was telling you about my chat with Grace. After discussing the Tuckers we moved on and evidently Upper Slaughter has a *Phantom Menace*."

"A what?"

"A *Phantom Menace*. Or that's what Grace Woolmer called him. "

"Tell me more," Phillip said as he turned right onto the B4078, heading for Sedgebarrow.

John shrugged. "There's not much to tell other than after Mrs Tucker killed herself, routine police enquiries revealed from a number of reliable sources that over a period of time a man had been seen hiding in bushes, wearing camouflaged clothing with his face blackened."

"Sounds like a bit of a crank."

"Exactly, and that's the conclusion the police came up with. Evidently there hasn't been a burglary, a flasher or any form of assault in Upper Slaughter for at least ten years."

"You said has or had a *Phantom Menace?* Presumably there haven't been any recent sightings."

"Not that I know of but about six months ago, a few months before you and Sarah moved in, Elspeth and I came home from a night out somewhere and she was sure somebody had been in the cottage."

Without realising it Phillip took his foot off the accelerator and put it on the brake. "Run that past me again?" he said.

"It was nothing really. I didn't sense anything. There was nothing missing and no sign that anybody had been there." John sniggered. "Elspeth reckoned she could smell him."

Steering the car towards the entrance to a field, Phillip applied the handbrake and turned off the ignition.

"You're not going to believe this, John, but exactly the same thing happened to us last night."

"What do you mean?"

"I mean that when we got home after leaving you, Sarah was convinced somebody had been in the cottage and, wait for this – she reckoned she could smell whoever it was."

"You're joking."

"It's not something you joke about, is it?"

"You checked, obviously?"

"Every door, window, even the cellar, and there was nothing. It got to Sarah though because I don't think she had much sleep."

"You don't think our places are haunted do you?"

Phillip looked at him. "I don't believe in such things but I do think it's just a little too much of a coincidence, don't you?"

"I admit it's strange, although there's bound to be an explanation that –"

"That could suggest this *Phantom Menace* is more than just a Peeping Tom? Perhaps he's bolder than people think."

"You're not serious."

It was Phillip's turn to shrug. "It would be an explanation wouldn't it? I'd better have a word with Sarah because she often walks around the bedroom with nothing on and the curtains open. It's so private at the back."

"You're not going to tell her about the *Phantom Menace*, are you? Wouldn't that spook her even more?"

"Doesn't Elspeth know?"

John shook his head. "I've deliberately not mentioned it to her, and as she's never said anything to me I decided to leave well alone. But she might know, especially after her chats with Grace Woolmer."

"Probably best if I do the same," Phillip said, resuming their journey to Evesham.

Michael waited and watched.

That man got his car out of the garage and drove up Church Lane, which meant Mrs Preston was now on her own.

She hadn't appeared at the bedroom window yet.

He only had an hour before catching the bus into Evesham. Going into town on a Saturday morning was one of his routines. When he went to work it was different, because there was no time for him to walk in his favourite places. Walking by the river was the main attraction but he didn't like it if there were too many people around, in fact being completely on his own was what he really wanted. Work was all right because they left him alone now ... most of the time. Of course, his is den and the surrounding area offered him the ideal.

He could be totally on his own there ... well, away from other people.

But he also went to Evesham on a Saturday to buy provisions: not a lot of things but food and stuff that wouldn't go off. Chocolate, biscuits and bottles of lemonade and Coca Cola were his main purchases as well as tinned stuff. He never took anything from the fridge or store cupboard at home because it would be missed. The tins of food he bought – curries and stews – he kept for a very long time.

This morning his mother hadn't returned by the time he left the house. Even if she had she would have gone straight to bed without even bothering to see whether he was in the house or not. Because he was catching the ten o'clock bus, his camouflage clothing was not an option, so he was wearing his jeans and dark jacket – they were good enough. He might be stupid but not that stupid, regardless of what his mother still told him. She said many nasty things to him but he was used to it … it didn't matter most of the time.

He knew she was with her boyfriend: Friday nights normally meant he was alone in the house. She went there on a Friday and sometimes her boyfriend came to the house during the week. However, normally it meant Michael had the house to himself. On a Friday, he could do whatever he wanted: eat what he wanted, watch programmes and videos on the big TV. If there was a girlfriend on the scene he could have taken her to the house on a Friday.

He didn't have a girlfriend and he didn't want a girlfriend.

Not yet.

Girls just made fun of him, pointing at him and laughing.

If he had to be with people then being at work with just men was a good thing. It seemed to be the only place where he was treated as though he was normal. There were only six of them and their supervisor.

Michael didn't mind doing the same thing over and over again, boredom was a word he rarely used. Proud of what he produced, he simply took great pleasure in doing things with his hands and woodwork was his favourite. Making legs for tables and chairs, sometimes fifty a day, was what he loved most.

What the supervisor didn't know was that Michael marked every leg he made in the same place, just a little nick. Unless somebody knew where to look, his mark was impossible to find.

But he knew that every chair, every table which was supported by the legs he made was special. He could go into anybody's house and tell them whether he had made the legs on their tables and chairs. That meant he was different.

It also meant that what he made was different too.

He was daydreaming.

He must not take his eyes from her window.

But if she was there he would have noticed.

He hadn't missed her.

She would be there.

A sudden movement distracted him, but it wasn't at the bedroom window. There was somebody walking down Church Lane. It was the Warrington woman. He could only see her head and shoulders, bobbing along above the wall. She was smiling and wearing sunglasses. Where was she going? There was nobody further down Church Lane for her so she must be going to Primrose Cottage. Because he couldn't see the front door of the cottage he moved round to the other side of the garage so that he could see if she carried on down Church Lane or not.

She didn't. She stopped at Primrose Cottage.

Michael disliked the Warrington woman.

He had never liked her from the moment she arrived in the village. She never said hello to him the way his Mrs Preston said hello. He remembered one day, before he visited her cottage, seeing her coming towards him down the High Street. She crossed over to the other side of the road so that she didn't have to say hello. He remembered the look she gave him and didn't like her from that moment on.

When he went to her cottage up by the green, he was very tempted to break something. He wanted to pay her back, but he didn't. He knew other things about her as well, that she wasn't married but she was still living with a man. His mother was sort of doing that since his father left, but Michael knew it was wrong in the eyes of God.

He didn't go to church because people stared at him, but he did believe in God. Well, he thought he believed in God. He wasn't too sure.

But he did visit the Warrington woman's bedroom and saw her clothes and touched her private things. Maybe he had touched what she was wearing now and that made him smile.

The Warrington woman and Mrs Preston were coming out of the back door of Primrose Cottage.

Because he wasn't wearing his camouflage clothing he was a little further back in the woods than usual, so there was more foliage between him and the back garden. He certainly didn't want to be seen.

They were laughing and the Warrington woman had her arm round Mrs Preston's shoulders. They were going to the garage to get Mrs Preston's car to go somewhere. It didn't matter because he had to catch the bus but he wouldn't leave until they drove away.

Mrs Preston was wearing a pair of pretty pink trousers that reached to just below her knees. They were tight but being so slim she was able to wear tight things. A white shirt was hanging over the top of her trousers. She was carrying a coat. Her hair was swept back over her ears and she had gold studs in them.

She looked pretty, very pretty.

He remembered seeing that shirt in her wardrobe just a few hours ago. He remembered touching that shirt as he touched all the others. Now that she was wearing it, Michael felt as though he was part of her. Even when she washed it he would still know he had touched it.

The Warrington woman was taller and bigger and wouldn't have been able to wear the same clothes as Mrs

Preston. She was wearing jeans and a white long-sleeved top. Her bottom was a lot bigger than Mrs Preston's.

They reached the garage and were opening the doors. They were not very far from him now, so close he was sure he could smell Mrs Preston's perfume.

The Warrington woman wasn't as pretty. She probably thought she was pretty, being blonde and taller, but she wasn't.

Anyway he knew her secrets.

Her secrets were different from Mrs Preston's.

"Sorry about using your car, Sarah," Elspeth said as she swung the garage door open. "But I do hate driving that bloody great thing of John's. It drinks petrol and it's so bloody difficult to park."

She put her arm round Sarah's shoulder in a sisterly way, but even that disturbed Sarah and gave her the same feeling she had when their hands touched, when Elspeth had brushed her fingers against her breast. For a fleeting moment the images she'd seen when Phillip was making love to her flooded back. She shuddered slightly, but hopefully not so that Elspeth would notice.

"It's not a problem," she said quietly, unlocking the door of her white Renault Clio. "I need to fill it up before Monday anyway. Don't get in yet. It's a bit tight against that wall. I'll get it out."

She turned round when Elspeth didn't reply. She couldn't see her so she left the keys in the car door and went back outside. Elspeth was standing at the side of the garage.

"What are you doing?" Sarah asked, walking over to her.

Folding her arms defensively, Elspeth said, "Nothing, but I got the weirdest feeling that we were being watched."

"What do you mean?"

Elspeth shrugged. "I don't know, Sarah, but I just ..."

Michael watched the Warrington woman move away from the garage and stand by the wall. She was too close. He lowered himself even further into the undergrowth, wishing that he had put on his combat clothing and blackened his face. He could have got a later bus.

She was looking straight at him.

Discovery was not an option.

It was what he did.

His entire life revolved around what he was now doing.

"I just ... I thought we were being watched."

"I can't see anyone," Sarah said, looking in the same direction. The woods behind the cottage were beautiful, especially now as autumn approached but when the sun went down they became a little disquieting. They could hide anything or anybody. Quite often she heard rustling and animal noises in the dark shadows.

"Perhaps it's just me, I feel a bit on edge this morning," Elspeth said, turning away from the wall.

"Why? Is there any particular reason?" Sarah asked, biting her lip.

"I didn't have a good night's sleep."

"You and me the same."

"Right, Sarah. And the therapy for a bad night's sleep is shopping. Whether we want anything or not, we're going to shop until we drop."

"Thank God," Michael whispered to himself having learnt his lesson.

He would never be so stupid again.

But then a smile spread across his face.

He now knew her name was Sarah. Sarah Preston.

What a lovely name.

Michael caught the bus but only because it was late.

He was so worried about his near escape when watching Sarah and the Warrington woman that he lost track of time. After they drove away up Church Lane, he stayed where he was for a while.

He didn't trust them or himself.

Sarah Preston – he was so pleased he now knew her full name – was all right; she hadn't sensed anything, but the Warrington woman, she was too smart. She was like a vixen sniffing the air, trying to detect danger.

He didn't like the fact that his Sarah Preston was friends with the Warrington woman. If the Warrington woman had been nice to him as well, then it wouldn't be so bad.

He gazed out of the bus window at the countryside, beautiful and now bathed in sunshine. That was where he belonged, out there in the wild mingling with nature. He didn't want what everybody else wanted. He didn't need television, videos, loud music and ... and he didn't really need people. All he needed was nature: the woods, the fields, the wild animals and the weather.

He loved the times he spent in his den watching, waiting, hoping and perhaps seeing rain. He loved the sound of raindrops on the trees and on the roof of his den. He was disappointed when he discovered he had done too good a job with the roof and it didn't leak.

But the animals in their burrows wouldn't be getting wet either and he was one of them.

One evening when it was raining he took off all his clothes and sat cross-legged in the woods so that he could feel like a real animal, letting the rain fall on him as it was falling on the rest of nature. It made him feel part of something; he felt wanted and he felt accepted. The trees didn't tell him he was stupid, the rabbits didn't cross over to the other side of the wood so they didn't have to be near him. The family of badgers that were his next-door neighbours treated him as though he was part of the community, nature's community. That was where he belonged and that was what he would show Sarah Preston when the time came. He would respect her as he respected nature. He didn't abuse his position when he was in the woods and he would not abuse her.

114

Nature was beautiful as she was beautiful. Sarah Preston and nature needed to meet and he was going to be the one to do the introductions – soon.

It would be soon but first he had to do something about that man.

"They'll kill us," Sarah said when they eventually decided to take a breather from their shopping and stop for lunch.

"Why? They can both afford it," Elspeth said, quickly adding, "because we're worth it."

Sarah giggled. "I know but –"

"But nothing. The palace party is next weekend and we need something to wear."

"I know but –"

"Will you stop saying *I know but*. If they hadn't wanted us to spend money they wouldn't have let us come shopping together."

"I know ... I'm sorry."

Sarah searched Elspeth's eyes, hoping to see something that would tell her what was going on.

"Right, what do you fancy?" Elspeth said, breaking eye contact.

Sarah breathed in deeply and sighed. My God, she thought, I'm not going to be able to stand much more of this. "Something light," she said. "I want to be able to get into the dress I bought for the party."

"It looked gorgeous, and sod the cost."

"I hope Phillip agrees with you. Don't you think it's a bit revealing?"

"Revealing? What's the point in having boobs if we don't show them off?"

"If I were more like you then I'd agree but –"

"That's the beauty of the dress, Sarah dear. It does wonders." She held up her hand. "Not that I'm saying –"

"It's all right, I know my boobs are small so there's no need for you to apologise."

"I know but ..."

They burst out laughing forgetting the waitress who was hovering at their table being totally ignored during their exchange.

"Would you like to order?" the waitress asked politely.

"Oh, yes," Sarah said. "I'm sorry, we didn't see you there."

"That's probably because my boobs aren't big enough," the waitress said with a straight face.

Sarah put on a sheepish face and noticed Elspeth was doing the same. They exchanged glances, their eyes doing the laughing. "I'll have a Caesar salad and a still water, please," Sarah said.

The waitress wrote on her pad and turned to Elspeth.

"The same, please."

Sarah's mobile rang. She looked around. "I hate it when it rings in public," she said, reaching into her bag.

"Then turn it off."

"It normally is turned off," she said. She looked at the phone and saw that it was Phillip. "Yes?" she whispered into the mouthpiece.

"That's a nice greeting," Phillip said. "Where are you? In a morgue?"

"No, of course not, we're in El Fredo's."

"Lucky El Fredo. How far have you got?"

"What do you mean?"

"With your shopping. John and I have played squash and had lunch, but if you two are going to be a while yet we wouldn't mind going up to a garage in Bromsgrove to look at some Beamers. I think I may have persuaded John to change his allegiance."

"What are you on about?"

"Doesn't matter. What about meeting later for a meal? Nothing fancy, it'll save anybody cooking."

"Well, yes, hang on a minute." Sarah held the phone away from her ear. "It's Phillip, and he's suggesting we meet up for a meal later. They're going to Bromsgrove to look at BMWs."

116

"Are they?" Elspeth said, looking pleased. "Tell him *The Olde Black Bear* in Tewkesbury at six-thirty. John knows where it is."

Sarah nodded as her head spun with the thought of having another five hours or more on her own with Elspeth.

"Elspeth suggests *The Olde Black Bear* in Tewkesbury at six-thirty. She says John will know where it is."

"Okay, *The Olde Black Bear* it is. Don't spend too much."

"We won't, "bye."

Sarah closed the call and put the phone back in her bag. "We've got another five hours to spend money. Any suggestions where we should go?"

"A couple," Elspeth said with an impish smile.

Michael changed his mind about walking along the riverside in Evesham. The close escape with Sarah and the Warrington woman had scared him more than he realised. He needed to regain his confidence and the only place he could do that was in his den.

He always felt secure there.

As soon as he reached the terminus he caught the next bus to Bourton-on-the-Water and walked the extra few miles back to Upper Slaughter via Lower Slaughter using Warden's Way, a well-used footpath that connected the two villages.

He went home first to change.

He had not expected his mother to be in.

"I wondered where you were," she said as he let himself in through the back door. She was pouring hot water into a couple of mugs, a cigarette hanging from her lips.

Regardless of what she called him, he loved his mother but he knew he was nothing more than an embarrassment to her, especially as his brother and sister were doing so well. He was frequently told, perhaps once too often, that if his mother's wishes had been answered he would have been aborted the moment she realised she was pregnant. She had also told him he was conceived as a result of one of his father's drunken sexual attacks on her. Michael knew enough to ask her how she could be so certain, but was told the only time her father ever fancied her after the first two were born, was when he was drunk.

Mary Griffiths didn't consider herself an unattractive woman. In her late forties, and with dyed blonde hair, she thought even after three children she still had a good figure and hopefully, since her husband had walked out, she was still attractive to men. She needed a man in her life and the one for whom she was making the coffee was a possibility. He was divorced, had a good job and seemed to fancy her even when he was sober.

That was a start.

Like Michael, Mary worked in Evesham but her shift pattern with the supermarket hardly ever coincided with Michael's movements to and from work, which pleased her.

Why did the only child still at home have to be so stupid?

She hadn't wanted him in the first place because his brother and sister had been enough, but she was persuaded under the threat of violence from her husband to keep him. Peter wanted another son with whom he could go to football matches and the pub. Michael was therefore a big disappointment to him as well. Mary, in a weird way, was grateful to Michael for being the way he was because she believed that it played a big part in her husband walking out – and good riddance.

However, she resented the fact that Michael still lived at home. She managed to rid herself of a violent and drunken husband and now she wanted rid of his idiot son.

But who would have him?

No girl in her right mind would look at him twice. Having said that, she had to admit he was not a bad looking lad. If anything he was quite handsome: tall with brown curly hair, a good physique, if not a little too slim, and, she accepted reluctantly, a certain charm. But he was simple. It wouldn't take a girl very long to realise that he had nothing to offer. He was a complete loner. She had no idea where he disappeared off to for hours on end, but she didn't care either. He was out of the house and that was all she wanted. She accepted that he was talented with his hands. The job in Evesham was a bonus and Michael seemed happy there.

Pouring hot water onto the instant coffee in the mug, she looked at him standing just inside the back door. If Derek came up trumps she would move out and leave Michael to his own devices. He looked after himself most of the time anyway.

"So where have you been?" she asked her son, not really caring whether he answered or not.

"Out," he replied.

"I can see that. I don't want you going in the front room," she said, picking up the mugs, "I'm entertaining."

Michael had no intention of going in the front room. He never went into the front room when she was there. There was never any need for him to go into the front room.

He watched his mother leave the kitchen, a mug of coffee in each hand and the cigarette still hanging from her lips. All he wanted to do was go to his room and change so that he could get the hell out of the house.

He knew what his mother meant by *entertaining*; he had often heard her *entertaining*. He always tried to block out the grunts and other noises by putting his head under the pillow, like he used to do when he heard his father come home drunk.

It was disgusting.

He still hated his father.

But he loved his mother and every time she rejected him he would go to his room and cry. All he wanted was to be held. All he ever wanted was to feel needed.

He knew he wasn't clever. He knew he was never going to be what she wanted. But he needed her and it took a very long time for him to realise that she didn't need him.

In his room he took the risk and changed into his combat clothing before retrieving Sarah Preston's red pants from where he hid them in the bottom drawer, and then left as quickly as he could.

He used one of his many secret routes out from the back garden making sure he never approached his private world the same way.

As he crossed the fields keeping close to the hedgerows, he thought about what he needed to do.

It worried him.

He didn't know whether he was capable of hurting another human being, but if he was going to get rid of that man he didn't have any choice but to hurt him. He never doubted that the opportunity would arise but he did doubt his own ability to go through with whatever method he decided to use to kill him.

As he was moving up the hedgerow towards the edge of the wood he disturbed some rabbits. They were only small, and when they sensed danger they scurried away. That was when he decided he must do something to give him the confidence to do what needed to be done. The image of the rabbit he killed always returned to him, and he hated himself but that was because it was part of nature, the nature he understood and now knew so well. The rabbits were part of his private world, but there were other things, other animals that were not. There was Mrs Proctor's fat cat for example. It was no more part of his private world than any other animal he saw in the village.

Other than the foxes, that is.

The foxes were different and he admired them.

He saw foxes in the village quite often but they didn't see him: they rifled dustbins and they raided the chickens in Top Farm.

Less than an hour later he crawled into his den.

There was nobody about.

He was safe.

By the time he lowered himself into the den, Michael had formulated his plan.

He would use Mrs Proctor's fat cat as a test.

If killing a cat he knew went without a problem there were plenty of other cats and dogs in the village to practice on.

Smiling to himself, he went to one of the wooden shelves where he kept his food supply and selected a tin of his favourite soup, but not before he put Sarah Preston's red pants in a small box, placing it back on the same shelf.

He had always known the empty box would come in useful.

Chapter Eight

"So what have you spent my money on?" Phillip asked, taking the shopping bags from Sarah and placing them against the wall of *The Olde Black Bear* dining room.

"*Your* money? What do you mean your money? I used my money and because it was my money you'll have to wait to find out," she said as she sat down.

Phillip held up his hands defensively and smiled at John and Elspeth. It was just a bit of marital banter yet he sensed an undertone in Sarah's voice. "All right, all right," he said, "I was only joking."

"We had a great time and what we spent is incidental," Elspeth added. "Anyway, who won the squash?"

"I don't think it's a question of who won but who lost," John said, looking smug. "What would you all like to drink?"

After John had taken the orders and gone to the bar, Sarah looked at Phillip quizzically.

"You look preoccupied. What is it?"

He shook his head. "Oh, nothing, but ... I suppose if it's anything I was thinking about the meeting I've got on Monday and whether I'm doing the right thing."

"Why? What are you doing?" Elspeth asked, casting a furtive glance at Sarah. She had deliberately trivialised what they had bought because she wanted to give a secret message to Sarah. The trouble was she thought it was a secret only she knew about.

Having thoroughly enjoyed the time she'd spent with Sarah, she believed she was now in a different world. After

122

she had analysed her dream from last night she looked upon her friend completely differently.

How can you discover you are in love with somebody and not regard them differently the next time you see them? As they shopped and relaxed she found that she was watching Sarah for telltale signs and mannerisms that before she may have ignored or just smiled at, but now were endearing and thought provoking.

She felt like a schoolgirl with a crush.

So was history repeating itself?

Throughout the day she managed to walk as close to Sarah as she dared and when possible she consciously allowed their hips to touch. When she watched Sarah appear from the changing cubicle, with apprehension written all over her face and wearing the dress she eventually bought for the cocktail party, Elspeth had wanted to hug her and tell her she would look wonderful in anything. As it was she smiled and nodded, and then watched the apprehension become sheer delight as Sarah soaked up her approval.

How she had wanted to sneak into the cubicle and steal just one kiss.

Elspeth looked up, suddenly aware that Phillip was talking.

"... should be some time Monday afternoon," he said, looking at her for a reaction.

"I'm sorry, Phillip but I didn't catch what you said."

Phillip looked sideways at Sarah.

"I was saying that I'm meeting a representative from a firm called Kwong Tsun Wo. They are based in Hong Kong and are trying to persuade me to import rosewood furniture and sell it in my shops. I've yet to be convinced."

Elspeth tried to look interested. She liked Phillip and was pleased he and John had become good friends, but she did find him a little tedious on occasions, especially when he started talking about antiques. She and John had a simple rule at home: no talking shop, not from either of them. They showed an interest in what the other did but that was different, and anyway, John's job was steeped in confidentiality. She had a feeling that Phillip was about to launch into the pros and cons of something about which she wasn't in the slightest bit interested. What she actually wanted to do was manoeuvre her legs under the table so that at least a knee was touching Sarah.

"That's interesting," she said, looking towards the bar and wishing John would hurry up. She could do with a drink.

Sarah did not miss the look Elspeth gave her but she did misinterpret it.

Rather than regarding it as a private and caring moment between the two of them, she thought it was dismissive.

She was convinced her feelings towards Elspeth were wrong and having sensed a change in her, Elspeth was telling her she wasn't interested after all.

It was not normal. What she thought about early that morning when she and Phillip were making love surely wasn't natural. It wasn't only not natural it was morally wrong. She was not like that. She had never been like that.

It was quite straightforward. After the move to Upper Slaughter, she wanted friendship and Elspeth was the first to offer it to her. She was grateful but she was allowing her appreciation to run away with her. She loved Phillip, she wanted Phillip and she certainly wasn't going to do anything that might jeopardise their future together. And whatever problems they had, perceived or not, were solvable.

So what she thought was her business.

What she did though, could affect other people she really cared about.

Phillip guessed from the way Elspeth had said *that's interesting* that she meant the complete opposite.

He looked at her as she turned her head towards the bar.

His mind immediately went back to early this morning when he imagined it was Elspeth he was making love to and not Sarah. Looking at her profile, he understood why he found her so damned attractive but now for some reason he felt guilty.

He loved Sarah.

But in the last twenty-four hours, and especially at just after four o'clock in the morning he had sensed a change in her, a change that worried him. He ought to look upon what happened in a positive way but something was stopping him.

He glanced at Sarah but she had her head bowed so rather than asking questions he stood up and went to help John with the drinks.

Watching Phillip walking slowly towards the bar, Sarah was confused.

Why did she feel so pleased that even for just a few seconds she was once again alone with Elspeth?

Elspeth saw in Sarah's eyes something that was not there before. What was it? Regret?

She was so happy earlier when they were shopping and having lunch but as they approached Tewkesbury after leaving Gloucester, Sarah had become quieter and less communicative.

She had sensed then that something wasn't quite right.

Instinctively, she reached for Sarah's hand.

"What's the matter, Sarah? Something's wrong."

Sarah looked down at her hand in Elspeth's. She ought to take her hand away but she couldn't. "Nothing's the matter," she said quietly, fighting back her tears.

"I am female, don't forget," Elspeth said, "so I know what a woman means when she says *nothing*. And nothing makes you want to cry, does it?"

She held Sarah's hand even tighter.

"I'm not crying because I'm sad," Sarah said, looking deeply into Elspeth's eyes. "I'm crying because I'm so happy."

She didn't know why she said it. The words had just come out but it worried her that she meant it. She wanted to communicate her feelings to her friend but found she couldn't say anything more. She hoped the look in her eyes would tell Elspeth everything, including her confusion.

Hector, Mrs Proctor's Siamese cat, followed his usual route from the back door.

Michael was lying in wait.

Hector wasn't as sprightly as his age would have suggested because he was overfed.

Michael and Hector had met before.

In fact Hector – until that Warrington woman scared him earlier in the day – had been the source of Michael's biggest shock since he started watching people and going into their houses.

Because the Proctors were such a nice couple and had lived in the village for many years, they were one of Michael's first visits.

They were an early test case but he had hoped they were a safe one.

Before Mr Proctor died he was in Michael's eyes a special man. He was one of the few villagers who befriended him. Whenever they met in the village Mr Proctor always stopped for a chat. He didn't make Michael feel stupid; he talked to him as though he was an equal. Their chats were normally brief and rather one-sided but at least they happened. Mr Proctor used to ask him how he was, how work was going and did he have a girlfriend yet? They also talked about the countryside, about things that Michael understood. The only thing that made him feel awkward was when he asked whether there was a girlfriend on the scene yet.

About two years ago, several weeks went by without him seeing Mr Proctor. At first, he thought the Proctors might be on holiday, but when the weeks became months he began to worry.

He watched their house for hours but not once did he see Mr Proctor leave it or come home. On the other hand, he saw Mrs Proctor on a number of occasions. She had many visitors, some of whom he recognised, but he never saw Mr Proctor again.

Although he wanted to ask his mother what might have happened, he knew she would want to know why he was asking, and he didn't want to tell her.

It was private.

His chats with Mr Proctor were very private, almost as private as the things Wendy and Sharon did to him in the churchyard and what he saw them doing to themselves.

No, he was wrong to compare Mr Proctor with the churchyard incident because he was a genuine person whereas Wendy and Sharon were false and rude.

Michael never found out what happened to Mr Proctor, so he assumed his old friend had died.

He would always remember Mr Proctor's grey hair and his droopy grey moustache. The pipe he smoked, and for reasons he could never work out, made Michael trust him from the first time they talked. He always wore black boots and a collar and tie. Mr Proctor was from a different age but he was also like the father or grandfather he always wished he could have had.

Michael also wished that he had been able to say goodbye.

The night he decided Mr Proctor must have died Michael went home and cried.

He had lost a friend: he had lost his only friend in the village.

One night soon after Mr Proctor died, Michael had been watching Mrs Proctor's house for about an hour when Hector scared the living daylights out of him.

He justified watching Mrs Proctor's house for reasons that were different to those that drove him to watch other houses: as well as wishing his father could have been like Mr

Proctor he also wished his mother's house could have been like theirs. And by watching the house after Mr Proctor died he felt he was in some small way protecting Mrs Proctor. He wasn't sure what he was protecting her from but he still felt good doing it.

On this occasion though, he was just about to leave when he sensed that he was the one under scrutiny.

He was in the undergrowth at the rear of Mrs Proctor's house, looking over a stone wall at the back when he was sure he was not alone. He froze, hoping that whoever it was had merely stopped to light a cigarette or something.

But the sensation didn't go away.

When he eventually plucked up courage to look round he saw Hector sitting just a few feet away from him, watching him. It was dusk but still fairly warm, yet a shiver ran down his spine. He reached towards the cat but it merely sniffed his fingers and strolled through the broken gate towards Mrs Proctor's back door.

Hector was a lot slimmer in those days.

Michael had watched him growing bigger and bigger over time.

Invariably he continued to see Hector during his visits and the trust between them grew on each occasion. He started taking titbits from the fridge at home to feed Hector, so he felt partially responsible for the cat's weight problem. When he fed Hector and stroked him he did it because he was doing what he guessed Mr Proctor always did.

For just a short while it brought his old friend Mr Proctor back to him.

That was why Michael decided that if he were able to kill Hector then he would be able to do the same to that man. Killing Hector would be like killing the memories of his special friendship with Mr Proctor, but it was a necessary test.

If he were capable of disposing of Hector then he would be capable of anything.

Hector stopped when he saw Michael but just as quickly recognised a source of more food and waddled purring towards him. Michael had brought some tuna fish he found in his mother's fridge that he didn't think would be missed. He took the foil parcel from his pocket and unwrapped it. Hector immediately stuck his nose in it, then his mouth. Even when the fish had gone Hector continued to lick the foil, attempting to purr at the same time.

Michael reached down and stroked Hector's head and then his neck. He coaxed him closer and when he was close enough he put his hand under the cat's ribcage and lifted him up, pulling him towards his own chest. Hector was a lot heavier than he had expected. The cat could still smell the fish so it pushed its nose into Michael's pocket.

After standing up slowly, Michael moved away from the back of the house and melted into the darkening gloom.

Hector didn't seem to mind being carried.

Wishing he had brought some more fish to keep the cat occupied on the way back to his den, Michael walked on. He decided he would kill Hector in the den because it would be an additional test, and then bury the fat cat's body in the woods.

The den was where he felt secure.

It was where he would bring Sarah Preston.

He had to build up his confidence.

Hector's grave was ready and the cross made. The grave was well away from the den and close to where he had buried the rabbit. If a fox, a stoat or a weasel started digging at the grave after Hector was buried it would not matter.

Half way back to the den Hector started to feel quite heavy even for a cat. As they left the village, Hector seemed to sense something was different because he started struggling and Michael had to tighten his grip. The cat then quietened for a while but once in the wood he struggled again and for a moment Michael thought he was going to have to stop and kill Hector right then.

However, they reached the den without further incident.

Once inside the den and with the faint glow from one of the lamps, Hector behaved as though nothing was unusual. He walked slowly round the earthen floor, sniffing at everything and every now and again casting a furtive glance at Michael.

Michael poured some milk into a small bowl and put it down on the floor. The cat sniffed at the milk and lapped it enthusiastically. Michael reached for the wire noose he had made earlier and widened the circle so that it would fit over the cat's neck.

It would be quick.

He would make sure it was quick.

Just because he needed to kill Hector didn't mean that the cat needed to suffer.

It may as well be now. Why wait?

He slipped off the stump of wood he had hand carved into a stool and onto his knees. For a moment Hector stopped lapping to look up at him but quickly went back to the milk. With the noose hanging from his right hand, Michael shuffled a bit closer to the cat. He checked that the loop was the right size.

Slowly he lowered the noose. He touched one of Hector's ears and it twitched. He lowered the noose down further in front of Hector's eyes and over his nose. The wire tapped against the bowl before dipping into the milk.

Now. Do it now. Quickly!

Hector stopped lapping the milk. Slowly turning his head he looked up at Michael in the dim light. Michael closed his eyes as he saw Mr Proctor's face and not Hector's.

He hesitated.

Would he be breaking a trust?

As he realised he could no more kill Hector than kill another rabbit, he accepted that he had failed.

But if he wasn't capable of killing a cat how was he ever going to kill that man?

Slowly he retrieved the noose from in front of Hector's head and sat back on his haunches. Hector gave him a cursory look, blinked, then lapped up the last drops of milk.

Tears rolled down Michael's cheeks and Hector became a blur.

He had failed and with his failure he had lost Sarah Preston.

Sarah Preston would never look at him if that man were still around, and without the hope that Sarah Preston could one day be his, he didn't want to live. He had no reason to live.

His dream was shattered.

If he could have Mrs Tucker's courage, he might be able to go through with it, but he didn't have her courage.

Hector would be all right now. Cats were smart. Cats were bright. Hector would find his own way back to Mrs Proctor's.

Not like him. He was stupid.

He was even more stupid than people thought.

Perhaps he should end it all, here and now, while he had the chance.

Sarah stared at herself in the mirror. The dress had looked so nice in the shop. Elspeth liked it and when she showed it to Phillip he made all the right noises. But she was the one who had to wear it. She had never worn anything so daring before, well not in public.

She admitted the style was all right because it really suited her, but ...

The off-white colour with tinges of charcoal grey was certainly unusual and the silk-satin mix felt cool against her skin. It was long and two-piece; the top was almost backless and had a thin tie round her neck. What made it so sensual and eye-catching was that the top was the lacing at the sides.

Turning sideways, she looked again, concerned that it was too revealing.

Well, perhaps it wasn't so bad after all. Yves St Laurent was expensive but he knew how to make a woman feel good. Now she had to decide whether she ought to wear any underwear: pants maybe but a bra? The straps would be seen through the lacing at the sides. A thong would be better because there wouldn't be any lines. Yes, the dress was daring because it revealed more than she was used to but ... but maybe it wasn't that revealing.

She checked the digital alarm clock on Phillip's bedside table.

Elspeth and John would be calling for them in just over an hour so she ought to have a bath now. She slipped off the dress and hung it on the wardrobe, smoothing the front with the backs of her fingers. She wanted to look good for Elspeth ... no, she wanted to look good for Phillip.

The previous Saturday she wished she'd been able to tell Elspeth why her happiness made her cry, but John and Phillip had returned to the table before she could pluck up the courage and the opportunity didn't arise again.

Her time would come. She just hoped that Elspeth would understand and wouldn't laugh at her. She wasn't sure how she would tell her and what words she would use.

"They'll be here in an hour, Phillip," she shouted from the top of the stairs.

"I know," he shouted back.

As she went to the bathroom, Sarah could see the flickering of the computer screen. His Monday meeting had gone well which meant he was pleased with the deal agreed with Kwong Tsun Wo, though she sensed that under the veneer of satisfaction was apprehension. He would have committed a lot of capital to the venture and now he was on the Internet checking out other suppliers and retailers.

She was pleased he'd agreed to the computer being downstairs. He had wanted to use one of the bedrooms but the room he chose was the one she wanted for a nursery when the time came.

If the time ever came.

"I'm going to have a bath."

"All right, I'll be up in a minute."

She didn't want Phillip with her. She wanted to lie in the bath and think ... think of Elspeth and what she ought to say to her.

Was that so wrong?

It felt wrong but she could not help herself. She needed to be on her own to sort out her confusion. There had never been a reason to doubt her sexuality before.

"Don't rush," she shouted down to Phillip. "I've got to wash my hair and we haven't got time for anything else."

She waited for a reply, but when she didn't get one she turned on the taps, leaving Phillip to his rosewood furniture.

And leaving her to ... what?

Elspeth was enjoying the powerful jets of water from her shower. She loved the sensation, especially when she put the showerhead on pulse and let it massage her shoulders.

Her week had been reasonable and there were another twenty thousand words on her laptop as testament to her productivity. The email on Monday morning from her publishing agent had goaded her into action.

Although there were periods of frenzied typing during the week she admitted she spent far too long daydreaming or maybe it was just wishful thinking. She could only guess at what Sarah was trying to tell her the previous Saturday. When she said she could guess even then she knew she was being a little too presumptuous. Sarah didn't actually say or do anything that supported her conclusions but there was sufficient evidence in Sarah's body language and in her eyes to prop up her hopes.

Even if it was only guesswork, she still couldn't believe what she was thinking. The idea was fantasy and fantasy was why she wrote stories. It wasn't real.

She so enjoyed the time she and Sarah spent together in Gloucester, and although Sarah said she enjoyed it too, it must have been for different reasons. That was until Sarah's mood changed and she saw the tears in her eyes.

Was it just possible – could it be possible – that her own feelings were being mirrored, were being reciprocated?

Had Sarah been trying to tell her she felt the same? For a moment, she held her breath …

No, of course she wasn't. There was nothing in anything Sarah said or did to support the suggestion. If she felt the same, Elspeth would have detected it long ago.

No, she really was being fanciful … but Sarah did say that she was crying because she was happy. When Phillip asked her what was wrong she told him there was something in her eye, but Elspeth saw the look Sarah gave her. The look was for her and for her alone, not for Phillip. Sarah was trying to tell her something.

She turned off the shower and stepping out of the cubicle she looked at herself in the full-length mirror on the wall. She remembered Sarah implying that she was envious of her figure but Elspeth thought she needed to lose a few pounds. If she did, John would be disappointed but then she wouldn't be doing it for John. Whenever they made love John always seemed transfixed by her breasts. She didn't mind, but there were occasions when she wanted to tell him to leave them alone, get on with what he was doing and then when he finished let her go to sleep.

It wasn't because she found sex with John repellent; on the contrary, she did enjoy their sessions together. After her first unexpected experience with the girl at school, she experimented as she tried to come to terms with whatever her sexuality was.

The first time she went with a boy – because that's all he was – she did not enjoy the experience. Besides hurting she found it a non-event and wondered what all the fuss was about. Belinda, the girl with whom she experienced her brief affair, was far more caring and loving, far more knowledgeable. But Elspeth listened to the other girls bragging among themselves about the boys they had been

134

with, their relative sizes and whether this mattered or not. At the time she was only seventeen but regardless of her experience with Belinda, she thought she was being left out.

After listening to the girlie gossip, she selected a boy she thought would be the best bet and made him very aware that she was available. His name was Josh. He was also seventeen but supposedly the heartthrob of the sixth form. He played rugby, did weight training, excelled on the athletics track and looked, she supposed, how a man ought to look.

It took him a while to cotton on to what Elspeth was offering but eventually he plucked up the courage to ask her out. On their third date he began his fumblings in the back of his father's car. She decided very quickly that his dexterousness was sorely wanting. He appeared incapable of undoing buttons with one hand, and then when he attempted to undo her bra she almost burst out laughing. Anybody would have thought he was being asked to conduct some complicated experiment in the physics laboratory.

After much grunting and groaning, getting legs and arms trapped in between seats and headrests, they managed to manoeuvre into what she decided had to be called the acrobat's position. It was dark so she couldn't see him, not that she particularly wanted to, but after a couple of feeble attempts by him she took hold of him and guided him towards his goal.

The pain hit her and she screamed.

Josh took this as being an indication of her enjoyment, and thrust even harder. She was bloody uncomfortable, her legs splayed, her neck and head twisted between the door and the seat, her right arm caught underneath her and her breasts were being handled as though they were basketballs. Fortunately it lasted less than two minutes. With a final grunt Josh collapsed on top of her.

The pain receded, but it was accompanied by the realisation that she was no longer a virgin. It was not something she was going to brag about. She tried to push

Josh off but it wasn't until they untangled their arms and legs that she was able to breathe properly.

She hoped he wasn't going to ask how it was for her.

Josh sat next to her on the back seat, a smug smile on his face. She peered down at him and in the dim moonlight she had her first glimpse of what had done the damage.

It was then that she realised she was bleeding.

She pushed backwards against the seat trying to lift herself from the ever-increasing stickiness of her own blood.

"I'm bleeding," she said, more to herself than Josh.

"You're what?"

"I'm bleeding."

"Why?" Josh asked accusingly, turning to face her.

"Probably because it was my first time," Elspeth said innocently.

"Fucking hell!" Josh shouted as he opened the back door and almost fell out of the car. "Are you telling me you were a fucking virgin?"

"Not quite the way I would describe me, and now not technically accurate," Elspeth said quietly as she tried to soak up some of the blood with her discarded pants. "I was until you stuck that thing in me."

Her sarcasm was lost on Josh.

"My father will fucking kill me. How are we going to get that out of the back seat?"

"Tell him you cut your finger, it's probably about the same size!"

Fortunately, Josh decided that after their first encounter he and Elspeth were history. Not wishing to repeat the experience she contemplated becoming a nun but eventually things got better. By the time she met John she had slept with five other men, not boys, and her belief that she was *normal* grew with each experience. Although none of the relationships lasted for more than a couple of months, she discovered that men could be gentle and caring, after all. However, her memories of her experience with Belinda were never far away.

She never asked herself why she was the one who finished the relationships ... not just with Belinda, but with all the men too.

Elspeth turned round so that she could look at her bottom.

She approved of her bottom and hips. She thought both were beautifully proportioned and probably her best assets and she considered they made her look very feminine unlike some of the fashionably straight-hipped girls around nowadays.

"Sorry, Sarah," she said to the mirror as she realised she had inadvertently criticised her friend's hips. Maybe if Sarah put on a bit of weight the curves would follow.

The dress Elspeth was going to wear that evening would show her bottom and hips at their best. She smiled to herself when she imagined the ogling that would go on, and not only from the men. The men would try to picture her naked, but the women would be envious. There was one woman who didn't need to be envious because if she felt the way Elspeth prayed she did, then she would soon be seeing what Elspeth was looking at now.

If only.

At the very thought of Sarah touching her she tensed her thighs and bottom. Oh, if only she could be sure it really was going to happen.

She turned around again and began drying herself, rubbing her hair gently. She didn't care what she looked like for other people, she just wanted to look good for Sarah. Her naturally blonde hair was also one of her best features. She liked the way it was cut, falling straight to her shoulders. Lowering her eyes, she glanced down over her stomach and smiled again when she pictured Sarah looking at her. Her long slim legs and small feet were very feminine, her toes slender and neat. Yes, she looked good and in about thirty minutes she would look even better.

"Are you finished in there?" John asked through the bathroom door.

"Just drying myself," she replied, looking at herself in the mirror a final time before opening the door.

It was a dry, warm evening as Sarah walked with Phillip, John and Elspeth down Church Lane from Primrose Cottage on the way to Clifton House. Elspeth and John, having been to one of Hilary's cocktail parties before, looked reasonably blasé and Phillip appeared ambivalent about the whole experience, although Sarah couldn't help noticing that he seemed more interested than usual in Elspeth's dress.

"Well, what do you think?" Elspeth said, linking her arm in Sarah's.

"You mean your dress?"

"Of course."

"It's gorgeous, but –"

"A little revealing?" Elspeth suggested

"It does show rather a lot of you, yes."

"I told you ages ago that it was the only way to have a good evening at one of these parties," she said tightening her grip on Sarah's arm.

When she saw what Elspeth was wearing Sarah was both envious and disapproving. Envious because Elspeth was able to wear a dress like that and get away with it, but disapproving because she wondered why she felt the need to reveal so much.

As they were crossing the stone footbridge by the ford Elspeth gave Sarah's arm a slight tug, bringing her to a stop. Elspeth looked furtively at John and Phillip, who were by then twenty or so yards ahead, and then back at Sarah.

"We must talk, not now, but we must talk."

"What about?" Sarah felt goose pimples erupt on her arms.

"Us," Elspeth said. "We haven't had a chance since last Saturday, but we must talk."

"Us?" Sarah tilted her head to one side. Inside she was screaming.

"Yes, us, you and me. Stop being so evasive, Sarah."

138

"I'm not sure –"

"Not now, but sooner rather than later." Elspeth stole another look at the men, then bent forward and kissed Sarah on the cheek. "And sooner is this evening."

At six thirty-five, John led the way up the steps to the ornate front door of Clifton House. Sarah, unlike the others, was nervous, and not just because of the thought of trying to make polite conversation for a couple of hours.

The front door opened and a tall, handsome, grey-haired man in tails greeted them.

"Good evening, sirs and madams," he said stepping back to let them pass through the door. "May I ask your names?"

John spoke for them all.

"John Davidson, Elspeth Warrington and Mr and Mrs Phillip Preston," he said as they all handed their coats to a formally bedecked girl who stood to one side of the butler. Sarah had never met a real butler before, regardless of having been to many formal functions with her parents.

"Thank you," the butler said, "please follow me."

He led them through open double doors, beyond which was the buzz of many voices. To one side of the doors was a table where other guests had deposited their gifts, so Sarah and Elspeth followed suit. When Sarah looked up they were at the top of three steps that led down into what could only be described as a baronial hall.

"Mr and Mrs Phillip Preston, Miss Elspeth Warrington and Mr John Davidson," the butler announced. Sarah was sure there was a lowering of voices as people turned to look at them.

Just inside the door in a welcoming line were Hilary Bond-Smithers, a man who Sarah assumed was her husband Jeremy, and two others she thought must be their adult children, Belinda, and Charles.

Phillip ushered Sarah towards their hosts.

"Sarah, my dear," Hilary said, extending her hand. "I'm so pleased you could come." She looked at Phillip. "And you must be Phillip," she said.

139

Phillip took her hand and Sarah was a little surprised when he bowed slightly. She knew he would feel foolish when he realised what he had done.

"That's me," Phillip said.

"I'm so sorry we haven't met before but time has rushed by." Hilary turned to the man next to her. "And this is Jeremy, my husband, and of course Belinda and Charles."

Sarah moved with Phillip to stand briefly in front of Jeremy, which left Hilary to greet Elspeth and John.

"Good evening," Jeremy said to them both.

He wasn't unlike the butler to look at, probably a little shorter but an equivalent age. Sarah took in the cut of Jeremy's suit, concluding that it would probably have cost at least a thousand pounds. Phillip's suit she knew wasn't cheap but it was off the peg.

"Good evening," they said together, reaching across each other to shake hands with Belinda and Charles.

Belinda was the image of her mother. From what she'd been told Sarah guessed she was in her early twenties but she already looked middle-aged. She remembered Hilary telling her that Belinda was a close friend of Abigail Tucker's, so maybe there had been a price to pay. Switching her attention to Charles, she decided he was probably one of the most handsome men she had ever seen, taller than his father, deeply tanned with jet black hair and a rugged complexion. She guessed his age at about thirty.

"You're from Primrose Cottage, aren't you?" Jeremy said, lifting his eyes rather obviously from the front of Sarah's dress.

"Yes, we are," she replied, reluctantly looking away from Charles' face.

He smiled at her knowingly.

"You've settled in I hope," Belinda said.

"We had to," Sarah said. "I went back to work this week."

"Where's that?

"Gloucester. I work in a solicitors' office."

140

"Oh, how nice," Jeremy said before turning his attention to Elspeth and John. "Elspeth, my dear," he said, "how nice it is to see you again. As lovely as ever I see."

Sarah and Phillip nodded to Belinda and Charles before moving further into the room.

A couple of waitresses stood opposite each other like book-ends, holding trays with a colourful assortment of drinks.

Sarah selected what she hoped was a straight orange juice and Phillip took a gin and tonic.

Sarah surveyed the room. About thirty people stood around in small groups as waitresses passed among them with trays of canapés.

"Let's go over there," Phillip suggested, "over by that window."

Walking across the expensive shag pile carpets scattered randomly on the large flagstone floor, they found a convenient spot next to one of three huge sash-windows overlooking a courtyard, from which Sarah could just see the top of the footbridge over the river. Deep red velvet curtains were draped on either side of the windows and between each window hung ornately framed oil paintings of men and women sitting on what could easily be mistaken for thrones.

A large stone fireplace dominated the stone wall on the far side of the room from where they stood sipping their drinks. On either side of the fireplace were full size shields in front of crossed swords and lances. Sarah noticed that the furniture had been moved against the walls and some of the guests, most of whom looked as though they were worth a bob or two, were sitting down.

"So what do you think of the palace?" Elspeth asked as she and John joined them.

"The only word I can think of at the moment is, wow!" Sarah said, still in awe of the pictures and the enormous chandeliers.

"I could think of another word," Phillip said, "but where do they keep their telly?"

John looked at him sideways and laughed. "People like this don't have tellies. They have theatres. It's small admittedly, but it's still a theatre."

"And no doubt there's an indoor pool somewhere," Phillip said.

"Good God, yes. Go through that door over there," he said pointing to the far corner of the room, "down the corridor and you'll come to one of the biggest bloody conservatories you've ever seen with a ten-metre pool as its centrepiece."

"If you behave yourselves tonight you might just get invited back to one of their costume dinners and by costume I don't mean fancy dress," Elspeth added.

"What, you get invited for a swim?" Phillip asked.

"Yes, before and in-between courses, and then for dessert things have been known to get a little risqué."

"Have you been?" Sarah asked Elspeth.

"Once, about three months after we arrived. It was just before poor Abigail was killed."

"And?" Phillip said, encouraging her.

"Yes, some of the guests did strip off for a skinny-dip but no I didn't," Elspeth said, looking Phillip straight in the eye without a hint of a smile, "And neither did John. That's probably why we haven't been invited to one of their costume dinners again."

Sarah saw John's knowing smile as he looked at Phillip and raised his eyebrows.

Elspeth turned to Sarah. "Anyway, unless we circulate you'll not even make bonfire night. You take Phillip that way, John, and I'll go this way with Sarah. We'll meet near the fire place in about half an hour."

"But –"

"No buts, John. Look over there," Elspeth said pointing at a group near one of the other windows. "There's Penelope

Crowthorne and you know you like her, especially when she's almost wearing a dress."

Before John could argue Elspeth took Sarah's arm and guided her in the opposite direction. More guests were arriving and the hall was filling up. There must have been well over fifty people there now, all trying to talk over each other.

After stopping at the first group of guests for a few minutes, Elspeth steered Sarah towards a door that led down a short corridor to another door that she opened onto what appeared to be an unused bedroom. There was a single unmade bed, a chest-of-drawers, a wardrobe, a bedside table cum locker and a chair, but other than that the room was stark and obviously unoccupied.

"What are we doing in here?" Sarah asked as Elspeth closed the door and moved to the window that overlooked the side of the orchard. Sarah stayed at the door, her earlier nervousness turning to anxiety.

"As I said, Sarah, we have to talk."

"But why here?"

"Privacy."

"Phillip and John will wonder where we are."

"Not if Penelope Crowthorne has her way. She'll keep them occupied for the time we need."

"Who's Penelope Crowthorne?"

"It doesn't matter who she is, as long as she serves her purpose." Elspeth turned from the window and faced Sarah. Folding her arms, she leant against the radiator. "So what are we going to do?"

Sarah frowned, feigning confusion. "About what? What are you talking about? Is this –?"

"Sarah, please don't fight your feelings, you know exactly what I'm saying. We need to talk about us. If I thought it was only me then we wouldn't be here, but I saw how you were last Saturday and it was you who said you were crying because you were so happy." Elspeth extracted a cigarette from her evening bag and lit it. She looked for something to use as an ashtray.

"I can't," Sarah said.

"You can't what?" Elspeth reached behind her and opened the window a little.

"I don't know what or how I feel."

Exhaling out of the corner of her mouth, Elspeth's eyes narrowed as she looked at Sarah.

"All right, I appreciate that maybe you're confused, and so am I, so let me try to help us both. If I were to tell you that I want to be with you, can I be more honest than that?"

Sarah moved towards the chair. "And I want to be with you but ..."

Elspeth grinned. "But I don't mean as friends. And if you're being honest I don't think you do either."

Sarah sat down, her mind in a turmoil. This wasn't right. No matter how she really felt, this could not be right. "But we are friends," she whispered, her voice catching.

"Of course we're friends but I think, like me, you want more than just friendship." Elspeth threw the cigarette out of the window and lit another one. "Can we stop beating around the bush and start being honest with each other? I've fallen in love with you, Sarah, and I think you feel the same about me."

"I love Phillip," Sarah said.

"Of course you do and in a way I love John, but neither of us feel for them the way we feel for each other."

Sarah shook her head. "This isn't for real. It's not happening," she said as her eyes misted over.

"It is and it is. I'm here and you're here. If we turn away from our feelings now we'll regret it for the rest of our lives."

The second half-smoked cigarette followed the first.

Elspeth carefully closed the window before crossing the small room. She knelt in front of Sarah and reached for both her hands.

Sarah did not resist.

"Sarah, since the first day I came to see you I've known there was something special between us. I sensed it in you too. The way we feel isn't something we have to hide nowadays, it's something we must face head on and do what needs to be done."

Sarah lifted her head as tears began running down her cheeks.

"I'm married, Elspeth. I'm married to a man I love. We're trying to have a child. We're trying to have children. I admit that I'm very fond of you and the way I feel is scary, but I mustn't allow my feelings to change what I really want."

The grip on Sarah's hands tightened.

"And what do you really want? Do you actually know?" Elspeth asked.

"I want a family: I want a son and a daughter. I want to be a mother and then a grandmother. I want security. I want to be happy." Sarah lowered her eyes.

Elspeth put a finger under Sarah's chin, lifting her head gently. "I could make you happy," she said.

"This is wrong. I'm a married woman and it's Phillip I want to be with."

"Is it?" Elspeth leaned forward.

Sarah knew what was going to happen, but she couldn't stop it. It had only happened in her imagination before and she had loved the sensation. But this time Elspeth's lips on hers were for real, the pressure gentle and reassuring. A shiver ran down her spine and she closed her eyes: what was happening was so natural ... yet so wrong.

She wanted to return the kiss, she wanted ...

"No," she whispered, pulling away, "this is ..." She opened her eyes.

Elspeth's face was only an inch from hers, her hand on Sarah's shoulder.

"Don't fight it, Sarah, it's what we both want," Elspeth said as she tried to kiss Sarah again. But Sarah turned her head away.

"No, Elspeth, we mustn't, we can't."

"We must and we can."

"No." Sarah reached for Elspeth's hand and moved it from her shoulder. "No, Elspeth, we must not."

Elspeth sat back on her haunches. Her hands fell to her sides.

"All right, perhaps I expected too much from you but you cannot, you must not deny your feelings," she said softly. "I don't feel foolish telling you I'm in love with you because I believe if you were being honest with yourself and me, you would admit you feel the same about me. But maybe I'm expecting too much too quickly." She took hold of Sarah's hand and lifted it to her lips.

Tears rolled down both their faces. "I'm in love with you, Sarah," Elspeth said softly. "And one day you will be mine."

Chapter Nine

After repairing their makeup as best they could, Sarah and Elspeth rejoined the party, moving slowly from group to group until they reached the fireplace. Other than the normal looks and leers, nobody took any real notice of them.

Phillip and John were with them seconds later.

"You managed to tear yourselves away from Penelope Crowthorne then?" Elspeth said, searching John's face to see if he noticed that she had been crying.

Sarah could not bring herself to say anything.

She couldn't bring herself to even look at Phillip.

To some extent, the kiss they had shared and what was said were irrelevant. It was her belief that Elspeth could be right that was covering Sarah with guilt and confusion.

She was also beginning to think that she did feel the same but still knew it was wrong.

Although she didn't go to church every Sunday, she believed in God, in the commandments and the sacraments. The vows that accompanied the marriage ceremony were sacrosanct. So her current feelings were alien to the married person she really was.

Until a few minutes ago she also believed that her feelings for Elspeth were nothing more than a very good friendship. It was a little more than that after her experience just under a week earlier, but that had been a fantasy: fantasies are impossible or improbable and they certainly don't become a reality.

Or was she lying to herself?

Was she in denial of the truth?

Was she really two people, both struggling for possession?

Each time their hands touched, each time she looked at Elspeth, when she thought about spending another hour, another minute with her, the sensation that ran through her was testament to her utter confusion.

And then just a few minutes ago there was that kiss.

How did she feel then? Impossible or improbable?

No, her imagination, her fantasy *was* now a reality.

When Elspeth kissed her on the lips she felt elated. She had wanted the intimacy to go on and on.

But she should not have felt the way she did because she was married to Phillip. As she turned her face away so that Elspeth couldn't kiss her again and although she told Elspeth what they were doing was wrong, what she really wanted was the opposite. She wanted Elspeth to kiss her and she wanted to kiss Elspeth: to be touched and to touch.

With Phillip standing next to her she realised she was and probably had been living a lie since moving to Upper Slaughter, living in a world she thought she ought to be living in. Elspeth's kiss had demanded so many explanations, uncovered so many truths. Up to that point she had thought the man who was now only a few inches from her was the truth.

She could not look at him.

She could not bring herself to see what she was possibly going to destroy. Everything they were working towards, all their plans, everything she believed she wanted – were they all now in the past?

That morning she had woken up with the man she believed was her future.

A few hours later, she was no longer so sure.

Or was her confusion generating unbelievable thoughts which were only adding to her total bewilderment?

"That outrageous woman was already pissed," John said, trying to explain things to Sarah and Elspeth. "I thought I'd better get Phillip away from her. Even *he* wasn't safe."

"Thanks," Phillip retorted, glancing at Sarah. Something was wrong, he could tell, but he also knew it was not always wise to ask.

Phillip looked around the room hoping the next hour would pass more quickly than the first. He found the people he and John spoke to boring, only wanting to talk about themselves, and if not boring they were the opposite – too inquisitive. One woman – he couldn't remember her name – assumed that because he and John were circulating together they actually were together in the strict sense of the word. She even told them she didn't disapprove of homosexuality. Her comment, as well as being highly amusing, made him think – why were he and John circulating together, and where were Sarah and Elspeth?

Looking round the room he could not see them. He was just about to go and find them when John pulled his arm, guiding him towards the group containing the infamous Penelope Crowthorne.

He grabbed another gin and tonic from a passing waitress before shaking Penelope by the hand. She was wearing what he assumed those in the know would call a *creation*. Although her dress was fastened in a bow at the neck, there wasn't a lot of material between the bow and her navel. Not wishing to satisfy her rather obvious self-image, he lifted his eyes to her face. She was talking to a lone man as he and John approached but this man drifted away, appearing relieved to escape.

"Hello, John," Penelope said. "Who's this?" she asked, after she took hold of Phillip's hand.

"Phillip, Phillip Preston. He and his wife Sarah moved into Primrose Cottage just over a month ago. This is Penelope Crowthorne, Phillip."

"Hello, Phillip."

"Penelope," he said with a slight nod.

149

"And what do you do?" she added, hanging onto his hand a little too long. Once again, he tried not to allow his eyes to drift down the front of Penelope's dress, but failed. She was about five feet six inches tall, probably fortyish, with short auburn hair and almost jet black eyes. She was slim but the dress she was wearing left little to the imagination. Phillip decided she was attractive but obvious – and therefore very dangerous.

"I buy and sell antiques," he told her.

"Oh, how fascinating, and where do you do that?"

She asked her question in such a way that she could have been enquiring about the price of eggs.

"In Gloucester," he said.

"Really! I must come and see you."

"Please do."

"Do you have a card?"

"Not on me."

"But you ought to, especially at one of Hilary's parties."

"This is the first one he and Sarah have been to," John said.

Penelope was very tactile; she touched hands and arms as she spoke. Phillip had already had three gin and tonics. He decided she was even more attractive in an even more obvious sort of way and, he thought, smiling to himself, probably adventurous rather than dangerous.

"And is your husband with you?" Phillip asked.

"Good Lord, no," she said with a slight titter. "He's in Thailand."

When she didn't add a reason Phillip thought it might be best not to enquire why he was in Thailand.

"Which one is your wife? Sarah, I think John said her name was?"

"Yes," Phillip confirmed, "it's Sarah." He looked around the room again. "She's with Elspeth somewhere, but I can't see them at the moment."

He sneaked a look at John, frowning.

150

John shrugged. "Elspeth has probably gone somewhere for a cigarette and taken Sarah with her."

"Enough of your wives," Penelope said, emptying her glass. "No, sorry, John, Elspeth isn't your wife, is she?"

"She may as well be," John said.

Penelope wasn't slurring her words but it was obvious that she was already tipsy. She looked around for a waitress but Phillip having spotted one close by replaced the drink for her. As she lifted her arm to take the glass, what little there was for Phillip's imagination to dwell on was swiftly made unnecessary.

From her smile he concluded it had been deliberate.

"Are you still soliciting?" Penelope asked John with a mischievous grin.

John smiled at her. "I wish I was, Penelope. It would be a far more pleasurable way of earning a living than being a solicitor."

She was listening but her eyes were still on Phillip.

When another couple wandered over Penelope looked disappointed but introduced them as Alexandra and Christian Hammersley. After exchanging polite conversation for a few minutes John and Phillip managed to move on, but only after promising they would return before the party ended.

Penelope gave Phillip an inviting look, telling him she really did like antiques and would be paying him a visit.

"And who have you two met?" Phillip asked.

He was still concerned about Sarah's demeanour. It was almost as though she was in some sort of trance: her face was expressionless, her shoulders slumped and her head bowed.

"A lot of boring people full of their own self-importance," Elspeth said as she glanced at Sarah. "So no change from previous experiences."

"Any bum-pinchers this year?" John asked, looking around the room.

151

"No, no pinchers this year but the odd patter," Elspeth said with a weak smile on her lips. "I must admit I did escape to have a cigarette for part of the time."

"I thought as much," John said. "What about you, Sarah? Anybody pat your bottom?"

Sarah was looking at the floor, her hands crossed in front of her.

"Sarah?"

She slowly lifted her head. "Yes?" Phillip wondered why she looked more confused than ever.

"I asked whether anybody patted your bottom."

"Why ... why would anybody want to do that?" She shook her head, seemingly trying to rid herself of something.

Phillip reached for her hand. "Are you all right?"

She snatched her hand away. "No, I'm not. Will you take me home please?" She took a step back and waited.

The others exchanged bewildered looks. "We can't leave yet, it –"

"Phillip, I want to go now, please." Sarah looked up and her eyes were watering. "Please."

"What is it?"

She turned her head away.

"All right, if you –"

He reached for her arm. "I'm coming with you," he said looking over his shoulder at the other two. "I'm sorry," he mouthed.

Elspeth smiled ruefully. "Don't worry, we'll tell the Bond-Smithers that Sarah felt unwell. What's wrong?" she added so that Sarah didn't hear her:

Phillip shook his head, "Don't know," he mouthed back.

Sarah stayed silent all the way back to Primrose Cottage.

It was just after eight o'clock and dusk had settled. The wind was blowing harder and the branches on the old oak trees by the ford were swaying, the leaves rustling, the branches squeaking.

"Looks like rain," Phillip said.

152

She heard him but did not respond. She saw nothing but the ground in front of her as she walked up the hill, her hands thrust deeply into her coat pockets for security, her head in an absolute turmoil.

In her mind the way she had previously felt about Elspeth had been some sort of game – a fantasy. But like many a fantasy which suddenly moved onto life's stage and became a reality, she didn't know how to cope with it. She was confused and full of guilt, and yet she was not guilty of anything other than refusing Elspeth's advances.

Nevertheless, perhaps Elspeth had spoken the truth. Perhaps she did share her feelings. But it was only perhaps.

Once again tears welled up in her eyes and she turned away from Phillip. He mustn't see her tears.

Phillip?

What was she going to do and what were *they* going to do?

They would have to move, they would have to go back to Evesham, to Gloucester, anywhere that was away from Upper Slaughter.

But she didn't want to leave. She didn't want to throw away the friendship Elspeth had given her. Perhaps they could go back to the way they were before. Perhaps they could recover the situation. She wanted to be with Elspeth as a friend, but she didn't want to ruin what she had with Phillip. Regardless of what she might have thought earlier, Phillip *was* her future.

Wasn't he?

But she *did* want to touch Elspeth in the same way she wanted Elspeth to touch her. She couldn't lie, not to herself. It was the shock brought about by realising what the truth actually was that was causing her to react the way she did.

She *did* want to feel the gentleness, the tenderness, the understanding. She *did* want to feel part of somebody else.

For as many years as she could remember, she was either ambivalent or sympathetic towards gay relationships. It depended on what the people involved were like. She

153

never read anything more than tolerance into her attitude, but that was before she met Elspeth. Now she was questioning her own sexuality not somebody else's.

Society would judge her as it always sat in judgement and more often than not was very quick in reaching a verdict. But modern society, unlike thirty or forty years ago, now told her the way she thought she felt was acceptable. She was part of a minority community who were full of doubts but one that had the right to do whatever its members wanted.

Such relationships were now accepted without prejudice.

That was all very well from society's perspective but when it came down to individual relationships such deviances still violated some people's social norms and could still shatter lives. Tolerance and understanding were only possible as standards. Few people – regardless of what turned them on in their own fantasies – accepted such behaviour if it affected their immediate lives.

That was the way Phillip would react.

If she confessed to him about her feelings for Elspeth, it would be worse than if she confessed to wanting to be with another man. He would accuse her of living a lie. He would internalise such an admission and blame himself. He would ask where he might have gone wrong when in reality he had done nothing wrong. Indeed, if it hadn't been for him then maybe the fantasy which was now almost reality, would have happened a long time ago, but she didn't want to lose him and she didn't want to have to watch him as she confessed her feelings for Elspeth.

In a relationship, a fantasy can be kept secret to be used repeatedly.

The truth had to be faced head on.

Phillip opened the front door and stood back to let Sarah in.

He'd had no response to his attempt at breaking into her silence. Something was very wrong. He learnt very early on in their relationship that when Sarah was in a mood it was better to let her find her own way out of it.

154

Now he believed she couldn't see a way out of wherever she was. Asking her again what was wrong would only make matters worse. He knew her well enough to know she was in some kind of mental maze and whichever way she turned she would find she was facing a dead end. He wished he knew why she was in this maze. It could be something he had done but on this occasion he doubted it.

Whenever Sarah felt down, worried or bored, he always assumed that he was to blame or he had to do something about it. During a previous argument, she told him she could never work out whether his attitude was unfettered arrogance or genuine concern and she wasn't sure he could either.

"What would you like for supper?" he asked, hesitating at the kitchen door as he saw Sarah going upstairs. "Those canapés were nice enough but not particularly filling."

She stopped, hesitated, then came back down the stairs a little way and sat on the bottom step.

She buried her head in her hands and started to cry.

"What is it? What's happened?" he asked softly, sitting next to her and putting his arm round her shoulders.

She sniffed, shaking her head. "Nothing ... nothing, and I know that sounds stupid but it's absolutely nothing."

Taking his handkerchief from his pocket he tried to wipe Sarah's tears away. "How can it be nothing? Something happened at that party. You were fine before and on the way down. What was it?"

"I'm just very low at the moment. I've let everything get on top of me. It's nothing."

"It's got to be something. Why are you so low?"

"Don't ... please don't ask, Phillip. I'm just being me. I've got to think things through. I'll tell you when I'm ready to talk. You know what I'm like."

She pressed her face into his shoulder, wishing she had the courage to tell him right now.

What was there to tell him?

My best friend told me that she's in love with me and wants to be with me, but I don't know what I want ... yet?

She felt him squeeze her shoulder.

"When you're ready I'll be here. Why don't you go and have a lie down for an hour or so? I'll throw a meal together when you've rested."

Sarah nodded. "Yes, I think I will." She twisted her head so that she could look into his eyes. "I love you, Phillip, please don't ever doubt that, no matter what happens."

Phillip conjured up a weak smile "That sounds rather ominous but whatever it is, we'll get through it."

She kissed him.

I hope to God you're right, she thought, taking off her shoes and walking slowly upstairs. She hoped that very soon she would be able to look back on this evening and wonder why she let it get to her this way.

From the moment Sarah left the party, Elspeth felt her mood change for the worse. Ever since her poorly timed admission, she'd been worried by Sarah's silence.

What an impetuous fool she was.

Seeing Sarah leave the party with Phillip made her feel as though she was walking out of her life for good. Her intentions had been the opposite, but she had managed to get everything very wrong.

After Sarah and Phillip left the party she went over to one of the large windows and could just see them crossing the footbridge by the ford. Sarah's shoulders were slumped, her body language even from that distance obvious and it communicated her sadness.

When she and John left an hour later and offered their thanks to the Bond-Smithers, they also apologised for the Prestons having to leave early but it was obvious to Elspeth, if not to John, that Hilary Bond-Smithers' mind was fortunately on other things.

She probably didn't even know the Prestons had left early.

Once they got home John broke the silence.

"So," he said slumping down into a chair in the living room, "what the hell was the matter with Sarah this evening?"

He was going to ask on the way back up Church Lane but decided to leave his question until they got home. He saw Elspeth stare at Primrose Cottage as they passed it on their way up the hill and sensed even then that maybe his question was already answered.

Throwing her cape onto the back of the sofa Elspeth went over to the cupboard where they kept the bottles of drink. "You know what we females can be like," she said. "Whisky?"

"Please. What sort of answer is that?" John picked up the remote control and flicked on the television.

"Do we have to have that on?" Elspeth said, passing him his drink.

"Sorry." He turned it off. "Does that mean you want to talk?"

Elspeth sat down in the chair opposite him, kicked off her shoes and tucked her feet under her.

"I must have a cigarette," she said, reaching for her bag. "Bloody parties where there's no smoking are hell."

"And a lot better for you," he said.

"You're not going to start lecturing me, are you?"

"No, just passing a comment. Anyway, Sarah apart, what's got into *you*?" John took a sip of the whisky, screwing up his face as he swallowed. "Do I detect a connection between Sarah's behaviour and your mood?"

Elspeth looked at him for a second or two before looking away. He knew nothing about her relationship with the girl at school; she had never had a reason to tell him. But about three weeks before Abigail Tucker was killed in the riding accident, John had witnessed something perfectly harmless

157

between her and Abigail and she wondered if he was making a somewhat tenuous connection.

She had become friends with Abigail soon after they moved to Upper Slaughter. Abigail was nearly ten years younger than Elspeth but they had met while Elspeth was strolling round the village trying to find inspiration for the book she was writing about a family of elves that lived on a river bank among the rushes. She was on her way home when she stopped on the footbridge by the ford to stare into the flowing water. She hadn't seen Abigail walking down Church Lane but became aware that she was not alone.

"Hello," Elspeth said, "you are Abigail Tucker aren't you?"

"Yes," Abigail said, leaning on the hand rail a few feet away. "And you're Elspeth Warrington?"

"There are no secrets in Upper Slaughter, are there?" Elspeth said turning towards the girl. "Have you been riding?"

"Yes, I've been exercising Bluey."

"Bluey?"

"He's one of the Bond-Smithers' horses." Abigail nodded towards the big house beyond the river. "Have you met Hilary Bond-Smithers yet?"

"Oh yes, I've had a visit."

Abigail smiled. "She's a very nice woman," she said.

Elspeth put her hand on the girl's arm. "I hope I didn't imply otherwise."

Still smiling, Abigail looked down at the water flowing under the low bridge beneath her feet. "Do you mind if I ask you a personal question?"

"Not at all, as long you don't mind if I give you an honest answer."

"I've seen you walking round the village before –"

"I do quite often, just to try to get inspiration."

"For your books?"

"How did you know that?"

158

"Hilary told me. You must have mentioned what you do when she came to see you."

Elspeth thought for a moment. "Yes, I think I did but ... why are you interested in what I do?"

"It's something I always thought I might like to do. I would like to write children's stories about horses, well a particular horse," Abigail said.

"Bluey?"

"No. It would be a pony, a sort of Lassie type pony."

"Sounds intriguing," Elspeth said.

Very quickly after this short meeting they became close friends. There was never even a hint of impropriety but situations can be misinterpreted and that was exactly what happened only a week later.

She had nearly finished the story about the family of elves. As she woke in the morning, she felt inspired and after a quick breakfast she sat at her laptop for most of the day only stopping for a quick sandwich at lunchtime. She was just typing the final word of the final chapter when there was a knock at the front door.

It was Abigail and for once she wasn't dressed in her jodhpurs and riding hat. She stood on the front door step looking very distressed.

"Abigail, what's the matter?" Elspeth stood back as Abigail rushed past her.

In the kitchen, Abigail sat down at the table with her head in her hands.

"I've got to talk to somebody."

"About what?" Elspeth asked, switching on the kettle.

"I didn't mean somebody, I meant you," Abigail said ignoring Elspeth's question.

"Coffee?" Elspeth reached for her cigarettes and lit one.

"Can I have one?"

"Of course." She passed the packet and lighter across the table.

As Abigail lit a cigarette Elspeth noticed that her hands were shaking. The way she inhaled and then exhaled suggested the girl had been smoking for quite a while. Elspeth wondered how she kept the secret from her parents, if indeed she did.

"Calm down. Whatever it is can't be as bad as all that."

"It is," Abigail said, looking up at Elspeth.

"So what is it?"

Abigail drew deeply on her cigarette. "I was with a man last night and he –"

"Hang on a minute, Abigail, let me make the coffee and then you'll have my full attention."

Elspeth put the two steaming mugs on the table and sat down.

"Okay," she said, "are you happy in here or do you want to go somewhere more comfortable?"

"No, it's fine here, thank you."

"All right. You were saying that you were with a man last night, so what happened?"

"That's the point, nothing happened." Abigail picked up her coffee after stubbing out the half-smoked cigarette. "Did I do the right thing?"

"You've lost me. How about starting from the beginning and then I'll try to tell you whether you did the right thing or not. Let's start with who this man was."

Abigail calmed down a little. She took a deep breath: "You know I'm taking a gap year before going to university?" Elspeth nodded. "I enrolled on an IT course at the FE College in Evesham –"

"Yes, you told me that."

"Sorry. Well, I've been seeing one of the lecturers – well he's not really a lecturer because he runs the gymnasium. We've been out a few times but last night he tried it on."

"You mean he tried to have sex with you?"

Abigail lowered her head. "Yes," she said.

"So what happened?"

"I said no."

Elspeth put her hand in front of her mouth to cover her smile. "So what's the problem with that? You didn't want to have sex so you said no. Well done you."

Abigail sipped her coffee, fingering the cigarette packet in front of her. "But I did want to. I'm eighteen for God's sake."

"Sorry, Abigail, but you've lost me again. You were with this man, he wanted to have sex with you, you wanted to have sex with him but you said no. So what's the problem? Far better to have said no and meant yes, than to have said yes and meant no."

"But ... but I really wanted him to, you know ..."

This time Elspeth didn't hide her smile. "There's nothing wrong with wanting to do something but then not doing it because it may be wrong. You're lucky he listened to you."

"That's what worries me, he's really nice. He might not want to see me again."

"How old is he?"

"Twenty-four."

"If he's got any sense he'll respect you for what you did, or in this case didn't do. If seeing you again or not is based purely on whether you have sex or not, then you're better off without him." Elspeth took out another cigarette and lit it. "Have another if you want one."

Abigail shook her head. "How old were you?"

"What, when I first had sex with a man or in my case a boy?"

"Yes."

"Seventeen, it was in the back of a car and it was horrible."

"But I'm eighteen."

"So what? There isn't a law that says you have to lose your virginity by a particular age. It's when you're ready, and from what you've told me, you're not ready."

"I suppose I'm not, it's just that ..."

"I know what you mean, you feel under pressure." Abigail nodded. "Tell me, why are you here rather than talking this over with your mother?"

Abigail looked up, shock written all over her face. "My mother!" she exclaimed. "I couldn't discuss anything like this with my mother."

"I see. If it's any help I had the same sort of relationship with my mother. What about Belinda? Don't you two discuss such things when you're together?"

"I've tried to but she's useless. I don't think she's ever kissed a boy let alone allowed anyone to touch her."

"So you came to me. I'm not sure whether that's a compliment or not," Elspeth said jokingly.

"Oh, I didn't mean that. I just thought ..."

"I know you didn't."

Abigail smiled. "Thank you. So you think I did the right thing?"

"On this occasion, yes, you did the right thing. The next time, or the next time after that, you'll know when it's the right time."

Abigail reached across the table so she could put her hand on Elspeth's. "Thank you," she said, smiling for the first time.

"Will you see him again?"

"Next Saturday. It's the College Christmas ball. He's asked me."

"So he hasn't dumped you?"

"No."

"I suggest you hang on to your gymnast, he sounds as though he's a rare breed. Another coffee?"

"Please."

"So what are you wearing?"

"I don't know yet, I haven't been to a ball before."

"Okay, what size are you? Ten, twelve?"

"Twelve on the bottom and fourteen on the top." Abigail looked down at herself. "I'm out of proportion."

"Me too." They giggled. "Look, I've got a few things upstairs that may be suitable. We are the same size and the same height. If there's something you like then I'll happily lend it to you. Do you want to see them?"

"No, I couldn't."

"Why not?"

Upstairs Abigail sat on the bed while Elspeth rummaged through her wardrobe, extracting four old but still very wearable evening dresses. The legal functions she went to with John were always formal, and after just a year her collection had grown. The labels were not well known and the dresses were simple in both design and colour.

Elspeth hung the dresses on the wardrobe door. "There you are," she said. "Do you like any of them?"

"They're beautiful. I think we have similar tastes."

"Want to try them on?"

"Can I?"

"Let's take them downstairs, it's warmer down there than up here." Elspeth gathered the dresses and led the way downstairs.

"Which one first?"

"That long black woollen one is lovely."

Abigail took off her fleece and then without any embarrassment undid and wriggled out of her jeans.

"Should I take my T-shirt off as well?"

"Might be better," Elspeth said.

She thought Abigail's legs were probably a little longer than hers, her hips narrower and her waist a little fuller but the dresses should still fit in the right places. Abigail had long brown hair, which most of the time she wore in a ponytail but as she took off her T-shirt she pulled the band with it allowing her hair to fall down her back. Pulling the dress over her head, she smoothed the material over her hips and waist.

"How does it look?" she asked Elspeth.

"Go and look for yourself, there's a long mirror in the hall."

Coming back into the living room a couple of minutes later, with her nose screwed up, she said: "It isn't right, is it?"

"It's fine on top but I agree, the bottom doesn't hang properly."

"Pity," Abigail said, pulling the dress over her head and shaking her hair.

"I think this one would be perfect," Elspeth suggested, handing her another black dress. "I always liked the feel of velvet against the skin."

Undoing the zip Abigail stepped into the dress and fastened the halter-neck collar. Elspeth watched her glide into the hall and then twirl a couple of times in front of the mirror. Realising the dress was backless Abigail undid the halter-neck so that she could take off her bra.

"It really is gorgeous," she shouted from the hall, "and it fits so beautifully."

"It's not too old fashioned for you, is it?"

"Not at all."

"I think you've made your choice then." Elspeth smiled, feeling genuinely pleased. "What about shoes?"

"I'll have to get a pair," Abigail said, undoing the halter-neck.

"I'm a five."

"So am I." Abigail stepped out of the dress and handed it to Elspeth. "I left my bra in the hall."

As Abigail was picking up her bra from the hall table John walked in through the front door. She made a vain attempt to cover herself.

"John," she spluttered.

"Abigail," he said as his eyes travelled from the poor girl's bare feet to her staring eyes.

"Abigail," Elspeth said from behind her, "go into the living room and put some clothes on and John, put your tongue away and close your mouth."

Abigail turned and fled past Elspeth, her hands still clutching at her breasts.

164

Elspeth smiled. "That's what you get for coming home early so perhaps you'll do it more often now," she said, folding her arms defensively.

"What precisely …?"

"Not what you think, or more correctly not what you would like to think," Elspeth said, staring defiantly at him.

"And what precisely am I supposed to be thinking?" John asked, putting his briefcase down and taking off his coat.

Elspeth ignored him. "Abigail was simply trying on some of my dresses. She's going to a ball on Saturday and didn't know what to wear."

"So why was she standing in the hall with next to nothing on?" John asked in a stage whisper.

Elspeth shook her head. "The explanation is quite simple John, but shall we save the poor girl any further embarrassment."

Pulling on her fleece Abigail appeared behind Elspeth.

"I'm awfully sorry about that," she said, looking from John to Elspeth and back again. "It –"

"There's no need, Abigail," Elspeth told her. "Have you got the dress?"

"No, I left it …"

"I need to put a couple of stitches in it, so I'll bring it down to you later in the week."

"Thank you," Abigail said and turning to John she added, "I'm really sorry."

He smiled. "Don't be," he said. "I think it was more a pleasure for me than it was for you."

She scurried past him and let herself out.

Elspeth took the dresses upstairs, then joined John in the kitchen.

"So what brought you home so early?" she asked, sitting down at the kitchen table.

John finished pouring boiling water into the teapot.

"I don't know, I just thought I'd surprise you for a change, and I certainly did that."

He took a couple of mugs out of the cupboard.

"What precisely do you mean by that?" Elspeth asked, lighting a cigarette.

"Well, you have to admit ... well, if you'd walked in and there was a naked boy in the hallway, you'd have wondered, wouldn't you?"

Still not looking at Elspeth he went to the fridge to get the milk.

She guessed he was half winding her up but maybe part of him did question whether he was being told the whole truth or not.

"It would be unlikely that an eighteen-year old boy would be trying your clothes on," Elspeth suggested. "Anyway, I don't see why I should be expected to explain myself. Abigail popped in for a chat and tried on a couple of dresses, there's no more to it than that despite what your perverted mind may think."

Elspeth thought it best not to mention what Abigail had wanted to talk about as it might add fat to the fire that was probably already burning in John's head.

"Okay," he said, smiling as he put the mugs on the table. "If that's what you say happened, then that's the way it was."

"You don't sound convinced."

"Oh, I am where Abigail is concerned."

Elspeth decided not to ask him what the hell he meant by that.

It had been a good day up to that point and she wasn't going to let him spoil it.

Chapter Ten

"What did you say?" Elspeth asked.

"I asked whether Sarah's behaviour and your mood were connected," John said.

He waited for Elspeth to say something.

Early on in their relationship, John thought Elspeth was his future. She was everything he wanted in a woman, a wife and possibly a mother, but after just six months into their relationship he had begun to feel less certain. She quite often seemed distant, uncommunicative and just a little reluctant. She also made it perfectly clear that she never intended having any children, which he thought strange considering she wrote children's books for a living. But whenever they argued he found it a little incongruous that she always seemed to resort to accusations about their sex life rather than sticking to the main topic of the argument. The exchange was always the same.

"If I don't satisfy you, you'd better look elsewhere."

"What?"

"You know exactly what I'm saying."

"I do?"

Initially he was shocked and just a little scared by what she said but now he was used to it. The possibility of marriage was discussed but each time it was decided to wait a couple of years before committing themselves to a long-term relationship. Neither set of parents was happy with them living together but when it was obvious there wasn't going to be an immediate change, the hints and looks disappeared ... almost.

Then Sarah and John Preston arrived in the village.

John admitted they were a lovely couple and great fun to be with – he particularly enjoyed the fact that he and Phillip had so much in common – but for some reason which he could not quite put his finger on, he watched Elspeth when Sarah was around, and then he started watching Sarah too. Elspeth had changed overnight and the change was dramatic. She had been in some sort of rut before Sarah arrived. Her writing was suffering, she was miserable and always spoiling for a fight. But after she met Sarah and started helping her sort out Primrose Cottage, it was as though she had found a new zest for life. She was full of energy and, John admitted to himself, she was happier than he had ever seen her previously.

He never doubted Elspeth and although there were the usual arguments, he never doubted her honesty or her feelings for him. But something had changed, not in her attitude towards him but in her life generally. Something had given her a new goal, something to aim for. When he commented on the change in her she smiled and said he was imagining things. Deep down he was intrigued about what the reason could be, although he was more than content that she was now full of life and full of purpose.

He then noticed she was taking more care of herself.

In the past she always opted for the casual look and the only time he saw her in what he referred to as her smart clothes, was when she went with him to one of the dinner parties organised by his chambers. He loved the way she was but he put it down to the fact that she was a writer and her life was more connected to the fictitious characters she created than to her real self and real people. But since Phillip and Sarah's arrival things had changed. Whereas before Elspeth could be ready to go out at least ten minutes early, now she inevitably took a good deal longer. Initially, he thought she might fancy Phillip but the looks, touches and innuendoes weren't there so he switched his attention to Sarah.

168

He watched them closely every time they were together.

When talking their eye contact was obvious, to the extent that when either Elspeth or Sarah said anything to him or Phillip, they broke eye contact and tended to look down at their hands. When out they always made sure they were walking side-by-side, and as close as possible. Indeed, whenever they were to be with Phillip and Sarah, Elspeth started talking about what they would be doing hours before they were due to see each other.

His observations made him think.

He didn't believe anything was going on between the two women, other than in their heads, although in many ways that was more dangerous. Although it had happened a while ago, he still had doubts about what Elspeth told him happened with Abigail. Elspeth, like many others who knew Abigail well, took the girl's untimely death very badly, locking herself away in her study for hours on end. John hated himself for thinking it, but more recently after watching Elspeth and Sarah he found himself beginning to question what the truth really was.

He noticed that Sarah's moods fluctuated when they were all together. There were times when she was completely animated, the life and soul of the party. But at other times she was withdrawn, appeared dejected and confused by what was happening – whatever that might be. If he was right about what might be happening, Sarah wasn't coping with the discovery as well as Elspeth.

He did not feel rejected. He was surprisingly sanguine about what he now believed to be the truth. He had never attended any official courses in understanding human behaviour and body language but his job brought him into a great deal of contact with the general public. Being able to see through the many fantastic stories which were all part of his daily work, and quite educational. Innocence, even when perceived, was a great advantage and it was amazing the stories people concocted to try to prove a right to such a

169

desirable quality, regardless of how guilty they were of the crime.

The previous weekend he did contemplate raising his concerns with Phillip. He decided to leave well alone: Phillip, if he was not aware of anything that might be going on would be devastated, and for all John knew he could inadvertently sow seeds of unnecessary doubt that might lead to the break-up of what was, on the surface, a very happy marriage.

For him, the cocktail party had dismissed any residual doubt. Elspeth suggesting she and Sarah circulate on their own, confirmed his previous suspicions. He watched them and when they disappeared through the door at the far end of the room, he closed his eyes and for the first time felt genuinely worried. He was only given food for thought before and he admitted he did allow his imagination to take over, so there was every chance he may have got it all wrong. But that simple act after they arrived at the party was all the proof he needed.

He knew he was terrible company for Phillip during the party. He did the necessary introductions but then stood back and waited for Sarah and Elspeth to return. When they did appear it was obvious that Sarah was confused, even distressed, and Elspeth looked equally worried and upset. Whatever went on for the fifteen minutes they were missing, he guessed that Elspeth would have taken the lead. She was by far the stronger of the two. It was also obvious they had both been crying.

Something happened, something very serious and he was determined to find out what it was.

"What do you mean?" Elspeth said, trying to delay the answer she was going to have to give eventually.

"I think you know what I mean, Elspeth. I'm not blind. Watching and understanding people is part of my job and I know when I'm not being told the truth."

He sipped his whisky and waited.

"You're talking in riddles. What precisely are you getting at?" She could not look at him. She knew exactly what he was getting at and the fact that he may have guessed was a shock.

John went over to the sideboard to pour himself another whisky.

"I'm neither blind nor an idiot, so please don't treat me as though I am. Phillip might be living in blissful ignorance, but I'm not."

Elspeth sat back in the chair and crossed her legs. Every nerve ending was on edge. She did not want this. Why did she feel like a naughty child who had been found out?

What the hell had she done to make him suspicious?

She squeezed her eyes shut, gripping the glass in her hands as tightly as she dared.

"How long have you known?" She asked the question before she could decide what she actually wanted to say.

John leant against the sideboard, looking down at her.

"Known?" he repeated. "Probably an hour or so for sure, but I've had my suspicions for quite a while."

"What suspicions? I don't understand."

"Abigail," John said.

"What? You thought she and I were having ... that's ridiculous."

"The evidence suggested –"

"What evidence? What I told you that day was the truth. Abigail was an innocent mixed-up child. How dare you try to dirty her memory."

John hesitated and held up his hand. "All right, maybe I got that wrong but you and Sarah, are you saying I'm wrong there too?"

"No and I'm so sorry," Elspeth said quietly.

"It depends what there is to be sorry about, and from a purely selfish perspective, how it's going to affect me."

Elspeth lit a cigarette before draining her glass. This was not supposed to happen. It was the second thing which was not supposed to happen this evening. "I don't know how it's going to affect you, it depends on how ..." Tears gushed into her eyes. "I didn't want ... any of this to happen," she said as she attempted to stub out her cigarette. "I tried ... I tried to stop it ... but it just happened."

John moved away from the sideboard, took the cigarette from her fingers and put it out in the ashtray. "So you woke up one morning, having decided you preferred women to men. Is it really as simple as that?" he said as he went back to the sideboard.

"Don't be so silly, of course it's not as simple as that. It's not ... it's not like that at all. I didn't set out to deceive you ... I ..."

Elspeth very rarely cried but now that she was crying, she wasn't thinking straight. Sarah had rejected her and now John was on the point of doing the same. In a matter of hours her whole life was going to be turned upside down and she was responsible. There was nobody else to blame.

She was afraid of being alone. She tried to give the impression that she exuded confidence but deep down she was dependent on others. She got her strength from others. Without others she was weak.

"I do love you, John," she said as more tears flowed down her cheeks. "You have to believe me."

John shook his head. "Love? I'm not sure you know what love is. Has everything we've done together been a charade? Was I simply a convenience while you were trying to sort out in your mind whether you preferred women to men?" He knocked back the remains of the whisky. "Is Sarah the first or have you been pulling the wool over my eyes for as long as we've been together?"

She dabbed her eyes with a tissue: "There hasn't been anybody else, John, I promise you. I told you the truth about Abigail."

She stood up and walked across the room to John. Wrapping her arms round his neck she rested her head against his shoulder, her tears wetting his shirt.

He didn't resist.

172

"I don't know what's happening, John. I don't understand why I feel the way I do. I'm so unhappy."

He put his hands on her waist. "Does Sarah feel the same about you?" he asked softly.

She shuddered. "No, I don't think she does."

"Then whether you believe me or not, I feel very sorry for you," he said.

She looked up at his face. Tears were still streaming down her cheeks. "Do you really mean that?"

He smiled. "You were made the way you are. If you meant it when you said you loved me then I have a chance. I'm not going to give you up without a fight."

"I don't know what's happening," she said.

"And at the moment, neither do I."

Chapter Eleven

Sarah woke at just after five in the morning.

The short rest before eating that Phillip had suggested, turned into the whole night. It was the most fitful night's sleep she had ever experienced. Images, some recognisable and some grotesque had leapt out at her from every corner of her mind. She didn't remember Phillip coming to bed but as her eyes became accustomed to the darkness in the room she was aware of his surprisingly relaxed breathing next to her. He must be very worried and didn't deserve what she was doing to him, but until she was able to understand what was happening herself there was no way she could discuss it with him.

Discuss?

It wasn't the sort of thing she could imagine sitting down and discussing with her husband.

Explain?

How do explain that what you believed was nothing more than a very strong friendship had turned into something that was pulling at your heartstrings? How do you explain that the feelings delved so deeply into your soul that the very thought of being away from that person made you want to curl up and disappear?

Confess?

Would she have the strength to plead guilty? What would she plead guilty to? Her feelings for this other woman were so strong but ...

It was the way she thought she had felt about Phillip.

Moving the duvet slowly to one side, she swung her legs off the bed. She picked up the clothes she'd discarded before

174

getting ready for the cocktail party, and turning the door handle as quietly as she could she left the bedroom. All she would need were her Barbour, scarf, woolly hat and walking boots. She would not be going far, but far enough so that she could think. She needed to be on her own, she needed to feel the breeze against her face; she needed to see the sun rise and she needed to decide what she really wanted.

She got dressed downstairs and with the spare key they kept in the cutlery drawer she let herself out through the back door. Outside she stood and breathed in the fresh cool morning air.

Where could she go?

She didn't want to be seen, although she doubted there would be anybody else about at this time of the morning.

Should she have left a note?

If she left a note she would also have to leave an explanation of why she was out walking so early, something she never usually did alone.

She wouldn't be long. How long do you need to decide what the hell you should do with the rest of your life? She wanted to be with Elspeth but she didn't want to leave Phillip.

But she couldn't have them both.

Opening the side gate, she moved slowly towards Church Lane, peering up and down the road until she was sure there was nobody about. After wrapping the Barbour round her body, tucking her chin deeply into the scarf and pulling the woolly hat over her ears, she headed down the lane towards the ford.

Just before the river she took the track to the left, went past the old wooden bench on the right and then into the wood which ran along by the water for nearly half a mile. The canopy created by the trees didn't entirely mask the light rising in the east, but it did play games with the shadows. The breeze was light but it was sufficient to make the leaves above her rustle. Twigs snapped under her feet as she walked and something swished in the undergrowth. She should have

175

brought a torch, maybe going back for one would be a good idea. But she walked on, deeper into the enveloping darkness.

Something snapped behind her. She turned round quickly, her eyes wide open, peering into the greyness, seeing the outlines of the trees she knew so well – but only in daylight.

This was madness, then again so was the reason she was here.

It was all madness.

Having managed to stay on the track and in less than five minutes, she felt more confident. The sky was getting lighter and the track twisted its way out of the wood. She could hear the river and see the field beyond the line of trees. She and Phillip had used a fallen tree to cross the river just beyond the edge of the wood. She would use that and then head up through the fields to the farmer's track that ran along the ridge high above the village. Perhaps by looking down on what her life was now she could find some inspiration for what it should be in the future.

After the climb, he reached the track and sat down on a stile to catch her breath. The warmth of the sun was now on her cheeks. It was a blazing orange semi-circle peeking above the distant horizon. As she wished Phillip were there to see it with her, she watched it moving inch by inch, getting bigger every second.

Phillip?

Why did she immediately think of Phillip? Why wasn't it Elspeth she imagined being with her rather than Phillip?

When they were on holiday, she and Phillip often sat and watched the sunrise and sunset. Wherever they went they always made a point of seeing at least one day start and another end. She remembered something Phillip said as they watched a particularly spectacular sunrise when on holiday in Bali. He put his arm round her and said: "When I see the sun rise it's the start of another day which means I can tell you I love you more today than I did yesterday."

She said something like: "Where on earth did you get that one from?" But she still loved him for saying it.

Her eyes filled with tears at the memory. She shook her head and stood up. She must be sensible: she must not let such memories cloud her judgement. If her decision was that she wanted to be with Phillip it must be because of the future not the past.

Climbing over the stile, she took a deep breath and headed up the track, climbing slowly until she was adjacent to Upper Slaughter. A light mist covered parts of the village but she could just see the top of the church spire. Not far from there Phillip was still asleep, she hoped. She could see the roof of their cottage but Elspeth's roof was hidden beneath the mist.

Was everything she was looking at trying to tell her something?

The mist, the church, the fact that she couldn't see Elspeth's cottage roof: were they all signs?

Of course they weren't, she was being silly.

She was the only person who could decide.

Back on the track she started walking slowly away from the village. On the horizon she could see the outline of Copper's Ridge woods. If her mind was not made up by the time she reached the woods she would turn round and go home. She might even get back before Phillip was up: he always had a lie in on Sunday morning. If he woke early he would think she was downstairs. She would not be long, maybe another hour or so.

An hour or so to decide what to do with the rest of her life. What the hell did that mean?

Michael spotted a figure in the distance, about half a mile away from Copper's Ridge woods. He wondered who it could be, since nobody was usually silly enough to be out walking this early in the morning.

Returning Hector the cat unharmed to Mrs Proctor's garden had not presented a problem. Afterwards he went back to his den to spend the night there. He was very annoyed with himself because killing the cat should have been easy, especially as Hector was one cat he did not particularly like.

The whole episode was an adventure for Hector and a disaster for him. It had been a stupid and immature idea.

Because he had had a disturbed night's sleep he was about to leave the woods earlier than usual by one of his secret routes, but it was then he spotted the distant figure. He always checked the track that ran along the ridge but only used it himself when he felt lazy. This particular Sunday morning he felt lazy. He was cold, hungry and miserable. He just wanted to get back to the warmth of his mother's house and go to bed.

After seeing whoever it was moving along the track, Michael returned to his den, collected his binoculars and then went to one of his observation points just inside the line of trees not far from Mrs Tucker's and Abigail's oak tree. He adjusted the binoculars until the person coming along the track was in focus. He could tell it was a female from the way she walked, but she had the collar of her coat up and a scarf wrapped round the bottom half of her face. Her woolly hat was pulled down over her ears against the early morning cold.

She was walking slowly, looking from side to side.

He checked where the sun was so that he could ensure it didn't catch the lenses of his binoculars: he didn't want this woman to become inquisitive.

He held the binoculars steadily in his hands.

There was something very familiar about the way she was walking.

Sarah spotted the lone tree about half way along the front of the wood.

She decided to walk as far as the tree and then turn round and go back. The tree was on a grassy hump and its branches on one side almost touched the ground. She checked her watch; it was nearly six-thirty, an hour and a half since she'd woken up and still she had not made a decision.

Was she expecting too much of herself?

A decision that could alter her entire life does not transpire just because of an early morning walk, she told herself. This time twenty-four hours ago, the possibility of a future without Phillip had not even entered her head. Why did she think she was brave enough to even attempt a decision?

She was being silly. She was infatuated with Elspeth, but she was in love with Phillip.

What did that make her?

Bisexual? Was that the word?

Don't be ridiculous, of course she wasn't bisexual.

If she were bisexual, she would have known ages ago. There would have been someone else, another female who she was attracted to in that way. She was just obsessed with the thought of another woman being in love with her, not just loving her, but being *in love* with her.

It was different.

Did she want to be with Elspeth? Of course she did, she was the most inspirational person anyone could ever want to meet, so of course she wanted to be with her.

But that was all. There was nothing else. She didn't want to do anything else ... did she? Of course she didn't. The thought of being touched intimately by another woman was repulsive: the thought of touching another woman intimately was equally repellent ... wasn't it?

Of course it was. So had she decided? Was it as simple as that?

Was it really all about sex?

Were her thoughts telling her what she wanted? Or was she just trying to find excuses so that she could maintain the status quo? The status quo would be the best because it was something she knew, something she understood, something she could cope with, even control ... and something she could work on.

So that was it. Better the devil you know than the one you don't. The decision was made ... wasn't it?

The tree was only fifty yards or so away.

Sarah wished she had a flask of tea or even a nip of whisky or brandy with her. She decided to sit by the tree for five minutes and then head back.

Her decision was made.

Phillip will be worried. He's bound to be up now having sensed she wasn't in bed next to him, and having checked the house he will be extremely anxious.

A few minutes ago a decision was going to be impossible, but now it was made.

She wanted to be with Phillip. Elspeth was a fantasy.

Wasn't she?

She sat down, drew her knees up under her chin, wrapped her arms round her legs and cried.

She was totally confused. She didn't know what she wanted.

Michael almost dropped the binoculars when he realised who he was looking at.

"My God it's her. What is she doing up here in the middle of nowhere?" he whispered.

His wish had come true.

She was only a hundred yards away and she was walking towards him.

Why?

He didn't know what to do.

She was walking towards the tree – *the* tree. Where Abigail and her mother died. Where he watched Mrs Tucker kill herself. She killed herself so that she could be with her daughter. He understood that. If he loved somebody as much as Mrs Tucker had loved her daughter, he would want to be with them too.

180

He watched Sarah Preston come closer and closer. She reached the tree, looked around her and sat down at almost the exact spot where Mrs Tucker had died.

She had come to him.

The person, the only person he really loved was here.

If she was here to die as well, maybe to get away from that man, he would kill himself to be with her. He might not be able to kill a rabbit or even Hector the cat, but if Sarah Preston died he would not have a problem with killing himself to be with her.

He shook his head. He was being stupid again because he was letting his imagination and his euphoria run away with his thoughts. Of course she wasn't here to die.

But she *was* crying.

She needed looking after. She needed holding the way his mother held him once when he was very young, when he was hurt and before she decided he was stupid. His mother stopped holding him a long time ago. That was all he ever wanted ... to be held because when he was held he was being loved. The memory was indelibly inscribed on his mind.

All he ever wanted was to love and be loved.

He loved Sarah Preston.

She was here, very close. Maybe she could love him. Maybe she would hold him. Maybe ...

He took the binoculars from around his neck and pushed them into his pocket. He would go and speak to her. He would not frighten her. He just wanted to speak to her.

Moving behind the bush from which he had watched her progress along the track, he crawled slowly through the long grass until the tree trunk hid her from view.

He didn't want to frighten her. He would get close before he said anything.

What should he say?

He wanted to impress her.

Crawling on his stomach, he approached the tree. She was wearing one of those green waterproof jackets he saw many people in the village wearing. He had also seen them hanging up in the houses he explored.

His hand touched the tree trunk. The bark was rough.

She was just on the other side.

What should he say?

He didn't want to frighten her and he didn't want to hurt her. If he hurt her she would not love him.

What should he say?

Slowly and silently he got to his feet.

Sarah froze.

She wasn't alone. Somebody or something was very close. She squeezed her eyes shut.

God, what should she do?

Maybe it was an animal. Maybe a fox, a badger, a rabbit or a deer was watching her. If she kept perfectly still and turned her head very slowly she would see it. It must be very close. She was sure she could hear it breathing.

Slowly she sat upright and turned her head in the direction she thought the animal would be.

Then she saw him.

She saw a man, a very dishevelled looking young man with a dirty face and hands.

He smiled and said hello.

Sarah screamed.

Chapter Twelve

Phillip opened his eyes with a start, immediately aware that Sarah was not by his side.

He stretched and yawned as he wondered where she was. He couldn't hear any movement in the bathroom so he assumed she was downstairs making the tea. She always brought him a mug of tea on a Sunday morning as he took her one during the week. If she were sticking to their routine then when she came up maybe she would be ready to talk, ready to tell him what was really troubling her. He wanted to know but on this occasion it was with a little foreboding.

Looking down at Sarah last night as he went to bed he could tell from her body posture and the odd whimper that although she was sleeping she was not really resting.

His own mind was also in turmoil.

He got into bed and wanted so much to take her in his arms but he didn't want to disturb her. He lay in the dark with his hands behind his head and worried until sleep eventually came to him. It was an unsettled night, but each time he woke she was there. As is often the case his deepest sleep pattern was during the two hours before he woke up properly.

Absentmindedly he let his hand drop onto her side of the bed. Something wasn't right but his brain didn't initially tell him what it was. He moved his hand around a little, and then it came to him.

Her side of the bed was cold. The duvet was thrown back and the sheet was cold. If she had only just got up it would still be warm. She didn't normally get up this early, not on a Sunday morning, not even to make a mug of tea.

Whatever had been troubling her the previous evening must still be on her mind and that would explain why she was out of bed so early.

Leaping out of bed, he checked the other bedrooms, but she wasn't in either the spare room or the guest room.

After flinging on his dressing gown, he padded down the stairs, frowning when he reached the bottom.

There wasn't a sound. The radio in the kitchen wasn't on, nor was the television. The light was on in the kitchen but that was all. He went from room to room. He called her name.

Nothing.

He felt the kettle. The water wasn't even warm. He shook his head and sat down at the kitchen table.

Where was she?

"Sarah?" he called again. "Sarah, love."

No response.

On impulse, he checked under the stairs. Her Barbour, scarf, woolly hat and walking boots were missing.

That was it. She was out for a walk. She'd needed some fresh air, maybe to think.

Walking on her own wasn't something she did very often, certainly not at this time of the morning, so he made himself a coffee and went back to bed, wondering if he should call her mobile.

No, she wouldn't want to be disturbed on her walk so he would give her an hour or so and if she wasn't back he would call her. He had no idea what time she went out but he was sure she would be back soon.

He reached for his book and settled down to read a chapter or two, but concentration was impossible.

Elspeth woke at just after six.

Her first thought after opening her eyes was the same as her last thought before succumbing to sleep – Sarah.

John was snoring next to her with one of his legs draped across her ankles. She moved her feet as slowly as she could so as not to disturb him.

As well as being surprised that John had been so understanding, she was also completely thrown when he seemed to know exactly what was going on.

So what *was* going on? Nothing and that was one of her problems.

She thought she was being so careful and yet he knew. He was right about the eye contact in the same way that he was right about walking as close to Sarah as possible. Two very simple and unobtrusive actions, but he quite rightly managed to put two and two together. Perhaps he did watch people closely, too closely as far as she was concerned.

But why was he so understanding? Would the accusations follow later?

So many questions but the only ones she knew the answers to were why they had gone to bed and made love, and why she had let him. He needed to cling onto a semblance of normality, she supposed. They always made love on a Saturday evening and just because she was giving him every reason to reject her, maybe he was fighting for what he really wanted – her. She had told him she loved him, and she did, and for him that was something to hang on to, something that gave him hope.

But was she right to let him cling onto that hope?

Last night John was more caring than normal. He spent a long time kissing, touching and stroking her. She responded to his touch, which for her was proof that under the circumstances, she did still have strong feelings for him. She would have let him make love to her anyway. She believed she owed it to him, but she didn't expect to feel the way she did.

The experience made her more confused.

She thought during their exchange the previous evening that he would probably choose to sleep in the spare room, but not John. Perhaps because he knew what was going on he had already decided long before confronting her how he was going to play things.

Now she was awake and Sarah was back on her mind.

Making love with John didn't change anything because she still felt the longing. She still wanted to be with Sarah, to talk to her, to walk with her, to eat and drink with her and to sleep with her. But Sarah's reaction at the party meant that it would never happen, not unless she could think of some other way to handle the situation rather than head on.

She was the one who felt rejected.

Having freed her feet from John's leg, she swung her legs out of bed and sat there for a while feeling the autumnal chill engulfing her naked body. With her eyes closed she ran her hands down her thighs, wondering what she should do next. Perhaps it was not her decision: perhaps there was no decision to make. John had said he would fight to keep her so maybe there was no reason for him to fight after all.

Perhaps the decision was already made.

She tiptoed out of the bedroom, avoiding the floorboards that squeaked. She filled the bath and for at least an hour she soaked herself in aromatic oils, topping up the hot water every now and again so that the heat made her perspire.

Whatever was in her, whatever made her feel the way she did, it needed to be expunged. She needed to sort out her body and her mind. Perhaps by talking about her feelings with John it would be a new beginning for them, a new understanding. Of course they talked, but rarely did they discuss their real feelings, seldom did they examine what was going on in their minds. Perhaps by sharing more of their intimate thoughts they would get through the shock her confession had caused them both.

Perhaps …

As Sarah screamed, he almost fell backwards, an expression of total shock on his face. She thought he was going to cry he looked so overcome.

The rooks in the trees behind him had also been disturbed: they were still circling and cawing their disapproval.

She was sure she knew him from somewhere.

Leaning against the tree with one hand, she closed her eyes momentarily as she tried to regain her composure. For some reason she felt as though it was all her fault.

All he had said was, hello.

Now she felt the need to apologise.

"I'm sorry," she said quietly, "but I didn't know you were there."

He was only a few feet from her, staring at her with unblinking eyes as though nobody had ever apologised to him before, embarrassed under her gaze.

"I'm sorry," she said again. "I thought I was alone." She tilted her head to one side, trying to work out not only who he was but also why she hadn't been aware that he was there before he spoke to her. She thought she ought to feel threatened but she didn't; for some reason she felt compassion instead.

She had no idea why.

He was a nice looking young man, in need of a shave and a wash but there was nothing menacing about him.

He was shy.

Unable to make eye contact, his eyes were looking at her hands.

No, she didn't feel threatened.

"I know you, don't I?" she asked.

He nodded slowly, his eyes still downcast.

"I've seen you in the village once or twice, haven't I?"

He nodded again.

Having left his camouflage clothes in the den, Michael was wearing his jeans, a T-shirt, a scruffy anorak and trainers. He was aware of the way he looked but how could he have known he was going to see her?

"What's your name?" Sarah Preston asked.

187

He wondered why she was asking his name as though she was speaking to a young boy and not a grown man.

Shuffling from one foot to the other, he hesitated. This was not how it was supposed to be. He knew the words he wanted to use because he had rehearsed them often enough, but now the time had arrived, the words would not come out.

"Michael," he whispered, lifting his head to look at her

"I'm sorry, I didn't hear you."

"Michael," he said again.

"Hello, Michael, I'm Sarah. We have met, haven't we?" She put her hands in her pockets.

He shook his head. They had not met before, so why was she saying they had?

She frowned. "Oh, I'm sorry I thought we had. I've seen you though, haven't I?"

This time he nodded. Yes, she had seen him once but he had seen her many times.

"Do you live in Upper Slaughter?"

He nodded again.

"You're not very talkative, are you?"

She was still speaking to him as though he was a child.

"Yes," he said looking at her lovely face. She was beautiful. Even in that old coat, she was beautiful. Her face was as he imagined an angel's would be. And she was being so nice to him. The woolly hat she was wearing looked like a little girl's.

She was talking to him.

He tried to smile, to say thank you.

Being so nervous didn't help.

"What do you mean, Michael? Do you mean you *are* talkative?"

He was confused. He didn't know why he had said yes. He thought he was telling her that he did live in Upper Slaughter, the same village she lived in. He shook his head slowly.

"No," he said and then he waited, but she just smiled.

188

He wanted to put his fingers on her lips and touch her smile. People didn't smile at him, they laughed at him but they never smiled. Her smile was so lovely.

It lit up her face.

Her beautiful face became even more beautiful.

He closed his eyes slowly and opened them again. She was still there and that beautiful face was still smiling at him.

"I ..." he started to say.

"Yes, go on Michael, you what?"

She moved a little closer to him, and he was startled when she took one hand out of her pocket and put it on his arm.

"What did you want to tell me, Michael?"

He wanted her to wrap her arms round him and tell him everything would be all right. It would take his sadness away.

"I think ... I think you're beautiful," he said in a rush.

She took a step back, biting her lip as a sudden feeling of wariness came over her.

"Well ... thank you, Michael. And I have to say that you're a very good looking young man."

She was on her guard but for some reason she actually found his praise quite endearing and not at all threatening.

She smiled. "So, Michael, what are you doing up on Copper's Ridge at this time on a Sunday morning?" She felt secure enough to touch his arm again. "Shall we sit down?"

He shook his head vigorously. "No ... no ... I ... I don't want to sit down, I want to ... I want to show you something," he said.

"Show me something? What do you want to show me, Michael?"

"My den."

"Where is your den?"

He pointed towards the woods. "In there," he said.

"In the woods?"

He nodded.

189

She checked her watch. It was nearly eight o'clock. She was obviously dealing with a grown man who had the mind of a child. She wondered why in such a small village as Upper Slaughter she wasn't aware of him already. Wherever she went either with or without Phillip she always finished up chatting with somebody and each time she did she heard a little more about something or someone in the village. But she had never been told about a young man called Michael who ... who what? How should she describe him? He had learning difficulties. Was that the politically correct description to use nowadays?

She checked her watch again. She really did need to be heading back to the village.

"I need to go home, Michael. Will it take long to show me your den?"

She still didn't feel threatened, and showing her his den was obviously very important to him. Another five minutes wouldn't make any difference.

"All right, show me your den and then ..." She thought for a second, "... and then shall we walk back to the village together?"

He looked up.

He did not want her to go back to the village.

If they went back to the village she would go back to her cottage. That man was in the cottage. She would tell that man about him, and ... and he wouldn't understand.

Nobody would understand.

His den had to be her secret.

He wanted her to go to his den with him and ... and stay in the den with him. He wanted to see her. Not just her beautiful face, he wanted to see her properly, the way he had seen her before ... at the window. She was so beautiful. He wanted to touch her the way Sharon and Wendy had allowed him to touch them. He wanted Sarah Preston to touch him. She was more beautiful than Sharon and Wendy, they were just pretty: Sarah Preston was beautiful.

190

Michael half turned towards the woods.

"Shall I follow you, Michael?"

He nodded.

What should he do? Should he take her there on one of his secret paths, or should he take her directly to the den. If he took her by the secret route it would not be a secret anymore. But if he took her straight there she could find it again.

Did it matter?

If he told her it was a secret would she keep it to herself? He wanted to share his secrets with her. He wanted to share everything with her.

He started to walk towards the woods.

"I'm right behind you, Michael," Sarah said, feeling confident that by humouring him for a few more minutes it would mean he would be happy and then she could head for home.

Michael led the way through the first line of trees.

The undergrowth was thick up to that point, but once inside the tree line the going became easier. He was moving slowly, looking round every few seconds to make sure she was still there. At one point she was so intent on looking around her she didn't see a prominent root sticking out of the ground. Her toe struck the root and she stumbled and fell. The next thing she felt was a pair of strong hands under her arms lifting her to her feet. He almost lifted her off the ground before she was able to regain her balance.

"Thank you, Michael, that was very kind of you."

She was surprised by his strength. Although he was slim he was well built, but she certainly didn't expect to feel as though she was no heavier than a feather. He was gentle, but there was no doubting just how strong he was.

His look of concern was so genuine she was tempted to reach up and kiss him on the cheek, but before she could he lifted his hand and with a grubby finger he moved a few strands of hair that had fallen over her face. He looked at her as though they had known each other for ages and it was uncanny how secure she felt in the company of this young man who she only vaguely remembered but knew nothing about.

Was she being utterly stupid?

Why was she walking into the woods with a complete stranger? Why wasn't she running in the opposite direction?

She followed him as they snaked through the woods, sometimes following paths made by animals, sometimes on what appeared to be fresh ground. She was sure they doubled back on themselves a few times but after about five minutes, he stopped.

"Wait here," he said.

Doing as she was asked, she hunched down by a tree to rest and watched Michael as he disappeared from view behind a large bush.

She had come to Copper's Ridge to be alone and by sheer chance Michael – whatever-his-name was – just happened to be here at the same time. He was young and good-looking but appeared to have the mind of a ten-year old.

Did that make him dangerous? He was too innocent to be dangerous. Anyway, meeting him had for a while taken her mind off the real reason why she was here.

After all, her mind was already made up, wasn't it? All she needed to do now was work out whether she could maintain that decision by staying in Upper Slaughter or whether she would have to find a plausible reason to move back to Evesham or Gloucester or wherever. She doubted whether she could stay knowing Elspeth was only a few minutes' walk away. That would not be fair on either of them.

By coming to see Michael's den she felt she was doing him a favour. He was obviously a very lonely young man and, from what she had seen and heard, understandably so. She could not see him having many friends in the village. She wondered where he lived.

192

She had a feeling she had seen him walking round the village. He was a harmless kid in an adult's body and if showing her his den made him happy then that was the least she could do. He sounded so innocent when he told her she was beautiful.

She was musing over her assumption when he returned, but this time from the other side of the bush. He moved like a wild animal, slowly, silently and ever watchful but completely at home in the countryside. As he reached her he knelt down in front of her and his frowning blue eyes seemed to be asking so many questions.

"Follow ... follow me," he said.

Reaching for her hand, he helped her up. As she stood up his eyes stayed on her face, her hand was still in his. The skin at the base of his fingers was hard. His hands were large, full of strength and hers felt small and weak by comparison.

Turning slowly he led her by the hand round the bush. They were close to the edge of the woods, but wherever they were going was screened from view by more bushes.

Without warning he let go of her hand and stooped down. He plucked a large firm circle of compressed moss, grass, twigs and leaves from in front of him. Sarah looked over his crouched body: she saw a mound but nothing else.

Surely this wasn't his den?

She could have been only feet away and she would have walked straight past it. He jumped down into the uncovered hole the edge of which came half way up his chest. He was Phillip's height, maybe a little shorter. She would disappear completely if she had to climb down into the hole.

He ducked down and then turned round, holding up his hands to help her do the same. She felt strange and for the first time was uncertain about what to do. She didn't know whether it was apprehension or fear, or maybe a combination of the two. His grip on her hands tightened as he pulled her towards him. She had little choice but to move. She put one foot over the edge and then sat down, curling her leg round to one side as she jumped, joining Michael in the hole. The edge was almost at the top of her head.

She felt a twinge of apprehension. She had made a commitment the moment she agreed to follow him into the woods. It wasn't fear of what might happen if she didn't do as he asked, but more a belief that if she complied he would do her no harm. It was too late now.

He let go of her hands and ducked down again as he stepped into the mound. She slowly followed him.

It was dark, very dark. This was utter madness. Slits of light came from parts of the den but not enough to see where she was going. She felt him brush past her, the column of light disappearing as he replaced the circular cover to the entrance.

"You ... you can sit down," he said from behind her.

"Where? I can't see anything."

Once again his strong hands guided her a few feet away from where she was standing. He turned her round and gently lowered her onto what she thought was a stool. The den was damp and smelt of mildew and wet earth. She heard the rustling of matches, saw the sudden flash and the glare as the wick flared into a bright light. He lit two more lamps, and his den came alive.

She looked around, her mouth open, not really believing what she was seeing.

It was amazing. It wasn't a den: it was a home.

The underground room – the only word she could think of to describe it – was more like an oval with rounded corners than a rectangle. There was a table with one of the lamps standing on it, and two small chairs. Shelves were cut into the earthen walls, and on them were tins of beans, spaghetti, soup, curry, stew and fruit.

The shelves on the other side held plastic storage jars. On the earthen floor below the shelves were three large containers of what she assumed was water. On the other wall there was a shelf with two plates, bowls, mugs, a couple of small saucepans and a camping stove.

A small table stood by the entrance, and stretching almost from wall to wall was a wooden framed single bed, with a sleeping bag and a pillow.

Next to where she sat there was a metal bucket and she screwed up her nose as she guessed what that was for. She looked down at the earthen floor and noted it was level and hard. A small rush mat lay almost in its centre. The roof was made of finely interwoven sticks and small branches, and there seemed to be a black covering above the sticks. In the middle was a hole about a foot across. A chimney she thought. He had even built a chimney.

She was mesmerised. How could anyone build something like this under the noses of whoever owned the woods? She didn't know much about construction work but it appeared to her to be an amazing feat.

He was watching her, the glow of the lamp making him look older than he was. The shadows on his face, under his eyes and nose gave him a ghoulish look and the apprehension she felt minutes earlier turned suddenly to fear.

This was not a den, not a room, not a home. This was a cell, a prison.

She was trapped.

Chapter Thirteen

Phillip put the book back on the bedside table then picked up his watch. He couldn't concentrate and frowned when he saw it was nearly half past eight. He must have dozed off again. If Sarah had only gone for a walk she should have been back by now. He had been awake well over an hour and she must have left the cottage long before that.

His earlier concern, as well as feeling annoyed because she had gone out without him, turned to worry. Her behaviour was strange the previous evening but disappearing for as long as this without even leaving a note was too much out of the ordinary.

He sat up in bed, trying to decide what to do. She could have gone anywhere. He reached for his mobile. He called her number but was told her phone was switched off.

They often walked together in the surrounding countryside and around the village and he could not remember them taking the same route more than once. There were so many footpaths and tracks to follow. He recalled Sarah saying that if they lived in the village for ten years there would always be somewhere new to explore.

Phillip leapt off the bed, grabbed his jeans and sweatshirt from the back of the chair, threw them on and scrambled round looking for his socks and slip-on shoes. He almost tripped down the step just outside the door and he flew down the stairs.

Before leaving the cottage, he checked every room again and the only significant item he found in the living room was the T-shirt Sarah had worn to bed the previous night. He went to the back door, reached up for the key that was hanging on a hook on the wall and stopped. If the key was there, which door had she used?

He ran back down the hall to the front door. The security chain was in place. She must have left by the back door. In the kitchen, he checked the cutlery drawer. The spare key was missing.

Well that answered one question but generated a good deal more. He opened the back door, locking it again as soon as he was outside. It was a cool morning and he shivered as he headed for the side of the cottage. He hoped his shaking was because of the temperature and not some omen of impending bad news.

As he stepped into Church Lane he started up the hill towards the village green and John and Elspeth's cottage. He prayed that he would meet Sarah on her way back, running down the lane towards him and saying how sorry she was.

Old Greg was standing at his gate.

He gave the usual nod in answer to Phillip's "good morning."

Phillip thought about asking him whether he had seen Sarah but he didn't want to suggest that his wife was missing.

Knocking on John and Elspeth's door he realised how early it was on a Sunday morning to be calling even on close friends, but he was sure they wouldn't mind as this could be an emergency.

"Phillip!" Elspeth said, smiling as she opened the door. "What can we do for you at this ... er ... time of the morning?"

She was still in her dressing gown having not gone back upstairs because she didn't want to disturb John. Regardless of having made love before going to sleep, she was not looking forward to dealing with either his silence or further questioning. There was no way they could act as though nothing was happening.

"Sorry," Phillip said as he pushed past her into the hallway, "but this is important." He headed straight for the kitchen and spun round as Elspeth followed him into the room.

"What is it, Phillip?"

"Is John up?" he asked, pulling out a chair from the table and slumping down onto it.

"No, not yet. The last time I looked he was still in the land of nod. Would you like a coffee?" she asked.

"Yes, yes I would and a strong one please."

She flicked the kettle on and turned to face Phillip.

Something was very wrong and it was obvious who it involved.

What could have happened? Sarah might have said something. Perhaps Phillip was now more aware of what was going on than she had thought.

"Are you going to tell me what it is?"

He lifted his head. She was amazed to see that his eyes were brimming with tears. "It's ... it's Sarah," he said, his voice a tremor. "She's disappeared."

Elspeth's hands fell to her sides. "Disappeared? What do you mean disappeared?" She knew she sounded accusatory, but that was exactly how she felt.

"I mean I don't know where she is."

Elspeth moved to the table and sat down next to Phillip.

"I'm sorry if I'm being a little slow but can you tell me exactly what you mean by disappeared." Her heart was pounding and the hairs on the back of her neck were prickling.

"I mean," Phillip said, his voice still catching with emotion, "that ... that she isn't at home and I don't know where she is. When I woke up this morning she wasn't there. I thought she'd gone out for an early morning walk. Her boots and jacket are missing, but that was well over an hour ago."

198

"An hour?" she said, feeling the relief spread through her. "You and Sarah normally go walking for a lot longer than that. An hour is nothing."

"It's much more than an hour. When I woke up her side of the bed was cold. She'd already been gone for quite a while. I've no idea how long but it must be more like a couple of hours, if not longer."

He drummed his fingers on the table.

"Well, maybe not an hour then," Elspeth said. "Maybe an hour and a half, two hours. That's still not very long for you two."

The kettle clicked off. She ignored it.

"That's my point, Elspeth. Two hours isn't very long when we go walking together but Sarah has never gone on her own before, not for this long. There isn't a note, there's nothing to tell me where she's gone and for how long."

"I see," Elspeth said as calmly as she could, the earlier relief being replaced once again by anxiety. She thought for a few seconds but she needed to ask him something. "Did you have a row last night?"

Phillip frowned. "No. She was acting a little strangely. In fact when we got home she went straight to bed. She didn't even have a meal."

Thank God, Elspeth thought. He doesn't know.

"There was nothing said or not said that might have put her in a mood?"

"She was already in a mood and a half: I've learned over the years that when she's like that it's best if I say nothing. You were with her most of the time at the party, so didn't you see what might have caused the change in her?"

"No," she said quickly. "There were some pretty pretentious people there, but no, there was nothing."

"She gave no hint to you what it might have been?"

"None at all." Elspeth forced a smile though it felt as though her face would crack. Oh God, it was her fault. It was *all* her fault. She shouldn't have acted so quickly, she should not have been so damned impulsive.

"Are you sure?"

"Of course I'm sure. Have you any idea which way she might have gone?"

Phillip spread his hands. "Pick any direction from north through south and back to north again. There are so many possibilities. I wouldn't know where to start."

Elspeth couldn't bear the tension any longer. "All right," she said, standing up and walking to the door. "You make the coffee and I'll go and wake John."

"Thanks," Phillip said, slumping even further into the chair.

Elspeth walked into the bedroom and this time she deliberately stepped on the floorboard that squeaked. John stirred and lifted his head off the pillow although his eyes were still closed.

"Please get up, John. We've got a bit of an emergency," she said, taking off her dressing gown before opening her underwear drawer.

"Emergency," he said. "It's not even nine o'clock and it is Sunday morning, you know."

"It might be," she said as she fastened her bra and reached for her pants. "But Phillip's downstairs. Sarah's missing."

He was instantly wide-awake. "Missing? What do you mean missing?"

"Phillip hasn't the faintest idea where she is and he hasn't seen her for a couple of hours."

"But it's Sunday morning."

"So bloody what, and will you stop saying it's Sunday morning. Sarah's missing and we're going to help Phillip find her." She pulled a polo-neck jumper over her head and shook her hair loose.

John was half out of bed. "I think I'll remember this weekend for –"

"Don't start, John, please," Elspeth said, wriggling into a pair of brown cords.

200

"What was said last night is insignificant compared with how Phillip is feeling at the right now."

"Does he know what –?"

"No, he bloody doesn't and he's not going to know, not from us anyway. Now will you get dressed please, and hurry."

Zipping up her cords she went to the bedroom door.

"Oh, and John, thank you for last night. If that's the way you do your fighting then I can't wait for the war."

She left the room.

Although the three burning lamps generated some heat, Sarah shivered. Michael had stared at her for almost a minute before gesturing that she should stand up. He gripped her arm but not as gently as before, and took her over to one of the slits that acted as a limited source of natural light.

Sarah looked through the slit, the brighter light on the outside temporarily blinding her.

"That ... that tree, over there ... there, between those bushes," Michael said pointing with his other hand, "that's where you were sitting."

She heard his words but it took a few seconds for their significance to sink in. He had taken her in a complete circle. They had walked for over five minutes and gone nowhere. Seeing the tree made her feel a little happier. Perhaps she was safe after all. She knew his name and by now, she knew every inch of his face. If he meant her any harm then surely he would have disguised himself by wearing some sort of mask, a balaclava or something. He would not have told her his name and he would not be showing her where his den was in relation to a tree that she could easily find again. But nobody knew where she was, and from what Michael had told her she was being introduced to his secret life. Being a good judge of character she had come to the conclusion that he was nothing more than a simple young man who was proud of something he had achieved on his own ... and wanted to share it with someone.

She relaxed a little and as she did she felt the grip on her arm slacken.

"It's a beautiful tree," she said, deciding that humouring him was now probably her best ploy.

Why did she need a ploy?

"It's ... it's seen the deaths ... the deaths of two people," he explained, his voice sounding more mature.

Shocked by what he said she suddenly remembered – Abigail Tucker and her mother. That must be the tree where Mrs Tucker committed suicide. She had never wanted to go anywhere near it when out walking but from the description she'd been given she had believed it was another half mile or so along the track.

"Yes, I know," she said.

Michael turned his head back and looked at her. "She ... she hung herself from that ... that branch on the right. I ... I saw it happen."

The fear returned. "What? You saw Mrs Tucker commit suicide?"

He nodded. "She ... she didn't want to do it. She ... she changed her mind but she ... she fell."

"Where were you? In here?"

"No, out ... out there," he said. "I ... I was a few yards ... a few yards from the tree."

"You mean ..." She stopped herself from asking the obvious question. God, the emotional twists and turns he was putting her through were like the route he had taken to his den. She must be careful not to antagonise him or add to her own fears.

"Sit ... sit down." It sounded like an order. "I'll make ... I'll make you a drink."

Michael felt the impatience building up inside him.

Yet his confidence had grown the moment they had set foot in his world. He was pleased he was able speak those words because he had often rehearsed what he would say. Never having spoken to anyone in his den before, he surprised himself when he was able to say so much. He was aware he was stuttering but she understood what he had said. He had said more in the last five minutes than in the last few weeks.

She was so close he wanted to touch her.

But he sensed that she was scared and she mustn't be. She was here because she wanted to see his den. She could have said she didn't want to. He would have been disappointed but he would not have made her do anything against her will. It was really her fault she was scared. He had done nothing to make her feel scared. The rabbits were scared of him when he first came to the wood but now the ones that lived nearby trusted him. They didn't scurry away the moment they saw him. They didn't trust him enough to come and visit him but they were happy to be his neighbours.

He moved the camping stove onto the table and lit it, poured water into one of the saucepans and put it carefully on the stove. He took the mugs and one of the plastic storage jars from the earthen shelf. When he had decided that one day Mrs Preston would be with him in his den, he bought one extra of everything, so he now had two plates, two mugs, two bowls and extra cutlery.

His planning had not been in vain.

He understood why she needed to go home but not yet, not for a little while. There was only one way he could be sure of that.

He turned to face Sarah. "Take your boots off."

"I'm sorry?"

Another twist.

It was as though a switch had been thrown. He had gone from being a timid young boy to a man who was scaring the hell out of her. She was now ensnared but she reminded herself she did walk into the trap of her own free will.

"Take your boots off," he said again. His voice was a monotone like one of those recorded messages on the phone.

The fear grew.

203

Was she misjudging him yet again? With trembling fingers she began unlacing her boots. When they were unlaced she sat back.

"Take ... take them off."

Keeping her eyes on him she did as she was told. They were only her boots. Or was she being terribly naive?

He bent down in front of her to pick up the boots. He did it slowly, almost as though he was caressing them as he touched the leather. He took the boots and placed them at the entrance of the den.

Stepping back towards her he looked down at her feet.

"Now ... now your socks," he said.

"Michael, why –?"

"Your socks," he said, his voice becoming louder and firmer. "Take ... take them off."

Never once looking away from him, she hooked her thumbs into the backs of her socks and pulled them over her heels. She felt the fear building up in her. He picked up the socks, held them against his cheek before taking them to where he had put her boots.

"The toilet is ... is there," he told her, pointing to the bucket she had already seen.

"I'm all right, thank you," she said, trying not to let her voice shake too much.

"You've ... you've got very ... very pretty feet," he said before turning back to the table and making what smelt like her favourite instant coffee. He handed her a steaming mug.

"No ... no milk," he said.

"Thank you." Sarah clutched the mug, getting a little comfort from its warmth. Her feet were cold against the earthen floor.

"So Sarah's walked out on you, has she?" John enquired as he walked into the kitchen. He was attempting to make light of what could be a very serious situation but realised how flippant his question was under the circumstances.

"Sorry," he added quickly, averting his eyes from Elspeth's accusing glare. "Tell me what's happened."

Phillip related what Elspeth already knew. "I haven't the faintest idea where to look," he added. "She could be anywhere. Maybe she's fallen and hurt herself, unable to walk. I don't know."

"Have you tried her mobile?"

"It's switched off."

"Don't worry, we'll find her. Let me get some caffeine inside me then we'll start looking."

Elspeth sipped her coffee. "Is there really nothing to go on?" she asked. "No clue at all?"

Phillip shook his head. "Saying she's gone for a walk is no more than an assumption."

"Did you check her car? Was it in the garage?"

John joined them at the table. "Did she take anything else, you know, a flask or something?"

"I didn't check her car but I'd have heard the garage door and no, I didn't check whether the flask had gone. I wasn't thinking."

Elspeth lit a cigarette. "I'd have been the same," she said, putting a hand on his arm. "But perhaps we ought to check a few things before we start clutching at straws or going on wild goose chases. She could have gone in any one of hundreds of directions."

Phillip nodded. "Of course."

"Is there nothing she said last night that could be of help?" John asked.

Elspeth frowned at him.

"No, she became very quiet. Well, you saw it while we were at the party. And Elspeth said she saw nothing that would have put Sarah into that sort of mood ..."

John stole another look at Elspeth.

"Once we'd left Clifton House she hardly said a word before she went upstairs to bed. I told her I'd cook a meal when she was ready but when she hadn't come down after a couple of hours I went and checked on her and she was out for the count."

"Have you no idea at all what caused the change in her last night?" Elspeth asked, knowing the question was on John's lips. She felt guilty enough already but she was sure that Phillip, even if he'd been lying earlier, would not be able to hide for a second time the fact that Sarah had told him what happened at the party.

Phillip looked at Elspeth and shook his head. "No," he said as he picked up his mug and drained the coffee. "You'd probably know better than me." He glanced at John.

"Elspeth and I have been through this. Sarah spent most of the time we were at the party with her but she didn't detect anything. Did you?" John said, looking at Elspeth for confirmation.

"Other than making a few disparaging remarks about the people who were there, I can't think of anything." Elspeth narrowed her eyes, daring John to take what she said any further. "She went with me when I escaped for a few minutes to have a cigarette but ..."

"Was there anything other than bottom patting?" John asked her.

"There wasn't really any of that. The usual reprobates were well behaved for a change. We both received the usual *I'm imagining you without any clothes on* looks, but other than that, no. There was nothing I could pinpoint that might have upset Sarah."

You dare, she thought as she looked at John.

"And none of that would have put her into a mood," Phillip said. "We all know she's used to being looked at by both men and women."

John stood up. "All right. Shall we start with her car? I suggest you let us look in the cottage as well. There may be something you missed."

"Good idea."

Phillip sounded completely wretched, almost as though he already feared the worst.

206

Old Greg stood by his gate.

He nodded, and Elspeth, John and Phillip nodded back.

As they walked past him he watched Elspeth's bottom.

He smiled. Elspeth was a bit of all right. One of the reasons he stood at his gate for so long was so that he could look at the women as they walked through his village. He liked Elspeth because she had an old-fashioned figure, complete with child-bearing hips, not straight up and down like some of them.

Lifting his gaze from Elspeth's rear he watched as the trio walked down Church Lane.

Something's up, he thought.

Just the three of them, where's the little one? Her husband was on his own earlier. Maybe there's a connection.

Sarah Preston's all right as well but maybe a bit thin. Pretty though.

He chuckled.

Both cars were still in the garage and the bonnet of Sarah's car was cold.

In the cottage they went from room to room. Elspeth picked up the T-shirt Phillip saw in the living room. When the men's backs were turned she lifted the garment to her nose, smelling Sarah and almost bursting into tears. When Phillip turned round she snatched the T-shirt away from her face.

"What's this doing in here?" she asked to cover her embarrassment at almost being caught.

"She wore that in bed last night," Phillip said.

"She always wears a T-shirt?"

"That and others like it."

"Why would it be in here?"

Phillip and John looked at her. "Why wouldn't it?" John said. "I can't see what Sarah wears in bed as being relevant. She may have come in here to get something and just threw it on the chair."

"Exactly," Elspeth said enthusiastically. "If she did, what did she come in here to get?"

"Hang on a minute."

Phillip went over to the writing desk in the corner and opened the drawer in which they kept the Ordnance survey maps of the area. He took them out and sorted through them.

"No," he then said despondently, "they're all here."

Elspeth sat down on the arm of the chair nearest to her.

"But surely even that tells us something. Do you normally take a map with you when you go walking?"

"Yes," Phillip said a little more enthusiastically. "Sarah likes to be sure she makes full use of walkers' rights. If a map says there's a footpath she will take it regardless of what sort of field it crosses."

"Okay," Elspeth added, glancing across at John who was leaning against the door jamb with a slight smile on his face. "By not taking a map, she either didn't intend going very far or she took a route she knew well."

"We've been on so many."

"Yes, but is there one special walk she was particularly keen on?"

Phillip thought for a moment. He shook his head. "She just loves walking. She always enthuses about everything she sees."

"But think ... no wait, where have you been most recently?"

"The last one was ten days or so ago. We followed the Warden's Way down to Lower Slaughter. We hadn't walked it before. It's only a couple of miles there and back. We went to get some fresh air before we ate."

"Then that's where I think we should start," Elspeth said, getting to her feet.

"Good thinking," Phillip said. "We both enjoyed it and Sarah said we should do it again."

"That settles it," Elspeth said. "Let's go."

After checking that the flask Phillip and Sarah normally took with them when out walking was still in the kitchen cupboard – and it was – Phillip, John and Elspeth set off for Warden's Way.

Michael said nothing for at least five minutes.

Sitting at the small table drinking his coffee, he could not take his eyes from Sarah's feet. He had never seen such delicate feet or such tiny toes.

They were like a small child's.

He wanted to pick them up one by one and kiss them and hold them against his face, gently of course because he didn't want to hurt her. He wanted to put her toes in his mouth. He saw a man doing that on a film he hired from the shop in Evesham and watched secretly in his bedroom. The woman appeared to enjoy it because she was smiling, although she made funny noises.

At the time he thought it was a strange thing to do.

But now he wanted to do the same to Sarah Preston.

Sarah was a beautiful name for a beautiful woman, and she had agreed to come to his den with him. He had not put her under any pressure. She had readily agreed. But he wouldn't do anything else to her unless she asked him to.

In his mind that was the way things were done.

That day in the churchyard Wendy and Sharon asked him to touch them because they took his hands and put them on their bodies. He would not have touched them without them asking him to.

Men should never do anything to a woman unless that was what she wanted them to.

He hated parts of another film he tried to watch. He fast-forwarded it when he got to those scenes.

They were so violent.

The woman did not ask the man to touch her, but he more than touched her. He did awful things to her, making her scream. When he first watched the film, Michael screamed with her wishing he could get into the film and hurt the man.

Women and girls were too fragile to handle the way that man in the film violated the woman.

That man?

Sarah Preston was married to *that man*.

Did he touch her when she didn't want him to?

Michael was sure he did.

If he did he was as bad as the man in the film.

He did not need proof because he knew.

He may not have been able to hurt Hector but that man was different.

Sarah Preston was so close to him. She was even more beautiful than he ever imagined. Having touched her hands and touched her boots and socks, he knew that if he lived with her, if he were married to her, he would always be touching her but only if she wanted him to. He would be as proud of her as he had once been proud of the model he built of the church.

He hated to think of any man touching her. He didn't want her to let any man do anything to her. She was so beautiful and beautiful things were there to be admired and cared for, not to be violated and forced to do things they didn't want to do.

"I think it's time I was going," Sarah said.

Watching him sitting at the table staring at her was very unnerving.

"Your den is magnificent," she said. "You're a clever man to have built it. Thank you for letting me see it but I really think it's time I was going."

Sarah was trying hard to stop herself shaking, or allowing him to see that her fear had turned to panic at the thought of having to spend another five minutes with him in his underground den.

The way he was looking at her was telling her only one thing.

He wanted her. He was planning. She had often seen that look in other men's eyes. They made it so obvious.

But on every other occasion she had been free to ignore their leering looks. This time she was trapped.

No!

The word screamed out in Michael's head.

No.

She can't leave.

If she leaves she will never come back. She was here because she wanted to be here. Hadn't she followed him to his den? She sat down and drank his coffee then took her boots and socks off when he asked her. That's when she showed him her beautiful feet.

No!

Sarah saw the expression on Michael's face change.

She could get up and run, but she wouldn't get as far as the entrance to the den before he caught her and even if she did she wouldn't be able to get through the entrance hole on her own.

Tears welled in her eyes. She began to shake. She must not speak again. If she spoke he would sense how frightened she was and that might be what he wanted. Power was what men wanted ...

What an absolute fool. What the hell was she doing here? She never wanted to come this far along Copper's Ridge because of what happened to Abigail Tucker and her mother. What made her come here this morning?

She only had herself to blame.

At just after ten o'clock Phillip, John and Elspeth reached the outskirts of Lower Slaughter. Phillip led them quickly along Warden's Way, hoping they would meet somebody who may have seen Sarah. More importantly he hoped they would meet Sarah herself.

He looked closely at the river, praying he wouldn't see anything that even hinted that further investigation might be necessary.

In silence they passed the old mill with its small gift shop. They walked along the narrow footpath that bordered the River Eye, in silence. They passed the terraced stone houses and the two footbridges, crossed the Upper Slaughter road, rejoined the footpath under a huge weeping willow and found a bench that looked over the river towards the gardens at the back of the Washbourne Court Hotel – in silence.

Phillip glanced at the other two. Like him their shoulders were slumped and they were also dragging their feet. He felt as though they had walked a hundred miles, not just one. Little was said until he led them to the bench.

"Well," he said, stretching his legs out in front of him, "that was a waste of time."

Elspeth lit a cigarette. "That was my fault because I was the one who suggested we come this way."

"It was a gamble," Phillip said. "Somebody had to make a decision. It could have happened whichever way we'd chosen to go."

He noted that John had said little during the short walk. He seemed content to peer behind bushes, in gullies, over gateways, in the river; everywhere that could have hidden somebody who might be injured or ... or dead. He and Elspeth did at least exchange a few words of reassurance.

"We didn't leave a note, did we?" John said, breaking into his thoughts.

"What?" Phillip and Elspeth asked in unison.

"A note," John said, leaning forward with his chin in his hands. "We didn't leave a note for Sarah in case she turned up while we were away."

Phillip took his mobile from his pocket. "I'll ring the house," he said. "I'm so bloody wound up that any common sense I had has left me." He selected the number and waited. "Damn. The answer phone cut in so she's not there."

"You did say you'd tried Sarah's mobile, didn't you, Phillip?" Elspeth said.

"Yes, of course I did, before we left to look for her and a couple of times on the way down here. I'll try it again. She reluctantly agreed to carry one in her bag but she never turns it on."

Phillip pressed a key then listened, holding the phone away from his ear so the others could hear. *"The number you have dialled is currently unobtainable, please try later."* He pressed the cancel button. "Shit. As usual the damn thing's not turned on."

John held his head in his hands. "If she does have her phone with her and she's lying somewhere injured or lost, why hasn't she turned it on and rung you?"

Phillip said nothing. Elspeth lit another cigarette.

"John, how long does somebody have to be missing before we can go to the police?" Phillip said.

"I don't think there's a time frame. I'd hazard a guess that it's a question of circumstances."

He stood up and marched away from the bench. "I think we ought to go home and then I'll drive into Stow. That's the nearest police station. Will you two come with me?"

"Of course we will," Elspeth said. "But don't let's give up hope. Sarah might be walking up Church Lane at this very moment."

Phillip turned and looked at her. She smiled – a weak smile that told him she didn't believe what she had just said.

Chapter Fourteen

"Can I have my socks and boots please, Michael?"

He was puzzled. She had stopped shaking but her eyes were still full of tears. She looked so sad but he didn't understand why. He wasn't going to harm her.

"I ... I want you to stay ... a little longer," he said, with as much understanding in his voice as he could manage because he wanted her to be as happy as he was. "It ... it's Sunday, so can't you stay for another ... another hour or so?"

If he became cross she would go.

He didn't want her to go.

If she went for her boots and socks there was nothing he could do about it. He would have to let her go. The tears and the shaking both meant that she was frightened of him.

Why was she frightened?

Was she frightened because he asked her to take off her boots and socks? There was nothing wrong with that. Would it help if he took his trainers and socks off as well? But he couldn't. His socks had holes in them and his feet were dirty. Hers were clean. Her nails were painted a beautiful red colour.

"Thank you for asking so nicely, Michael, but Phillip will be wondering where I am, and ..."

He heard the name but it took a few seconds for it to register. He didn't want a name. A name would make that man more personal. Hearing her talking about that man wasn't what he wanted

"Phillip," he repeated under his breath.

"Sorry, Michael, what did you say?"

He looked at her. "I ... I don't want you to go, not yet."

Humour him, Sarah thought. Keep him happy then he won't get aggressive. Try to say what he wants to hear.

"And I don't want to go, Michael. I've really enjoyed meeting you and seeing your beautiful den, but –"

"If you have enjoyed meeting ... meeting me and seeing my den, why are you crying?"

Her mind went into over-drive as she tried to think of a plausible reason.

There wasn't one. What the hell could she say?

"Because I'm sad, Michael," she said, thinking it would buy her a little time.

"Why are you sad?"

"I'm sad for you."

That stopped him. She saw it in his eyes – he didn't understand.

Why?

What had he done to make her feel sad for him?

Was it because he was dirty and because his clothes were dirty? That wouldn't make her sad, not so sad that she needed to cry. He knew how sad you needed to be before you cried because he cried a lot when he was young after being told he was different. He cried a lot more when he informed he was not like other boys of his age. It hurt most of all when his mother told him she didn't want him and he was stupid. She told him she was *ashamed* of him. He knew what ashamed meant ... she would be happier if he didn't exist. But as he got older he learnt not to cry so much. What his mother said didn't matter anymore. What other people said didn't matter anymore.

No, that wasn't true.

What Sarah Preston said mattered, and she had just said she was sad for him.

Why?

When his father smashed the model of the church he cried, and when Mr Proctor died he cried. He was very sad then.

"Why ... why?" Michael said. "Why are you sad ... sad for me?"

Sarah's nails bit into the palms of her hands. She needed to stay calm. She needed to talk her way out of this nightmare.

"Because," she said as quietly as she could, "you're a lovely man, a very handsome man, Michael, but I think you're very lonely."

"And ... and because you think I'm lonely, you are sad?" He shook his head.

"Yes."

"Sad enough for me to make you cry?"

"Yes."

"Do ... do you love me, Sarah Preston?"

Oh, shit! Why did he suddenly come out with that? Shit! Shit! Shit!

"I've only known you for an hour or so, Michael. That isn't long enough to get to know you even a little bit."

"I love ... I love you, Sarah Preston."

She breathed in fast and so deeply that she felt dizzy. Her efforts were making matters worse not better. "I'm flattered that you feel that way, Michael."

"I've seen ... seen you."

"I've seen you too, Michael, in the village. I would also be flattered if you would walk with me now – back to the village."

She prayed that she had said the right thing but he ignored her, looking angry as though she had interrupted his train of thought.

"I've ... I've seen you at your window," he said.

"My window?"

He nodded. He was smiling.

"I've seen you at your ... your bedroom window."

"What do you mean?"

216

"In the morning, at your window. I've seen you."

"Where were you?"

"In ... in the woods."

"Behind my cottage?"

"Yes, in the woods. By the church."

"Have you been there often?"

"Yes."

Dear God! What the hell was she dealing with? She shuddered. How often and when was he there? That morning she went shopping with Elspeth. Elspeth thought they were being watched.

"Does that man ... touch you?" Michael said.

"I'm sorry, what did you say?"

"That man ... does he touch you?"

"Who do you mean? Who is *that man*?"

This was getting completely out of hand. She was not handling the situation at all well. Trapped underground in an amazing but perilous tomb and she had to get out.

"The man ... the man you live with."

"Phillip?"

He nodded.

"He's my husband."

"Does ... does he touch you?"

"Of course he touches me and I touch him."

This was getting totally ridiculous, and judging by the sudden change in his expression she had once again said the wrong thing. How long was this going to go on for?

"Michael, you have to understand that I'm married to Phillip. He's my husband. He loves me and I love him. He will be worried now, wondering where I am."

"Where ... where does he touch you?"

"Michael, I really think –"

"Where does he touch you?"

"Michael –"

"Where?"

He stood up and glared at her. The sudden movement almost made her fall off the stool.

217

"Where does he touch you?" he shouted.

The tears were back, and the shaking. She clasped her arms round her knees, tried to curl up into a small ball, her mind screaming for somebody to find her, somebody to take her out of this nightmare. But she could scream as loud as she could and nobody would hear her.

And she had a feeling the real nightmare was about to start.

Phillip waved wildly at the empty taxi leaving the Lower Slaughter Manor hotel. There was little to gain from backtracking along Warden's Way. If Sarah was between the two villages they would have found her during the walk down.

Back in Primrose Cottage he checked his watch and grabbed his car keys. "Five hours. That's damn well long enough. Let's go."

"Why go to Stow?" Elspeth said. "Why not phone?"

He nodded and reached for the phone.

"Michael, I think we must stop this before it –"

She grabbed her throat. The feeling had been in the pit of her stomach for some time but now the control disappeared. Her mouth opened and her head shot forward. Again and again she wretched. Her throat hurt with the effort, yet nothing but stinging bile came out.

Michael sat and watched her.

What was the matter?

Why was she being ill?

He hadn't touched her. He only asked her a question.

What could he do?

What would his mother do for him if he was being sick?

Water.

She would give him some water.

He looked at the mug he had used for his coffee: there was nothing else he could use. Her mug was at her feet,

218

much too close. He got up and tipped the water container up to fill his mug.

"Drink this," he said.

He went as close as he dared. Her head was between her legs but she seemed to have stopped being sick.

"Here, some water," he said.

Sarah gulped the liquid down her burning throat. Slowly the nausea passed and she sat up.

"Michael," she said huskily, "you've done nothing wrong … there's nothing to be scared of." She closed her eyes and took a deep breath. "If we go back to the village now –"

"*No!*" his voice boomed. "*No!*"

She screwed up her face as she took another sip of water. "Michael, why are you doing this? I came to see your den with you, but now I must go –"

"No!"

She had to get out. If she didn't only two things were going to happen.

Rape and then murder.

She threw the mug at Michael and sprang off the stool. Running towards the entrance to the den her forehead cracked against something hard and she fell backwards onto the floor. She wanted to scream but didn't have time before blackness engulfed her.

The mug missed him, making a dull thud against the earthen wall.

As she raced for the entrance he tried to warn her about the thick branch that supported the weight of the roof, but it was too late.

She was lying on the floor now and blood was oozing from her forehead.

Why had she done that?

He did not mean she couldn't go. He just told her he didn't want her to go.

Slowly he moved over to where Sarah lay unconscious.

He knelt down beside her. Her eyes were closed. Her right leg was caught under her. The soles of her delicate feet were dirty from the earthen floor and her arms were stretched out at her sides. He picked up her small hand in his. It was warm. He lifted it to his cheek, rubbing her nails against his skin. He pressed her fingers against his lips and kissed them gently.

"Wake up," he whispered, his voice catching. "Please ... please wake up."

"They'll be here in about thirty minutes," Phillip said as he put the phone down.

"So what do we do in the meantime?" Elspeth looked from Phillip to John.

"What can we do?" Phillip said.

"Try her mobile again?" John suggested.

Phillip reached for the phone. After only a couple of seconds he shook his head. "It's still switched off."

"D'you know where she keeps it?"

"In her bag."

"And where's that?"

Phillip closed his eyes. Idiot, he said to himself as he got up and went into the hall. He opened the under-stairs cupboard where he looked earlier to see if Sarah's coat was missing. The bag she used most days was hanging on the hook at the back of the door. He took it down and felt inside. The first thing he touched was her mobile phone. He took it out and held it up for the others to see.

"How could I be so stupid?" he said.

"Have you had anything to eat?" Elspeth asked as she got up from the table. Her expression suggested the discovery of Sarah's mobile phone was the worst omen yet.

Phillip shook his head.

"I'll make us all a sandwich before the police arrive."

Sarah shivered.

She was lying down and there was a musty smell in her nostrils.

Where was she?

Her head ached, her forehead throbbed and her mouth felt like sandpaper. She tried to touch her head but her hand wouldn't move, neither would her other hand. Opening her eyes the darkness hit her.

Her feet were even colder than the rest of her.

She tried to move her feet but couldn't.

The awful musty smell was right under her nose.

What the hell was it?

Slowly her eyes became accustomed to the dark. She moved her head sideways and saw slits of light above her as the horror of where she was rushed back to her.

She was not dreaming because everything was too real. Tugging at her hands and feet again, they still wouldn't move. She wriggled her fingers and toes but her wrists and ankles were tied to something. The musty smell grew stronger. As she moved her head her nose touched cold metal.

She moved her head from side to side. It was the zip on the sleeping bag she had seen on the makeshift bed.

He had tied her to the bed.

Where was he? Where could he have gone?

God, her head hurt. She screwed up her eyes, feeling crustiness on her forehead. She had made a dash for the entrance but she remembered nothing after that.

This time the scream started in her stomach and vibrated throughout her body.

"I wonder what we're going to be faced with, Debbie," PC Tony Martin said, turning right towards the village.

"It's probably all going to be a waste of time," his new sidekick said. "Some rich middle-class bimbo pissed off with her husband so she decides to teach him a lesson."

"The sergeant doesn't normally get it wrong. He wouldn't have sent us out if he thought it wasn't worth it."

Tony peered through the windscreen, looking for some indication of where they needed to go.

"Hang on a second I'll ask this bloke where Primrose Cottage is."

Tony stopped the police car by the entrance to the Lords of the Manor Hotel and lowered the window.

"'Scuse me ,sir, can you tell us where Primrose Cottage is?"

"Sorry ... sorry," the man said.

"Primrose Cottage?" Tony repeated. "Can you tell me where it is?"

The man looked extremely nervous. Scruffy too, as though he hadn't washed for a week. He pointed towards the village green.

"Back ... back there and ... and down ... down Church Lane ... to the right."

"Thank you, sir." Tony closed the window before slipping the car into gear and reversing into the hotel gateway.

"Who was that or should I say what was that? The village idiot?" Debbie said.

"It takes all kinds to make a world," Tony said.

"Does it? There's Church Lane, down there. God, this place is like something out a history book."

Old Greg frowned as he saw the police car go down Church Lane.

He then looked back down the High Street and saw Michael Griffiths staring up the road.

"Bet "e's in a bit o' a flap," he muttered to himself.

Michael watched the police car turn right at the green and disappear.

Why were the police going to Primrose Cottage?

Had something happened to that man?

He hoped so.

Sarah Preston was still unconscious when he left her.

He had come back as quickly as he could to the village to get a bandage and some ointment for her head. After lifting her onto the bed he had covered her with the sleeping bag. As an afterthought he fastened her wrists and ankles to the bed because he was worried that if she woke, and he wasn't there, she might panic and fall and hurt herself again. He never left the den without turning the lamps out. Some animal might get in and knock them over. When he got back, he would bandage her head and then if she was well enough he would help her return to the village. He didn't want to do it but she was so worried, and now that she had hurt herself ... well, he didn't want to blame her but she did hurt herself, it wasn't him. Why had she tried to get out of the den without asking for his help?

He would have helped her if she had asked.

After seeing the police car turn down Church Lane, he turned round and broke into a jog. Seeing the police really worried him. He hoped his mother was not at home. He would take a bandage and some cream ... and an aspirin ... and ... whatever else he could think of.

"Mr Preston?" PC Tony Martin asked as the front door opened.

"Yes, thank you for getting here so quickly, please come in." Phillip opened the door further and stood back.

"I'm PC Tony Martin and this is PC Debbie Gould," Tony told him as they moved into the hall.

Phillip and Debbie Gould exchanged nods and polite smiles.

"Please, go straight through."

They all trooped into the kitchen.

"This is Elspeth Warrington and John Davidson, very good friends of mine. PC Martin and PC Gould."

More nods and brief smiles were exchanged.

"Would you like a cup of tea or coffee?" Phillip asked.

"That's very kind of you, sir. Coffee for me, milk and one sugar and ..."

223

"Coffee, please sir," Debbie added., "Black, no sugar."

"Right, please sit down."

John moved closer to the window to let the police constables sit down. They took their hats off and PC Martin extracted his notebook from his pocket.

"You wanted to report a missing person, sir."

"Yes," Phillip replied turning round and knocking the jar of coffee over.

"Come on, Phillip," Elspeth said, "you sit down and I'll get the coffee."

"Yes," Phillip said again, "my wife, Sarah."

"Can you tell us why you think she's missing, sir?"

Phillip told them what had happened and added that he and the other two were just back from Lower Slaughter after searching for Sarah.

"And there was no sign of her, sir?" PC Martin asked the questions while PC Gould gazed around the kitchen as if coveting the *Le Creuset* saucepans, the *Rangemaster* stove and the sleek wall units.

"No."

What an inane question Phillip wanted to add. If they had found Sarah the police wouldn't be here. What was the point in calling the police when they send a man who isn't bright enough to make sergeant by the time he is fifty and a young girl who isn't old enough to know where to start.

"Is it possible that your wife may just have gone for a long walk?"

Phillip closed his eyes and shook his head. John sat with his back against the wall, his face expressionless, and Elspeth made the coffee.

"Of course it's possible but it's now nearly midday and she's been missing for over six hours. If she normally went for long walks on her own I wouldn't have phoned."

"We understand ..."

"Did you have an argument, sir?" It was Debbie Gould's first question.

"If –"

"Here's your coffee," Elspeth said, putting the mugs down. "Mr Preston would not have called the police if he didn't have just cause. Mr Davidson and I know Mrs Preston very well and we are equally worried."

"Thank you, Mrs Warrington." PC Martin glared at his young companion. "But in situations such as this we have to ask some rather obvious questions in order to eliminate some of the possibilities. Facts may be obvious to you, but at this stage we know very little. PC Gould's question may have seemed perfunctory but if the answer had been yes, then we might have been able to use our experience of other similar cases to try to second-guess where Mrs Preston might be."

PC Martin spoke slowly and quietly, and his choice of words took the others by surprise.

"Yes, I'm sorry. No, my wife and I did not have an argument last night. In fact we said very little to each other. We'd been to a party in the village and when we got home she went straight to bed."

"What time did you get back from the party, sir?"

PC Martin flipped to a clean page in his notebook.

"Just before eight."

PC Martin looked a little surprised. "That's a bit early to come home from a party, isn't it, sir?"

"It wasn't that sort of party," Elspeth said. "It was a cocktail party and was only supposed to be for a couple of hours."

"Were you at the same party, Madam?"

"Yes."

"What time did you get home?"

Elspeth looked across at John, who was still sitting with his back to the wall just listening. "About nine fifteen, wasn't it John?"

"Give or take a few minutes, yes," he said.

"Thank you." PC Martin made a pencilled note. "So although it wasn't that sort of party you and your wife still came home early, Mr Preston?" There was no suggestion of sarcasm in his voice.

225

"Well yes, I suppose we did."

"Was there any particular reason?"

Elspeth and John looked at each other momentarily, Elspeth giving a slight shake of her head.

"I don't think the reason would be relevant ..."

"Try me, sir." PC Martin looked up from his notebook, his blue eyes fixed on Phillip.

"Well, when we went to the party she was fine. The four of us," he added, indicating Elspeth and John, "went together. But after we'd been there an hour or so, Sarah suddenly became very morose, almost upset by something."

"Suddenly, you say. Did you see anything that may have caused her change in mood?"

"When I say suddenly I mean, well, she was all right when she went off with Elspeth here, but when I next saw her she'd changed."

"Went off with Elspeth, sir? What exactly do you mean?"

Elspeth spoke before Phillip could say anything else. "Mrs Preston and I decided to circulate together at the party. I wanted to introduce her to a few people I knew. We popped out of the room where the party was being held so that I could have a cigarette."

"I see, thank you. I must ask you then," he said, looking at Elspeth, "did you see anything or hear anything that may have upset her?"

Elspeth took a deep breath and closed her eyes for a moment before looking at Phillip.

"I'm sorry, Phillip, but having thought about it I think I know what she was upset about. I'm sorry for not mentioning it before."

"What?" Phillip asked quietly.

"I think perhaps we ought –"

"No, if it's relevant then everyone here should know. What was it?"

Again Elspeth looked at John and his expression suggested that he could not believe she was going to tell them.

"You've been trying to start a family haven't you?" she asked Phillip.

"For about the last ten years, yes, but I can't see ..."

"She thinks she's let you down. It's been building up inside her. I think that might be why she was the way she was. There was a lot of *children* talk at the party and I think it might have got to her. She was asked by everyone we met whether she had any children and one idiot, when Sarah said she hadn't, suggested at her age she ought to hurry up."

Elspeth wasn't lying because Sarah had told her about her perceived inability to become pregnant and about how depressed she felt as a result, but she was lying about the time and location.

Elspeth heard John's sigh of relief.

"And Mrs Preston said nothing to you about this last night before going to bed?" PC Martin's question was directed at Phillip.

"No, nothing. I knew she felt bad about it but ..."

Phillip did not believe for one second that Elspeth's conclusion was accurate, but if everybody they met at the party started talking about their own children, he accepted it could have sparked something.

"Had you ever talked about it, sir?" PC Gould said.

"Of course we'd talked about it. You don't spend ten years trying to have a baby without talking about it."

"No, sorry, sir, that's not what I meant. Presumably you've both had tests and there's something wrong with Mrs Preston that is stopping her from becoming pregnant."

"What?" Phillip said not believing what he had just heard.

His wife was missing and here was a young kid in uniform asking intimate questions about Sarah's ability to conceive. Everyone was looking at him so he forced himself to calm down.

"Yes, something like that."

"I see," PC Gould said.

"It doesn't make sense that she should wander off on her own because of that," Phillip said.

"We won't know until we find her, sir."

After collecting the bandage and ointment from the bathroom in his mother's house, Michael walked along the river to the bottom of Church Lane. Looking up the lane from the other side of the bridge he could just see the front of the police car parked outside Primrose Cottage. He turned round, walked quickly back along the river and then left the village in the opposite direction to Copper's Ridge.

He would have to use one of his longer secret routes because taking care was now his priority. Being over confident would mean he might start making mistakes.

As he walked he thought.

He had done nothing wrong but nobody would believe him.

Sarah Preston went to Copper's Ridge of her own free will. She went to his den because she wanted to and not because he forced her. The accident was not his fault: she was the one who banged her head against the branch. She was frightened but not because of anything he did.

That must be why the police were at Primrose Cottage.

Somebody had reported her missing.

But nobody would believe him.

Sarah Preston would tell them the truth. Or would she?

When she asked him if she could leave he couldn't let her go then because he needed to talk to her. But he couldn't find the right words and he didn't want to feel stupid in front of her. He liked just looking at her because she was so beautiful.

What did he do to make her sick?

When she hit her head and he put her on the bed, he cleaned her face and neck as best he could. He was tempted to take off her coat and top, but she had not told him he

228

could, so he didn't. When he was wiping her chin, he deliberately let the back of his hand brush against her breasts.

What could he do now?

When he left Sarah Preston in the den she was breathing well enough. He felt for a pulse on her neck, and that seemed all right. As his fingers touched her skin its softness made him feel so happy.

He had not hurt her in any way. She knocked herself out. He had not done anything to make her hit her head.

As he walked his eyes began to water. None of this was his fault. Yes, he might have planned to hurt that man but he would never have been able to go through with it because Hector the cat was proof of that. He could no more harm that man than anyone or anything else. He was incapable of inflicting pain on anyone, except on himself. His thoughts always caused him pain.

He wanted to be normal. He wanted to have a girlfriend, then a wife, and even children. What chance did he stand? Everybody thought he was stupid.

It was all too late.

Even at work, although he was good at his job, all the others made fun of him, though not always intentionally. What did he hear Mr Masters call it? Banter – he said it was just banter and it happened all the time when people worked closely together. But when some of the others were involved *in a bit of banter*, Michael couldn't join in. He understood what was happening but he either couldn't or didn't want to be part of it.

Mr Masters didn't join in either.

If Mr Masters was around the others never made fun of him. He was a good man. He was the manager because he was a good man and because he knew how to handle people. He worked in an office not on the shop floor with the others. After Mr Proctor, Michael liked Mr Masters the most.

Approaching Copper's Ridge from the east and keeping inside the tree line, he checked whether there was anybody else about but he only saw a couple of people in the far distance walking their dog. Mr Jones the farmer from Lower Slaughter was in his field, also with his dog but neither he nor his dog saw him.

He wiped away a tear and smiled.

Stupid he might be but he was invisible.

After lowering himself into the den, he replaced the cover and waited until his eyes became accustomed to the darkness. While he waited he listened. Other than the slight rustle of leaves in the breeze he could not hear a thing.

"Sarah Preston?" he said as quietly as he could in case he frightened her.

He listened.

Nothing.

"Mrs Preston …"

Sarah lay on the bed, listening to his ridiculous voice.

Sarah Preston! Mrs Preston! He sounded like a five-year-old calling for his mother. God, what time was it?

What a mess.

How was she going to persuade him to release her? The stink from the sleeping bag was bad enough but being tied to the bed was unbearable.

There was a sudden glare as Michael struck a match and lit one of the lamps.

Michael swung the lamp round so that he could see the bed.

Sarah Preston was still there. She looked straight at him, her eyes black in the dim light.

She looked so fragile. He must release her wrists and ankles. Would she believe he only tied them to the bed for her own safety?

He lit the second lamp and then the third.

"Don't you ever leave me in the fucking dark again," she said. "I was terrified."

He almost dropped the lamp he was carrying. She sounded just like his mother did when she used that word.

230

"I'm ... I'm sorry," he said kneeling down next to the bed.

"And get this fucking stinking thing off me."

"I'm ... I'm sorry."

After moving the sleeping bag away from her, he reached for her wrists and undid the knots. "I'm ... I'm sorry," he said again.

"Stop saying you're fucking sorry and undo whatever is tied to my ankles."

As he undid the knots at her feet, he wished she would stop swearing. She wasn't so beautiful when she was swearing. There was no need for her to swear at him.

Her feet were free.

She shot off the bed, her hands like claws as she attacked his face, his neck, his arms – any bit of him within her reach.

"You fucking bastard, how dare you!"

She was on top of him, her arms and legs flailing.

The lamp on the floor fell over but went out straightaway with a pop. She was like a wild animal, clawing at his eyes, kicking him, her spittle covering his face.

"You fucking bastard!"

He grabbed her wrists and forced her hands away from his face, but still she struggled, trying to get her knee between his legs. She was red in the face and making a growling noise as she wrestled with him. But he was too strong and her initial surge of energy was gone. She slumped down on top of him.

"Let me go," she whimpered, "please let me go."

She was crying.

He released her wrists and like a rag doll she flopped even closer to him; he felt her face brush against his. Slowly he moved his arms so that they went round her shoulders onto her back.

He hugged her as she cried.

231

About half an hour before she heard Michael returning, Sarah had worked herself into such a state of panic that she started tugging even harder at her restraints. Only when the pain became unbearable did she stop.

The thought of being tied up and left in a pitch black underground den in the middle of a wood miles from anywhere terrified her.

She heard a tractor in the distance, an animal snuffling round above her and she was sure she heard voices, children's voices. She filled her lungs and screamed as loudly as she could for as long as she could, but all she achieved was added soreness to her throat. Nobody came to save her.

She could not understand Michael's reason for leaving her tied up. Eventually the headache dissipated but when the blood on her forehead dried and began to itch, she was unable to scratch it. She was convinced she was going to die, no not just die, she was going to be raped and then murdered.

Lying on the stinking bed, she imagined what it was like to be killed.

Would she feel the pain before she died?

Would he mutilate her before he killed her? Would he threaten her and then laugh as he slashed at her body with a knife?

She wondered what it was like to be strangled, throttled, unable to breathe, the temporary hysteria as her lungs craved for oxygen, the blackness as she passed out. Then she imagined she was having an out of body experience as she watched her naked corpse being buried in some hollow in the ground only to be uncovered and consumed by animals. Maybe she would be dismembered: her arms, legs and head severed. She saw him carrying her decapitated head by its hair, blood dripping from the neck, the eyes wide open and staring.

One day a piece of her would be found and her DNA would tell them who she was – who she once was.

How long would it be before she was found? Some women, who disappeared presumed murdered, were never found.

She began to plan her escape.

There would be no rape, no murder and no dismembering.

Michael was stupid and he was simple.

She could outthink him and outwit him.

She would escape ...

So where did it all go wrong?

Why wasn't she running, escaping barefooted through the grass along Copper's Ridge?

Why was she lying on top of him feeling the stubble on his face against her cheek, his arms holding her gently, soothing her?

Her heart beating at twice its normal rate, why?

Why were tears running down her cheeks?

She was supposed to be free, why wasn't she?

"Right then, sir," PC Martin said as Phillip opened the front door. "I won't say not to worry because it'd be a bit glib but what I will tell you, sir, is that nine times out of ten the person reported missing turns up within forty-eight hours."

"Does that mean you're not going to do anything until tomorrow?"

"Not at all, sir, before we leave the village, we'll call on a few of your close neighbours to see if they saw Mrs Preston this morning. Trouble is –"

"I'd prefer it if you didn't –" Phillip said.

"Do you want your wife found, sir?"

"Of course I do."

"Then leave us to our job, sir."

PC Gould went down the path towards the front gate but stopped and walked back to the front door. "Mr Preston?" she said.

PC Martin gave her a swift sideways look.

"Yes?" Phillip said.

PC Gould glanced at PC Martin and then back at Phillip.

"Mr Preston, am I right in saying your friends live together?"

"Yes, they do. I'm sorry, I thought that was obvious."

"I heard PC Martin call her Mrs Warrington and I just wanted to make sure."

"Oh, I see. Well yes, they do live together."

"Would you say that your wife and Miss Warrington are ... good friends or is it just a neighbourly sort of friendship?"

Phillip frowned. "I would say they're very good friends, very close. Sarah was lucky to find someone like her in a village of this size. Why, what are you getting at?"

"I'm not getting at anything, sir. I'm just confirming an observation, that's all," PC Gould said and headed back to the front gate.

PC Martin put his cap back on his head. "Right, sir, I can't tell you not to worry because you will, but in the majority of cases –"

"I know, they're back within forty-eight hours."

"Exactly, sir."

"When can I expect to hear from somebody again?"

"I'll radio a report in from the car, sir, and then the sergeant can decide what should be done."

"All right, thanks," Phillip said, feeling far from happy about the way things were being left.

In the police car, PC Martin put his hat on the dash before lighting a cigarette.

"What was that all about?" he said.

"What?" Debbie said as she turned the key in the ignition.

She thought it strange that when they were together he always drove to an incident and she drove away from it while he had a cigarette.

"That business about the Warrington woman and Mrs Preston?" he said, exhaling out of the open window. "You know damn well what I'm asking."

"Oh," she said, "that. I think we're dealing with more than just a good friendship there, Tony."

He narrowed his eyes. "Are you suggesting what I think you're suggesting?"

She smiled. "I'm suggesting exactly what you're thinking, not what I'm suggesting." She glanced sideways.

"What? They're having an affair? They are, you know …"

"Lesbians? I don't *know,* Tony but I would certainly hazard a guess it could be a possibility. Where to?"

"Clifton House. Through the ford at the bottom and then left. I want to know what happened at that party."

As the car moved slowly down the hill, Tony Martin mulled over what Debbie had said.

He smiled to himself.

"I suppose we could have pinned Elspeth Warrington down a bit more," Debbie suggested, breaking into his thoughts.

"What? You mean whether she's, you know, closer to Sarah Preston than a normal friendship would suggest?"

"No, of course not. But what happened at the party … what really happened."

"We did ask if you remember, but you're suggesting she was lying."

"I'm not suggesting this time, Tony, I'm telling you. Miss Elspeth Warrington was lying through her teeth."

Michael didn't know what to do.

She was still on top of him, the fight having left her but he was scared that if he moved she would start again. He could feel the side of his face burning where she scratched him.

Why had she attacked him? It was like fighting off a wild animal.

He tried to ease himself from under her. She wasn't heavy. He could easily lift her off but he didn't want to

235

annoy her. Slowly he moved his hands to her shoulders and lifted as gently as he could. Her head lolled against his chest, so he lifted her a little further. In the dim light he saw that there was spittle all around her mouth and her head was bleeding. Her eyes were closed and her breathing was slow but steady.

He thought she might have passed out again.

Inch by inch he eased himself from under her. When he was free he turned her over. She could be asleep or maybe she had hit her head harder than he thought and was unconscious again. She was as light as a feather so he picked her up and carried her to the bed, laying her down on her back.

He took the antiseptic wipes from his pocket but instead of wiping his own torn cheek, he attended to Sarah Preston first.

With the lightest possible touch he wiped her mouth then her chin and her neck. The cuts on her forehead were not deep but even in the poor light he could see bruising already coming out. He took the antiseptic cream from his pocket and smeared some on the cuts and bruises. He didn't know if it would do any good.

She was lying on an old mattress his mother had thrown out about six months ago. He had tied it up and carried it to his den. He bent down and sniffed the mattress. It smelt of damp but was nowhere near as bad as the sleeping bag. Next he checked the lamp he had dropped when she attacked him. Luckily, the spilt kerosene did not catch fire.

After trimming the lamp's wick he lit it, put it back on the table and sat down to wait.

The police presence in the village worried him. She must have been reported missing, but why so soon? She was an adult and had only been gone a few hours. Even if she hadn't stopped at the tree she might still have been walking, so why had the police been called?

It wasn't his fault.

He was doing all he could to help her.

236

There was no reason for her to be frightened because he would never hurt her.

But who would believe him?

He looked down at Sarah Preston.

Her face was towards him, her lips slightly apart. Her chest was rising and falling. She was so beautiful, so very, very beautiful that it took his breath away, but he would not touch her. He would never touch her unless she asked him to.

"Well, what did they say?" John asked as Phillip returned to the kitchen.

Phillip slumped down onto a chair. "Not a lot but basically they reckon it's far too early. The bloke kept on about what might happen in the first forty-eight hours and what bloody statistics told him was likely to happen next. And yes, basically they're going to do fuck all until tomorrow." He looked at Elspeth. "Sorry."

"Don't mind me. You swear as much as you like, I'll be joining you soon." She took a deep breath. "In fact I'll join you now: anyone got any fucking ideas?"

"Well, I for one can't sit here and wait for the police to tell me to start worrying. That point was passed long ago." Phillip rose slowly as if all the stuffing had gone out of him. "I'm going back out there," he said pointing to the front door. "At least if I'm searching I'll feel as though I'm doing something positive."

"Where do you suggest?" John asked.

"We've tried south, so I'm going north this time."

"Can I make a suggestion?"

"Of course, anything's better than nothing."

"Can I suggest we go and get my wagon? We can cover more ground with a four-wheel drive and if we open the roof you'll be able to see far more from up there."

"Good idea."

"Do you want me to come?" Elspeth asked.

The men exchanged looks. "Would you mind staying here just in case she returns?" Phillip said.

237

Elspeth smiled. "Of course I wouldn't."

Setting off down Church Lane in John's Landrover Freelander, Phillip looked across the river and spotted the police car outside Clifton House.

"I didn't expect that," he said. "I wonder why they went there first."

John shrugged as he slowly applied the brakes. "Probably because it's as good a starting place as any. We told them that's where the party was."

"You're probably right but that reminds me. That female PC asked me what sort of friends Sarah and Elspeth were."

John's foot almost slipped off the accelerator. "What sort of friends?"

"Whether they were good friends or not."

"What did you say?"

"Well, I said they were very good friends, what else? What do you think she was getting at?"

"I've no idea," John said. "If we're going up to Copper's Ridge we need to cross the water somewhere. Any ideas?"

"Keep to this track and about half a mile past where Sarah and I cross the river using that fallen tree, there a farmer's bridge that connects the fields either side of the river. You must have seen it. Under the circumstances I'm sure he won't mind us using it.

Elspeth stood at the window in the guest bedroom, craning her neck as she watched John's Freelander turn left before the ford and disappear from view.

As soon as she was certain they would not return, she hurried across the landing and into the main bedroom. She had helped decorate the whole cottage so she knew every corner, every crack, every patch where perhaps the paint had not covered the wall as well as they hoped it would.

She could still hear Sarah's laughter and her own as together they experienced such fun, real fun. After having one glass too many at the end of an exhausting day, they

238

would try to say they had *dwunk two too many wines today too*.

Her writing suffered during those first few weeks but it was for the right reasons. Being with Sarah satisfied all her needs for escapism, for her fantasizing, for her dreams.

Where were her dreams now?

She crossed over to the glass-fronted wardrobe. Sliding the door along its runners she took in at a glance the array of clothes. She moved closer so that she could smell Sarah. Her tears had started soon after the men left the cottage, and she was still crying. She was surprised she'd been able to hold them back for so long but now they ran in streams down her cheeks. She wasn't crying, she was weeping: weeping and wondering.

On top of a pile of folded jumpers she saw the one she thought suited Sarah most of all. She picked it up and let the folds fall out. She held it at arm's length, its blurred image making her close her eyes. She imagined Sarah wearing it, imagined her happy smiling face and the look in her lovely eyes. She imagined the indescribable feeling of love that was all consuming whenever she was near her.

Sitting down on the bed she held the jumper close to her, burying her face into the soft wool. As her tears flowed she was overcome by a sensation of immense loss. A loss from which she would never recover: a loss from which she would never want to recover because to recover would mean the memory had already faded.

She was not ready to lose anybody but least of all Sarah.

Lying back on the bed she put her head on the pillow where only hours earlier Sarah's head had lain. The silent weeping changed to agonising crying and the crying became a wail. She didn't care who heard her: she didn't care who knew because her life was never going to be the same. Her life had changed and was beyond the point of recovery. What this meant didn't matter, not anymore.

The two of them had never stood a chance.

Michael sat and watched her as she slept.

He heard her every breath, her every whimper, drinking it in so that it would be imprinted forever in his memory. When saliva dribbled from the corner of her mouth he gently wiped it away but quickly returned to his seat in case he disturbed her. She tossed and turned, her head moving from side to side on the pillow. She tried to speak in her sleep, her words strange and unintelligible.

He could not believe she was so close to him and yet so far away. He wanted to talk to her. He wanted to tell her about the bad things in his earlier life and what was happening inside his head now.

He knew he was better than all those other people made him feel. The words he needed were important because if he was clumsy with the words he might scare her again.

And he must try to stop stuttering.

If he thought before he spoke and then spoke slowly, he was sure he could do it.

He smiled to himself. He admired what she tried to do when she attempted to escape.

Escape?

Why was he using that word? There was no need for her to escape. She could leave whenever she wanted. So, he didn't understand why she had done it.

She was strong, there was ... what was it his mother used to say about his sister? ... there was fire in her belly, that was it. When Sarah Preston started fighting and she scratched his face and eyes, he felt exhilarated, he felt excited because she was so close to him. When she collapsed on top of him he didn't want her to move, ever. Her face was next to his, her hair across his face and her body hard against his. It was what his dreams, his fantasies had been made of ...

But she was not well and he had to help her. She must have hit her head harder than he first thought.

He went back to the bed and put his fingers against her bruised forehead. He was shocked to feel how hot she was.

She was too hot.

The perspiration made her face and her neck wet. Her head was moving from side to side on the pillow and she was still saying those indecipherable words.

He stopped and cocked his head.

There was a noise … a noise outside that should not be there.

Turning his head slightly he tried to identify the noise.

It was an engine – an engine revving as it moved along the track on Copper's Ridge.

He listened, as alert as the wild animal he believed he was.

It wasn't a tractor, or the farmer's Landrover.

He lifted the cover from the entrance. Through narrowed eyes he peered out towards the edge of the wood. Seeing nothing he lifted the cover a little higher and jumped out, allowing it to fall back into place, then headed for the edge of the wood, staying low and moving almost soundlessly and ending up at the spot where he could see most of Copper's Ridge. It was not far from Mrs Tucker's tree and he could also see the track running in both directions across the top of the ridge.

Then he saw it.

He recognised the vehicle. He had watched it being driven through the village with Sarah Preston sometimes sitting in the back. Oh yes, he knew that vehicle and he knew who would be driving it. A man was standing up, with half his body sticking out through the roof. The vehicle was moving slowly along the track towards him

How did they know where to find him?

Nobody could have seen him so how did they know?

He watched the vehicle's slow progress. Even if they did know, he was safe. His den was invisible. Even the farmer who owned Copper's Ridge wood once walked within yards of his den and did not spot it.

They would never find him and they would never find his Sarah Preston.

But he would watch.

He would wait and see what they did.

Glancing back towards the village, he saw that the clouds were darkening: it would be raining soon.

Chapter Fifteen

Hilary Bond-Smithers took an instant dislike to PC Tony Martin. He was the epitome of what she loathed most about some members of the police force. For a start there was little evidence of any breeding and if he was any good why was he still a constable at his age? She objected to being questioned by a mere constable and his assistant, a plain slip of a girl who didn't look old enough to be out of school let alone wearing a police uniform. If she needed to be questioned then she expected at least a Chief Inspector and preferably a Superintendent to come to see her.

This really was most objectionable and most inconvenient.

"How many guests did you have at your party, Madam?" PC Martin asked Hilary Bond-Smithers.

"What difference will knowing that make?" she replied.

"Because, *Madam*," Tony Martin said, "we are investigating the possible disappearance of one of your party guests, and knowing how many people were here last night will give me an idea of how many people we'll need to speak to. In other words what resources we'll need to allocate should Mrs Preston be officially declared missing."

"You're not going to question all my guests, surely?" Hilary asked indignantly.

"If that becomes necessary, Madam, yes we will need to speak to all of them. How many were there?"

"What makes you think it was something that happened here which may have caused this gel to go missing?"

"Madam, we don't know. We don't even know for certain that Mrs Preston is missing, but her husband is very worried. From what he told us, Mrs Preston may have experienced something during your party that upset her."

"What are you suggesting?"

"I'm not suggesting anything, Madam, merely making preliminary enquiries."

"If my husband were here, he would –"

"Madam, I'm sorry if my question is difficult to answer but it's quite simple really. All I need from you at this stage is how many guests attended so that when our enquiries start, should it come to that, we know how many officers to allocate. If that question is too difficult to answer then maybe you could call on somebody who could answer it."

"The insolence!" Hilary spat at him.

"I mean you no disrespect, Mrs Bond-Smithers. It's a simple question which I'm sure has a simple answer. Should we need to question your guests we will ensure we are discreet, but unfortunately in a case such as this, it may be necessary to speak to them all."

"The gel has only been missing a few hours ..."

"Mrs Bond-Smithers, please answer my question and we'll leave you in peace. How many?"

Hilary folded her arms and puffed out her chest. "Well, we invited just over a hundred from all over the county of course, but only eighty were actually able to come."

"Eighty. Thank you, Madam. The fact that some of your guests travelled a reasonable distance will not generate a problem."

"You're not serious about ..."

"If it becomes necessary we will be very serious, Madam."

PC Martin took his cap from under his arm. "Just one further question before we go. How well do you know Mrs Preston?"

"I don't know her very well at all, actually. I went to see her soon after she and her husband arrived in the village but other than seeing each other at a distance we've had no occasion to meet since then."

"Thank you. And Miss Warrington?"

"Elspeth? Elspeth has been a friend of the family for well over a year, she writes books, you know and rides."

"Does she?"

Tony Martin would have liked nothing more than to find a reason to arrest Mrs Bond-Smithers for obstructing the police but he decided that in so doing he might be placing his career on the line. He would not be surprised to discover that the Chief Constable had been a guest at Mrs Bond-Smithers' party.

"We don't need a list at this stage, Madam," he said, "but if Mrs Preston is declared a missing person we will need one then. If you could prepare a list it could save time later. Thank you for your trouble." Tony Martin deliberately put his cap on before smiling at Hilary.

He turned and went to the front door.

He had expected Debbie Gould to follow him but he should have known better.

"Madam," he heard her say behind him, "when you're drawing up this list, could you annotate it to show who was with whom when they arrived at your party and then who was with whom when they left?"

Debbie smiled before following him out.

Tony Martin suppressed a smile when he looked over his shoulder and saw Hilary Bond-Smithers standing at the door with her mouth open.

"You can be a right little madam yourself," Tony said as they headed back to the police car.

"Did you see the way she looked at you? She thought you were —"

"All right, thank you, Debbie."

He opened the car door.

"There's more to Clifton House than meets the eye. She was too defensive too early. Without wishing Sarah Preston any harm, I half wish we'll have a reason to come back here."

245

"I don't think it's anything to do with Clifton bloody House, or Mrs Hilary bloody Bond-Smithers. Call it female intuition but I still think Elspeth Warrington knows more than she's saying."

"What do you mean? You've already suggested Elspeth Warrington and Sarah Preston are more than just good friends or have you changed your mind?"

Debbie Gould smiled and shook her head. "I don't know what I mean but I was watching her and she was hiding something. John thingy, her partner, was very quiet too. I reckon we need look no further than the two of them."

"So it's a threesome now is it and those two know where Sarah Preston is, do they?"

"I'm not saying that but I think they know why she's where she is."

"If that's feminine intuition then I think I'll stick with the facts."

"And what are they?"

"We could have a missing person on our hands but I'm not even prepared to say so just yet."

"Those are facts, are they?" Debbie Gould said.

"It's all there is at the moment."

John and Phillip drove along the track on Copper's Ridge in silence, which eventually Phillip broke as he dropped down from his vantage point back onto his seat.

"Sarah and I have only been this far along Copper's Ridge. She had this thing about the Tucker woman and her daughter."

John slowed down. "Well, that prominent lone tree coming up on the left is where it all happened."

"Really? I thought it was a lot further along."

John drove on for another fifty yards then pulled in by the tree and turned off the engine.

"Why are we stopping?"

John shrugged. "If Sarah didn't want to come along here when she was with you, it's unlikely she would come this far on her own." He opened his door. "Do you want to see where the Tucker woman topped herself?"

"You're being a bit macabre," Phillip said as he got out of the car.

John moved round to the other side of the Freelander. "Not a lot happens in Upper Slaughter. I just thought while we were here you might like to see a bit of its past."

Michael watched the two men get out of the vehicle and walk over to the tree. Even without recognising the four-by-four he would have known immediately who they were.

They must know something. Why else would they come up to the ridge?

Had he been seen after all?

If he had, then surely the police would be with them.

He put his hands under his jacket, trying to stop them from shaking.

He needed to go back to the village. Sarah Preston wasn't well and he needed to get some medicine. He would get some bedding as well. Once when he wasn't well his mother, in one of her more caring moments, told him to stay warm. It was one of the only times she ever showed any concern for him.

The two men were talking. The one who lived with the Warrington woman was pointing at the tree and waving his arms about. Michael prayed that he had not left any footprints and more importantly, he hoped Sarah Preston hadn't either. He was normally careful not to leave any signs. But he was still shaking.

What could he do?

If he told them what had happened they would not believe him. He didn't know the words anyway, so he would stutter and stammer and they would think he was an idiot. But he could lead them to Sarah Preston and they could take her home in the car, put her to bed and make her better.

What would happen then?

When she was better she would tell them the truth. The police would come and take him away. He would lose his job. Even when he was eventually released because he had not done anything wrong, he would still lose his job. The others were always looking for reasons to criticise him and say his work was poor. Although he liked working with the men he knew deep down they didn't like working alongside an idiot who was better at their jobs than they were. They said his work was poor but his work was not poor.

He was good at what he did and better than most of those he worked with. If he was arrested even his few friends at work would not want to know him. Even Mr Masters would not be able to help him.

If he tried to explain everything to the men they would lose their tempers. They could even become violent. Although he would put up a fight but they would get the better of him eventually.

They would beat him up.

He could look after Sarah Preston. He could give her some medicine and keep her warm. Then when she was better he could help her walk back to the village.

But what then?

Would the police believe her?

He shook his head.

What should he do?

A few minutes later the two men got back into the four-by-four, turned it round and headed back along the track towards the village.

It was too late now.

They had made up his mind for him.

He would have to look after Sarah Preston. Helping her get better would make her grateful to him. She would tell the truth and then he could just go back to being the way he was. The little time he was with her would stay with him forever but that was all he ever wanted.

He just wanted to spend a little time with her – just the two of them together. His imagination had got the better of him and he had allowed his frustration to make him think other things were possible, but now he knew they would never happen.

Just being with her a little longer would make him happy.

He waited until the four-by-four disappeared before returning to his den.

Sarah Preston was still asleep, but she seemed more settled. Her head was not moving as much. He touched her forehead with the back of his fingers. She was still hotter than she should be, but not as hot as she was previously. He was worried about keeping her warm because the sleeping bag could not be used now. He lifted an old paraffin heater out from under the table and lit it, making sure he placed it under the chimney in the roof. It would help but he still needed to go back to the village.

Looking down at her sleeping face, he wondered whether he should tie her up again. He didn't want her to harm herself – perhaps just her wrists but not her feet. If he tied her wrists to the bed-frame, she would not fall off the bed.

He would not be long, perhaps an hour or so.

Elspeth heard men's voices.

Where was she?

It was a strange room. Her dressing table was not where it should be, the window was too big and the bed too small. She was clutching something – a jumper?

Then it dawned on her.

It was Sarah and Phillip's room.

She must have cried herself to sleep. She swung her legs off the bed and the movement made her feel giddy. She felt as though she was drugged.

"Elspeth?" It was John's voice. "Elspeth, are you upstairs?"

"Yes," she shouted, "down in a minute."

She quickly folded the jumper and put it back on top of the pile in the wardrobe. After sitting down at Sarah's dressing table and she looked at herself in the mirror.

The face she saw looking back at her told the complete story.

"Did you find anything, Phillip? See anything?" Elspeth asked breezily. It was just as well he was too tied up with his own thoughts to notice what she looked like.

"Absolutely nothing. Were there any calls while we were out?" John asked.

"Not one," Elspeth said.

Phillip sat at the kitchen table with his head in his hands and his body slumped forward. "Where can she be?" he said. "I didn't expect to find her up on Copper's Ridge, but in my heart I thought that when we got back home she would be here. I know I mustn't give up hope but ..."

Elspeth crossed to the table. She placed a hand on Phillip's shoulder. "She'll come home."

He looked up, tears in his eyes. "When? And why did she have to go away in the first place?"

It was suddenly all too much for Elspeth.

She rushed out of the kitchen and out of the cottage.

The first thing Sarah was aware of was a smell of burning.

She opened her eyes. She was cold.

When she attempted to move her hands she couldn't but this time she wasn't surprised so she didn't panic.

She twisted her head and looked around for the source of the smell.

She saw it straightaway.

The lamp on the table was smoking and the flame was burning yellow. Surely that wasn't how it should be. She tried to move her feet, expecting them to be tied as well but they were not. Her feet and toes were colder than the rest of her. She wondered what the time was. There was no way of telling, although there seemed to be some light coming through the slits above her head.

She looked at her wrists. They were only loosely tied so maybe she could reach the knots with her teeth. She moved her head and the throbbing started – behind her eyes, her temples, everywhere.

She rested back on the pillow and closed her eyes.

Michael let himself into the house by the back door.

His mother's car wasn't parked outside which meant he would get everything he needed without answering any questions. Having taken one of the longer routes back to the village meant he had less time than he really needed. He had not seen anybody but people might be watching him from behind the many net curtains in the village streets. He was not that worried who saw him because he knew he had done nothing wrong.

Watching people was not a crime.

Well, yes, he visited some of their houses, he saw their houses from the other side of the net curtains, but he never took anything.

Except from Sarah Preston, but that was different.

He recovered his bedroom door key from its hiding place under the carpet. He would take his quilt, the sheets and the pillows.

What could he put them in?

One of the black rubbish bags his mother kept in the pantry would be ideal. He ought to take two so that he could put one inside the other because they were not very strong. He ran back upstairs and stuffed the bedding into the bags.

What else?

Aspirins and … and Sarah Preston would need some more clothes. Something to keep her warm. He knew where all her clothes were kept. He closed his eyes and pictured the room, the wardrobe and the drawers. He could not take a lot but she would be pleased if he took her a few things. There was enough food and water at the den for another two days.

251

The water was a bit old but he was sure that would not matter.

He moved his wardrobe away from the wall. Behind it was a hole in the plasterboard and inside the hole was the box where he kept the keys he had made. They were labelled with house numbers or names. He picked one up without looking at the label and put it in his pocket.

What should he do? Leave the bedding in his room or take it and hide it somewhere? He decided to hide it in a secret place down by the stream in case his mother came home before he could get back.

As an afterthought he decided to have a shower. He scrubbed his entire body and washed his hair twice until it was squeaky clean. The shower gave him extra energy. Afterwards he applied deodorant and brushed his teeth.

Walking up through the village, he saw a few people at a distance but nobody he recognised. As he passed the village green, he looked at the row of cottages where that Warrington woman lived. He hoped she was there. He hoped they were all there. He would only need a couple of minutes because he knew where everything was.

His step faltered when he saw that the four-by-four was not parked in its usual place. They may have gone somewhere but he hoped they were not down at the Prestons' cottage.

He was so intent on thinking about what he should do next that he didn't notice he was being watched, but he should have known. Carelessness was not an option.

Old Greg was at his gate, his hat on the back of his head, his pipe in his mouth. Michael liked Old Greg. They had never talked but he thought Old Greg was probably a lot like him. Michael lifted his right hand a little and after a couple of seconds Old Greg nodded as he blew out a stream of smoke.

Michael admonished himself again for being so careless.

Old Greg was always watching.

Leaving the village after making doubly sure he was not being watched again, Michael climbed over a gate and crossed a couple of fields before entering the small wood by the church at the back of Primrose Cottage. He moved silently through the wood until he reached the Prestons' garage. He saw movement in the kitchen.

He screwed his eyes closed in frustration.

But he could wait – not for long, but he could wait.

When the rain started to fall he was pleased he'd put on his waterproof jacket before leaving home. He pulled the hood over his head and thought of Sarah Preston, praying that she was all right. He had thought he would only be an hour, but it would be longer. He had left the lamps burning this time so that she wouldn't be scared.

Phillip sprang up from the table. "I'm going to phone the police," he said, marching to the window and back again.

John checked his watch. "What good is that going to do? They said they'd come back some time after six if you hadn't called. It's nearly five now. They'll be here in just over an hour."

"You're right." Phillip bowed his head, his hand resting on the phone. "But I feel so useless. There must be something I can do."

"All any of us can do is wait." John said. "What about Sarah's parents? You could ring them and see if she's there ... but she would have let you know, wouldn't she?"

"Yes, I'm sure she would," Phillip said. "The police already have that information but I told them I didn't want her mum and dad or any of her friends contacted, until much later. I didn't want to worry any of them unnecessarily."

"On second thoughts," John said. "What if Sarah's been there all the time? Couldn't you ring about something else? If she is there, they're bound to tell you."

Phillip thought for a few seconds. "If she was with her parents or friends I'm sure she'd have let me know. Anyway,

253

I hardly ever ring her parents. They're bound to think something's wrong if I do."

John got up from the table. "Isn't it Sarah's birthday next month?"

"Yes, why?"

"Couldn't you ring on the pretext you want to discuss a present you were thinking of buying her?"

"It'd be the first time in the last ten years but I suppose I could. What could I suggest buying her that would need her mother's advice?"

"I don't know but Elspeth would."

Phillip brightened a little. "It's a long shot but it's worth a try. Do you think we could disturb Elspeth? You did say it might be best to leave her alone for a while."

"She'd do anything to bring Sarah home."

"You're sure?"

"I'm certain."

Michael didn't see Phillip and John leave the cottage but he did hear the Freelander's engine start. Watching the vehicle moving slowly up Church Lane towards the village green, he realised how lucky he was, he had expected to wait a lot longer.

Speed was now a necessity.

Before opening the back door he took off his waterproof and his trainers. They would get even wetter if he left them outside but he had no choice. Letting himself into the kitchen, he noticed the mugs on the table, the ashtray with three cigarette ends in it, and an open packet of biscuits by the kettle.

He moved across the kitchen into the hall before running up the stairs two at a time. Going straight into the main bedroom, he stopped just inside the doorway.

What could he take that would not be missed? He must not do anything that would suggest he or anyone else had been here. But he needed to take clothes to keep her warm.

And what could he put them in?

He hadn't thought this through properly.

They might be back any minute.

Sliding the mirrored door to one side he gasped when he saw just how many clothes he was faced with. There was an old brown bag stuffed into the bottom of the wardrobe, so he grabbed it, hoping it was empty. He thrust his hand inside.

Shoes.

After stuffing the shoes onto the racks under her dresses he selected a jumper from the top of the pile on the middle shelf. He chose a black pair of trousers that looked thick and warm and quickly moved the hangers to get rid of the gap he had created.

He was beginning to panic.

They could be back at any moment.

Opening the drawer he knew contained her underwear, he chose a bra and a pair of pants and flung them into the bag, wishing he had time to hold them.

What else?

Her things on the dressing table and from the bathroom would be missed.

Joggers – they would be better than trousers.

She must have some joggers somewhere, everybody does. They would be warm. She would need joggers and a top, a warm top. He couldn't see any in her bedroom so he quickly went into another bedroom and there to his delight, lying on an unmade bed, were some discarded clothes including a pair of joggers. He scooped up the joggers with what he thought was a warm top and put them in the bag.

Two minutes later he was out of the cottage.

Backtracking through the woods, he passed the church on his right as he went towards the road

Then he stopped.

He was being stupid.

Going that way he would have to pass the Warrington woman's cottage and Old Greg's. He didn't have a bag with him when Old Greg saw him before and if he saw him with one this time even Old Greg might start asking questions.

He was being very stupid.

People were right.

He turned round and took the path by the river back to where he had hidden the bedding.

The lamp on the table had gone out. There was now only a faint smell of burning.

The headache had eased. She moved her head slowly hoping the throbbing would not return. Swivelling onto one side she tried to swing her legs off the bed but it was too difficult so she tried a different tack. By edging across slowly she managed to get her face close enough to her left wrist so that she could get her teeth onto the cord.

The cord was soft. She stretched as far as she could until her right arm felt as though it was being pulled from its socket. The looser the knot became the more frantically she pulled and after a final mighty tug her left wrist was free.

With a smile of satisfaction she let her head drop back onto the pillow. She was ready now to free her right wrist. Sitting on the side of the bed, massaging her wrists and her feet, she looked around the room, surprised that she felt so alert though she was sure she was running a temperature. She lifted one hand to her forehead. Scabs were forming where she cracked her head and it was painful but not too bad.

She was bursting for the loo but her first priority was to escape.

The light was dim but good enough to make her way across to the entrance. Her first disappointment was that her boots and socks were not there. She went back for one of the lamps, but it merely confirmed her frustration. The smelly sleeping bag was there, a few leaves, stones and bits of paper but no boots and socks. Well, she would just have to walk in bare feet.

She looked up and screwing up her eyes she searched for the outline of the cover. Putting her hands onto the centre she exerted all her strength.

It was like pushing against a brick wall.

Going back into the den, she managed to drag the heavy log-come-stool to the entrance. She stood on it and fell off straightaway but once she had made it as level as possible she was able to put her shoulders against the cover, which she pushed as hard as she could until she was exhausted.

It was too much, too difficult.

After another concerted effort she finally gave up.

"Shit," she said, sitting down on the stool. "Fucking shit, shit. shit!"

The lamp on the floor just inside the den was fading. She looked at it without having the faintest idea how to keep it going. If the lamps went out she would have to give up, but at least this time he had left them burning for her. She picked up the lamp and turned a furled knob which merely made the dying flame more yellow. Tentatively she pulled the plunger out then slowly pushed it back in. She did this again, quickly this time and the flame brightened and turned blue.

Carrying the lamp to the spot where Michael had told her the toilet was, she squatted over the bucket, balancing herself by holding a root jutting out from the floor.

As she finished she heard what sounded like an animal scraping the cover over the entrance. She quickly hobbled away from the bucket, pulling up her pants and jeans as best she could. In the shaft of dim light over the entrance she saw a pair of legs emerge. Holding her breath she watched Michael's feet touch the stool. As he stumbled into the den she thought of making a dash for the entrance while the cover was off. It might be her only chance, but he was blocking the way.

Their eyes met, but without comment he moved the stool back to the table and pointed at the bed.

"Sit down," he said.

Deciding it might be better for the time being if she did as she was told, she went across to the bed and sat down. Michael turned his back and pulled some bags into the den from the entrance.

She immediately recognised the brown bag her mother had given her when she first went away to boarding school. It was one of those things you no longer used but could not, for sentimental reasons, throw away. She kept it for shoes she no longer wore.

"Where did you get that?" she asked, pointing at the bag.

He looked at her but said nothing. Picking up all the lamps he put them on the table and pumped them back to brightness.

She was still wearing her coat. Her hands were clasped on her lap. Her knees were together with her beautiful grubby bare feet touching the floor.

Why was she still here?

She had managed to free herself but she had not left although she would have been able to get out of the den on her own. Hiding her boots and socks just outside the entrance was the only obstacle he had put in her way. He had not wanted to do it but ... but now he didn't know why he had. He had made sure the knots round her wrists were loose so that she would not be frightened.

"Where did you get the bag?" she asked again.

He took a deep breath because he was determined not to stutter. "From your bedroom," he said.

Her eyes widened. "How did you get into my bedroom?"

He felt in his jacket pocket for the key and showed it to Sarah.

"Is that a key to my cottage?" she asked slowly.

He nodded.

"What are you doing with a key to my cottage?"

"I made it," he said.

She looked at the floor, unable to meet his eyes, shaking with the knowledge of what he had done. How did he get into the cottage without being seen? Where was Phillip?

He said he had made the key?

How had he made it?

Why had he made it?

That night when she and Phillip arrived home from the evening out with Elspeth and John, she had been convinced that somebody had been in the cottage.

Once more she felt her confidence ebbing away. "Have you been to my cottage before, Michael?" she said quietly.

He nodded, dropping the key back into his pocket.

"How often have you been into my cottage?"

He was not happy with the questions she was asking. It didn't matter how often he had been to her cottage. It was what he was doing now that mattered. Picking up the brown bag he took it over to her and dropped it at her feet before withdrawing towards the entrance. He watched her unzip the bag and put each item one by one on the bed.

How could a complete stranger walk into her cottage – her bedroom – and pack a bag as though she was going away for a weekend? Her favourite jumper, her joggers, the old sweatshirt she sometimes wore when she was decorating, a pair of pants, a bra and a screwed up vest?

How did he know where to find them? She looked up at him. His eyes were asking her to be pleased with his choices.

Afraid of how he would react she didn't know whether she ought to say what needed to be said. "Thank you, Michael. It was very kind of you to get me these things but … but I really ought to go home. My husband will be very worried."

"He already is."

"Sorry?"

"The police."

"What about the police?"

"They were there."

"Where?"

"At your cottage."

It was a simple exchange but it was the equivalent of crossing the Rubicon. In a flash she understood what the hell was going on. She had not just been stupid to follow Michael into his private sanctuary – she had been downright imbecilic. Maybe, just maybe, during the first hour or so she might have been able to persuade him to let her go but now it was not just she who was trapped. He was also trapped – trapped by his own actions.

She didn't believe he meant her any harm.

He was simply obsessed with her.

If her situation was not so serious she would have laughed.

On the day she went shopping with Elspeth and after the incident by the garage, Elspeth had related a story about somebody in the village who had been dubbed the *Phantom Menace*. She had decided not to mention it to Phillip because he would think she was being silly, especially after she was sure somebody had been in their cottage while they were out.

She was now looking at this somebody and he looked no more like a *Phantom Menace* than the village vicar. He was a young, handsome half-wit who was infatuated with her. As a result of her own actions she had walked into the tangled maze of his life, like a fly into a spider's web. If Elspeth had not chosen the cocktail party to open her heart she wouldn't be where she was now. She was not blaming Elspeth. Elspeth didn't tell her to get up before dawn and walk up to Copper's Ridge. Elspeth didn't tell her to follow Michael into the wood and Elspeth didn't tell her to climb into a hole in the ground.

Phillip must have called the police. What else did she expect him to do? He must be out of his mind with worry.

Calling the police probably removed the last chance she could possibly have had at talking her way out of what she had actually managed to talk her way into. Michael had seen the police. He was scared.

He was also trapped.

Nobody would believe him. Nobody would understand *his* version of what happened but they *would* believe her. The truth could become her means of escape.

"You saw the police at my cottage?"

"Yes."

"My husband will be very worried."

She was so close, tantalizingly close. She must not go, not yet.

It would never happen again. He had been willing to kill to get her to where she was now: the fact that his willingness didn't match his ability was neither here nor there – he had planned to kill, to murder.

For her.

But *she* came up to Copper's Ridge looking for *him*.

Why else would she have been here?

"The police," he said.

The police were now involved and they were there because of him.

"I'll tell them the truth," she said, leaning forward. "There's nothing for you to worry about. You have done nothing wrong. I'll tell them I was lost, that you helped me, that you looked after me. There's nothing to be scared of because I'll tell the police the truth."

He shook his head and took a deep breath. "I want you to stay for just a little longer."

"I know you do, Michael, and under different circumstances I would love to stay. But because of other things, things you know nothing about, I must go home. I –"

No, she had to stay a little longer and there was only one way of keeping her here.

"Take your coat off," he said.

"Michael, I –"

"Take your coat off." Anger was building up inside him but he didn't know why. He had never felt it before, not like this, so he didn't know how to control it.

"Why, I –"

He took another deep breath. "I said take your coat off. If you can't take it off I'll come over there and take it off for you."

261

His mind was in a whirl. What was he saying?

The words he heard were not his words – they were words his father had used. He was always saying things like, "take that smile off your face, if you don't I'll take it off for you."

She had such a pretty face, such lovely eyes.

"Take it off."

Stunned and confused, Sarah wondered why he had suddenly changed. She had been sure she could persuade him that he wouldn't be in any trouble.

"You don't mean that, Michael do you? It's cold in here and my coat –"

"Take it off."

If she took any of her clothes off it would not stop there.

"No, Michael, I'm not going to take my coat off. You're going to get me my socks and boots, I'm going to put them on and then I am going with you back to the village."

It felt as though his head was going to burst.

She was supposed to do what he said. He had always done what his father told him to do. He only needed to feel the belt cutting into his flesh a few times before he realised that by doing what he was told there would be less pain.

Why wasn't she doing what he told her?

It was for her own good. He wanted her to stay a little longer. But if he asked her properly now, she wouldn't do it.

He didn't want to hurt her, but if she didn't do as he asked he might have to.

No, he couldn't. He would never hurt her.

"Take your coat off." He reached beneath his jacket for the buckle on his belt.

Sarah followed his movement. It could only mean one thing. Her skin began to creep and once more bile burned the back of her throat.

What had happened? She had been so sure.

Slowly she moved her fingers to the zip on her Barbour, her eyes not leaving his as she lowered the zip. She shrugged the coat from her shoulders, letting it fall on the bed behind her. Was it better to do as she was told or risk ... risk what? If it was inevitable then just maybe it was better to –

"Michael, nothing has happened yet and the police will be told the truth. Please don't make things worse for yourself."

"Take your jeans off."

"Michael –"

"Your jeans."

"Michael, please –"

"Your jeans." His voice had become metallic, adding to the chill that was already in the air.

She undid the button on the top of her jeans, then the zip. "Michael –"

"Off."

She stood up and lowered her jeans to her ankles. The cold attacked her legs but it was nothing compared with the icy horror that was engulfing her entire body.

Stepping out of her jeans she waited.

His staring eyes left hers and travelled down her legs to her feet and back up again. The top she was wearing was quite long and it fell half way down her thighs.

The anger left him.

It was replaced by a throbbing sensation. It was the same stirring that happened every time he went to bed and let his mind wander. Every time he thought about Sarah Preston. The throbbing became more intense and more uncomfortable.

She was looking at his face.

"Why are you making me do this?" Her voice was almost a whisper.

"Your top, take it off."

"Michael please, I –"

"Off."

263

She crossed her arms and lifted the top over her head.

He was shaking, he wanted her, he needed her but ... but he could not do it. He wanted to touch her, he wanted her to touch him ... but he must not do it. Since his experience in the churchyard with Sharon and Wendy he had not touched and he had not been touched.

She was beautiful, so beautiful, but he could not do it.

She watched his eyes consume her body.

Standing in front of her, his hands at his side, he looked so pathetic and yet so innocent, but it was his innocence that made him so dangerous.

It was going to happen.

Should she fight him or should she just let him rape her? Maybe if she didn't fight him he would let her go. But she was not thinking straight. Even now, she would be willing to tell the police he had done her no harm. Making her undress so he could look at her was part of his innocence. If he was going to rape her he would already have done it.

"Put the joggers on."

"Michael ... I –"

"Put the joggers on and the jumper."

"What?"

He moved to the bed and picked up the joggers and held them out to her. "These. Put them on."

Relief gushed over her and she did as he ordered. She pulled the joggers up to her waist and put on the jumper. When she was dressed, she sat on the bed.

She looked up at him. "Michael ..." – but she couldn't think what she should say.

He picked up the black plastic bag and emptied it on the bed. She stared at the duvet, sheets and pillows. The mattress she was sitting on was cold and damp but clean, unlike that stinking sleeping bag. The bed linen was clean too. Why had he brought bed linen? Kidnappers and rapists don't ...

But he was neither.

She had not been kidnapped and he had not raped her.

264

Picking up the other clothes he put them back in the brown bag. "Sit over there," he said, pointing at the stool.

Doing as she was told she watched in further amazement as he proceeded to make the bed. He worked slowly but methodically, folding the sheet under the mattress, shaking the two pillows into the cases and placing them carefully at the head of the bed. He stretched the duvet out on top, smoothing down the cover until he was satisfied it was wrinkle-free.

Looking at the bed she realised it could only mean one thing; she was not going to be allowed to leave until the following day ... if at all.

After moving round the den pumping the lamps and checking the small paraffin heater, he selected a couple of tins from the shelves. She sat watching him, her eyes wide as she followed his every movement. She wanted to speak but she was afraid that if she did she might say something wrong again. He was unpredictable but at the moment she believed she was once again reasonably safe ... for the time being.

He turned round from the shelf, holding the tins in his hand. "Curry," he said.

"We're going to eat curry?"

He nodded as he pointed at the bed and said, "Sit there."

She sat on the bed with her back against the earthen wall. Her feet were frozen so she pulled the duvet over them. The situation was not just bizarre, it was like a dream, a nightmare, but not one from which she was going to wake up. Her own thoughts were becoming bizarre too: she was concerned that the mud stains on her feet would get onto the sheets. She was imprisoned in a hole in the ground, her captor was opening a tin of curry, and she was worried about getting the sheets dirty? She had gone from being terrified only a few minutes earlier to being ridiculously calm. The moment he told her to put on her joggers she knew he really didn't mean her any harm.

He emptied the contents of the tins into a metal pot, which he put on the camping stove. He filled the mugs with water and passed one to her. She had not realised how thirsty she was. After a couple of minutes he ladled the curry into two bowls and handed one to her, without once making eye contact. After turning off the stove he sat on the stool and started eating.

She kept her eyes on him. The food was just warm, not properly heated through, but it didn't matter. As well as being thirsty she was also very hungry, not having eaten properly for over twenty-four hours.

They ate in silence and quickly.

She watched him and he watched her. They were like a couple of wild animals at a watering hole: nourishment was the priority, neither really trusting the other.

As she put the last morsel she could scrape from the bowl into her mouth, she managed a brief smile.

"Thank you," she said as she held the bowl out so that he could take it from her. He put the bowls on the table and resumed his seat.

He sipped his water.

Taking a deep breath she closed her eyes.

"I think we should talk, Michael, don't you?"

The food although not hot, had warmed her. She pulled the duvet up to her knees.

"This is a very unusual situation for us both. I've never been anywhere like this before and I'm assuming that I'm your first visitor."

She was choosing her words carefully, aware that the slightest error could undo the progress of the last hour.

"I think you've been very clever building somewhere like this and I can understand why you needed it," she said, trying to get something out of him, some sort of commitment that would hopefully lead to her release. "By letting me see it, you've shown your trust in me. It means you trust me not to tell anyone about it."

Thinking he was going to speak she hesitated but when he just looked at her, she carried on.

"I promise you, Michael, no-one will know about your den from me. Nobody will know about you from me. Nobody will know we've been together. It'll be our secret. I'll tell my husband and the police that I stayed the night in a pub somewhere and I will refuse to tell them where it was, so they won't be able to check."

While eating she had come to accept that there was no way she was going to leave his den tonight, but she was sure that if she handled the situation correctly she *would* be leaving it in the morning.

"I'd be lying if I said you hadn't scared me," she went on. "I was scared earlier but not anymore. I think you are a very kind and considerate man. You have looked after me very well, and the fact that you went and got me some clothes and this bedding is proof of just how considerate you are."

His face remained expressionless.

"And medicine," he said.

"Medicine?" she repeated.

"Your forehead, the cream and the wipes."

She lifted her hand to her head and for the first time she realised what he had done. "You did this?" she said. It was a stupid question. Who else could have done it?

"Yes."

"Michael, you are even kinder than I thought. You are a wonderful young man."

"Thank you," he said. "I have some aspirins too."

She smiled. "May I have a couple?"

He reached into his pocket and gave her the sleeve of pills. She popped two out and swallowed them with some water.

"My head is a lot better, thanks to you but I still have a slight headache, so that was very thoughtful of you."

"I hope they work," he said.

"I'm sure they will." She paused. "In the morning I'll walk back to Upper Slaughter, back to Primrose Cottage and explain that I had needed to be on my own to think. I'll tell them that I walked for miles and miles, and by the time I stopped walking it was too late to start for home. I'll apologise for making everybody so worried and I suppose I'll also have to say I'm sorry for wasting the police's time."

She smiled. It was a completely inadequate explanation and she would have to think further, but she hoped for now that Michael would accept what she was saying.

"Where I really was and who I was with will be our secret. I promise you Michael, it will be our secret."

Michael listened to everything Sarah Preston said.

He believed that she meant every word. He believed he could trust her. If she said it would be their secret then that was the way it would be.

Sharing a secret with somebody else was new to him and he liked it. If he needed to choose anybody to share a secret with, it would be with her. Nobody else knew his den existed. She was the only one and she would always be the only one.

"Tomorrow," Michael said.

"What about tomorrow, Michael?"

"You will go home tomorrow."

A wave of relief started in her toes, the tips of her fingers, and swiftly enveloped her. Her whole body tingled with excitement.

She was going to be free. It was almost over. She was going home tomorrow, going home to the security of her own kitchen, her own bathroom, her own bedroom. She would be back with Phillip.

The memory of the strangest and yet most horrifying twelve hours of her life began to recede straight away. She was already sitting at her kitchen table sipping a cup of hot tea with lots of sugar.

In another twelve hours it would all be over.

"Thank you, Michael, thank you," she said.

She was safe.

Sergeant Laura Craig looked around the Preston's kitchen. She hated being out this late on a Sunday evening and hoped she'd be able to get away soon.

She had made up her mind straightaway about the type of people she was dealing with.

"As was explained to you earlier on the phone, Mr Preston, your wife has only been gone for thirteen hours so –"

"I'm well aware of how long she's been gone, Sergeant, but –"

"Sir, I fully appreciate just how worried you must be, but from my experience people who are thought to be missing turn up within forty-eight hours. May I sit down?"

"Yes, of course. Would you like coffee or a cup of tea?"

"No, thank you."

"PC Martin, who came earlier, told me about this forty-eight hour business but I've checked everywhere with no results. I know my wife, Sergeant. She wouldn't be away this long without letting me know where she is."

"That might be ..."

Sergeant Craig stopped talking as Elspeth walked into the kitchen.

Phillip saw the confusion on Elspeth's face.

"Sorry, Sergeant, this is Elspeth Warrington – a very good friend of ours and a particularly good friend of Sarah's. She was up in the bathroom when you arrived."

Sergeant Craig stood up and held out her hand. ""Miss Warrington. Sergeant Craig, Madam."

"Sergeant." Elspeth took her hand and shook it gently. "Do you mind if I have a quick word in private with Mr Preston?"

Sergeant Craig looked a little surprised. "Of course not," she said, standing up to leave. "I'll wait in –"

"There's no need. You wait here. Phillip, will you come with me please?"

269

Elspeth took Phillip's hand and led him out of the kitchen and up the stairs.

"Elspeth? What –?"

"Wait, Phillip, please."

The light was already on in the main bedroom. He followed her in.

"When you and John went looking for Sarah I came up here to see if there was anything you may have missed, you know what I mean." She stood in front of the wardrobe. "Have you been in here since then?"

He looked at the exposed shelving. "No," he said.

"At least one of her jumpers has gone."

"What?"

"When I was in here before, Sarah's favourite jumper was on top of this pile. You know the long one, wool, high collar, russet coloured?"

"It may have –"

"It's not in the wardrobe, Phillip, I've checked. And," she said, brushing past him, "this drawer was slightly open and I hope you don't mind but I looked inside."

"Of course I don't mind, but ..."

Elspeth opened the drawer. "It's where Sarah keeps her undies and I can tell you that some items are missing."

He frowned. "How on earth do you know that?"

"Because I'm a woman. And look at these gaps. Here and here. Open any woman's undies drawer and I can almost guarantee you won't find gaps."

"Are you saying she's been back? While I was with you and John, she's been back?"

"It certainly looks like that."

He thought for a moment, then went to the top of the stairs.

"Sergeant Craig," he shouted, "will you come up here for a minute?"

In no time Sergeant Craig appeared at the top of the stairs.

270

"Will you come into the bedroom, please? We think Sarah has been here – and recently."

"Why?"

"Some of her clothes are missing and they were here only a couple of hours ago," Elspeth said.

"What's missing?"

"At least one jumper and some underwear."

"You're sure?"

Phillip looked at Elspeth.

"Yes, we are."

"Anything else?" Sergeant Craig asked.

"I haven't really checked," Phillip said.

"Would you mind doing so now, sir?"

Phillip went over to the wardrobe and sorted through the hangers.

"I don't know," he said over his shoulder, "there aren't any empty hangers but I don't know what's in the wash or the cleaners. There could be other things missing."

Sergeant Craig looked down at the rack of shoes.

"What about her shoes?"

Phillip quickly scanned the rack. "No, nothing ... wait a minute. There was a brown bag here. Sarah uses it for shoes she's considering throwing out." He picked up a shoe. "The shoes are here but the bag is missing."

Elspeth had moved over to Sarah's dressing table. "What about her creams and things?"

Phillip joined her. "I wouldn't know but there doesn't seem to be anything missing."

"Would you mind checking the bathroom, sir," Sergeant Craig said, "to see if her toothbrush is still there?" I know it sounds a bit silly, sir, but would you mind?"

"It's still there, and her toothpaste, deodorant and her other bits and pieces," Phillip said, coming out of the en-suite shower-room.

He glanced at Elspeth who was standing in front of one of the spare bedrooms, the door was open and the light was shining on the bed.

271

"Her joggers," he said as he went into the room followed by Sergeant Craig and Elspeth. "On the bed. She always puts her joggers on the bed, you know, her work-out clothes. They're all missing."

"I'll go down and put the kettle on again, Phillip. We can talk downstairs."

Having accepted the second offer of a coffee Sergeant Craig was sitting with Phillip at the table. She looked at Elspeth's back.

"It's me who must ask to speak to you in private this time, Mr Preston."

"No, Sergeant, Miss Warrington is a good friend. Anything you want to say can be said in front of her. And I think I know what you are going to say."

"Will you talk to me, Michael?"

He looked down at his hands.

Being asked to talk was his worst nightmare. He could never find the words. They were in his head but he could never say them. He understood what people said to him but when he had to speak, the words would not move from his mind to his mouth. If he could talk properly with people things would be so different. But it was Sarah who was asking him to talk. Being asked by Sarah Preston was different. She had not made fun of him when he couldn't find the words, when he made a mistake, when he stuttered.

She would understand.

"What about?" he said.

"You and me," she added. "If you want to."

"I'll try," he said, still inspecting his hands.

"Look at me, Michael. Please look at me."

He slowly lifted his head.

She smiled. "That's better. First, do you have any coffee left?"

He nodded.

"May I have some, please?"

While he was making the coffee she pulled the duvet further up her body and for the first time in hours she was warm. Warm and more secure than since she left Primrose Cottage that morning. She was no longer scared. She realised now that she had generated her own fear. Michael had not done anything, not intentionally, to make her feel scared.

Once the coffee was made, Michael sat on the stool, a steaming mug in his hands.

"What's your second name?" Sarah said.

"Griffiths."

"Michael Griffiths, I like that. And you live in Upper Slaughter?" When he looked up, frowning, she added quickly: "You can trust me, Michael. What I said earlier was the truth. This is all our secret."

He seemed satisfied. "Yes."

"Where do you live?"

"Down by the river."

"Which end? The ford end or the other end?"

The frown returned so Sarah thought it might be better to ask closed questions. "The other end?"

"Yes."

"By the road to Lower Swell?"

"Yes ... yes, but ..."

"I know where you mean, on the road that runs parallel ... that runs alongside –"

"I know what parallel means."

"Of course you do, I'm sorry." She sipped her coffee. It was very bitter but nonetheless welcome. "Do you live on your own?" Damn she thought, and started to ask, "Do you live with your –"

"I live with my mother."

"And father?"

"No, he ... he left a long time ago."

"So just your mother?"

"Sometimes her boyfriend is there."

273

She detected in the tone of his voice that it might be better not to ask any more questions about his father. "And do you work?"

"Yes, in Evesham."

"What do you do?"

"Mr Preston, I'm sorry to have to ask you this, but is there any possibility that your wife could be having an affair?" Sergeant Craig paused but only for a second. Phillip held his breath. "I'm sorry, Mr Preston, but your answer could determine which way our enquiries go, if indeed there remains a need to conduct any enquiries."

The question stunned Phillip. Not just the question but the possibility.

The likelihood that Sarah would even contemplate let alone actually have an affair had never entered his head. It was too incredible to even consider as an explanation. But from an outsider's perspective it would seem to be a possibility, even a probability.

Only one doubt existed, the only negative aspect to their relationship, but surely her inability to conceive would not even suggest that she might be having an affair. After all, it was not him that –

No, it was wrong to think like that. Apportioning blame under the circumstances and before the truth was known, was wrong.

Glancing at Elspeth, Phillip shook his head. "That isn't a possibility. There's no way my wife is having an affair. I would have known before now."

"Can you provide another explanation of why she would come back for her clothes, sir?"

Elspeth reached for her cigarettes. Phillip disapproved of her smoking in his house but Sarah always turned a blind eye. God, she thought, why can't John hurry up on that phone. And why did his mother have to ring this evening. It had been over half an hour so what could they be talking about?

274

Probably her. It didn't take much for John's mother to start on about her dislike for her son's partner. Perhaps dislike was not strictly fair. Disapproval was a better word. In John's mother's opinion no respectable woman lived and slept with a man unless they were married. If John's mother knew the truth she would not only disapprove of Elspeth, she would have an apoplexy.

Elspeth saw Sergeant Craig watching her as she puffed on the cigarette.

"Do you mind if I have a cigarette?" the sergeant said, looking at both Phillip and Elspeth. "I know it's not ..."

Elspeth pushed the packet towards her.

"Feel free," Philip said, "one more won't make any difference."

He stood up and went to the cupboard. He needed a drink.

"This is ridiculous," he said, reaching for the whisky bottle. "There's no way my wife is having an affair and it's you who should be giving me an explanation, not the reverse."

"I'm sorry, sir, but I can't think –"

"Of another reason she would come back for her clothes? Is that what you were going to say?" He used the glass to point at her. "Is that a female talking or an experienced police sergeant?"

"Phillip, I don't think –"

"Oh come on, Elspeth, you would know if Sarah were having an affair wouldn't you? After all, sometimes I think she's closer to you than she is to me." He paused. "So is she? Is Sarah having an affair?"

"Not that I'm aware of," Elspeth replied without a hint of hesitation. "But you're right, I think I would know. Can I have one of those?"

Phillip poured a generous tot of whisky into a fresh glass.

275

"The lemonade's in the fridge. What about you, Sergeant?" he asked, the whisky bottle still in his hand.

"No thank you, sir." Sergeant Craig stubbed out the half-smoked cigarette, trying to think of what she could say without antagonising the situation further.

It was the most obvious explanation and she was not willing, not yet, to commit half the station to an investigation that looked like it might yet be another domestic problem. It might be serious, but if Sarah Preston was having an affair, it was none of her business.

"I understand why the suggestion is unacceptable, sir, but in view of what we've discovered, I do think we ought to leave things until the morning."

What she did not say was that there was a distinct likelihood that Sarah would ring either later that evening or in the morning. From what she had also gleaned by looking around, she seemed to be a very reasonable, tidy and caring woman, who, if she were having an affair, would not want her husband to worry more than was necessary, regardless of what the longer term outcome might be. But if she was having an affair why hadn't she taken her clothes with her in the first place? Why had she come back for them? Her toothbrush and cosmetics could be replicated wherever she was, but ...

"The *morning*?" Phillip said. "I see. My wife could be out there having been attacked and raped by some pervert and all you can say is that we ought to leave it until the morning. Is that what the police are for? To act as bloody welfare officers? My wife could be lying in a ditch somewhere, dead or not far from it. If she isn't already dead, further inaction would ensure she dies of hypothermia."

"I don't think, sir –"

"All right," he said holding up his hands, "if that's the way you operate then there's sod all I can do about it. But I have a witness to the fact that based on –"

He stopped and closed his eyes as the sheer horror of what could be the truth hit him. She had gone. He didn't want to hear the truth but the facts spoke for themselves.

Sarah had left him. She had left him for another man. She was not lying in a ditch; she had not been raped or murdered because she was out there somewhere in the arms of another man and she was there of her own free will.

Facts were facts.

"Please leave," he said quietly, "please leave now."

"I'll see you out," he heard Elspeth say to Sergeant Craig.

When he sensed he was alone he opened his eyes and refilled his glass. There was no other explanation: she had gone and he had been so blind, so tied up in his own little world he had not sensed things had reached such a pitch.

As the front door closed he swallowed the whisky, then reached again for the bottle.

Sergeant Craig stopped just beyond the door to put on her hat.

"Tell me, Sergeant," Elspeth said. "Do you honestly believe that Mrs Preston has run off with another man?"

The sergeant turned slowly to face Elspeth. "I don't know what to think just yet," she replied, examining Elspeth's face in a most disconcerting way. "It does seem to be the only logical explanation. But there are certain inconsistencies —"

"But why would she come back for her clothes? If what you suggest is true, surely she would have taken what she wanted with her in the first place?"

Sergeant Craig inclined her head. "Exactly, so we'll see what the morning brings, Miss Warrington."

She stopped as John appeared at the gate.

"Sorry about that, Elspeth," John said, "Mum was in one of her moods." He looked at Sergeant Craig and held out his hand, "I'm John Davidson, has anything happened?"

"I'm sorry, sir, who —"

277

"He's my partner, Sergeant. We live together."

"Oh, I see. Well, sir, I'll leave Miss Warrington to bring you up to speed. I'll be here about nine in the morning. Please tell Mr Preston."

Sergeant Craig looked from John to Elspeth and then went briskly through the gate to the police car.

"So what's happened?" John asked, following Elspeth back into the cottage.

Chapter Sixteen

Trying to keep the conversation centred on Michael rather than on herself was not easy.

And she was tired.

She would rather be sleeping than talking. Her nervous energy had been sapped and she was mentally and physically shattered. Thinking of the right questions to ask Michael had taken a lot out of her as well, and although she still didn't feel threatened, his monosyllabic answers made any form of conversation very difficult. But there had been progress and she knew more than before. She still couldn't come to terms with where she was and what she was doing here.

What was going on back at Primrose Cottage was causing her increasing concern. Michael said he saw the police car parked outside. She needed to think through what she was going to say when she got back because what she told Michael she was going to say was too simplistic. She would be tripped up too easily.

The promises she had made to Michael she would keep: he didn't deserve to be pilloried by either the police or the villagers, or even Phillip. He was a simple soul who led a simple life. It was not his fault that she had blustered into the world in which he felt most secure. He had handled the situation the best way he could. In fact, Sarah thought, he had shown a lot more consideration towards her than many of her male associates who called themselves gentlemen.

Previously, looking beyond the next few hours had not been an option, but it was important now to make sure she had a feasible story to tell Phillip – and possibly the police –

about what had happened. She hoped it was not going to be as difficult as she first thought.

The only real problem would be coming up with a rational reason for going walking so early. What happened since she left Primrose Cottage would be easy by comparison. The real reason for the need for solitude would never be divulged, although she assumed Elspeth will have guessed.

She had left the cottage before six that morning. Walking at two miles an hour with the odd break she would have been twenty miles away by the time she booked into a pub or hotel. The area was rural in places but walking twenty miles without being seen would have tested anyone.

She shook her head.

No, that would be a silly explanation. It would soon be discovered that she hadn't been anywhere near the place.

Damn. It was going to be more difficult than she first thought. There would be question after question and she was not a good liar.

The feasibility of what she was planning was weak.

She would wait: she had all night to think of the explanations she needed. She might not be a good liar, but she had an imagination.

"What time is it, Michael? My watch seems to have stopped."

"About eleven," he said.

"I'm feeling very tired, would it be all right if I went to sleep."

He nodded but the disappointment showed on his face.

"We'll have time to talk some more before I leave in the morning," she said, smiling. "I must go to the loo again before ..."

Michael carried one of the lamps across to the recess where the bucket was, and sat down again with his back to her.

He was offering her a modicum of privacy.

"Thank you, Michael, that was very considerate of you."

"Where the fuck is she?" Phillip said, slurring his words. "That policewoman was talking a load of fucking crap. D'you know, John, she said Sarah had gone off with some other fucking bloke?"

"Yes, Phillip, I know. Elspeth told me."

Elspeth looked across the kitchen table at Phillip, wildly waving his empty whisky glass while she and John nursed their mugs of black coffee. Allowing Phillip to drink himself into an uncharacteristic stupor was a deliberate ploy.

Elspeth wished that she was in a position to do the same thing.

"Fucking rubbish. If she was having a … a fucking affair, I would have known. You would have known. You can fucking tell, can't you, when somebody's cheating on you. No way is she cheating on me and no way would she ever fucking cheat on me."

Elspeth and John exchanged looks, both raising their eyebrows though Elspeth knew it was for different reasons. She had been sure Sarah would return before it got dark. Her insides were churning over with worry and how she stopped herself from crying in front of Phillip she didn't know. With each second her guilt grew and grew. She would do anything to go back and change everything.

It was all her fault.

She was a bloody idiot. If she had kept her feelings to herself none of this would have happened.

She knew only too well that no matter how strongly one feels about another human being, in certain circumstances those feelings can never be expressed.

It had all gone wrong. Not only had she expected Sarah to cope with her admission, she had expected her to reciprocate her feelings.

And look what was happening as a result of her stupidity.

Regardless of her need for thinking and her need for sleep, Sarah and Michael continued to talk, albeit their conversation was one-sided.

During a pause Michael suddenly asked a question: "How is your head?"

It came to Sarah in a flash of inspiration but as she thought about it, it was more a case of the blindingly obvious and, surprisingly, it was Michael's simple question that put the idea there in the first place.

She was aware when she furrowed her brow that the bruising was still there but other than that the pain was now only slight.

"Fine, thank you."

She automatically lifted her finger to the bruising and that was when the idea came to her.

There was no need to concoct stories that might generate questions that could prove difficult to answer. Why didn't she stick to the truth ... well, some of the truth? When she hit her head she had knocked herself out, hadn't she? So why couldn't her period of unconsciousness have been longer and why couldn't it have caused temporary amnesia? If you don't remember anything it makes it a lot easier when you don't know the answers to probing questions. It was the most logical explanation for everything and there were the cuts and bruises as proof. She smiled to herself, so pleased that she had at last found the solution in spite of it having stared at her in the face in more ways than one.

"Thank you," she said again, "you've just solved a problem."

Michael looked confused but she decided not to elaborate. "You were telling me about the work you do. You must be very clever. Did you make all the furniture in here?"

He nodded.

"It's very good and this bed is very comfortable." She thought for a moment. "Are you going to give me the key you made for my cottage?"

His head drooped.

282

"It would be better if you did, Michael, and then nobody would be able to link you to anything, would they?"

"All right," he said reluctantly.

"Thank you. You can give it to me in the morning."

"All right," he said again.

"How many houses have you been into?"

He shrugged. "I've lost count, fifteen or twenty, maybe more."

"Why did you feel the need to go into these houses?"

Michael slumped down on the stool.

Sarah Preston was asking too many questions.

He didn't mind the questions, not about his work and things, but she was asking about his private world. Although she was the only person ever to be with him in his private world, he didn't want to say anymore. He was in his den and she would stay with him until the morning, it was as simple as that.

What he did was only for him.

Going into other people's houses told him ... told him how other people lived. That was why he had gone into her cottage, well that and because he was in love with her. He was not in love with any of the others. If she knew more about him then she would have more to hide, she would have more for him to trust her with.

He did trust her but ...

"To see," he said.

"To see what, Michael?"

"To see what people are really like. To see their secrets."

"You think what we see of people outside their houses is different?"

"Yes."

"Did you see anything in my cottage that made me different?"

"No."

"There was nothing that made me different?"

"No."

283

"Where did you go in my cottage, Michael? You knew today where to find my clothes and my underwear. Is that where you looked before?"

"Yes."

"You were in my bedroom?"

He nodded.

"Do you think now that it was wrong to go into my cottage and my bedroom?"

After a couple of seconds, he nodded again.

"You looked in my bedroom. Where else did you go?"

Lifting his head, he said: "Nowhere. I only went to your room."

"But it's not only my room, Michael, because it's my husband's as well."

"I know."

"Did you take anything?"

His eyes flashed to the small box on the shelf.

Should he tell her?

"No. I never take anything. I just look." He hoped she would not see his blush of embarrassment.

Then he changed his mind. They trusted each other so lying to her was wrong.

He got up slowly and taking the box from the shelf, he handed it to her. She looked at it and then at him before taking the top off. She pulled out the pair of red pants.

"You took these from my bedroom?"

"Yes," he said, "I'm sorry."

"This is all you took?"

"Yes."

"Why did you take them?"

"I wanted something of yours so I could ..."

"Could what, Michael?"

"I just wanted ... wanted to have ... to have something of yours to hold," he said as tears filled his eyes.

"I understand," she said, "but thank you for giving them back to me." She paused. "So in all the other houses you just go to look?"

284

"Yes, and touch."

"And you touched all my clothes?"

"Yes."

"What else do you do?"

"Watch people."

"What? Around the village?"

"Everywhere."

"Do you like the people you watch?"

"Sometimes I do."

"Who do you like to watch the most?"

"Anybody."

"But do you prefer to watch men or women?"

"Anybody. I watch everybody."

As he was answering her questions, a gush of relief washed over him. It was as though he was cleansing his soul to the only person he trusted enough to listen to him.

"So, you just watch them going about their everyday lives, you don't intrude ... I mean you don't watch them in their private lives?"

"Sometimes."

"Have you ever watched me? No, I didn't mean to ask ..."

"Yes, I have watched you a lot of times."

"Where was I?"

"I've watched you in the village, out walking but also at your window. I tried to tell you before but ..."

"You saw me at the bedroom window?"

"Yes."

"Why were you watching me?"

"To see you. I wanted to see you."

"How often have you watched me at the window?"

"A lot of times, I wanted to see you ... you know, without any clothes on."

"And did you?" she asked.

"Yes, once at the window. You looked beautiful."

"Thank you, Michael, but you understand what you did was wrong?"

"Yes, I do now. But ... but not because I saw you, because I didn't ask you if I could."

"What do you mean?"

"I think you are beautiful ... all of you is beautiful ... not just your face."

"That's a very kind thing to say, but ..."

"I'm sorry I looked at you without asking," he said quietly.

"That's all right, but now we are friends, will you need to watch me in the future?"

He could not give her an answer because he didn't know. She would be leaving in the morning and he didn't know if he would be able to stop what he loved doing most.

"Michael, it's important. I've told you that you can trust me. Nobody will ever know about us being together, but in return I must be able to trust you. Do you understand?"

If she asked him not to do something and he said he would do as she asked and then he broke that promise, he would also break that trust.

"Do you trust me, Michael?"

He nodded because he wanted her to trust him but ...

"Do you want me to trust you?"

"Yes."

"Then I do. From this moment forward I trust you, Michael."

He looked up.

A tear rolled down his cheek.

A promise was a promise..

"We're going to have to tell him," John said as he walked back into the kitchen with Elspeth.

Phillip had eventually collapsed face down on the table. With Elspeth's help, John had manhandled him upstairs and put him to bed.

Elspeth lit a cigarette. "I don't see the point," she said, pacing the kitchen from one end to the other and puffing nervously on her cigarette.

286

"The point is that if this comes out later he'll wonder why the bloody hell we kept it to ourselves. He won't only wonder he'll be bloody furious. He thinks Sarah is having an affair for Christ's sake and she's not. Well," he said, pausing slightly, "not in the strictest sense."

"I still think it's the sort of thing we should keep to ourselves." Elspeth swung away from him. "Nothing has happened."

"Hasn't it? So why is Sarah missing?"

"What good would it do now?"

"It might –"

"Might what?" She stubbed out her cigarette and stood facing John. "Sarah's missing and although it's probably all my fault, what happened between us might have caused her to go but it doesn't explain why she's still out there somewhere. And it doesn't explain why she came back for some clothes."

"I still think Phillip has the right to know."

"So, that's it? We tell all and suffer the consequences, the fall out?"

"Yes. I think that's the only way forward." John saw Elspeth's reaction and thought it best to move on. "Who's going to stay with him tonight? We can't leave him alone, not in that state."

"I will," she said. "You've got work in the morning."

"I would take the day off but I've got a couple of important meetings in preparation for a difficult case."

"I'm sure you have. I'll stay with him."

"I really am very tired now, Michael. I'm going to lie down and try to get some sleep. Is that okay?"

"Yes."

"In the morning it might be better if I make my own way back to the village."

He watched her move down the bed and so that she could rest her head on the pillow. It was so natural ... so normal.

"What about you? Where will you sleep?" she asked.

Sleep would mean she was not with him. She would be wherever her dreams took her, but he would still be able to watch her as she slept. He could move closer and watch her breathing as she slept. Except when he was cleaning her forehead and face he had still not touched her.

He wanted to touch her.

Seeing her at the bedroom window and just now, before he told her to put on the joggers, the urge had been so strong. He saw her pale smooth skin that he so badly wanted to touch. He saw her lovely slim legs, her flat tummy, her navel and the tops of her breasts. He wished she had taken off her underwear but now it was too late. They trusted each other and people who trust each other do not do anything to upset that trust.

Who would he talk to in the future?

There was no-one.

She talked to him: nobody had ever talked to him like that before. The words he wanted to use did not come readily to him, but she had helped him. He hadn't stuttered ... well, not a lot. She had been interested in what he said. Nobody had ever been interested in him before. She asked him what he did and she said how clever he was.

When she started asking questions about him going into other people's houses he didn't want to tell her but then he changed his mind. He did want to tell her, he did want her to know what he did in his private world. If he could not share with her the way he was, then who was there to share it with? Now he had somebody to tell his secrets to.

Yes, Sarah Preston was exactly as he thought she would be.

He looked at her pretty face and sighed.

Should he ask her if he could have the red pants back? He only wanted them so that part of her would always be with him. Would she understand his need? He was pleased he had owned up to taking them. She hadn't scolded him. She understood why he took them.

Her eyelids were drooping.

She was falling asleep and she was leaving him.

Soon her mind would not be with him but she would still be here.

She was so beautiful.

Her lovely head on the pillow, her hair framing her gorgeous face, her eyes closing with her lips parted. How he would like to touch her face, let his fingers brush over her skin, stroke her lips, her hair and put his lips on hers.

She was breathing steadily now, sleep had taken her but she trusted him.

"Goodnight, Sarah Preston. Sleep tight, Sarah Preston. When you dream, dream of me, Sarah Preston." He whispered the words. "If you dream of me I will be with you."

He allowed the gathering tears to roll down his cheeks. She was asleep now so she would not see him crying.

How could he let her go in the morning?

After she left she would be gone forever. She would go back to that man, she would live with that man, eat with that man and sleep with that man.

If he let her go, would she ever think of him?

Would she ever want to see him again?

When she saw him in the village would she cross to the other side of the street so she didn't have to look at him or speak to him?

She was asleep.

Slowly he stood up and going to the lamps he pumped each one as quietly as he could. He sat down again and watched her sleep. Staying awake all night would mean he could watch her sleep.

In the morning he would decide.

Elspeth checked on Phillip.

He was asleep but was very restless. The duvet was on the floor and he was lying in the foetal position with an arm thrown out to one side. When she and John had put him to bed they had left him in his boxer shorts. She sat on the side of the bed and pulled the duvet back onto the bed, covering him as best she could. She was worried about the amount he had drunk. It must have been at least half a bottle of whisky. He was suffering but no more than she was suffering, although she could not anaesthetise her feelings with alcohol. She would wait a few minutes just to make sure he was all right.

She lay down on the other side of the bed and looked at the ceiling as she tried to call out to Sarah. They all wanted to know where she was. Why, why, why had she come back for some clothes without contacting any of them?

Elspeth closed her eyes and in a few seconds was overcome by sheer mental exhaustion.

John lay in bed wondering what the future held for him. He did not want any harm to come to Sarah but even if the worst situation were to materialise it wouldn't change anything.

Eventually Elspeth would find somebody else.

Was his relationship with her really at an end? Would it be possible to recover what they once had? Was their relationship worth fighting for when he knew the battle was already lost?

He drifted into a troubled sleep.

Sarah woke with a start.

The only light was from the lamp on the table but that was failing quite quickly. She hadn't the faintest idea what time it was. Lifting her head she wondered where Michael was but then she saw him, curled up on the rush mat on the floor.

"Michael," she whispered. "Are you all right?"

When there was no response she slipped off the bed and went over to him. His eyes were closed and he was breathing steadily, his head resting on his outstretched arm.

He must be freezing.

She knelt on the earthen floor.

290

"Michael," she said again, touching his shoulder. His head moved but he did not wake up. She lifted his wrist and twisted it towards the dim light so that she could see his watch. It was nearly three-thirty. What should she do? She couldn't leave him on the floor.

She took off his trainers and undid the buttons on his jacket. He opened his eyes as she tried to lift his shoulder to ease his jacket off.

"What ...?"

"It's all right, Michael, you were asleep on the floor. You'll catch your death of cold and it'll be another three hours before it starts to get light. There's room for both of us on the bed." She tugged at his jacket. "Come on, give me a hand."

He sat up so that she could pull off his jacket.

"I'll go on the inside," she said.

She got onto the bed, then held the duvet back so that he could lie next to her.

She sensed his hesitation..

"Come on. There's room for both of us. Don't be scared. You can go straight back to sleep."

He didn't look at her as he lowered himself onto the bed. "Right," she said softly, "pull the duvet over yourself and let's get some sleep."

Facing the mud wall, Sarah was aware that by letting him join her she was placing more trust in him than she should have. But she believed that if he had planned to do anything to her, he would have done it ages ago. She could feel his hip against her thigh and sensed that he was tense with self-doubt.

"Relax," she whispered.

In a few hours she would be home and facing whatever was going to be thrown at her. But as long as she stuck to her story they will have little choice but to believe her. There was nothing to be gained from telling them the truth.

The truth?

The absolute truth?

291

The real truth was why she was up on Copper's Ridge in the first place. Had her adventure – she no longer thought of it as a nightmare – changed anything? Had it told her what she really wanted? She shook her head. That was never going to happen. She was a married woman who wanted to have children. What had made her think there was any alternative? She loved Elspeth in her own way but her love was not nearly strong enough to take her away from the real world. Her real world was with Phillip – and the children she was determined to have. How could she ever have doubted that?

Closing her eyes she willed herself back towards the unconscious world of sleep. Everything would be all right. Everything would turn out for the best –

Her eyes shot open as Michael's hand slipped under her jumper and moved slowly over her ribcage towards her breast.

She froze.

If she over-reacted, it might make matters worse. His hand was on the front of her bra. She would pretend to be asleep.

His hand stopped with his fingertips against the top of her breast.

She dare not move … breathe normally … think about the consequences.

What an idiot!

Michael turned onto his side so that Sarah's back and thighs were contoured into his own body.

His face was next to her neck.

With his fingertips he touched her breast, it was so delicate and soft.

She hadn't told him to stop.

Her smell was like the roses in Mrs Lancaster's garden and her hair against his cheek was like the feathers of the injured baby thrush he once found and fed.

Moving his head he touched her ear with his lips, the tip of his tongue was against her skin. He needed to clench his

292

thighs as he became uncomfortable. Nothing else must happen unless she told him he could. The bed was so small he had little choice but to touch her. By inviting him onto the bed she was saying he could touch her, but nothing else.

Her body was tense against his.

What was she doing?

She was moving, not away from him but onto her back. His lips brushed against her cheek, then her nose and then her lips found his.

He had never kissed a woman before, not properly.

But she was kissing him. She was pushing her lips against his.

And now her tongue was against his mouth, moving slowly from side to side.

He tried to control his shaking. Nothing like this had ever happened before. It was what his dreams were for: it can't be for real, not with Sarah Preston.

But it was for real.

His dreams had been so inadequate.

She was really kissing him.

Little electric shocks shot through her body as his fingers touched her breast. His touch was not the touch of somebody abusing her. It was gentle and caring. Rather than wanting him to stop she wished for more. She wanted him to touch her.

He was shaking with apprehension, he needed some encouragement. She moved onto her back so she could kiss him. It seemed the most natural thing to do. The real world would never know they had ever met, so what was happening and what might happen was another fantasy in a whole stream of fantasies.

She needed to stop his shaking so she deepened her kiss.

His fingers stopped moving against her and his lips were not responding to hers. He needed to be shown what to do, he needed her guidance.

She felt for his hand. His fingers were as rigid as the rest of him. At first he resisted as she steered his hand under her bra and fully onto her breast, holding his hand against her.

Rolling her body towards his she lifted the jumper over her head, then she unclipped her bra and dropped it onto the earthen floor. After pulling off his T-shirt, she lowered herself and pushed the warmth of her body against his.

What was she doing? What should *he* do?

He could feel her breath only inches from his face, and then her lips were on his again, her hands moving over his bare shoulders.

She was lying on top of him, her breasts against him, so soft, so warm, but what should he do? He was hurting.

Clenching his thighs didn't help. It was hurting, he needed to ... what was she doing now?

Her hand reached down. She was touching him.

And now, in the dim light, he saw Sarah Preston move so that she was sitting astride him. Her eyes were sparkling as she looked down at him and she was smiling. She reached for his belt and then the zip on his jeans.

Her fingers were on him again.

She was touching him.

She could not stop now.

It was too late.

She wanted it to happen, she would not rest until it happened. Taking him only so far and then stopping would be so cruel ... and not just for him. She was already committed. Her joggers and pants joined the jumper and bra on the floor. Soon there was no need to guide his hands any more as his body closed in on hers.

The sensation seemed to start in every part of her body at the same time. It was as though she was suspended above the bed and she almost stopped breathing as she realised what was happening. Like a glow it spread slowly through her entire body, its epicentre between her thighs. A tingling, a throbbing that became a rhythmic pounding, it was like a balloon that had been over-inflated, waiting to burst.

Then it did burst and she screamed.

It was as though she was having an out of body experience. She could feel everything and yet feel nothing. Her scream seemed to echo round the earthen room. She had never felt anything like it before.

For what seemed like an hour neither of them moved. It would be his and her secret – to add to their other secrets – but with this secret, she had the answer to her dilemma.

There was no longer a need to ask the question.

The answer was there, lying beneath her.

Chapter Seventeen

Phillip watched the sun's rays streaming in through the window.

The dust was dancing in the beams of light, as though the room was infested with millions of quivering fireflies.

His mouth was dry, his nose was blocked and his head was thumping.

He knew why.

Even as he drank the whisky he knew how he would feel in the morning but last night alcohol was the only answer.

But what was the question?

His wife whom he loved so much and trusted beyond trust had left him without even leaving a note. The alcohol was necessary to make him sleep. He didn't remember going to bed, he didn't remember very much at all, other than the knowledge that she had gone and this was his first morning without her. How he felt now was how he was going to feel every morning in the future.

He closed his eyes.

At some stage in the night he had imagined she was lying next to him. His imagination even told him he was touching her.

He opened his eyes again but only for long enough to see that it was six-thirty. The time told him his mental alarm worked even when he was troubled.

Twenty-four hours ago she was not here either. She had been gone a whole day.

Elspeth let the jets of water stab at her body, as hard and as hot as she could bear.

During the night, she heard the church clock strike every hour, every half-hour. Her imagination suggested Sarah was lying broken in a ditch, her body mutilated and her dead eyes staring into space. Sarah was screaming for help as some faceless pervert horribly abused her but her screams went unheard. Through Sarah's eyes she saw her last moments on this earth as she prayed for death to come quickly.

The blackness of death descended.

She also prayed for forgiveness. If she had not been so impulsive and just waited then it would be Sarah standing under the shower in Primrose Cottage, not her.

It was all her fault.

The main TV news was just finishing as John buttered his second slice of toast and poured his third cup of coffee. His night was fitful but he was surprised he'd slept at all. A hot bath and a shave helped him to feel reasonably normal.

As he was shaving he looked at himself in the mirror and smiled.

Elspeth had spent the night alone with another man and he hadn't been in the slightest bit worried. It was not a question of trust because trust was no longer relevant. He would speak to Elspeth before he left for work, he would try to explain why he needed some space. He needed to distance himself from her for a short while.

He needed time to think.

If Sarah had returned during the night Elspeth would already be home. In a selfish way he was pleased that she wasn't. He would ring before he went to work and he would find a good reason to be late home this evening. Maybe he ought to copy Sarah and do a runner. That would shock them all and generate a few questions.

Yes, that was not a bad idea.

He went upstairs to pack an overnight bag.

Sarah opened her eyes and stared at the greyness above her.

She wanted to feel guilty but she didn't.

Under the duvet she ran her hands over her naked body and felt a completeness she had never felt before. It was unbelievable: she was in a hole in the ground with a man who was still a stranger – a stranger she had thought was going to rape and murder her and yet she was the one who had initiated sex between them. Perhaps part of the unexpected thrill came from the realisation that Michael had never had sex before. He was a complete novice and she was responsible for helping him. The circumstances had generated a setting that would previously have been way beyond her imagination.

No, she did not feel guilty.

She felt relieved.

He was incredibly gentle.

She thought that once he became aware of what she was offering he would turn into an animal but he didn't. If anything, he became more gentle. A beginner he may be, but he was an incredibly considerate beginner. Now an arm lay protectively across her stomach and his hand was cupping her breast. His face was against her shoulder, his stubble against her skin.

Warmth and contentment consumed her. He had given her the answer that subconsciously she had been looking for.

"Are you still asleep?" she whispered.

He was awake.

She felt his lips on her shoulder and his hand run slowly down the entire length of her body. She heard a long slow sigh but then without a word he rolled off the bed and ran to the cover over the entrance. Light streamed in as she watched in awe a still naked Michael lever himself out of the den.

He sat on the fallen branch about twenty feet from the entrance to his den, watching the rabbits in the hedgerow. They moved slowly, dipping their noses into dew-soaked grass before slowly hopping a few more feet to another source of nourishment. He knew they were aware he was watching them: he watched them most mornings so they were used to him.

They trusted him because they knew he meant them no harm.

Sarah Preston trusted him because she now knew he meant her no harm.

He had never experienced anything like it.

What she had done for him was beyond his wildest imaginings, his most inventive dreams.

There were no words he could think of to describe the way she had made him feel, but on this occasion not having the words didn't concern him. It was like ... the words were not there but he could and always would remember how she had made him feel. With her beautiful smiling face looking down at him in the dim light, with his hands on her naked body, she made him feel like the man that he always knew he could be ... he was.

By giving to him and taking from him, she had worked a miracle.

And afterwards, when she held him he had felt secure ... so secure and loved for the first time in his life.

Once again tears rolled down his cheeks. But they were the tears of happiness, of joy: they were telling him he had a future. With this new dawn he could look forward to what could be, rather than backwards to what used to be.

He smiled through his tears as he realised that from this day forward he could be the man he always wanted to be. The man he had always known he was.

Sarah relieved herself over the bucket and wished she could clean her teeth and have a shower. She was cold but it didn't matter; on the inside was a warm glow – a warm glow of contentment, happiness and ... total fulfilment.

She poured some water into the old saucepan she had seen Michael use the night before to make a drink. There was sufficient natural light coming from the entrance now for her to see what she was doing, so she lit the camping stove, feeling the heat of the flames against her body. She wondered where he was. The shaft of light was still there so the cover was not back in place. He would not have gone far. She found her jumper under the bed, put it on and went to the entrance.

Using the stool to stand on, she was able to lift her head above ground level. She saw a naked Michael sitting on the branch, watching the rabbits. At that moment she had never seen anything so incredible before.

He looked so handsome, so thoughtful, and so dependable.

She knew now he could also be sensitive and caring.

His arms were resting on his thighs and his head was at an angle as he watched the rabbits feeding a few yards from where he was sitting. His beautiful face was in profile, the rising sun throwing shadows across his naked body, his posture almost godlike.

If only life could be like this all the time – cut off from reality, removed from the complexities, nothing material other than the basic necessities of life.

And the delights.

She didn't want to disturb him. Disturbing him would mean breaking the spell and they would have to move on to the next stage. It would take them closer to when it must all end. Other than the decision that she would leave on her own, nothing was planned, so nothing would be forced.

It would just happen.

As earlier, she had looked down on his face and his body she saw the real man who was below the surface of the callow youth whose insecurity had betrayed him. She had seen him change as he became less afraid and began to accept that what they were doing was really happening.

And then something quite unexpected and remarkable occurred.

At first she didn't know what it was, but it was how she remembered feeling once when she was thinking about Elspeth. This time it was different. She didn't know where it started but she knew how it would finish. As the sensation took hold of her it seemed once again to engulf her entire body, every pore, every nerve ending. It was something she had never experienced with a man before, not even with Phillip when their relationship was in its infancy and at its best. But when it was happening with Michael she wanted it to go on and on forever.

And it had happened so quickly.

The sensation had grown and grown until it exploded inside her body, every square inch of her skin tingled, every part of her body pulsated with ecstasy and fulfilment.

As she looked at him watching the rabbits she closed her eyes and relived those breath-taking few minutes that had gone on resonating through her body for the next half hour.

Michael sensed he was being watched, so he slowly turned to face her. Her eyes were closed, her hair dishevelled, but she was still the most beautiful thing he would ever look at. Everything in the wood was beautiful and natural, but she was even more beautiful and more natural.

What she had done for him was also beautiful and natural.

He was different now.

There was a future for him, a real future.

It was as though a door had opened and beyond it was a world he had never experienced before, a world he could walk into and close the door behind him on his old world. He would be shutting out his inhibitions, he would be putting the past where it should be, and then he would walk into this new world with an open and confident mind.

He lowered his head: sadly, he knew the magnificent and beautiful source of his enlightenment was only an hour or so from leaving him. She was responsible for him having a future, but he accepted now that she was not part of that future.

He had become a man at last.

Opening her eyes Sarah saw Michael looking at her.

He didn't need to say anything because there was no longer a need for words. His eyes spoke a thousand words, a million words: it didn't matter how many because there were no words to describe how either of them felt.

He had done something unimaginable for her. She knew that she had done something unimaginable for him.

But it must end.

She needed to face the harshness, the reality of what was happening less than two miles away where there were people who would not understand: people who, if they ever discovered the truth, would try to destroy what she and Michael had found in each other.

They would never know the truth; they must never know the truth.

Michael blinked as Sarah Preston ducked back down into the den.

Was it after all a dream?

No, not this time.

He looked once more at the rabbits, knowing that every time he saw them in the future he would think of this moment. This moment would never be repeated but it was a moment that would never leave him. Every day, every hour, every minute, every second he would think of this moment.

The memory of being wanted would never leave him, of being loved and held by somebody who really cared.

She was pouring hot water into the mugs when she heard him lower himself into the den. Her back was towards him. She dared not turn round: if she did she would break down. Tears were already in her eyes.

Tears?

They were genuine tears of regret, not because of what she had done but because it was coming to an end.

In an hour, in less than an hour she would walk away.

He stood still and gazed at her, trying to take in every detail to print the vision on the screen of his mind.

Her bare thighs, her shapely legs and tiny feet: her mere presence was intoxicating. He wanted to touch her again, to feel the silkiness of her skin against his, but it would be wrong.

The spell would be broken.

He would let her go but not before he found the words to tell her about the miracle. If he could find the words: she must not go away wondering what he was thinking.

"Coffee's ready," Sarah said, her voice breaking as she picked up the steaming mugs.

Turning round she saw him.

He took a pace towards her, but stopped, swallowing deeply before he spoke. "Thank you for what you did for me."

His smile was radiant – a kind of smile that was new to both of them – that seemed to symbolise their union so that neither of them would ever forget it.

"Your coffee," she said, handing him the mug, her fingers trembling as they touched his.

"Thank you," he said again. "For the coffee, for what you have done to me, for holding me and for loving me."

Sarah's grip on her mug tightened as though it was a life-line. "It's me who should be thanking you," she said slowly, her eyes never leaving his face, "for what *you* have done for *me*."

Elspeth didn't want to wake Phillip so she was using the main bathroom rather than the en suite shower room. She dried herself on a bath towel she found on the rail. She chose the pink one rather than the blue one. It had a slight whiff of Sarah.

She held it against her face, burying her nose in the soft material. It was the same with the jumper, the jumper that was now missing. It had also smelt of Sarah.

Sarah was out there somewhere.

303

Phillip crawled out of bed.

He needed the toilet, he needed to clean his teeth and then have a freezing cold shower. And afterwards he would have a very strong black coffee. He needed anything that would make the horrors of a very disturbed night go away.

With bleary eyes he padded to the en-suite bathroom, glancing back at the bed just once to make sure he had not simply woken up from the worst nightmare he had ever had.

She was not there.

After putting on his dressing gown, he opened the bedroom door to go downstairs and make himself that very strong coffee.

The main bathroom door was open.

Elspeth had her back to the door, one foot up on the toilet seat as she dried her toes.

"Ah," Phillip said, confused. "I'm sorry, I didn't realise ..."

She jumped at the sound of his voice but smiled at him over her shoulder. "No, I should apologise. I didn't close the door."

"What are you doing in ..."

"I stayed the night, just in case." She changed feet and carried on drying her toes.

"Well, thank you. I'm ... I'm going to make myself a coffee. Would you like a mug?"

"Please. I'll be down in a minute."

John picked up the phone and dialled the Prestons' number. It rang twice and Elspeth answered.

"Hello?" she said.

"It's me. I presume there's no news."

"No, nothing."

"How's Phillip?"

"Fine. Well, as fine as you'd expect. He's just made some life-saving coffee and he's disappeared somewhere again – outside getting some fresh air, I think."

"What about you?" he said.

"Me? Worried sick if that doesn't offend –"

"Don't, Elspeth, there's no need for that."

"For what?"

"You know what I mean."

"Do I? What time will you be home from work?" she asked.

John picked up on the word *home*, he wanted to say something sarcastic but decided not to.

"As soon as I'm ready," he replied, but thinking that maybe *home* was not such a good idea after all. "If anything happens you can ring Jennifer. I'm in meetings all day."

"Jennifer? What shall I tell her? That your best friend's wife has been found dead –"

"Stop it, Elspeth," he said patiently but feeling the opposite. "Just leave a message and I'll ring back you as soon as I can."

"Don't you think you're being just a little insensitive about this?"

"We won't discuss insensitivity if you don't mind. We've done all we can. The police must now be allowed to do what they can. I'm going to work but before you say anything else, I'm praying along with you and Phillip that Sarah is all right – wherever she might be."

He put the receiver down before Elspeth could comment.

As he checked the kitchen to make sure he had got everything, his thoughts went back to the day he went into the Tie Rack on Paddington Station and saw Elspeth for the first time.

Of course there was an animal attraction. What man doesn't look at a pretty girl in that way? But as he got to know her – could he say now that he had ever really known her? – she had become more and more part of his reason for living.

If that was love then yes, he was very much in love with Elspeth Warrington, and had always believed she felt the same about him.

Sarah might reappear and walk back into Phillip's life; if nothing was said he might never be any the wiser. But a chapter in John's life had come to an end and he was not too sure whether he wanted to turn to the next page.

He looked at the bag he had packed earlier.

Should he or shouldn't he?

He picked up the bag and his laptop and headed for the front door.

The bag was the catalyst. Without it he could not make a decision.

After putting both bag and laptop on the back seat, he climbed into the Freelander. As he prepared to move off he saw Old Greg at his gate, even at this time in the morning. John raised his hand in acknowledgement and was surprised when Old Greg did more than give him the usual almost undetectable nod in return. Instead Old Greg also lifted his hand, almost as though he wanted to say something, but then turned and shuffled back down the path to the front door of his cottage.

John shrugged as he turned the key in the ignition.

Sarah stood outside the den for the first time since she had entered it. Stepping closer to Michael she took his face in her hands and pulled him towards her. She had to stand on her tiptoes to kiss him.

"Thank you," she whispered, clinging to him for a few moments more. "You'll never know what you have done for me over the last twenty-four hours. Never!"

"I ..." he started to say but then faltered.

Putting her fingers against his lips, she said: "Don't ... don't speak. I want to remember you – us – the way we are. I know now why I was guided towards Copper's Ridge and I will always be grateful." Still looking into his eyes she picked up the brown bag. "I must go now."

He nodded and smiled. "Take our secrets with you, Sarah Preston," he said.

"Secrets and memories," she whispered. "Both will be with me forever." She reached into the brown bag. "Here," she said, giving him the little box that contained her red pants. "Keep these."

He looked down at the box and smiled. "Thank you. They will be our secret too," he said as she turned her head away and walked slowly out of the wood.

And out of his life.

He watched her as she went past the Tuckers' old oak tree.

She hesitated momentarily to take the coat out of the brown bag. She put it on followed by her woolly hat. Then she rifled through the bag as though she was checking what was in it.

But she didn't look back.

Chapter Eighteen

"What time did the police say they'd be here?" Phillip asked, staring into the mug of black coffee.

"She said she thought it would be some time after nine." Elspeth said.

She still had Sarah's pink towel from the shower wrapped around her. She had been chatting to Phillip for over an hour, not actually saying what she was thinking, and not knowing what he was thinking either.

Sarah was dead.

If she was not dead she was lying somewhere and was dying.

The most grotesque images were emblazoned on her mind and most certainly on Phillip's as well. It seemed that she was not the only one who chose to overlook the fact that some of Sarah's clothes had been collected. She also did not think or want to ask why Sarah had come back for her clothes but had left her make-up and toiletries.

Elspeth was sure they had both chosen to discount or ignore the most pertinent pieces of evidence because neither of them were accepting there might be somebody else. If there was no logic behind what had happened, then why had it happened? Ugly images of Sarah's mutilated body and staring eyes were preferable to the alternative scenario in which she would be alive – and perhaps happy with someone else.

It struck her that if she was able to say what she really thought, she might reach a more rational conclusion, and at the same time subject her own behaviour and thoughts to some of their joint analysis.

"I must go and get dressed," she said, looking down at the pink towel.

"Nine ?" Phillip checked his watch. "That's not for another hour. You would have thought –"

"They have to wait, Phillip. If they go chasing shadows after only a few hours they'd get nowhere. Anyway, they don't have the resources."

"It's been over twenty-four hours. I'd have thought that was long enough for them."

"They'll be here soon." She collected the coffee mugs from the table. "Do you want this?" she asked, indicating his coffee.

"No, no thanks."

"I presume you're not going to work."

"How could I? I'll give them a ring later."

She ran the tap, moving her fingers under the water until it was hot. "What about Sarah?"

"What d'you mean?"

"Her work. Are you going to tell them?"

"I hadn't even thought of that." He got up and started pacing the kitchen. "Tell them what? I don't know, I suppose they'll have to know some time. I'll say she's not well."

"We don't know any different, do we?" She reached for the tea towel.

"I think we do."

Phillip's eyes felt as though they had sunk deeper and deeper into their sockets. He needed that shave and a shower but he felt like having neither.

He stopped by the cooker and lowered his head into his hands. "God, what a fucking mess this is. What am I going to do?"

Elspeth threw the tea towel onto the drainer and moved across the kitchen to his side.

He felt her hands on the back of his neck. She smelt of soap. He had never been this close to her before, other than to give her a perfunctory peck on the cheek whenever they met. He let her pull his head down onto her bare shoulder as she wrapped her arms around him.

Sarah stopped only twice on her way back to Upper Slaughter.

First, she stopped by the oak tree to take her Barbour and woolly hat from the brown bag. The morning air was chilly but her body felt as though it was glowing – as though it had been gently massaged all over. She wanted to look back but she dare not. If she looked back, she would be tempted to go back.

She hated leaving Michael, seeing the look on his face for the last time. The village was too small for them not to bump into each again but it would never be the same. Her future wasn't with Michael, it was not with anybody but the man she married ten years earlier. Phillip would be distraught but in just over an hour she would be with him. It wouldn't be easy after what happened last night but it was a transition she had to make. A transition she wanted more than anything else to make – for both their sakes.

As she picked up the brown bag to move on, she stopped.

The bag?

If her story were to be believed, how was she going to explain the bag and the clothes? If she had just gone for a walk she would not have taken the bag with her. She contemplated going back and asking Michael to look after it but that would be silly.

No, she would have to hide it somewhere and then go back for it once things had settled down.

Where?

Where could she hide it?

She unzipped the bag again to check what was in it. Her joggers, the top she had worn the previous day and underwear. She wasn't wearing a bra so there were two in the bag. Should she put one on now? Could she put the other clothes under her Barbour and just hide the bag somewhere?

She started to walk and think – something was bound to come to her.

There was time.

Michael looked around his den with a feeling of great sorrow and loss, as though a vital part of him had been wrenched from his body.

If his future was going to be so different to his past then everything must stop: not just the spying and the visits, but the den as well.

He would leave everything as it was.

The bedding would have to be taken back to his mother's house but everything else would stay. He would replace the cover for the last time then walk away.

There was no need for his den anymore.

Not in his new life.

He was a man, and only boys have dens.

Dressing slowly he knew what he must do, but he didn't want to rush leaving what had been his life until now. He was not due in work until ten o'clock so there was plenty of time. The pan he used to heat the curry the previous evening was in the middle of the floor. One of his nature friends would find its way in and it could eat what was left. He would take away the used tins and any other rubbish in case it harmed the animals.

Once he was satisfied with his preparations he looked round for a last time before placing the black plastic bags with the bedding and rubbish outside the entrance. After climbing out he replaced the cover, ensuring that the rocks were in the right spots. He walked round to make sure it was still as invisible as ever and smiled.

The den had given him great pleasure over the years but nothing compared with the last twenty-four hours. He always knew that one day he would have to leave it because either somebody else discovered it or because he was moving away with his mother, but he would never have believed that in the end it would be because of Sarah Preston.

She had made him into the man he now was.

Sarah reached the beginning of the track which led down to the river and through the wood to the village.

As she walked along Copper's Ridge she kept a careful watch on the track ahead and on both sides just in case she saw anybody, but nobody seemed to be about.

It was a bright sunny morning with a clear blue sky and a cooling breeze coming from the south-west. The onset of autumn was evident in the trees, and the fields looked bleak, their crops long harvested.

But her spirits were high.

Once inside the line of trees in the wood she left the track to find somewhere to hide the bag. Soon she found a slight dip in the ground surrounded by undergrowth and bushes that was ideal.

Quickly she unzipped the bag, then glancing again at the contents she decided what she would do.

Looking around to make sure she was alone, she took off the Barbour, the top, jeans and boots and put on the second pair of pants and both bras. She looked down at her filthy feet and smiled as she pulled on the jeans followed by both tops and the jumper. After wrapping the joggers round her waist, she put on her socks, boots and Barbour and checked the bag to make sure there was nothing left in it.

After pushing the bag into the dip in the ground she covered it with dead bracken and fallen leaves, then stood back and checked her work. One corner of the bag could still be seen but unless somebody walked to that exact spot and knew what they were looking for they would not see it. Sarah didn't want to leave it there too long because of its sentimental value.

Once she had retraced her steps to the track, she stopped to take a breath.

Her hand went to her forehead to feel the crustiness of the scabbing. The injury must still be very evident and would provide the only explanation she was willing to give for her absence.

She pulled the woolly hat well down over her forehead.

"I can only guess what you must be going through," Elspeth said. "Sarah and I have become very close friends over the last couple of months and I'm extremely worried about her but for you it must be absolutely awful."

Philip lifted his head from her shoulder; her closeness, her warmth and her smell had acted like a tonic. He felt a little more positive and his hopes regained some of the lost ground. His hands were on her hips and hers were behind his neck.

Opening his eyes, he smiled.

Her face was only inches from his.

"Thank you," he said, "thank you for being here for me."

He bent forward to kiss her on the cheek but she moved her head so that his lips fell on hers.

Pulling back immediately, thinking the mistake had been his, he felt the pressure of Elspeth's hands on the back of his neck gently forcing his mouth back onto hers.

As they kissed she knew she had him exactly where she wanted him.

It was very devious but it might just work.

If Sarah was dead then nothing would be lost, but if she was alive then Elspeth knew there was everything to gain. The idea had come to her when she realised he was behind her as she was drying herself in the bathroom. If she had something on him then she would be able to use it to her advantage.

He had said nothing about the incident in the bathroom, not even saying he was sorry, so that was indicative. He had seen her stark naked and he didn't feel the need to apologise to her.

That could only mean one thing.

And *he* had kissed *her*, hadn't he?

313

She increased the pressure of her lips on his as she moved her hand to where the towel was tucked in, and pulled it loose.

The towel dropped to the floor but he was ahead of her, his hands already on her body. She could feel the need in him.

His wife was missing and yet he was prepared to have sex with her best friend.

She smiled to herself.

Either he had the morals of a guttersnipe or there were problems she knew nothing about.

This was going to be easier than she first thought.

As she got to the edge of the wood nearest the village Sarah stopped and looked towards Clifton House.

That was where it had all started.

She had felt insecure for a lot longer but it was Elspeth who had brought Sarah's insecurity to a head. If the incident at the party had not happened, if she had not had the earth shattering fantasy of Elspeth making love to her, she would not have felt the need to be alone in order to determine for once and all her sexuality. If she had not wanted to be alone she would not have gone up to Copper's Ridge and she would not have met Michael.

Without Elspeth and Michael she would probably still be in a total quandary about how to resolve the apparent shortcomings in her marriage.

But not anymore. Her indecision was now replaced by a new strength and commitment, a new determination to get on with her the rest of her life. It would now go in the direction she wanted it to go and that was all down to Michael Griffiths.

It was nothing to do with Elspeth.

Pulling the Barbour tightly round her body, she left the wood and began walking purposefully towards the bottom of Church Lane.

Regardless of how positive she was feeling, as she started up the incline for Primrose Cottage she felt her apprehension grow.

Why?

Frantically Phillip guided Elspeth towards a kitchen chair.

Even the area of his brain that was shouting at him to stop had given up. Nothing could stop him. He wanted her, he needed her, and it was going to happen here and now.

He sat down and Elspeth stood in front of him with her thighs either side of his. She put one hand behind his head and pulled him against her breasts.

"Are you sure you want this to happen?" she whispered.

"Of course, I do," he said. "You don't know how often – "

"Then shut up and let's get on with it," she said as she reached for him.

The shrillness of the front door bell ringing was like an alarm going off in his head, and no doubt in Elspeth's too.

It was a strange feeling, ringing her own doorbell. She could not remember ever having rung her own doorbell before. It sounded weird from the outside.

She thought about going round to the back door but that would have been too normal – nothing was going to be normal anymore. Her life with Phillip was going to change dramatically.

She rang the bell again.

After searching her Barbour in vain for the spare key she had taken from the kitchen drawer, she gave up believing it was buried deep in a pocket somewhere.

And where was the key Michael had made, the one he was supposed to give her?

Shaking her head, she realised her explanation about where she had been would cover everything, even a lost key. There was no need for her to worry.

"Fuck," Phillip said under his breath.

"Almost," Elspeth responded, letting go of him. "It'll be the police," she said.

She had him. It might not have happened but she had him.

"What –?"

She picked up the towel from the floor and wrapped it round her body before grabbing his dressing gown from the table and throwing it at him.

"I'll go upstairs. Put that on and answer the door," she said.

"What –?"

"Go on. Do it."

"Elspeth, I ... that didn't ..."

"Do it."

The bell rang again.

Phillip pulled on his dressing gown then followed Elspeth into the hall.

Fortunately the curtain was over the front door so the police would not see them. He watched Elspeth disappear up the stairs and into the main bedroom.

He took a deep breath, pulled back the curtain, unbolted the door and opened it.

"Good morn ... *Sarah!*"

"Hello Phillip."

"Sarah!"

"Will you stop saying my name and let me in?"

"What –?"

Sarah burst into tears and buried herself against his chest.

"I'm sorry," she sobbed. "I am so, so sorry, sorry, sorry."

Standing just inside the bedroom Elspeth listened to the exchange.

Hearing Sarah's voice took her breath away. She wanted to rush down the stairs, take Sarah in her arms, smother her with kisses and tell her that she too was sorry, so very, very sorry.

She closed her eyes.

Sarah.

She was home, she was not dead and lying mutilated in some ditch.

She must get dressed and go to her.

Phillip put his arm round Sarah's shoulders and gently led her to the kitchen. She sat on the chair where minutes earlier he was so close to doing the most stupid thing in his life.

He shuddered at the thought.

But looking down at Sarah everything else was forgotten when he realised this was no dream – she was really home. She looked tired, dishevelled and dirty but there was only one thing that mattered ... she was safe.

And she was home.

"I'm so sorry," Sarah said again, "you must have been –"

"Stop it," Phillip said softly, "there's no need now. The explanations can wait. The main thing is that you are all right ... you *are* all right, aren't you?"

He was gripping Sarah's hands as tightly as he dared, not believing he was actually touching her. He wanted to hug her, kiss her all over as his worst fears began to subside.

She lifted her head. "Yes, I'm all right except for this," she said, taking off the woolly hat.

"Your head," Phillip said, shocked by what he saw. "What on earth have you done to your head?" He put his fingers lightly against the bruising and the crusty scabbing. "What happened?"

She covered his fingers with hers. "It's part of what I have to tell you," she explained. "It's the reason why I have caused you so much worry."

"What –?"

"You said later, Phillip. For the moment just accept that I am all right, very tired and dirty but all right. I'm home. I

317

could murder a mug of strong coffee and I'll let you put three teaspoons of sugar in it as well."

"Well … yes, of course, as long as … but you don't take –"

"Phillip please, I'm all right but I'll be even better after that coffee."

"Of course ... sorry, yes, of course." He stood up.

Elspeth tiptoed down the stairs and waited just inside the dining room. She thought about trying to sneak out the front door but it could be seen from the kitchen and the door was open.

"Sarah?" she said walking slowly into the kitchen.

Phillip turned from the sink and Sarah looked up.

"Elspeth, what are you –?"

"I was upstairs," Elspeth told her, stepping further into the kitchen. "I thought –"

"I'm afraid I got pretty drunk last night," Phillip said, "and Elspeth stayed the night to make sure I was all right."

She held Sarah's gaze.

Sarah didn't know what to say or do.

Half of her wanted to rush over and hug her friend because she was so pleased to see her, but the other half wanted to shout at her for being the cause of everything that had happened.

She could never hate Elspeth but she could do with her not being here at this precise moment.

Anyway, why was she here? Phillip had mumbled something about getting drunk. He was in his dressing gown and looking very sheepish.

What was going on? Why had she really stayed the night?

At that moment her questions must go unanswered because she didn't want Elspeth to be here … regardless of the reason. Maybe at some stage she would be able to decide whether their friendship could survive or not, but not now,

318

not before she explained to Phillip where she had been and why.

"Hello," she said, wishing she had the courage to say what she was thinking.

Elspeth saw the confusion on Sarah's face.

She wanted to explain and say how sorry she was, but she couldn't, not in front of Phillip. There would be ... there had to be a right time.

And then?

Once she was forgiven – because she was sure she would be forgiven – her time would definitely come, especially now that she had a hold on the man who stood between them.

"Hello Sarah. I'm so pleased you're safe and that you've come home. John's gone to work," she said, more for the sake of saying something.

She saw Phillip watching her exchange with Sarah. He was frowning and it was obvious he didn't understand what was happening between the two of them.

She moved further into the kitchen.

Phillip was confused.

Why weren't they hugging each other like the friends they were? And especially after such a traumatic twenty-four hours.

He tried to catch Sarah's eye but she wasn't looking at him.

Instead she was glaring at Elspeth.

Why?

Sarah could not have seen what was happening in the kitchen before she rang the bell. The curtain was across the door.

Had she been round to the back of the house first and looked in through the kitchen window? No, if she had all hell would be breaking loose.

So what was it?

The atmosphere was very tense.

Why were they being so unfriendly? They were the best of friends so he would have thought they would be delighted to see each other.

Elspeth stood in front of Sarah and touched her hand.

"I'm so pleased you're safe," she said.

Sarah was relieved that Phillip could not see the look that Elspeth gave her.

She wanted to snatch her hand away but she mustn't, Philip must not be given reason to suspect anything. But maybe he already did. She didn't have the faintest idea what had or had not been said during the last twenty-four hours

Elspeth's fingers were on the back of her hand, stroking gently. She moved her head to make sure Phillip could not see her eyes and glared as hard as she could at Elspeth.

Go, she wanted to scream. *Get out!*

Elspeth lifted her fingers to the bruising on Sarah's forehead. "What happened?"

"We've already agreed that …" Phillip started to say.

"No, it's all right, Phillip."

Sarah reached up and moved Elspeth's hand away from her head.

"I went for walk. I didn't look where I was going and cracked my head on a low branch. For most of yesterday I was unconscious and when I woke up it was pitch black and I didn't have the faintest idea where I was –"

The lies had started but there was no way she was going to break her promise to Michael, or to herself.

"You poor thing," Elspeth whispered, "you poor, poor …"

Phillip joined them at the table.

"Sarah you must –"

"I know, go to the hospital and have myself checked out." She took her hand from Elspeth's. "Now, all I want is that cup of coffee and a long and very hot bath. I'm tired, I smell, and I –"

320

She could not stand it any longer.

She stood up, rushed from the kitchen and ran upstairs.

Michael held the bedding to his face. He did not want to wash it but he accepted that eventually it would have to be washed. He held it once more close to him then quickly pushed it into the washing machine and switched it on. His mother would not be suspicious because he normally did his own washing.

He stripped off, looked down at his body in wonder and stepped into the shower.

While in the shower, he thought about how he was going to dispose of his collection of keys and remembered he hadn't given the Primrose Cottage key to Sarah Preston.

He promised he would.

Elspeth moved into the hall and looked longingly up the stairs.

"I'd better go," she said. "Or do you want me here when the police arrive?"

"No," Phillip said. "I can manage."

"I'll go then."

"Elspeth," he said, putting his hand on her arm.

She turned round, guessing what he was going to say.

"Yes, Phillip."

"What happened earlier, I –" He was whispering.

"Why, what happened earlier?" she asked, with just a hint of a smile on her lips.

"Well –"

"Nothing happened earlier, that's what happened, nothing," she said and wanted to add, "You just go on telling yourself that nothing happened but my time will come, then we'll decide what should happen next," but didn't.

"Thank you," Phillip said.

"Thank you? If nothing happened there's nothing to thank me for, is there?"

"No, I suppose ..."

"I'll go." She unlatched the door. "Look after her, Phillip. She's obviously had quite an experience."

Walking down the path Elspeth hesitated and looked back at the cottage. Having seen the deception in her eyes, she knew Sarah had lied, or if not lied she had not told them the whole truth.

There would be an explanation of how she got the cuts and bruises on her forehead but it definitely did not happen the way they were told.

And what about the clothes that were missing?

The truth would come out eventually.

Phillip climbed the stairs with Sarah's mug of coffee in his hand. He couldn't wait to look at her because only then would he believe she was really back. Half way up the stairs he remembered he needed to phone to say he would not be in to work. Fortunately, there was nothing other than routine for him to go in for anyway. He also needed to let Sarah's chambers know. He would use the landline downstairs.

Going back down he checked the phone book and tapped out the number. While he waited he told himself what a bloody fool he had been. He was overjoyed that Sarah was back but his conscience was still playing hell with him regardless of what Elspeth had said.

"Bentley, Smythe and Crooks," an efficient voice said.

"Good morning, my name is Phillip Preston, Sarah's husband."

"Oh, good morning, Mr Preston, how can I help?"

"It's just to say that Sarah won't be in today and probably not tomorrow. She's not feeling too well."

"Oh, I'm sorry to hear that, Mr Preston but ... but we weren't expecting her in anyway."

"What do you mean?"

There were a few seconds of silence. "Well, er, it's just that Mrs Preston wasn't expected today."

"You've just told me that, why?"

322

"Well ... well I think it might be better if she tells you herself."

"All right," Phillip said patiently, "just tell me when you were expecting her."

"I think ... I think you need to speak to your wife, Mr Preston."

"Thank you," Phillip said, "you've been very helpful."

He replaced the receiver slowly and carried Sarah's mug of coffee upstairs.

Sarah was lying on the bed with her head to one side and her eyes closed. Her breathing suggested she was fast asleep. She was still fully clothed and she was still wearing her muddy boots.

Phillip looked down at her. A small tic was pulling at the corner of her mouth. Her face and hands were filthy. She must have experienced a living nightmare. She was home, that's what mattered. She was back with him and so his worst fears, whatever they may have been, were unfounded.

And he was not dreaming.

He bent down and as gently as he could, he unlaced her boots.

Taking them and her socks off at the same time, he moved her feet under the duvet but not before he noticed her feet; even the soles were as mud-stained as the rest of her.

He frowned. Why were her feet so dirty? Hands and face he could understand, but why her feet?

Sod the bed linen. That is why washing machines were invented.

He tried to undo the Barbour to take it off but was afraid of waking her so he just pulled the duvet over her to let her sleep.

He kissed her cheek, wishing he could soothe the bruises on her forehead, to take the pain away.

As he was going down the stairs, still cursing himself for his utter stupidity earlier but at the same time thanking God Sarah was, as far as he could tell, unharmed, the front door bell rang.

323

"Hello, Mr Preston," said Sergeant Craig. PC Martin and PC Gould stood behind her.

"She's come home," he said, not knowing whether to laugh or cry.

"When was that, sir?" PC Martin asked, his expression not changing.

"About half an hour ago. She's upstairs now, and fast asleep."

"That's excellent news, sir." Sergeant Craig glanced sideways at PC Martin. "Do you mind if we come in?"

"No, of course not, please," Phillip said.

"Shall we go into the kitchen?"

"Yes, yes, the kitchen, yes, please."

"So, Mr Preston, are you able to tell us what happened?" Sergeant Craig was standing next to the dresser, PC Martin was over by the backdoor and PC Gould had stayed at the kitchen door. They had all kept their hats on, which, under the circumstances, Phillip thought unnecessary.

"Not in any detail, Sergeant, but it appears as though she did go for an early morning walk and at some stage, somewhere, she managed to knock herself out on the branch of a tree. She's got one hell of a lot of cuts and bruising on her forehead."

"And then?"

"What do you mean?"

"Well, how long was she unconscious for?"

Phillip shook his head. "I don't know yet. She said it was dark when she woke up and she didn't know where she was, but does it matter? I think she's still in a bit of a daze. She's come home so she's no longer missing. Surely –"

"Do you mind if PC Gould and I just pop up and see her, Mr Preston?"

"I told you, she's fast asleep. I think –"

"We won't wake her?"

"Do you have to?"

324

"I'm afraid we do, sir." Sergeant Craig looked across at PC Martin and nodded. "PC Martin will stay with you, sir. Which room is she in?"

"Top of the stairs and straight on, the one you were in before."

"Thank you."

Sergeant Craig left the kitchen with PC Gould at her heel.

"She doesn't believe me, does she?" Phillip said to PC Martin who was still by the back door.

"It's not that, sir. We do have procedures to follow in situations such as this."

"You don't accept the first explanation you're given – is that your procedure?"

"That's not what I was –"

"No, I'm sorry," Phillip said, wringing his hands. "I report my wife missing, it's suggested that she's having an affair, I then say she's come home injured, I suppose ..."

"Something like that, yes."

He slumped down at the kitchen table, his head in his hands.

"That bruising is pretty nasty," Sergeant Craig said when she and PC Gould returned to the kitchen a few minutes later. "I'd suggest she gets checked as soon as possible."

"That's exactly what I intend doing when she wakes up."

"She's awake," Sergeant Craig said.

"But ..."

"No, we didn't. She woke up as we were leaving the room. She's going to have a bath, I would suggest that you ..."

"I have every intention of having her checked out, Sergeant." Phillip glanced at PC Martin. "I understand why you had to see her, but I can assure you that her injuries were not inflicted by me."

"We weren't suggesting that –"

"Of course you weren't." Then a little tentatively Phillip asked: "Did she say anything else?"

"What sort of the thing?" Sergeant Craig asked.

"Well, you know, she must have told you how she knocked herself out, but did she say anything else? Was there anybody else involved? Was she molested in anyway?" He closed his eyes and took a deep breath. "All right, was she raped?" he asked with a sigh.

Sergeant Craig leant back against the worktop and folded her arms. "As far as we could establish, Mr Preston, your wife did exactly what she told you. She went for an early morning walk and at some stage she cracked her head on a branch." She shrugged. "So no, Mr Preston, she didn't tell us anything which suggested there was anybody else involved or that she was molested or raped. In fact there appears to have been no third party involvement whatsoever."

"Thank God for that."

"Right, sir, we'll be going. Regardless of what you might think, we're actually very pleased that Mrs Preston has come home safely. Whatever her reasons might have been for leaving in the first place are not our business, but if she tells you anything which suggests there might have been a criminal act then we will need to know."

Phillip bristled. "Are you suggesting my wife didn't tell you the truth about what happened? What exactly are you implying?"

"Nothing, sir."

PC Martin and PC Gould exchanged looks, which further annoyed Phillip.

"It's just that any injury sustained to the head can cause more than just temporary memory loss," PC Martin said. "The trauma your wife has been through could result in her unknowingly blanking out any less palatable experiences."

"So you *are* suggesting there could be more to what happened than she's told us?" Phillip said, shaking his head.

"No, sir, I am merely saying that time may reveal a few things we don't already know or have been told. As far as we can ascertain there hasn't been a criminal act committed and the business about the missing clothes is something that maybe ought to remain personal between the two of you."

Sergeant Craig signalled to the others.

"Right, we'll be going now but we'll have to come back in a day or two to interview your wife so that her file can be closed."

"Or not, depending on what she says?" Phillip said.

He had not forgotten about the clothes but with Sarah home now, how and why the clothes had gone missing seemed less important.

"We'll call you in a day or so to arrange a visit," Sergeant Craig said, ignoring Phillip's question.

After the police officers left the bedroom for the second time, Sarah swung her legs off the bed. She stripped off the Barbour followed by all the other clothes she was wearing and put everything else in the laundry basket. For a minute or so she listened at the top of the stairs to Phillip talking to the police, then she went into the bathroom and turned on the hot water tap.

She had told the police exactly what she had told Phillip, so she just hoped they believed her as well.

The police car had disappeared beyond the village green before Phillip went back into the cottage, the concern he felt weighing on his mind.

Sergeant Craig had implied Sarah might not have told them or him the full story of where she had been and what had happened to her. Since she disappeared, the possibility that she had run off with another man had always been there but it would be obvious to a blind person that she had been through hell.

Maybe, just maybe, a rogue branch did not cause her injuries but there would be another acceptable explanation. If she had gone to meet somebody ... no. he didn't even want to think about it.

The most important thing was that she was home. She was back with him. The truth would come out eventually and until then he was quite happy with simply having her back.

Elspeth wouldn't say anything about what had happened between them, because she had just as much to lose.

As the police car passed the ever-present Old Greg by the village green, Tony Martin glanced in the rear-view mirror at Debbie Gould.

"So do you still think there's some sort of conspiracy going on?" he asked.

"I think we ought to have gone to see Elspeth Warrington," Debbie said.

"Why? We had no reason to go and see her after what Mrs Preston told us what happened."

Debbie shook her head. "I know, boss, but I still think she's implicated in some way. There's definitely something going on between the two of them."

Sergeant Craig kept her eye on the road. "Even if there is, Mrs Preston's explanation of what happened suggested there was no third party involvement. And what they do in their private life and their sexual preferences is nothing to do with us."

Sandra Gould shook her head. "No, boss. We may never know for sure but I'm certain there's something going on and I'm convinced there's a connection."

PC Martin caught her eye in the mirror. "Or are you looking for something you want to find that doesn't exist?"

Debbie leaned forward. "I don't think this is last time we'll be here, that's all I'm saying."

When Phillip entered the steam filled bathroom, Sarah's head was all that was visible above a mass of soapsuds. She seemed to be asleep but she stirred and smiled.

"I didn't think anything could feel so good," she said. "This is unadulterated luxury."

The bruising on her forehead was more prominent now, probably due to the heat and there was perspiration oozing from every pore on her face.

Sitting on the toilet seat cover Phillip leant towards her.

"I'm sorry if the police woke you up," he said.

She closed her eyes and sank a little lower allowing the bath water to cover her face for a moment. "Waking up to see a couple of policewomen in your bedroom is a little disconcerting, I must agree," she said, reaching for a hand towel to dry her eyes.

"Yes, I'm sorry. I did ask them to leave you to sleep. What did they say?"

"They asked me if you'd done this to me." She lifted a soapy hand out of the water and touched her forehead.

"And?"

She smiled. "I told them you'd clobbered me with a mallet so they could go away happy."

He returned her smile. "Didn't you wonder why they were here?"

"If you hadn't reported me missing after I'd been gone an hour I'd have been pretty pissed off."

"Anything else?"

"The young one, PC Gould I think it was, asked me whether there was anyone else involved."

"And?"

"Well of course there wasn't. I've told you what happened."

He bent over the bath and kissed her. "You had me unbelievably worried. I thought I'd lost you."

"No such luck, I'm afraid. But I bet you weren't half as worried as I was when I woke up in the middle of a wood not knowing who or where I was."

"It must have been awful. Where were you?"

"Not now, Phillip."

"Sorry."

"Do you know what I'd like?"

"What's that?"

"A plate of eggs, bacon, fried bread, mushrooms and tomatoes, oh and some baked beans. There's a tin in the cupboard."

"I think I can manage that," he said, kneeling down by the bath. He put his hand into the water.

"Then go and manage it," she told him lifting his hand out of the soapy water. "There'll be plenty of time for that later."

"I just wanted to know it's really you but all right, I'll go." He dried his hand on the blue towel and turned back to her at the door. "Two things," he said. "After we've eaten I'm taking you to hospital for a check-up. No, don't bother arguing, police orders. And I phoned work to say you wouldn't be in for a couple of days."

"Ah!" she said. "You know. What did they say?"

"That they weren't expecting you anyway."

She screwed up her face. "Yes, sorry about that, I should have told you on Friday. I took a couple more weeks' unpaid leave. They were very understanding."

"I'm sure they were, but why?"

"Go and cook my breakfast and I'll tell you."

He held up his hands. "Okay, as you wish."

Elspeth sat in her living room holding a mug of coffee. She saw the police car leave the village and all she wanted to do was rush down Church Lane and back to Sarah.

She remembered the look on her face, the loathing in her eyes.

The rejection.

What had really happened?

Elspeth knew she had made a complete mess of everything on Saturday evening but after that all she had seen on Sarah's face was confusion. She had not seen any hint of the disgust she had seen in Sarah's eyes only an hour ago. It looked as though she had survived some sort of horrendous encounter with God knows what, and whatever it was it had changed her.

Nothing added up: she had to be lying.

Somebody had been back to the cottage on Sunday afternoon, somebody had taken the jumper and the underwear and the other things Phillip had spotted were missing. If she was lying unconscious somewhere and spent the night God knows where, who had been to the cottage?

No, Sarah was lying. It was as simple as that.

She was injured, she could not fake that, but what else happened? Where was she for over twenty-four hours and who was she with?

She didn't believe for one minute that there was any truth in the suggestion that Sarah was having an affair because if she were she would have known. She would have been able to tell. But there had to be something more than they were being told and she fully intended finding out what it was.

She may have been a fool on Saturday evening but she was not going to give up that easily.

Chapter Nineteen

Michael walked through the village on his way to catching the bus to work. The key to Primrose Cottage was in his pocket. He was intent on keeping his promise to Sarah Preston.

How was he going to return it to her?

He would bury the other keys later. It was something he promised himself he would do because that part of his life was over now.

But the key in his pocket was important because there was no way he could bury her key. They trusted each other and they had their secrets. He promised to give the key to her. Maybe she would keep it as a spare, maybe each time she looked at it or used it she would think of him.

Before the wondrous moment when he found her on Copper's Ridge, she had been constantly on his mind. Now she was there for different reasons. Even if nothing had happened it would still be the same: she would still be constantly on his mind.

But something did happen.

She had wanted him and given herself to him.

It was incredible. He would never experience anything like it ever again. She had made him feel like the real man that he knew he was.

He stopped by the ford and up looked up Church Lane.

How could he return the key?

Crossing the footbridge he started walking up the lane. No cars were about other than a few parked further up the lane. He saw nothing to indicate there was anybody at the cottage. The kitchen and main bedroom were at the back of the house. If they were in, that was where they would be, not in the living room, not at this time.

He stopped again as the cottage came fully into view. Screwing up his eyes, he still felt confused. Previously, whenever he thought of the man she lived with he always seethed with hatred; he had even considered murder, but not anymore. That had been silly and immature. He was a man himself now and must start thinking and acting like one. The old feelings were no longer there. He was looking to the future now: he was looking beyond tomorrow.

Lowering his head he carried on walking up Church Lane.

He was almost there so he must be careful.

Scanning the front bedroom windows and then the living and dining room windows, he tried only to move his eyes just in case there was somebody there. If somebody was watching him he didn't want them to think he was deliberately looking at the cottage. He stopped when he was opposite the gate and bent down, pretending to tie the laces on his trainers.

The cottage looked empty.

Maybe they were out and he could leave the key now. He had promised and Sarah Preston would think he had broken his promise. Perhaps she was at the hospital having her head checked. He didn't think the injury she had needed stitches but he would have wanted her to have it checked.

Feeling in his pocket his fingers grasped the key. He looked up and down the lane, went across to the gate, lifted the latch slowly and slipped silently down the path to the front door.

He put the key against his lips and kissed it.

"Thank you, Sarah Preston," he whispered before carefully sliding the key through the letter-box.

As Sarah came down the stairs she heard the letter-box squeak.

"What was that?" Phillip called from the kitchen.

Sarah saw the key on the doormat. "It's just a circular," she said, bending down to pick up the key.

She looked at it and smiled, squeezing it tightly and pressing it to her lips before slipping it into her dressing gown pocket. Thank God she had been there. If Phillip had seen the key there would have been more questions to answer. Michael had been a bit silly just putting it through the letter-box but he would have wanted to keep his promise. Fortunately no harm had been done. She stopped by the phone table and ripped off a piece of paper from the notepad.

"Just a circular," she said again, screwing up the piece of paper as she walked into the kitchen. "God that smells good."

She went over to the rubbish bin and dropped the screwed up piece of paper into it. "I didn't think I could feel this hungry."

Phillip looked over his shoulder. "The eggs are almost ready. Sit down and pour yourself a coffee. It'll be ready in a jiffy."

"Thanks."

She sat down at the table, feeling a warm glow all over her body, whether it was from the recent bath or something else, she wasn't sure. No damn it, of course she was sure. She poured the coffee, breathing in deeply as she fought to suppress the wave of nostalgia as the bitter aroma filled her nostrils. Anybody would have thought she had been away from civilisation for months not just twenty-four hours. But what a twenty-four hours it had been. She closed her eyes and saw Michael's smiling face at the moment he had suddenly accepted what she was doing to him.

She smiled with him.

"What are you smiling at?" Phillip asked.

"Just so pleased to be home," she said.

Phillip piled bacon, sausages, black pudding, mushrooms, tomatoes, fried eggs, baked beans and fried bread onto two plates and deftly recovered the toast from the grill just before it burned.

334

"Right, if this doesn't put some strength back into you, nothing will."

"It's just what I wanted." She touched his arm. "Phillip, I'm so sorry," she said, trying desperately to drag herself away from the aura of Michael. It was time now to move on, to project herself into the new life Michael had made it possible for her to enter. "I must have really scared you."

He stopped pouring his coffee and looked at her. "Scared is an understatement but explanations can wait. Get that lot inside you and then we're going to the hospital."

"But –"

"No buts. Eat, dress, then hospital, and that's an order."

"Yes, sir," Sarah said, smiling again as she picked up her knife and fork.

The key was burning a hole in her dressing gown pocket.

Had the last twenty-four hours really happened, she wondered.

Of course they had.

Her heart skipped a beat.

John sat in the meeting only half listening to what was being said.

He hated meetings because they very rarely achieved anything other than to generate unnecessary work, and most of the time the decisions were taken before the meeting started, or they were changed once the meeting was over. He preferred to operate on his own, make his own decisions, make his own mistakes and then learn from them.

Had Elspeth been a mistake? Had he learnt anything with her?

These were questions he could not answer because he hadn't realised they needed to be asked until very recently. He had either pushed the suspicions to the back of his mind or he had tried to view them from a completely different angle.

His world was now upside down and he was unable to concentrate on anything else. He had driven to work that morning like a robot: he could not remember what the traffic was like, where the hold-ups were or the weather conditions.

He needed to think straight and decide what he should do. He wasn't an impetuous man: his profession made him think things through so that he could reach logical fact-based conclusions and therefore logical and accurate decisions.

When the meeting was finally over he went straight to his office, told Jennifer he didn't want to be disturbed and sat behind his desk with his head in his hands. After a few minutes he picked up a pen and started writing.

Fact: Elspeth is either bi-sexual or a closeted lesbian.

Fact: she doesn't seem to care what I do about it.

Fact: in the time we have lived together I have never really had any inkling that her sexual preference was for anybody but me ... for men.

Fact: Abigail: until now I've never doubted Elspeth's sexual orientation and the Abigail incident I witnessed meant nothing.

Fact: Sarah Preston is the catalyst.

Fact: ~~Phillip Preston doesn't know that his wife is a ... is a what?~~

He scribbled a line through this possible fact as he didn't know the answer.

Fact: I don't know whether Sarah reciprocates Elspeth's feelings.

Fact: I'm still in love with Elspeth.

Fact: I do not want to lose her.

Question: can I continue to live with Elspeth knowing the way she feels?

He screwed up the piece of paper and threw it in the bin. That little exercise had got him absolutely nowhere. Grabbing his coat from the back of the door, he went into the central office.

"I'm going out, Jennifer," he told his secretary. "I don't know how long I'll be."

"You've got an eleven o'clock appointment and a meeting at two o'clock," Jennifer said in her efficient high-pitched educated voice.

"Reschedule them both," he said as he started for the main door.

"What shall I –?"

"Whatever you need to say but reschedule them."

As he walked out of the office, he heard Jennifer sigh.

Sarah and Phillip returned from the hospital just after lunch.

They had spoken very little although it was obvious Phillip was bursting with questions. She was ready with some of the answers but didn't want to instigate the inevitable. The longer he waited the more she could think of answers and try to pre-empt everything he was going to ask.

"So, they gave you the all clear?" Phillip said as he opened the car door for her outside A&E.

"It seems that way. The bruising and cuts are superficial and there doesn't seem to be any damage elsewhere. But I've got to take it easy for twenty-four hours just in case. So I won't be able to use that as an excuse," she added, trying to sound whimsical.

"Excuse for what?"

He had sounded serious so she decided not to go there yet. Making love with Phillip was something she needed to do – and very soon, tomorrow maybe – in order to re-establish her physical relationship with her husband.

"Oh, nothing," she said.

For the rest of the journey he said nothing further ... there were no questions either ... Sarah was relieved, the quietness gave her time to think.

"Well," Philip said as they walked in through the back door, "we've got an unexpected half day together. Any ideas?"

She couldn't believe what he was saying.

"Any ideas?" she said, hoping her surprise was evident. "I would have thought ..."

"What?" Phillip said, putting the car keys on the table.

She took off her coat and threw it on the back of a chair. "What about welcoming me back?"

"I didn't know whether you were ..."

"According to the hospital I'm fine, so neither of us has got an excuse."

She moved across the kitchen towards him but he didn't react in the way she expected. His behaviour and body language told her he was being cautious.

She stopped.

"Phillip, what is it? Since I got back this morning, you've been acting very strangely. I know it's been a terrible twenty-four hours for you but ... well, I would have thought I had good reason but why are you ...?"

"Where were you last night?"

She spread her hands, tensing every muscle in her body. "I told you, somewhere up on Copper's Ridge."

"You didn't mention Copper's Ridge and I know what you told me but where were you really?"

She shuddered as an image of Michael's face and bare chest appeared in front of her: his eyes closed, his teeth clenched as his thighs lifted her, and the deep sighs as the spasms went on and on.

"If I could take you to where I was, I would," she said. "I thought I'd told you it was somewhere up on Copper's Ridge. How could I have got back if I didn't recognise something once it was daylight? I told you what happened. I know it sounds incredible and maybe a little pathetic but ..."

"I'm not sure what the *buts* are, Sarah. I was worried sick, so sure something had happened to you, but then Elspeth –"

"Elspeth? What's she been –?"

"Listen to me," Phillip said and there was urgency in his voice. "Just listen to me."

"All right. I'm sorry." Suddenly her legs seemed to lose their strength so she pulled a chair away from the table and sat down.

"John and I went out looking for you, well we all went looking for you at first but then John and I went out on our own. We actually went up onto Copper's Ridge, as far as the tree where Abigail and her mother died but there was no sign … no that's not what I mean, what I mean is that if you had been somewhere close I'm sure I would have sensed it. There was nothing, nothing at all."

"I think, and I don't mean to be critical, Phillip, but I think you're being a little too romantic. What makes you think you'd have *sensed* something?"

He looked down sheepishly. "You know what I mean," he said quickly. "Anyway, we walked down Warden's Way first and called the police as soon as we got back. It was the second time they were here when Elspeth –" he paused, "when Elspeth noticed that some of your ... some of your clothes were missing," he finished in a hurry.

Sarah had put the clothes Michael brought for her in the laundry basket before she bathed. She had been sure Phillip wouldn't have noticed they were missing. What man can go to his wife's wardrobe and tell which items of clothing are there and which are not? Most men couldn't remember what colour the walls and carpets were, let alone where their wives kept their clothes.

Phillip said it was Elspeth who noticed some clothing was missing. What had Elspeth been doing going through her wardrobe and drawers? And how had she known what was where anyway?

There were no answers, not yet. It was a little disconcerting that the clothing Michael had brought to her had been missed. It didn't matter who had noticed: as she hadn't expected to be asked the question she didn't have a ready answer – she didn't have an explanation. She had thought everything through but her *everything* was proving not to be enough.

All she could think of saying was: "Of course some clothes were missing, I didn't go out with nothing on."

"I'm being serious, Sarah," he said. "Between you leaving early yesterday morning and returning this morning, somebody came into the cottage and took some of your clothes. If it wasn't you then who was it?"

She swallowed hard. "What clothes? And how did Elspeth know what was there and what wasn't?"

He leant forward and put his elbows on the table.

"Some of your underwear was missing and a jumper, your joggers and sweatshirt, the ones you wear for working in the cottage."

"How did Elspeth ... no leave that for the moment. This clothing was supposed to have gone missing while I was lying unconscious in some dark wet wood. Is that what you're saying?"

"Yes."

"Did any of you think of looking in the laundry basket? I put my joggers and the sweatshirt you are referring to in there on Friday evening, and some underwear. I'd planned to do some washing yesterday when I got back but unfortunately I was temporarily –"

"There's no need to be sarcastic," he said.

"I'm not being sarcastic but I *am* a little annoyed and I *am* worried that you seem to think I was off on some pre-planned liaison. I –"

"I wasn't suggesting that –"

"You didn't have to because it was written all over your face. Look, I went for a walk, cracked my head on a branch, knocked myself out and then I didn't have the faintest idea who or where I was. How about giving me a bit of sympathy and understanding rather than making accusations?" She didn't have an explanation for the missing jumper, which was now back on top of the others, so she had to try to lead Phillip away from asking any more questions about the missing clothes.

"I'm not accusing you of anything."

"I think you are. It certainly sounds like it."

"It just seems a bit strange that you were away so long."

340

She let the tears come into her eyes. It was a ploy she mastered years earlier, and she could not remember a time when it failed to work. This time it wasn't a ploy, though, the tears were genuine.

"The next time I have an accident I'll try –"

"Now you're being silly," he said. "I was just sick with worry."

"And I'm ... I'm sorry," she said as she wiped away a tear. "I'm sorry I caused you that worry but now I'm home. Maybe with the clothing you thought was missing you had every right to be suspicious but I hope I've explained that things were not missing."

She paused to see if Phillip was going to question her explanation, but when he didn't she said: "Are you going to work?"

"Of course not."

"I mean tomorrow."

"No, I'm not. Are you ready to tell me –"

"About the unpaid leave?" She breathed a sigh of relief. They had moved on. If Elspeth had noticed clothes were missing she would have known her explanation about them being in the laundry basket couldn't be true. but it wasn't Elspeth she had to convince.

"Yes."

"I was going to tell you but because of yesterday ..."

"But why?"

"I needed time to think. The job is getting me down and I need a change. I thought if I –"

"But you had time off when we first moved in so why couldn't you have done your thinking then?"

She screwed up her eyes. He was still very suspicious and yet this time she was telling him the complete truth. A tear dropped onto her hand.

"Phillip, I want to know why you're being so suspicious. I took the time off to decorate this cottage for you, for us. It was only when I went back to work I realised just how much I hated that bloody job. That's why I took more leave and

341

that's why I went for that damned walk yesterday. I needed time to think."

He reached across the table and covered her hand with his.

"It's me who should be apologising. I'm sorry. I thought I had lost you. You have no idea the things that went through my mind. And the police didn't help. I ..."

"You thought I was having an affair?"

"Yes, that did go through my mind, I'm sorry. I thought you had left me." He went round the table and kissed her. "I'm sorry," he said again.

"How sorry?" she asked smiling.

"What do you mean?"

She stood up and taking his hand she led him from the kitchen.

Half way up the stairs she was still smiling. She wouldn't have believed she could be such a good liar. Perhaps she wasn't, maybe Phillip's innocence was playing a part. He really was so pleased to have her back he was willing to accept her explanations without further probing.

Only time would tell.

Michael got into work just after ten o'clock.

As he set about his tasks for the day he realised he had a fixed smile on his face because Sarah Preston was constantly on his mind. He had *never* been able to get Sarah Preston out of his mind, but before Sunday night it had all been a fantasy: his imagination had generated an expectation that deep down he believed would never be fulfilled.

But now he was able to picture her and think about her for such different reasons. He no longer needed to imagine what she was like. If he closed his eyes he could feel every contour of her body, see every freckle, every silky hair, touch the smoothness of her skin and taste the sweetness of her lips. She was the lovely person he had expected her to be.

He had witnessed all her emotions.

Seeing her smile and seeing her cry was wonderful but when she became violent, when she attacked him, that was something else. Hearing her swear wasn't very nice but ... well, it wasn't that often.

He had talked to her, cared for her and treated her injuries after she was hurt. In the space of just a few hours they had shared every emotion possible. It was as though in twenty-four hours they had experienced a complete relationship. And then there was that moment when she had ... her hands on his body, touching him, caressing him, stroking him, her fingers soft as velvet as every inch of his body reacted to her touch.

When he touched her he didn't think anything could feel so wonderful. Feeling the warmth of her thighs against his hips, her feet and toes resting on his legs as she moved slowly and rhythmically, her hands on his chest, her nails gently scratching his skin, her eyes looking down at him and the smile on her lips.

Yes, in just a few hours they had lived together and experienced everything together.

He would remember her always.

"What're you smilin' at, lad?" Ben Foster asked.

He worked next to Michael sometimes and he liked the boy. He thought of him as a boy because like most of his workmates he also thought he was simple in the head, but he liked him anyway. Being bloody good at his job meant the others ought to watch out.

"Michael's very good with 'is 'ands," he had told his wife after Michael had been there a couple of weeks. "If 'e weren't so stupid 'e could make 'imself a fortune with 'is 'ands. Good lookin' lad too. Bet the girls all wan' him, 'til they find out what 'e's like, that is. Don't talk much, in fact 'e rarely talks at all. Polite though, says please an' thank you unlike most of 'is generation. When 'e does speak it's strange cos 'e's got quite a posh voice."

343

Michael looked sideways at Mr Foster. "Just thinking," he said, still smiling.

Ben was surprised he got a response at all, but he saw in Michael's eyes that something must have happened.

Something to change him.

"What is it, Michael, what's 'appened."

Michael switched off his lathe.

The manager had gone out so it wouldn't matter for a couple of minutes. The others were elsewhere in the workshop assembling, varnishing and finishing off the furniture. He wanted to tell somebody, not who he had been with because that was a secret, but he wanted to tell somebody that he had done it.

He would never tell his mother and he didn't have any friends to tell, well other than his friends at work, but they weren't real friends because he only saw them at work. Should he tell Mr Foster? He was old enough to be his father, if not his grandfather so would he be annoyed?

"Go on, lad. What is it?" Ben persisted as he also switched off his lathe.

Michael looked around the workshop to make sure the others were out of earshot. "I …"

"You what? What d'you wan' to tell me, lad?"

"I … I did it, Mr Foster."

"Did you?" Ben said with a broad smile. "But what is *it?* What did you do?"

"I … I did it with a woman."

Ben raised his eyebrows in surprise, the smile still on his face.

"You did it with a woman, did you? You're a dark 'orse. Who was it, anybody I know?"

Michael looked away, vigorously shaking his head, embarrassed by Mr Foster's directness. "No, nobody you know," he said.

"So, lad, was that your first time?"

Michael nodded. "Yes."

344

"So you're experienced now, are you?"

Michael nodded again. "Yes."

"So you've got a girlfriend now, 'ave you?"

"No," Michael said, thinking it was a silly question.

Ben frowned. "So if you 'aven't got a girlfriend lad, who'd you do it with?"

Michael hesitated. "I can't tell you her name."

"But she has a name," Ben said. "And where does this young lady live?"

"She lives ... she lives in the village."

"Oh, does she? Somebody's young daughter, is she?"

Michael thought it was another silly question because every girl was somebody's daughter.

"Yes," he said, "And somebody's wife?"

Ben almost dropped the chisel he was holding.

"Somebody's wife? What you been up to, lad? You can't go round doin' it with other men's wives."

Michael smiled.

"I did," he said proudly.

Elspeth tried to concentrate.

She had drunk too much coffee and smoked too many cigarettes but still she couldn't think straight. It wasn't writer's block. She knew what she wanted to write but every time she started tapping the keys her thoughts would wander off and she found herself staring through the window.

Concentrate.

Her mind wouldn't let her forget what she had seen in Sarah's eyes. It was definitely a loathing, hatred: yes she would even go that far. She had seen hatred in Sarah's eyes.

But why?

What had happened?

Where had she really been?

Over and over again the same questions whirled round in her mind. She let her head loll back against the chair's headrest.

God, what a bloody mess!

How many times had she said that? Why had she been so stupid? She had achieved absolutely nothing. All she had managed to do was alienate Sarah and John, as well as making an absolute fool of herself with Phillip.

John?

He was more astute than she ever expected. So he had been watching them, had he? Watching the way they looked at each other, the way they walked, the way they talked. Poor John, poor innocent John. He still had the tie he bought the first time they met, the one she chose for him. What did he expect from her? She couldn't help feeling the way she did. She liked men *and* women. Was that her fault? Did that make her a freak? So what if she was in love with Sarah? She could still love John the way she always had.

John would not be a problem.

Once he got over the shock he would not be a problem. He had never been a problem about anything. As soon as it looked as though he was going to be difficult about something she knew she could wrap him round her little finger. She would give him a week to get over it and then they would be back to normal.

Normal?

Would anything ever be normal again knowing that Sarah was living so close by?

Phillip?

Elspeth could not believe he was so easy and was so willing to cheat on Sarah, especially with somebody he thought was her best friend. They hadn't gone all the way and ironically it had been Sarah who had seen to that, but if she had arrived only seconds later it would definitely have happened. With Sarah missing he had been ready to have full sex with his wife's best friend. But then she'd been more than willing to let him. Maybe he was like her; maybe it didn't matter. Maybe he needed to do it there and then with somebody, anybody, for some bizarre reason.

Bizarre?

Was it some form of defence mechanism? And why was she trying to find excuses for him? It had so nearly happened so what was the difference? He didn't stop what he was about to do – Sarah did. The intent was there, and the capability – sod him, he would have to live with his own conscience.

She had enough to contend with.

But she had still been a bloody fool.

Perhaps she ought to question her own motives. She didn't really find Phillip attractive, well not in that sort of way. He was good-looking enough but she thought he was a bit wet. No, wet was the wrong word, more languorous, laid back – no get-up-and-go.

Was she being unfair?

She was the one who had tested him, wanting to know how strong his relationship with Sarah really was. Why, when both of them were worried out of their minds had she chosen that moment to do it? Perhaps it was because they *were* so worried. Perhaps it was because they needed each other for exactly that reason.

But Sarah wasn't a typical best friend. Phillip had been and still was the competition. She would be quite happy to take Phillip's place, quite happy to move into Primrose Cottage, quite happy to move in anywhere as long as it was with Sarah. People would gossip, point fingers, spread rumours and do whatever people who are incapable of understanding do to others.

Men would leer at them, trying to picture them together and then go home and make love to their wives. It wouldn't matter though because nothing would matter as long as they were together. She needed Phillip to feel guilty; she needed that hold over him, a hold she could use to break his relationship with Sarah. Having sex with him had perhaps been going a little too far, because Sarah would know and she would know why she had done it.

She got up and walked across the room to the other window. She had claimed the second bedroom as her study.

One window looked out towards the road leading into the village and the other down towards the church. She could see the church spire but more importantly, she could also see the edge of the roof on Primrose Cottage.

She wanted to move her desk to that window so that every time she looked up she could see that roof, but her desk wouldn't fit in the small space available. Her study was hers and John knew he was never, ever to enter it. It was her private world, where she wrote, where she thought, where she could be herself.

Where she could dream.

Everything in the room was hers: her personality, her imagination and her fantasies could all have free rein.

So if she was where she could be herself, why couldn't she answer two simple questions? What did she really want and what was she willing to do to get what she really wanted?

She could answer the first question in part because the answer was Sarah, but did she really want John as well?

From the moment she first set eyes on John she knew he would fill a longstanding gap in her life, but had she always believed that John was only a temporary gap filler? She never liked being on her own and there was no need for her to be: she could always move in with her mother and father but that would have been regressive. She went to London to find herself but all she found was a sales assistant's job with Tie-Rack and a grotty bed-sit in Bayswater. All she wanted to do was write. Then she had no idea who she wanted to be with in order to share her passion in every sense of the word.

She had been told often enough how attractive she was, so why hadn't she had more relationships? Why hadn't she played the field? Tested herself – with men and women?

Maybe John was once the answer but now he wasn't. He was now only part of the answer. She had already established that. If she'd been asked what she really wanted six weeks, six months or six years earlier, she wouldn't have known.

Now she did.

Sarah – that's who she wanted.

Sarah, Sarah, Sarah, Sarah.

She must not give up.

Sharing was not an option: it had to be all or nothing. If she hadn't seen the confusion in Sarah she would not be pursuing her goal. If she believed Sarah wasn't in the slightest bit interested she would have backed off ... but Sarah *was* interested: she just needed convincing.

Lighting another cigarette Elspeth stared at the corner of the roof of Primrose Cottage.

There still had to be a way.

Sarah willed herself to start feeling something, anything.

From the moment they reached the bedroom and for the first time, she took control and Phillip was more than willing to let her.

But there was nothing.

No tingling, no throbbing, nothing.

When she had put Michael's hands on her body the sensation was immediate, a sensation that had grown and grown until she felt she was high on drugs. She would have done anything for the feeling to continue, for it never to stop.

Was it only because Michael was the forbidden fruit?

She had needed to make love with Phillip as soon as possible because he was her future. Michael had given her a future but Phillip *was* that future and it needed to start straightaway, not tomorrow or the day after.

But there was nothing.

She looked down at him and saw the look of contentment on his face.

For her it was as it had been on so many occasions in the past: she felt only as though she was being the dutiful wife.

"Wow!" Phillip gasped, opening his eyes. "That was amazing. If that's the way ..."

"I'm pleased for you," was all Sarah could bring herself to say.

"And you?" he said, still breathing heavily.

"As ever," she said, smiling.

"Then I'm pleased for you also."

Phillip closed his eyes.

A naked Elspeth appeared.

She was smiling but not because she was amused or happy. The smile became laughter as she ridiculed him. Thinking about what could have happened made him shudder. It had been so close and he would have done it ... but it hadn't happened.

He opened his eyes quickly to rid himself of the image and the guilt.

I wish you could be really pleased for me, Sarah wanted to say.

She felt very let down. She had gone to Copper's Ridge to make a decision, which was why the last twenty minutes had been so very important. She fully accepted that there was a lot more to her relationship with Phillip than just sex, even though she had been told on more than one occasion just how important it was for men. Why couldn't it be important for women too? What had just happened, or hadn't in her case, had been a key to letting her develop her decision. After all, without sex there would be no baby, or babies, and no true family.

What could she do now?

Perhaps she had expected too much. Maybe she should have waited. It was only twelve hours since Michael had worked his magic. Perhaps her unrealistic expectations were the reason she felt as she did. Maybe it would happen the next time, or the time after that.

It had to be wrong to be making comparisons.

"So," Phillip said, running his thumb up the inside of Sarah's thigh, "What's next? I think we should do something special to celebrate your safe return."

Sarah arched her back and looked at the ceiling for inspiration. She wanted to tell him the truth. Didn't she promise herself less than forty-eight hours ago that there would be no more secrets? Yet here she was keeping the biggest secret of her life from her husband. If only she could tell him that he had failed the one simple test when a pass would have secured their future for as many years as they had left. She felt his hands moving over her stomach, his finger tip playing with her navel.

She wanted to tell him to stop, not wanting him to touch her. It wasn't even the same, it was worse. Previously she had always needed to please him: all he had needed to do on this occasion was please her.

Suddenly she wanted neither.

She just wanted to be left alone. The decision she had made up on Copper's Ridge was now a problem again but for different reasons. Her mind began to whirl – it was all too much. Even her nakedness at that moment felt wrong. Feeling his hands on her body wasn't right either.

What an absolute mess.

"Well?"

"I don't know," she said, trying to dismiss the terrible thoughts from her mind. "Let me go and have a shower and I'll think."

He sat up, pulling her towards him.

"You had a bath only a couple of hours ago." He buried his face against her.

"You know I like to have a shower afterwards," she said, wishing she could grab hold of his hair and pull him away. She put her hands either side of his head and moved it away. "I'm also dying for the loo," she lied.

"But ..."

"Please, Phillip, we've got all day."

"If you insist."

"I'd love another coffee," she told him as she headed for the bathroom.

John parked in the long-term car park at Bristol Temple Meads railway station. He had no idea why he was here.

After collecting the Freelander he had driven aimlessly round and round the centre of the city before heading out to the A4.

Regardless, he was now in this station car park, so what was he going to do?

He looked over his shoulder at the overnight bag on the back seat. Elspeth won't have missed it and she certainly won't be missing him. She will be thinking about Sarah. He might get a passing thought, but no more.

What was the point? Had they been living a lie from the moment they moved in together? He smirked as he recollected his immediate reaction on hearing what he now thought he had known all along to be the truth.

Would he fight for her?

Would he do whatever was needed to win her back?

Bollocks!

Elspeth was history as he had been history for some time.

That was what really hurt. He felt used, well and truly used. She never intended to stay with him. He could almost understand it if she had found another man but being dumped for a woman! That was too much for his masculine pride.

So what was he going to do?

He looked out over the car park. It was packed. Commuters – what a life. Did they ever bother to calculate how long they spent on trains, day in day out? Sitting in the same seats and standing on the same square foot of platform as they waited for the same train, morning after morning.

Sad gits!

And what was it all for?

Materialism?

A better house, a better car, a better what?

They would have routines, miserable routines; sit at the same desks, next to the same people who also had their miserable routines; eat their sandwiches at a set time, or go for a jog at lunchtime or to the local gymnasium. They would feel better for that because they might live longer and be able to stick to their miserable routines for longer.

At the end of their supposed working day they would reverse the routine: same square foot, same seat, same evening paper. They would drive home from the station in the car they would replace every other year; check their watches as they opened the front door to see if their routine had been upset by a minute or two. They would shout at the dog, kiss their partner and spend, if they were lucky, a short while with the kids before they went to bed.

Having dinner at the same time was all part of the routine, as was sitting in the same place at the table, talking – if they did talk – about the same things. Perhaps a little television would follow before going to bed, and once in a while making love.

But what were they really thinking?

How often did they genuinely open their minds to each other? How often were they really honest with each other? If Elspeth had been honest with him from the outset, would it have made a difference? He doubted it. It was too serious to gloss over and too serious to talk through.

Maybe they should have tried …

"Oh, by the way John, I've fallen in love with my best friend. I thought you ought to know," Elspeth might have said, sipping her soup.

"Have you darling, that's nice."

"Yes, it just happened."

"These things do."

"I suppose they do. Do you like the soup?"

"Yes, thank you."

What was it all for? What was the point of it all? They would all die one day and be forgotten. Their kids would grow up and have their own routines: they too would have kids and so on, and so on.

Was there a purpose to life?

If there was a purpose, he wished somebody would bloody well tell him what it was. He might just be able to come to terms with what was happening.

He knew he was being unfair to the commuters, using them because he was at the railway station. His routines were probably far more obvious than theirs were.

He needed a drink.

A drink might help him think straight, or forget.

He got out of the car and pulled up the collar of his coat against the chilly wind and the slight drizzle that was falling from the grey, bleak sky.

He looked upwards.

"That's what life's really like," he said aloud. "Fucking depressing."

Chapter Twenty

After twenty minutes Phillip went to investigate why Sarah had not joined him in the kitchen.

She was lying on the bed with a towel still wrapped round her and she was fast asleep. One arm was lying across the pillow, her fingers resting against the bruise on her forehead, her hair still wet.

He stood at the end of the bed and looked down at her.

Although she looked exhausted, she seemed untroubled in her sleep so he wondered if the last forty hours had really happened. Regardless of the truth it was at times like this that he really began to understand and appreciate the feelings he had for her. Maybe he was taking her for granted too often, so that would have to stop. Almost losing something so precious was the warning he needed. The harsh realities of life had hit him like a sledgehammer. Things were going to change, he was going to change but there wasn't any need for her to change.

She was a good person, through and through.

He had never looked at her before the way he was looking at her now. How could he ever have doubted her? How could he ever have imagined let alone believed that she may have left him for another man?

He managed to remove the damp towel without disturbing her. He dabbed lightly at a few droplets of water she had missed on her shoulder before covering her with the duvet, then he bent down and kissed her wet hair and whispered, "I love you."

John was enjoying the unaccustomed exhilaration of doing over 100 mph in the middle lane on an unusually quiet M5, when a lorry pulled out in front of him to overtake a slower vehicle – without indicating.

"Fucking idiot … What the – *Shit!*" he said, swerving to avoid the lorry. But why were his front wheels behaving as though they had a will of its own?

It took him less than a second to react to the sudden skid.

He tugged at the steering wheel.

Why the hell was nothing he was doing having any fucking effect?

The Freelander was whizzing through the air, it was tipping and now it was flipping onto its roof.

Fucking hell!

There was crunch as the roof began to cave in.

He thought these fucking Freelanders were supposed to –

His head was forced down by the collapsed roof, his neck was being wrenched sideways against his left shoulder.

The pressure was so intense … God, it hurt.

And then – !

The lorry moved on.

The driver switched off his mobile phone.

"What was that?" he mumbled, and checking his inside mirror saw nothing in his rear vision except the side of his lorry and not the outside lane. He had previously noticed that somebody or something had knocked his right hand door mirror out of alignment and had decided to correct it the next time he stopped for a break.

But never mind that now.

He was late for his delivery so he had better put his foot down.

PC Martin and PC Gould were at the front desk in the police station in Stow when the report of a RTA on the M5 came in. The report was circulated to all police stations in the area.

They weren't tasked to go to the scene of the accident because it was not within their area of responsibility.

"Hmm. Only one vehicle involved by the look of it, a Freelander," PC Martin said, reading out the main points to PC Gould. "Excessive speed. Patch of oil on the road, possibly from a previous accident, but probably from the driver's car ... driving too close to the crash barrier, maybe." He shook his head. "Stupid idiot! Driver has been taken to Tewkesbury Hospital." He smirked. "A broken bottle of whisky was in the front of the car with the top unscrewed ... own bloody fault by the look of it. Guy's name was Davidson."

"What did you say?" PC Gould whispered. "Davidson and he was driving a Freelander?"

PC Martin grabbed the office phone. "Get me Tewkesbury Hospital A & E, please. Yes, it's urgent. I'll hold ..."

Elspeth was sitting at her laptop, trying to work.

She heard a car pull up but thought nothing of it. They were so close to where the tourists parked their cars that they had become used to not reacting to the noise.

The knock on the door a few minutes later brought her out of the fantasy world of the book she was trying to write.

PC Tony Martin and PC Debbie Gould were standing on the doorstep.

"Oh, hello," Elspeth said absentmindedly.

"Miss Warrington," PC Martin said, "do you mind if we come in?"

"Of course not," Elspeth said, stepping back from the door. "I presume you've come to finalise your enquiries into Mrs Preston's disappearance."

PC Martin took off his hat and waited to be shown where he should go.

"Would you sit down please, Miss Warrington?" PC Gould said politely. "We'd like to talk to you."

"Oh." Elspeth looked surprised. "Come through to the kitchen, it's the warmest room in the cottage. John always says –" She lifted her hand to her mouth. "Is it about my father?" she asked.

"No, it's not your father. I'm afraid there's been an accident in which Mr Davidson was involved and –"

"What's he gone and done now?"

"Miss Warrington, it is with much regret that we must inform you that Mr Davidson was killed in the accident."

During his time with the police, PC Martin had found it necessary to inform any number of people that a loved one had died and he believed in the direct approach.

There was little point in evading the truth, or beating round the bush.

Both he and PC Gould watched Elspeth closely.

Elspeth stared at them.

She had heard what they said but her brain was not willing to take on board the meaning of the words. She lowered her hand slowly to the table.

"Killed?" she whispered. "John's dead?"

"Yes," PC Martin said, "I'm afraid he is."

"What ... what happened?"

"He was –" PC Gould started to say.

"We're not too sure at the moment, Miss Warrington," PC Martin said hurriedly, glancing sideways at Debbie Gould. "The cause of such accidents is not always immediately apparent and as it occurred well out of our area the full details are not yet known."

"Where then, where did it happen?"

"On the M5, just north of the Michael Wood Service Station."

"Was ... was there anybody else involved?"

"No, there were no other vehicles involved and no other casualties."

"What on earth was he doing?"

"I'm sorry. As yet we don't have the –"

"Of course, you already said so."

"Would you like a drink?" PC Gould asked helpfully.

"What?"

"A drink, would you like a drink?"

"A drink, yes ... no ... yes, a drink. Yes, I would like a drink."

"I'll put the kettle on."

"No ... no, not that sort of drink, I need a ... a real drink. It's not every day that ..." Elspeth's eyes filled with tears. "... in the living room, on the side ... there's a bottle of brandy."

"I'll get it." Debbie Gould left the kitchen.

PC Martin sat down. "I really am sorry, Miss Warrington." He put his hand on hers.

Elspeth looked at his blurred image. "My name's Elspeth. Please, under the circumstances ... formalities seem ... inappropriate."

"Elspeth," PC Martin repeated. "Yes, Elspeth."

PC Gould came back into the kitchen with a tumbler in her hand. She put it on the table in front of Elspeth and sat down.

"Thank you," Elspeth said.

She stared at the glass for a few seconds then picked it up and gulped down the contents, screwing up her face as the alcohol burned the back of her throat.

"I don't usually drink at this time of day. I was working ... writing ... I write children's books ... good God, John dead. How do I ... what do people do? It's awful ... John dead, I can't believe it ... I ..."

"Is there anybody you'd like us to call?" Debbie Gould asked.

"Call? What ... what do you mean?"

"Is there anybody you'd like to be with you?"

"With me? No ... I mean, yes ..." She knew straightaway who she would like to be with her but ... "Yes ... Mrs Preston ... Sarah ... but I'll ..."

WPC Gould stood up. "I'll go and get her, Miss Warrington. Is she at home?"

"Elspeth. I told PC Martin to call me Elspeth. Er ... yes, would you mind? I ... I think she's at home."

Elspeth saw PC Gould give PC Martin a strange look as she left the kitchen.

Phillip was walking across the back garden when he heard the front door bell. He swore under his breath, but wiping his hands on a bit of old cloth he went quickly to the front door just in case the bell was rung again and woke Sarah.

"Ah," he said when he saw PC Gould. "I'm afraid my wife is –"

"Not here?"

"No, she's here but she's asleep."

Sergeant Craig had said they would ring to arrange a time to see Sarah to finalise their inquiries, so what was PC Gould doing on the doorstep without warning?

"Can it wait? Sergeant Craig said that you would want to ask her some more questions but –"

"It's not to do with yesterday, sir," PC Gould told him. "There's been an accident and Mr Davidson has been killed."

Phillip's jaw dropped. "Killed? Do you mean he's dead?"

"That's what ... yes, I'm afraid he is."

"What happened?"

"There was an accident on the M5."

"Jesus! John dead! You'd better come in."

He shook his head and closed the door.

"So ... er ... so you'd like my wife to be with Elspeth. Is that what you're saying?" he asked, once he regained a little of his composure.

"Yes, sir," Debbie Gould said. "Well not me. Miss Warrington asked if I would come and get her."

"As I said, my wife's asleep ... but, I suppose under the circumstances. Sorry, that sounded a bit heartless. As you know she's been through a lot herself, but I suppose ..."

360

He started up the stairs, still not believing what he had been told.

"Wait here, please. I'll go and wake her."

Sarah had kicked off the duvet but she was still fast asleep. He sat on the side of the bed and put his hand on her shoulder.

"Sarah," he said quietly. "Sarah, wake up."

She moved her head and groaned.

"What …?"

"Sorry to wake you but there's been an …"

She opened her eyes slowly, still full of sleep.

He ran his fingers down the side of her face. "I'm sorry to wake you, love, but …"

"I was …"

"I know, but Elspeth needs you."

"Elspeth?" she muttered, rolling over onto her back. "Why does Elspeth need me?"

"There's been an accident and John –"

"Accident? What sort of accident?"

"Sarah, will you listen please?" he said gently. "There's been an accident and John was killed."

"John … John killed? Oh, my God!"

She sat up.

"PC Gould is downstairs. She's come to ask if you'll go and be with Elspeth."

"Of course!" She swung her legs off the bed. "I'll get dressed. What happened?" she asked, grabbing her underwear from the back of the chair.

"I don't know, other than it happened somewhere on the M5."

"M5. God, I can't … I can't believe … John dead?"

She pulled a velour long-sleeved top over her head. "Where are my shoes?"

"Which ones?"

"It doesn't matter. Just go downstairs and tell PC Gould I won't be a few seconds."

361

Five minutes later Sarah and Debbie Gould left Primrose Cottage.

"I'll have a shower and then follow you up," Phillip said as they reached the gate.

Sarah stopped. "Give me half an hour or so, Phillip. I think it would be better if it was just me and Elspeth for a while."

He shrugged. "All right," he said but his relief was evident. "Give me a ring if you need me sooner."

Walking up Church Lane, Sarah's emotions were mixed. She wanted to be there for her friend at such a tragic time but was also apprehensive about being alone with Elspeth. She told herself she was being silly, yet she could not shake the uneasy feeling that was still with her.

Having slept well, only waking once or twice, she felt refreshed. She had expected demons to come out of every corner of her mind but they hadn't. She had dreamt but from the little she could remember there had not been anything that suggested her subconscious was beginning to plague her with guilt. Whether she ought to feel remorseful or not seemed irrelevant, because she didn't and she wouldn't.

What had happened had happened because she had wanted it to.

Michael would keep his promise.

Nobody would ever know.

If she had not wanted it to happen then she was sure it wouldn't have happened, she was also sure that Michael wouldn't have touched her if she hadn't wanted him to.

As she walked up Church Lane she did begin to feel guilty about the way she had treated Elspeth, and the guilt had not just been there for the last few minutes. The news of John's death was horrendous; it had not sunk in but Elspeth needed her as a friend and that is what she would be.

"Can you tell me any more about the accident?" Sarah asked, as they reached the corner before Old Greg's cottage.

PC Gould stopped, placing a hand on Sarah's arm.

"I'm not supposed to say anything but I think you ought to know that Mr Davidson's was the only vehicle involved."

"So what does that mean?"

"Evidently there were some witnesses on a bridge over the motorway and they told the police at the scene that Mr Davidson had allegedly been speeding. According to the witnesses, a lorry pulled out in front of him and when he swerved to miss it he just seemed to lose control."

"I see. So if this allegation of speeding is right, he was responsible for his own death?"

She could not believe what she was asking. John was dead for God's sake so why did it matter at that moment whether he was speeding or not?

"No, Mrs Preston, that's not what I'm saying, but if his speed was excessive then it could have been a contributing factor."

"Your tone suggests that you're aware of other ... of other contributing factors."

"Please keep what I'm going to tell you to yourself, Mrs Preston, but what I'm going to say was in the report that came through to the station. They got Mrs Davidson's address from his driving licence, so Stow then became more involved. The police at the scene found a broken bottle of whisky in the front of Mr Davidson's car. The top was unscrewed so they assumed –"

"Right." Sarah looked into the policewoman's eyes. "Thank you for telling me and I understand what you're saying. It's probably best that I know. Thank you."

Debbie Gould ignored the old man at his gate, although she noticed Sarah smiled rather nervously in reply to his nod.

She had seen this man on sentry duty at his gate during their previous visits to the village and each time she decided he was either an eccentric or a weirdo, or both, and was the sort of person to whom you gave a wide berth unless, of course, you had official business with him.

Old Greg watched the backs of the two women as they headed towards the end cottage.

He took a meaningful puff on his pipe.

"Summat's up," he said to himself.

After the two police officers left, Elspeth went back into the kitchen.

PC Martin had explained that because of the circumstances of the accident there would have to be an autopsy and a Coroner's Inquest. He also told her there were specialists available who could be with her but Elspeth declined the offer. Sarah was with her now and she needed nobody else.

"We'll keep you informed," PC Martin said as they left.

"Thank you," she said.

What was there to tell her? Knowing how and why John had died was not going to bring him back and neither was it going to change anything else. She blamed herself. In the same way she was responsible for Sarah's missing twenty-four hours she was now responsible for John's death.

"I ... I feel numb," she told Sarah. "I feel numb and ... and totally confused. I don't know how I should react. Should I scream and shout? I keep looking at the clock and thinking ... and thinking he'll be home soon."

She had retrieved the bottle of brandy from the living room and after pouring herself another glass she looked at Sarah.

"Why him? Why me?"

She was certain she knew the answers to both questions.

John was dead because of her.

"Can I get you a drink?" she asked Sarah.

Sarah nodded and Elspeth got another glass from the cupboard, poured the brandy and handed the glass to Sarah, making sure their fingers touched.

Yes, she knew why John had died. It was because of the way she felt about Sarah.

He might not have taken his own life – John wouldn't have the courage to do that – but she knew him well enough to know alcohol would be involved. It was normally his answer to any problem he was trying to face.

But why wasn't she feeling as though half of her had died with him? She would cry, of course she would cry, she would cry because he was dead and she was responsible. But not for any other reason.

She realised her thoughts were irrational, insensitive and selfish but she didn't know what else to think.

From the moment PC Gould left her at the door of the cottage, Sarah watched Elspeth very closely.

Closely and warily.

The news was devastating but her nervousness remained. She wanted to put her arms around her friend and console her but her apprehension put her on her guard.

The reason why she was here was awful but it did not change anything else. Since Saturday evening her life had been one continuous traumatic experience, even though she had no regrets about her time with Michael. As she had drifted off to sleep what seemed like hours ago, she prayed that the disturbing elements of her experiences had at last ended. Each time she woke up she even managed to explain away the frustration she had felt when making love with Phillip: her time with Michael had been so thrilling that she should have realised that so soon afterwards with Phillip was bound to be a disappointment. Nevertheless, she felt the situation was recoverable ... because it had to be.

John was dead.

John, the innocent party in everything that had gone on before, had been killed. Perhaps now was the time to try to recover the friendship she and Elspeth once had, to put behind them the silliness of what had subsequently happened between them.

Was it possible? Was the situation with Elspeth really recoverable? Could the shock of John's death be the turning point in their damaged friendship?

Elspeth sensed Sarah's dilemma.

She also sensed her own immediate ability to distance what had happened to John from what was happening here and now in her kitchen.

The next few minutes or so were going to be critical.

How could she be so heartless, so unfeeling? The man with whom she lived was dead, his body hardly cold and yet she was already planning, plotting and scheming to secure her own future happiness.

She was really sorry John was dead. Could she put it any other way? She was sorry he had to die in such horrific circumstances, but there was nothing she could do about that. Of course she would miss him, she would miss his companionship, his attempts at making her feel special, his ... what else was there? Oh, God. She'd drunk too much brandy. It was giving her weird thoughts but she was *compos mentis* enough to realise it was anaesthetising her true feelings for a man she must have loved.

Wasn't it?

It had to be the brandy because there was no other cause, no other excuse. Why was she looking for an excuse?

"What can I do to help?" Sarah asked nervously.

"What can anybody do?" Elspeth said. "I feel so useless, so responsible ..."

"Why do you feel responsible?"

"Because of you."

"Me?"

"Because of the way I feel about you."

"Elspeth, please don't go there. I've come ..."

"He knew."

"Sorry?"

"John knew."

366

"Knew what?"

"About us."

"Elspeth, there is no us."

"He thought there was."

"And you didn't –"

"He wouldn't listen."

"Are you saying what I think you're saying?"

"What? That he may have died because –"

"Elspeth, I really don't think I want to hear this."

"What, the truth?"

"There is no truth. I came here to give you support because I had just been told that John had been killed. I'm certainly not here to discuss your –"

"My what? My perverted feelings for you?"

"That's not what I said. All I'm saying is –"

"What you're saying and what you're feeling are not necessarily the same thing.

Elspeth was sitting on the opposite side of the kitchen, but suddenly she stood up and moved towards Sarah, gesticulating with her empty glass as she walked.

Sarah hated seeing anyone drunk. She tried to back away but the kitchen unit stopped her. "I ... I like you as a very ... very good friend, that's all," she said with a tremor in her voice.

Elspeth's eyes seemed to bore into hers. "That's all?" she said, her speech becoming more slurred by the minute and at the same time more biting. "So you're saying that your ... your little safari up to Copper's Ridge had nothing to do with me, is that right?" She was standing in front of Sarah, looking down at her. "I asked whether that was right."

"I don't know. I –"

"Don't know, Sarah or don't want to know? What don't you know?" She placed her glass on the work surface and snatched Sarah's glass from her. "Perhaps we ought to discuss what you do know, rather than what you don't know."

"Look, I'm not saying that ..." Sarah tried again to back away but there was nowhere for her to go.

Elspeth jammed two fingers against Sarah's lips. "Sshh," she said. "There's no need to hide your feelings, not now."

"But –"

Sarah's words were cut off as Elspeth lurched forward and kissed her on the lips. She tried to pull her head away but Elspeth put her hands on either side of Sarah's face and held her in a vice-like grip. The edge of the work surface behind her was digging into her back.

As the pressure on her lips increased she started shaking. Michael had started shaking when she had touched him, but this was very different.

This was not shaking in ecstasy but shaking in fear.

Chapter Twenty-One

Michael was still smiling as he sat in his usual seat on the bus.

It was the first time he had travelled home from work since the weekend's experience, and the memory was vivid in his mind. He could not believe how his whole outlook had changed. It was as though he had been injected with a drug called *confidence*. He saw the people he worked with looking at him, nudging each other as much to say: "What's happened to him? Is he on drugs?"

It wouldn't be long before they knew because Ben would tell them. He would not be able to keep it to himself. But it wasn't just down to what he had told Ben, it was a lot more than that. Sarah Preston had given him the confidence: she had been the drug because her intimacy had made sure of that. He also felt a new vibrancy, a new vitality. There was a future now, whereas before he lived for that day and sometimes the next, but never beyond.

Now things were different.

Very different.

It was almost as though the old Michael was outside his body and waving goodbye.

It's up to you now, mate, the old body was saying. *Make of it what you can.*

He was told so many times and for so many years either directly or indirectly that he was an idiot, he was a weirdo and he ought to have been aborted after all – that was his father – and reluctantly he had come to accept that all his critics must be right.

Now he knew differently, they were not right. He might be a bit slow but he was not an idiot, and if he were a weirdo Sarah Preston would never have wanted to touch him.

Or let him touch her.

Settling back in the seat, he let his imagination wander even further.

He would move out of his mother's house and find somewhere on his own, someplace where he could be himself. He would replace his den with a small flat, get another job, a job that would give him something more to aim for: maybe he could even work for himself. He could employ somebody to do the books because he would never be able to do those. Anything would be better than just doing what somebody else paid him to do. He had a talent that he could develop, a talent that others would appreciate.

Maybe he could start his own brand of furniture.

He could see it now, people talking:

"Hello, Mary. Wow! Is that a new coffee table?"

"Yes, it's by Michael."

"Not *the* Michael?"

"Yes, *the* Michael."

"God, it must have cost you a fortune."

"It did, but it was worth it just for the quality of workmanship."

Michael had to cover his mouth as he sniggered. "Eat your heart out, *Ercol.* If you can charge five hundred for a simple coffee table then so can I," he muttered under his breath.

Sarah Preston, you are a marvel.

She had worked one miracle already so perhaps there could be another. There was no need to keep on reliving his experiences with her because she had changed his life forever. If he did it again with her the spell might be broken and then ... well. He wanted to go forwards not back.

What happened was their secret, their miracle. He had hungered after Sarah Preston but now he was moving on. She was the one who was giving him the strength to look beyond something he thought he could never have. He did not want to question why she had been so willing to give herself to him because he felt it had been their destiny from the moment she said hello on the first day he saw her and she saw him.

It was meant to be.

It was the *beginning* that followed the *awakening*.

The bus slowed down as it approached one of the last stops before leaving the town. Michael was normally home by six o'clock but because he had started late, ate his sandwiches late and finished late he had caught a later bus. It was a lot more crowded than his usual bus. He watched the passengers getting on, paying at the front or showing their passes. Having a pass always made him feel important. He liked having a pass.

He saw her before she saw him.

Wendy Fletcher.

Since the incident in the churchyard seven years ago, whenever they saw each other in the village they never spoke. He knew she always looked at him and wondered, as he wondered about her, but there was never anything else.

The passengers moved down the bus looking for seats. The seat next to him was empty but they all moved towards the back. Previously he would have thought it was because they didn't like the look of him, but now he knew differently.

When Wendy reached him she confirmed his thoughts.

After looking towards the back of the bus she hesitated before sitting down next to him. She was wearing jeans and a jacket with a sort of fur collar. Her hair was different, shorter and darker. There was a small gold ring in the side of her nose and he smiled at his reflection in the misted window as he remembered the one through her navel. He had thought it was a stupid thing to do. He wondered now whether if she opened her mouth there would be a ring through her tongue.

That would be stupid as well.

And unhygienic.

He moved closer to the window and kept his head turned away. Then he reminded himself that he wasn't the same person anymore. Perhaps Wendy was the one he should experiment with. If she responded then maybe his plans about himself, about his future, really were within his reach.

The bus gathered speed.

"Hello, Wendy," he said without looking at her.

No response.

He turned his head and saw that she was staring straight ahead.

"Hello, Wendy," he said again.

The woman on the seat in front of him was taking an interest in what was going on. He could see her reflection in the window.

"Hello, Michael."

What could he say next? He had to think of something. "Where ... where've you been?"

"Wha' you wanna know for?"

"Just interested, Wendy, that's all."

She started fiddling with the small bag on her knees.

She's as nervous I am, he thought.

"Just finished me shift, have'n I?" Wendy said.

"Where do you work?"

"Supermarket."

"Which one?"

"Morrisons."

"My mother works there."

"I know."

"I'm late this evening. I haven't seen you on the bus before."

She looked at him for the first time. Her forehead was creased with confusion. "Where d'you work?" she asked.

"In the workshop at the back of the furniture shop called Banisters, in Mill Street down by the river. Do you know the one I mean?"

"I fink so. Wha' do you do?"

"I make the furniture they sell in the shop."

372

"Wha-?" Her eyes opened in surprise. "You make that stuff in the shop?"

"Yes, with others of course."

"But it's ..." her mouth stayed open as she faced him. "... it's nice stuff."

"Yes, we pride ourselves on good craftsmanship." He could not believe what he had just said. He had said *craftsmanship* and he hadn't stuttered, and he was having a conversation.

This was unbelievable.

"Do you?" she said, smiling.

"Yes." She looked away for a few seconds.

"Michael, you know what happened in the churchyard all them years ago. You never told nobody did you?"

"No, why would I? It was a long time ago." The woman's head in front turned even further towards them.

Being aware, as most other villagers were, of what she and Sharon had been up to since, he was surprised Wendy even remembered the incident let alone worried about it.

"Well, it were only a bi' of fun, wan it?"

"You're right, it was fun."

"We was ... well, you know."

"Yes, I know, having a bit of fun. How is Sharon?"

"We ain't talkin'."

"Oh, why not?"

"She pinched me boyfriend, the bitch."

"When?"

"Las' mumf."

"So you haven't found anyone new yet?"

"Na, bein' stuck in fuckin' Upper fuckin' Slaughter don' help."

He was shocked.

He didn't like people swearing at the best of times because when people swore all he could hear was his father all those years ago. His father always swore before he beat him with his belt. When Sarah Preston had used that word it was because she had banged her head. She had an excuse. He

373

looked around and some of the other passengers were glaring at Wendy. He wanted to apologise for her manners but he didn't want to embarrass her or himself. So instead he asked her: "There's nobody at work?"

"Nah, the men is eiver crinklies or they's boys wiv spots, those tha' would be interested anyway."

He closed his eyes and took a deep breath. This was going to be the biggest test. Wendy didn't speak well but she was pretty. Not as pretty as Sarah Preston, but she was pretty. He saw again the incident in the churchyard when she had pulled up her T-shirt. He also could feel her hand on him as though it had happened yesterday. It wasn't her though, not yesterday. Yesterday it was Sarah Preston.

"Would you like to go out with me?" he asked in a rush.

"What – wiv you?"

"Well, if you don't want …"

"I didn' say I didn' wanna. I fought after what we done to you, you wouldn' wanna. Specially the way we treated you since."

"No, I'd like to."

She looked deep in thought. "Yeah, okay, why not? What you wanna do?"

"I haven't got a car."

"That's okay. We can 'av a drink in the 'otel. Go in the public bar. Ain't bin in there for ages."

"Yes, that would be nice."

"What time? There ain't nuffin on telly tonight."

He shrugged. "What about meeting you by the village green at," he shrugged again, "eight?"

"Okay, Michael. You got a date."

Phillip looked at his watch. She had been gone more than an hour and there hadn't been a phone call. The evening was drawing in and he was thinking about what to get for a meal.

He would cook tonight.

Looking at his watch again, he wondered if he should ring. No, that would appear as though he was checking up on

374

her. He would go to the cottage because he needed to see Elspeth. If he didn't it would look as though he didn't care.

He did care though. John had been a good friend. They had quite a bit in common, but especially their love of sport. The battles on the squash court and their long chats afterwards were … had been great fun.

John had been a good friend.

Sarah had hated having to push Elspeth away so violently but when her hands started to invade every inch of her body a terrible rage came over her, supplanting her fear and giving her a strength she didn't know she possessed. Elspeth fell backwards almost hitting her head against the edge of the kitchen table, but she was so drunk that she did not hurt herself.

Sarah helped her up and guided her to a kitchen chair. For about five minutes Elspeth sat with her head down on the table with her hands covering the sides of her face. Sarah couldn't tell whether she had passed out or was sleeping … or maybe she was regretting what had happened … with them and John.

After pouring the remains of both glasses of brandy down the sink Sarah made two mugs of coffee.

What should she do now?

She couldn't sit here forever while Elspeth slept off her hangover … or whatever she was doing. On the other hand she didn't feel she could leave.

Suddenly Elspeth moved and slowly straightened up. Sarah could hardly dare to look at her. Her hair was dishevelled, her beautiful face streaked with smudged make-up and her eyes … she had never seen such a look in Elspeth's eyes – a look of total dejection.

"Wouldn't you like to take something and go to bed now, Elspeth?" Sarah said gently. "You look done in … and understandably so."

Elspeth said nothing, he look vacant and uncommunicative.

"Talk to me, Elspeth," Sarah said after another few minutes. "It'll help to talk. We also loved John –"

"I don't want to talk about John," she said. "Not now. I want to talk about … about … oh you know what I want to talk about …" She started to sob.

Sarah went to her side and pulled her to her feet. She wrapped her arms around her and held her tightly. Her own tears were mingling with Elspeth's as she felt a wave of pity for her friend.

"I'm sorry, Elspeth. I'm so very sorry …"

Elspeth lifted her head from Sarah's shoulder. "I did love him … and I would never ever have wished him any harm … but I just can't feel … what I know I ought to feel. What I do feel is guilty, so bloody guilty." Elspeth wiped a hand across her eyes. "I needed you so much, Sarah. I want you to know that ..." she said as another flood of tears overcame her.

"I understand," Sarah said, stretching onto her toes so that she could hug Elspeth again. It was a completely natural, spontaneous thing to do. She had never been able to see other people cry without crying herself.

They were standing in the middle of the kitchen with their arms round each other and still weeping when Sarah heard a knock on the door and Phillip's voice asking to be let in.

Sarah guided Elspeth to a chair and went to the door, wiping her eyes with the back of her hands. After opening the door, she silently led Phillip to the kitchen.

He went straight to Elspeth. "I'm so very sorry," he said. "I can't believe it."

Elspeth bowed her head.

"Neither ... neither can I," she said.

Phillip turned and for the first time looked at Sarah. Seeing her tears he hurried to her side and took her in his arms. Still holding her he saw Elspeth's look of utter despair. He beckoned her over to him and put his arm around her. They were both crying again and Phillip, who prided himself on being able to keep his emotions under control, also cried.

Chapter Twenty-Two

Wendy was his first ever real date so he had never needed to make the effort before. After a lengthy shower, he had sprayed on plenty of deodorant and applied some of the old aftershave his father had left in the bathroom cabinet.

He smartened up the stubble he always wore, put on clean underwear, a dark-blue long-sleeved jumper under his black leather jacket, and his best jeans. He could not remember the last time he wore the leather jacket. He thought about putting on his new trainers but opted for a pair of black leather slip-ons, his only proper shoes.

Looking at himself in the hall mirror he was happy with what he saw, so he was pleased when the first thing Wendy said to him after they met was: "You look ever so smart, Michael."

"Thank you," he said, feeling a little embarrassed. "You ... you look very pretty."

When Wendy arrived home from work she had wondered what the hell she had agreed to.

Michael was all right to look at, in fact he was very good looking and he had a nice bum, but he was a bit simple – everybody said that, even his mother.

She hadn't wanted to sit next to him on the bus but there was really no choice, there were no other seats. When he started talking to her she was absolutely gob-smacked. She had only spoken to him that once in the churchyard – which she regretted – and then he said no more than yes and no. Sharon had said it would be exciting and daring and when

Michael had appeared they were already worked up, but as she said to Michael on the bus, it was just a bit of fun.

Although it was so long ago, even to this day she always felt bad about it and that was one of the reasons she didn't want to sit next to him on the bus. When he asked her out she regarded it as an opportunity to perhaps make amends. Agreeing to a date was her way of saying sorry.

It was always Sharon who had made her walk on the opposite side of the road whenever they saw him in the village. She didn't like doing it because he always looked so sad and lonely.

Then that cow Sharon pinched her boyfriend and her humiliation was added to when she found out they had been carrying on behind her back for ages.

The cow!

She would show her.

When she got home from work she had tea with her mother and younger brother – her father was on the late shift. If he knew she was going out with Michael Griffiths he would have a fit. He was always calling him the village idiot but she thought describing Michael like that was unfair: he might be simple but he was not an idiot. That was borne out on the bus by what he told her he did. He was clever to be able to do that – something her father could never do.

Thinking about it now, she would accept she had always had a slight crush on Michael Griffiths, but never understood why. Now she was about to find out.

"What you rushing yer tea for?" her mother asked, picking up a chip with her fingers and nibbling at it.

"I'm goin' out."

"Who wiv?"

"None of your bloody business."

"Don' you speak ta me like that."

"Don' forget to put some knickers on," Wendy's brother, Dirk, chipped in.

"An' you can shurrup, you little prick."

"Don' you call me –"

379

"Be quiet the both of you," her mother said.

"'E started it."

"I fuckin' didn't."

"Yeah you fuckin' did." Wendy slammed her fork down on a half-eaten plate of food. "Fuck you!" she shouted as she stormed out of the kitchen.

"Better leave yer knickers off," Dirk shouted after her, "save time later."

"Shut the fuck up an' eat your tea," his mother yelled.

In her room – her sanctuary – Wendy looked at the row of cheap clothes hanging in her small wardrobe. She often thought she could do better. The sooner she could get out of this hellhole the more chance she would have. Getting away from it all was one of the reasons she was so bitter towards Sharon. She had thought that Mark was on the point of suggesting they move in together ... though God knows where.

Bloody cow!

What should she wear? They were only going for a drink so it didn't have to be anything special – but what about afterwards? Should she let him? He might not try anything but maybe *she* would.

He was bloody good looking and ... well.

She took a deep breath. He was good looking at fifteen but now at ... he must be twenty-two now ... he was even better. He was tall, slim and she liked his designer stubble. She wondered what the rest of him would look like. She hadn't seen him with any girls so she didn't know whether he had moved on since the incident in the churchyard.

She selected a mauve sequined top that was short enough to show off the ring through her navel. She was pleased with her flat tummy. She didn't exercise or anything but it stayed flat. The jeans she bought the previous week that hung on her hips helped, not to flatten her tummy but to show it off. It wasn't too cold but even if it was it didn't matter, they would be inside most of the time.

She stripped off and went into the bathroom for a shower.

Old Greg smiled to himself as he watched Michael and Wendy walk by. He had been watching them since they first met up by the village green. He didn't think he had ever seen Michael Griffiths with a girl before, so that was progress.

He was a good-looking lad. The girl he was with, Wendy whatever her name was, she was pretty too. Old Greg puffed a little harder on his pipe as he imagined what the two of them would be up to later.

He chuckled as misty memories flooded back to him. People think when you are old and crinkly that you should not appreciate a pretty face and admire a good figure. Well, all they had to do was wait until they were old and then they might realise such approval never wanes. Those who disapprove of the twinkle in an old man's eye have a lot to learn.

He chuckled again, remembering he still had to find out why that police car had been outside the end cottage and why that young policewoman had been to fetch the Preston woman. The looks on their faces spoke a thousand words.

"Summat's really up," he said to himself.

"So what are we going to do?" Phillip asked.

The atmosphere was slightly more relaxed since he persuaded Elspeth and Sarah to move to the living room where they were now sitting comfortably round the gas fire, each with a mug of coffee clutched in their hands.

"You could come back to the cottage and I could throw something together to eat," he added.

He stole a glance at Elspeth and even with what had happened to John, he was still rebuking himself for what had nearly taken place that morning. If Sarah hadn't come home it *would* have happened and then what? He just hoped it was simply a moment of madness on both their parts.

Elspeth shook her head. "I don't want to sit and mope. There'll be enough time for that. I really can't accept that ... that John's dead. I expect him to walk into the room any second. It's ... it's ..."

"You've got to eat something," Sarah said. "We all have."

"I know. What about going down to the hotel for a bar snack. It's not too late," Elspeth suggested.

"Are you sure you're up to it?" Phillip said, hoping his surprise wasn't too evident. Under the circumstances it was a very strange thing to suggest.

Elspeth nodded. "Yes, it'll be better than sitting here and getting drunk. Nobody will know what's happened yet and it'll be quiet on a Monday evening."

"If you're sure it's what you want?"

"I'm sure. I know it doesn't sound right but ..."

"I'd better go home and get changed," Sarah said, standing up and leaving her drink untouched.

"You'll be all right," Phillip told her. "We'll go in the public bar. Nobody will notice what you're wearing – if there's anybody else in there."

"What would you like to drink?" Michael asked Wendy as they entered the bar where a welcoming log fire was burning at the far end of the room.

He was petrified.

He'd never been into the public bar let alone the hotel and all he knew was that he had seen very smart and expensive cars in the car park and what looked like very rich people going through the front doors.

He relaxed a little as he looked around the bar.

"An orange Bacardi Breezer, please," Wendy said, slipping off her coat and heading for the fire.

There were only four other people in the bar that he could see, and other than looking up when they walked in they didn't pay them any further attention, although Michael was aware that the men gave Wendy a second look as she took off her coat.

Approaching the bar, Michael was relieved when a young man about his own age approached him and said: "Yes sir?"

"An ... an orange ... Bacardi Bleeder, please, and ..."

"I think you mean a Bacardi Breezer, sir."

"Yes, a Bacardi Breezer and a pint of lager, please."

"Which lager, sir?"

"Stella, please."

Michael liked Stella Artois because it was all he drank when on rare occasions he and his workmates went to a pub in Evesham.

"We'll go over there in a minute," Wendy told him as he reached the table, "I'm just gettin' a bit warm."

"Right," Michael said, looking in the direction Wendy had pointed.

It was a small alcove big enough for four people.

"I'll put the drinks over there. Would you like a glass with this?" he asked, indicating the bottle.

"Nah," Wendy said, smiling, "It don't taste the same ou' of a glass."

A few minutes later, Michael almost dropped his pint of lager when he saw who had just come in to the bar. From his position next to Wendy he was able to lean back but still see the other group. Fortunately Sarah Preston sat down near the fire with her back towards him.

He had fully expected to see her again because Upper Slaughter was too small not to but he thought it would be at a distance when he would have been able to duck into an alleyway or turn around and go the other way. It wasn't because he didn't want to see her – he owed her so much – but he made a promise to himself and therefore indirectly to her that he must move on and let her get on with her own life too. If it wasn't for her he would never have been able to move on.

So her didn't expect to see her so close, and not in less than forty-eight hours after she had worked her magic.

"Ain't that them toffs tha' live in Primrose Cottage?" Wendy asked, nudging Michael.

"Yes ... yes," he answered nervously, "and the woman who lives up by the Green. Her name's Elspeth Warrington."

"A coupla doors down from Old Greg and 'ow do you know wha' 'er name is?"

"Yes, they live at Number One and Old Greg is at Number Four and I know her name because I keep my ear to the ground."

"Do you? Bit scruffy ain't they?"

"This is much better," Elspeth said, sitting as close to Sarah as she dared.

Her mind was in a turmoil. She was in total denial: John was not dead he was just working late. How could somebody like John be dead?

Then there was what almost happened with Sarah just over an hour earlier. Was she in denial about that too?

"I suppose I ought to add *under the circumstances* to what I just said. Am I being really awful," she asked, looking from Sarah to Phillip, wondering what they were both thinking.

"Not at all," Phillip said. "I don't think what's happened has actually sunk in with any of us yet. I certainly can't get my head round it. And anyway, we all react differently to bad news so if being here helps you then ..."

"But we haven't been in here for ages and then, after what's happened I suggest we come here. It's not just insensitive it's totally thoughtless and absolutely surreal."

Sarah touched Elspeth's arm. "Look, you said yourself earlier that there'll be plenty of time for mourning but if we all have yet to accept that John ... that John is no longer with us, then we're all here for the same reason. It's not just you and you were right, there're very few people in here and none that any of us would recognise."

384

Elspeth smiled, grateful for Sarah's support.

She could only guess what was really being said to her. Sarah didn't mean there would be plenty of time for mourning; she meant there would be plenty of time for living.

She looked around the bar and her eyes rested on Michael and a girl she didn't recognise. "You said there was nobody in here we knew but isn't that Michael Griffiths? You know, the one everybody calls the village idiot. I've never seen him with a girl before."

Sarah felt as though a thousand volts had struck her.

She wanted to turn round and look but at the same time she wanted to run. This was unbelievable, incredible, fantastic and just a little bizarre. Why couldn't the floor open up and swallow her.

God, what would they do if they knew the truth?

But she was being silly. She had promised never to tell anybody about her meeting with Michael and definitely not what they did together. Did all this really happen to her? She could feel the back of her neck prickling and beads of perspiration were forming on her forehead.

Images of naked Michael flew suddenly appeared.

"Are you all right, Sarah?"

It was Phillip's voice but it was like an echo. Her eyes were squeezed shut, her fingers clenched so hard she could feel her nails cutting into the palms of her hands.

"Sarah?" Elspeth said.

"I'm ... I'm all right," she whispered, "I'm just feeling ..."

She rushed from the table, ignoring her chair as it crashed to the floor, and made it to the ladies' toilets just in time to be violently sick. She had eaten little, and the retching was painful. As she lowered her head over the bowl, spitting out the foul smelling liquid, she imagined she was back in Michael's den doing exactly the same thing.

"Sarah, are you all right?"

"Go away, Elspeth," Sarah muttered between convulsions.

"I'm not going anywhere. Will you unlock the door?"

Elspeth pushed gently on the door and it swung open enough for her to ease herself into the cubicle. She bent down and put an arm round Sarah's shoulders.

"What brought that on?" she asked sympathetically.

Sarah spat into the bowl.

"I don't …" She couldn't finish what she wanted to say as another convulsion racked her body.

"What is it, Sarah?" Elspeth said.

Wendy slid out of the alcove telling Michael she was going to the loo. She had seen what had happened at the other table and not being one for missing a bit of village gossip she wanted to know more. As she crossed the bar she glanced at the man the two women were with and saw that he was staring anxiously into the fire.

Slowly opening the main door to the ladies' toilets Wendy could see one of the women sitting on the cubicle floor, her head and body hidden from view. She opened the door further and silently slipped into one of the cubicles on the opposite side. She sat down on the toilet seat and waited.

"It was so sudden," Elspeth said. 'What caused it?"

"I don't know … what … it was," Sarah mumbled as she reached for the loo roll to wipe her mouth. She knew exactly what had caused the nausea but if just seeing Michael had that effect on her, how was she going to keep up any pretence?

"Here let me," Elspeth said, wiping Sarah's mouth. "Is that better? Has it passed?"

Sarah nodded slowly, "I think so ... I hope so."

"Come on, let's clean you up and if you can face it get some food inside you. It must have been the shock of what's happened over the last few days. Come on."

Elspeth helped Sarah over to the sinks and turned on the hot tap.

Wendy lifted her feet off the floor so they couldn't be seen under the door.

"Look at me, Sarah," Elspeth said, turning Sarah's face towards her. "You're still as white as a sheet."

"I –"

"Don't talk."

"But ..."

"Later, you can tell me later. You've had more thrown at you in the last few days than most people experience in a life time," she said, wiping Sarah's mouth again with a dampened tissue. "First you get lost up on Copper's Ridge where you knock yourself out. God knows what else happened up there but next we hear that poor dear John has been killed and then I make it even worse by wanting to make love to you. It's all been too much for you."

Wendy had expected to hear a bit of tittle-tattle but what she actually heard was way beyond her wildest expectations.

What the fuck was going on?

She didn't know anything about somebody being lost up on Copper's Ridge but maybe if it only happened at the weekend word hadn't got round yet. And what was that about somebody called John being killed? Who was John? She knew that Elspeth Warrington – that's what Michael had called her – lived with somebody who wasn't her husband because it had been the talk of the village when they first moved in, but Wendy had just found it amusing.

If this John was the man she lived with they wouldn't be sitting here drinking as though nothing had happened. But something had happened. It was the last thing one of the women had said that made her eyes open even wider.

But, how could it all be true? One lived with a bloke and the other one was married. This is fantastic, bloody amazing ... this'll keep the village going for ever.

"Is that better?"

"Yes, thank you and I'm sorry. I don't know what ..."

"Stop it." Elspeth put her hands either side of Sarah's face and smiled. "All you need to know is that I love you and want you. I don't care how long it takes but one day we'll be together."

Elspeth lowered her lips onto Sarah's before she could move away.

Although Wendy couldn't see what was going on it was obvious what they were doing. She waited until she heard them leave before she let herself out of the cubicle. She thought quickly. If she went back into the bar from the toilets they would know she had been in there at the same time as them, so she went out into the corridor to the fire door near the Gents' toilets and fortunately it was ajar. If she could get back round to the main door she would re-enter the bar from the opposite direction and then they would never know.

"Feeling better?" Phillip asked, standing up as he saw Sarah and Elspeth coming towards him.

"She's fine," Elspeth said. "It must have been a combination of Saturday and Sunday and hearing about poor John."

Sarah stole a glance towards Michael before she sat down.

He was looking straight at her.

Before she broke off eye contact he mouthed : "Are you all right?"

With a slight nod she allowed the faintest of smiles to cross her lips.

"Have I got summat to tell you later," Wendy said, sitting down. "It'll keep this village goin' forever." She picked up her half-empty Bacardi Breezer bottle and took a swig. "God," she said, "it were fuckin' freezin' out there." She took Michael's hand and put it on her midriff. "See wha' I mean?"

He could feel the ring through her navel. He wanted to rip it out, in the same way he wanted to rip out the one through her nose.

"Do you have to swear all the time?" he said, leaving his hand where she had put it. Wendy's eyes opened wide.

"I'm ... I'm sorry," she said with a slight shake in her voice.

Michael smiled. "Good. Would you like another Bacardi Breezer?"

"Yeah, why not."

"The word is *yes* not *yeah*," he told her before getting up and going to the bar. He glanced over towards Sarah again, She seemed all right, but he noticed Elspeth Warrington was watching him, she had a frown on her face.

He looked away.

As they left The Lords of the Manor fifteen minutes later, Wendy asked: "Where you wanna go now?"

She was a little hesitant about opening her mouth at all after being corrected so abruptly by Michael. She didn't know why his mood had changed and what he had to be so la-di-dah about as he was from a background no different from her own. Just because he spoke properly didn't mean to say he was going to change her.

She had been thinking their date would turn out to be more than just a one-off. Much to her surprise he was good company, asking all about her family and her job. She also had a lot to tell him. After the experience in the ladies' toilets, she found it difficult not to tell him straightaway what she had heard, but she thought it would be best to wait until they were alone.

But that's when his mood had changed.

Why, she wondered?

"Who's in your house?" he answered.

"Nah. That's no good. Me bruvver and muvver's there. "E's a little bugger. Soon as 'e 'ears me come in 'e'll be listenin' at the door. I've 'ad ta stick paper in the key 'ole in the past."

Wendy's voice was beginning to irritate Michael.

Although he did ask a lot of questions in the pub he still didn't feel confident to talk about himself. Whenever she asked him personal questions he changed the subject. He had managed it on the bus earlier that evening so what was stopping him now?

Wendy had something to tell him and he was sure it was about Sarah Preston. When Sarah had rushed out of the bar, he had wanted to follow her but knew he couldn't. Seeing her had unsettled him, so if Wendy did have something to say, he wanted to hear what it was.

"We could try my house," he said.

"Won' ya muvver be there?"

"Maybe, but she won't care."

After approaching the house, Michael looked through a gap in the curtains first and saw his mother lying on the sofa with her head on her boyfriend's lap, watching TV. She was wearing her dressing gown so Michael guessed she had taken advantage of him being out.

Wendy stood behind him as he turned the key in the lock. He opened the door slowly but it still squeaked on its hinges.

Once inside he closed the door and ushered Wendy up the stairs.

"That you, Michael?" his mother shouted from the front room.

"Yes, Mum," he shouted back from the top of the stairs.

"Put the kettle on, love."

"I'm going straight to bed."

It was his turn now.

"All right, love. Sleep well," she shouted back.

There were times when Mary Griffiths deliberately behaved as though she was a loving mother but it was mainly for her boy-friend's sake. She didn't want Derek to get the wrong idea about her.

"What are you smiling about?" he asked as he took his eyes from the TV for the first time in almost thirty minutes.

"I'm not sure but unless I'm very much mistaken, Michael had a girl with him."

"How do you know?"

"He forgot the light at the top of the stairs. I'm sure I saw two shadows on that wall."

"You should be a detective."

"And," Mary added, "he said more after coming through that door than he's said in the last week."

"Aren't you going to say anything to him?"

"Not until the morning. If my son has persuaded a girl to come home with him then things are looking up in more ways than one."

"You're awful."

"Maybe, but isn't that why you're here?"

"Could be," Derek said. "Now *you* can go and put the kettle on. I'm losing the plot," he added pointing at the television.

"You lost the plot a long time ago."

She lifted her head and kissed his chin.

At the bottom of the stairs she stopped and listened for a few seconds.

"Fu ... I mean, bloody 'ell, Michael, you room's tidier than mine."

"It's the way I like it."

Wendy was sitting on the bed. He had remade it with a fresh sheet and duvet cover from the airing cupboard. The ones he had washed were scrunched up in the waiting-to-be ironed basket downstairs. That basket was always full.

"But it's so dark, the walls I mean."

"It's the way I like it. Are you going to take your coat off?"

Wendy stood up and let her coat drop onto the bed. Michael picked it up and hung it on a hook at the back of the door. He put his leather jacket on a hanger he took from the wardrobe.

"So," Wendy said, resting her head against the wall, "what you wanna do first?"

"What do you mean?"

"'Ave a snog, stupid. Or d'you wanna 'ear what I 'eard when I were in the bog?"

Michael looked down at her.

She had drunk about four Bacardi Breezers, which meant he had spent most of the money he had taken out with him. She offered to buy a round but he didn't think it was right.

"Would you like another drink?"

"What you got?"

Michael opened the cupboard by his bed, realizing too late that his small bottle of whisky and a couple of cans of beer were resting on top of his magazines. Quickly he tried to close it.

"'Ang on a minute, them's dirty books in there –"

"No, they –"

"Yeah they was, give us a look. I'll 'ave a whisky wiv … 'ave you got any lemonade?"

"No."

"Water then. Go on give us a look."

Michael bent down to retrieve the bottle of whisky and the top magazine, his face burning with embarrassment. He handed her the magazine then quickly left the bedroom to go for some water. While he was in the bathroom he brushed his teeth and put on some more deodorant.

392

When he got back Wendy was lying under the duvet, her clothes and underwear scattered all over the floor.

Sarah was inwardly furious with Phillip for persuading Elspeth to stay the night with them in Primrose Cottage.

After resigning herself to the inevitable though, she thought it just might give her a golden opportunity to tell Elspeth in no uncertain terms and once and for all, that she wanted an end right now to her ridiculously mistaken idea that there was any future for them as a couple.

"You go up, Phillip," she said in the kitchen as she switched the kettle on. "I'm not tired and Elspeth wants to talk some more. You need a good night's sleep. I can have a lie-in in the morning if I need it."

"We never got round to discussing you and your work and I –"

"There'll be plenty of time for that but Elspeth could do with just me being with her for a while longer. I think she was right. The last forty-eight hours have been different to say the least."

Phillip shook his head. "Are you sure you're all right? You looked awful earlier."

"Thanks a lot," she said, punching his arm playfully. "Yes, I'm fine."

"If you're sure."

"I'm sure. I won't be long."

Elspeth was sitting in the living room listening to Sarah and Phillip talking in the kitchen. Every word made her want to scream. It was the expected exchange between two people, both of whom wanted to help each other as well as her, with the shock of losing John.

Why couldn't she appreciate what they were doing?

What mattered was what had nearly happened between her and Sarah after hearing of John's death, not the fact that he was dead. So either Sarah was a better actor than she appreciated or she had a bigger fight on her hands than she had expected.

But she had something to get to the bottom of first.

What really happened up on Copper's Ridge and with whom.

She looked up as Sarah walked back into the room, closing the door behind her with exaggerated slowness.

"Here's your coffee?" Sarah said, passing Elspeth a mug.

Everything seemed so utterly surreal.

Since the fiasco at the cocktail party on Saturday evening all their lives had changed, but maybe Phillip had come out of it the least hurt: he had just lost a friend. Sarah felt that she and Elspeth had lost touch with reality.

"Thank you," Elspeth said taking the mug and putting it down in the grate. "Will you sit down?" she added indicating the rug in front of her.

Sarah hesitated then sat down and curled her legs underneath her. Her arm accidentally brushed against Elspeth's legs. Elspeth put her hand into Sarah's hair and twirled it around her fingers.

"I think you have something to tell me," Elspeth said, speaking as though she already knew what she would be told.

Sarah tried to turn her head, but Elspeth's grip in her hair stopped her.

"What do you mean?"

"Don't come the innocent with me, Sarah. That young idiot of a man in the hotel, Michael Griffiths or whatever his name is, what's been going on? What is he to you?"

"I'm afraid I don't know what —"

"Sarah, I saw him look at you. I saw him ask if you were all right and I saw you smile and nod your head, and again when he went to the bar. So what is he to you?"

Once more Sarah tried to move her head. "Elspeth, that's hurting."

Elspeth loosened her grip a little, but Sarah's hair was still entwined in her fingers and she felt a wave of panic waft through her. God, what was she going to say? If Elspeth had seen the brief exchange she had with Michael, how could she deny it?

"Elspeth, I –"

"Don't even bother lying. If we're going to have a future then we need to be honest with each other from the outset."

"Will you stop saying we have a future because we damn well don't, and it's what's happened to poor John we should be talking about. Either way hurting me isn't going to help," she said, reaching up and trying in vain to pull Elspeth's hand out of her hair.

"There'll be plenty of time to talk about poor John," Elspeth said. "Just tell me what's been going on. As far as I know Michael Griffiths is the village half-wit, he has got a screw loose and he's mentally retarded. Do you want to know what else I've heard?"

"He's none of those," Sarah said without thinking, compelled to jump to Michael's defence.

"Ah, so you do know him. I suppose you're going to tell me you also know it's rumoured he's the village's *Phantom Menace*."

"Yes I –"

"And that he's the village Peeping Tom?"

"Yes. I –"

"How do you know?" she demanded. "What's he to you? We've never discussed him –"

"Let go of my hair and I'll tell you," Sarah said calmly.

Slowly Elspeth disentangled her fingers. "Don't lie to me, Sarah. Please don't lie to me. So, what is there to tell?"

Sarah moved so that she was kneeling on the rug in front of the fireplace. She lifted her head and looked Elspeth straight in the eyes.

"I know Michael because I've seen him a few times in the village. I felt sorry for him and I've talked to him."

Elspeth shook her head. "That could be true but you're still lying. What is the truth?"

Sarah wavered.

If Michael hadn't been concerned about her, none of this would have been necessary. She would be breaking a promise if she told Elspeth anything more, but if she didn't she would get herself tied up into so many knots she would finish up saying more than she wanted to. There was no need to tell Elspeth the whole truth, there was no need for her, or anybody else to know what really happened between her and Michael: that would forever remain a secret – a very precious secret.

After thinking for a moment, she bowed her head.

"I … I didn't get lost up on Copper's Ridge," she said, "and I didn't knock myself out. Well I did but it didn't happen the way I told you all. I … I was with Michael Griffiths."

She told the story almost exactly as it had happened starting with why she felt the need to go for a walk in the first place. She explained everything in detail but she did leave out exactly where Michael's den was and of course what had happened between them.

What really happened would always remain their secret.

"and then I 'eard 'er say that somebody called John were killed." Wendy was lying on her tummy against the wall, the duvet covering her bottom and her legs. She could not believe her luck.

She didn't have any regrets about going on a date with Michael Griffiths.

He was still very shy but he knew how to please a girl.

Mary Griffiths was passing the bottom of the stairs again when she heard some strange noises coming from upstairs – well they weren't strange but she had never expected to hear them uttered by a girl in her son's bedroom. Mary knew she ought to be concerned about what was going on but did it really matter? She had waited years for him, stupid though he was, to bring a girl home. By bringing a girl home there was a distinct possibility he would move out and give her a bit of freedom.

"Derek, I reckon you could learn a thing or two from what's going on upstairs," she said going back into the front room.

"Why?" Derek said without taking his eyes off the screen.

"Can't you hear her? That girl's either being throttled, faking it or having a marvellous time."

"I didn't hear nothing."

"You wouldn't know what it was even if you did hear it."

"If I heard what?"

Mary shook her head then plonked herself down on the sofa next to Derek. "Give me a bit of room you romantic sod you!"

Derek moved but his eyes were still on the TV.

"Michael, d'you know who this guy John is?"

John? Why was she asking about someone called John?

Michael was lying on his back, his hands behind his head, staring at the ceiling. With Wendy it had been very different but just as enjoyable. In some ways it had been better. She had helped him as Sarah Preston had helped him, but this time he felt more confident.

And he had managed to wait.

Sarah Preston had told him it was important for a man to wait

With his mother only one staircase away, he did not believe for one second that she didn't know there was a girl in his room, especially when Wendy began making those noises.

He liked the noises she made. He liked it when she screwed up her face and her eyes. Two days ago being with a woman was no more than a dream. He knew it would happen one day but never like this. Never within the space of less than forty-eight hours could he have imagined he would be with two women, two very different women, two fantastic women. It was incredible. Just think what he would be able to tell Mr Foster now!

He wondered if Mr Foster had ever been with two women in as many days. He wondered if anybody he worked with ...

"Yes, I think I do," he said at last. He knew exactly who this John was. He had seen him often enough and he'd seen the photographs in their cottage. Yes, he knew who John Davidson was and he knew who Elspeth Warrington was.

Michael had decided after his visits to their cottage and for reasons he couldn't explain, that he did not like Elspeth Warrington. He wasn't sure why, but there was something about her.

The last time he saw John Davidson was on Sunday when he and Phillip Preston were looking for Sarah Preston on Copper's Ridge.

But Wendy had said that John Davidson ... well somebody called John ... had been killed.

"Who was "e then?"

"If he's the John I think her is, he lives with one of the women you were listening to, Elspeth Warrington."

"Wha'? But she was drinkin' in the hotel as though nuffin 'ad 'appened."

"It takes all kinds," Michael said, repeating what he had heard his mother say so often. "Why? What happened?"

"I don' know but he don' live wiv her any more cos he's dead. But you wait till you 'ear wha' I 'eard next."

Wendy was kneeling in front of him now with her hands resting on her thighs. Michael's gaze drifted over her body. Her hips were boyish, her skin pale and he liked the way her hair was cut, so it swung like a shiny curtain. If only she would get rid of those rings. She had a large mole on her right shoulder and another at the top of her thigh.

Yes, she was a very pretty girl.

398

Her voice still grated but that was something he could work on; he could teach her to speak properly.

He wondered if she would be willing to be his girlfriend.

Wendy watched Michael as he gazed at her body not feeling in the slightest bit embarrassed. She remembered only ever feeling embarrassed with one man – he wasn't a boyfriend but that was because he was old enough to be her father. It was after the Christmas party last year. She was very drunk and he was very persuasive. Her experience in the car park at the back of The Bull in Evesham was not due a repeat, ever. He was very rough, smelt of beer and tobacco, had bad breath and as soon as it was over he just pulled up his trousers and walked away.

It was the first and only time Wendy had felt disgusted with herself since the incident in the churchyard with the man – yes, he was a man all right – she was now looking at. He was a young boy then, now he was a man and he had just proved it.

Her opinion of Michael Griffiths had changed very quickly. She wouldn't have had sex with him otherwise. He frightened her a little in the pub when he raised his voice, and there was still that look in his eyes.

Afterwards, when she thought about it, she realised the way he had spoken to her actually made her feel good, not frightened. She couldn't believe the young, immature boy she and Sharon abused all those years ago was now this handsome, well-spoken and attractive man. He always was attractive; it was just that they thought he was mental. She didn't know what may have happened but something certainly had and that was why she was in his bed having just experienced a little of what – if she had her way – would be happen again. Yes, she really liked Michael Griffiths and she just hoped he liked her.

"Anyway," she said, forcing herself to stop daydreaming, "I don't fink you're goin' to believe wha' I 'eard next."

Michael moved his gaze to her face. She was smiling.
"What was that?"
"Them's two is dykes."
"Which two?"
"That Elspeth Warrington woman and Sarah Preston."

Michael lifted his head off the pillow.

He thought he'd heard Wendy correctly. "What makes you think that?" he said calmly.

"I don't think it, I know it. They was kissin' and Elspeth Warrington told Sarah Preston that she was in love wiv 'er."

"You must have misheard ..."

"No, I know what I 'eard. The Elspeth woman told Sarah Preston that she loved 'er an' that one day they would be togevver."

"You must have –"

"Honest, Michael, that's what she said. I ain't jokin'."

"But ... "

"Why don't you believe me? And that's not all. It seems Sarah Preston were up on Copper's Ridge sometime over the weekend, an' she got lost and knocked 'erself out. I 'eard 'em say it, 'onest."

He wasn't so worried about Wendy hearing that Sarah Preston had been on Copper's Ridge because what she heard was what he and Sarah Preston had agreed would be her story. His name hadn't been mentioned, so Sarah Preston was keeping her promise.

He didn't have a story to tell because he wasn't there, was he?

But he was more worried – amazed and bewildered – about the revelation that Sarah Preston and Elspeth Warrington were – what had she called them, dykes? He had read about lesbians but the word *dykes* was a new word for him and most unattractive. He assumed the way Wendy was talking that dykes and lesbians were the same thing.

Anyway, it had to be a load of rubbish: Sarah Preston could not be a lesbian because she would not have done it with him in that case.

Wendy must have misheard.

Michael heard a light tap on the bedroom door.

Wendy's eyes almost popped out of her head before she scrambled under the duvet. Michael stared at the door with his mouth open.

The door was tapped again.

"Yes ... yes ..." Michael said, his voice shaking.

"There's a couple of mugs of Ovaltine on the floor out here," his mother said through the closed door. "Sleep tight, you two, good night."

"Goodnight," Michael said, his eyes wide open in disbelief.

Chapter Twenty-Three

Sarah was still kneeling on the carpet, her head bowed with her hands clasped in her lap.

Had she done the right thing?

Elspeth had less right than Phillip to know the half-truths she was willing to tell. She had promised herself and she had promised Michael that nobody would ever know, but now the promises were partially broken.

But only partially.

Nobody would ever know the whole truth.

With shock and disapproval Elspeth could not believe what she had just been told. She listened as Sarah's story unfolded, wanting to interrupt on countless occasions but didn't. From the moment Sarah had described the way she willingly went with Michael Griffiths to what she childishly described as his den, she was in little doubt about what really happened.

She was still only being given some of the truth.

As soon as Sarah told her why she had needed to go walking up Copper's Ridge on her own, she guessed there was a lot more to her disappearance than she had already said.

"What on earth did you think you were doing?" she asked, like a mother scolding her daughter. "Why did you need to dirty yourself by being with that half-wit?"

Sarah's head remained bowed so Elspeth couldn't see the tears in her eyes.

She had only broken one promise but was that one promise too many? With her confession had she destroyed a confidence and shattered a dream? Had she made a wonderful experience into a shameful nightmare? Elspeth could think what she liked but she would never know the whole truth.

Nobody would.

"I'm not surprised you can't look at me. All I did on Saturday evening was tell you how I felt about you. You didn't have to go off and fuck the first available thing in trousers to try and prove to yourself that you didn't want me. You only had to –"

"*Stop it,*" Sarah whispered through clenched teeth. "That is not what happened. He looked after me, he cared for me and then when I, not him, when *I* felt ready to come home I did. So stop it. I did knock myself out and he cared for me."

"Stop what? Stop telling you what a fucking stupid little slut you are? You are the –"

"Stop using that word, stop saying that word."

"What word?" Elspeth threw her head back and laughed. "Oh, you mean *fuck*. Is that what you mean? I sincerely hope you're not going to tell me that nothing happened between you and that idiot boy who, by the way, is almost young enough to be your son and who's unable to string two words together."

"Keep your voice down, Phillip will hear you."

Sarah's chin was still on her chest, the tears rolling down her cheeks.

"It would probably be a good thing if he did. Don't you think he's got a right to know what he's married to? You go for a walk to think and what do you finish up doing? You finish up fucking a half-wit –"

"*Stop it!*" Sarah screamed. "It wasn't like that. You're so wrong. And anyway, even if it had happened, which it didn't, are *you* any better? Do you need reminding that … that you lost John today … you know, the man you shared your bed with last night. He's dead, Elspeth, and what were you doing within an hour of finding out? Trying to make love to –"

"If I'd known what you've just told me I wouldn't have bothered –"

"Why won't you believe me, *nothing happened*!"

"Don't make me laugh, Sarah. Okay, so I did need you but not because of John, and certainly not before I knew what sort of woman you really are. I'm the one who feels disgusted now. I feel disgusted with you and I feel disgusted with myself."

"And ... and what sort of woman am I?" Sarah wiped a tear from her cheek. "I worshipped the ground you walked on. I had found a true friend. I would have done anything for you because you were the closest thing I'd ever had to a soul mate." Sarah lowered her head again. "When you ... when you told me you loved me, I ... I didn't know what to do. I did love you, Elspeth, you'll never know how much I loved you but not like that. A hug, a cuddle, a shoulder to cry on, anything but ... but I'd never imagined you wanted me like that. We could have shared so much but you ruined it."

Elspeth leant forward so that her mouth was inches from Sarah's ear. She spoke in a controlled voice, her tone sending a shiver down Sarah's spine.

"Is that why you fucked the village idiot, because you didn't want to lose me? Because you didn't think I'd find out?"

With shaking hands Sarah twisted her T-shirt in her fingers. "I've told you the truth," she said, "and I ... I was confused ..."

"And during this period of confusion where did Phillip fit in to it all? Did he enter your mind at all while you were letting that –?

"How *dare* you!" She spat the words at Elspeth. "How dare you sit there in judgement when you ... when you showed just what you're capable of –"

"Oh, so you're admitting it now."

"No, I'm ... I'm admitting nothing because I will not say something happened just because your warped mind wants me to. You should be judging yourself not me."

"I'll tell you why I can sit here in judgement, Sarah Preston. I'll tell you just exactly what's been going on."

Sarah raised her head, her eyes narrowed. "What are you talking about now?"

Elspeth looked down at Sarah. "If you'd walked back through that front door yesterday morning just a little later than you did –"

"I think you two have just about gone far enough, don't you?" Phillip said calmly, standing just inside the door.

He stepped further into the room.

Sarah's face was streaked with tears whereas Elspeth's was ashen. Both women were staring at him.

"I've heard enough for one night. I am not sure whether that poor sod who's lying dead in a morgue isn't better off than any of us. I invited you here tonight, Elspeth, because I actually thought you needed your friends close to you. It seems that Sarah and I are a very misguided couple of people."

He looked at Sarah, praying that she was going to understand.

"You're not the only one who's fallen prey to this supposed friend, Sarah. What she was about to tell you was that if you hadn't returned when you did yesterday morning, I would have made the biggest mistake of my life."

Sarah looked at Elspeth, her mouth still wide open. It was obvious that from what she'd seen she had concluded correctly what Phillip was about to admit.

"Is ... is that true?"

"He's lying," Elspeth sneered. "But it *would* have been the biggest mistake of his life." She took a deep breath and tears sprang into her eyes. "He was about to rape me."

"You really are a scheming bitch," Phillip said, shaking his head and with his mouth turned down in disgust.

"Am I?" Elspeth said, sniggering through her tears.

"Get out," Sarah said quietly. "Elspeth, get out now."

"But he –"

405

"You might think I'm a slut, and in some ways perhaps I am, especially after believing in you, but one thing I do know is my husband and he wouldn't do –"

"You don't believe him, do you?" Suddenly Elspeth sounded very frightened.

"If the devil incarnate was in this room, I'd believe him before I believed you. I told you to get out and if you're not gone in the next ten seconds I will not be responsible for what I do next."

Sarah rose slowly to her feet, her unblinking eyes fixed on Elspeth's.

"But John –"

"Using your own word," Sarah said calmly, "you couldn't give a *fuck* about John. I doubt if you ever have. I agree with Phillip, John's better off where he is."

"How –"

"*Get out!*" Sarah screamed.

Michael and Wendy sat naked and cross-legged at either end of the bed staring at each other with mugs of steaming Ovaltine in their hands.

"Is your mother fer real?" Wendy asked, unable to keep a smile from her face.

"I'm beginning to wonder that myself," Michael said, unbelievably happy for the second time in his life.

It was nearly midnight and almost exactly seventy-two hours since he had crept into his den the previous Friday night. If he had lazed daydreaming on his homemade bed looking at the flickering light playing with the black plastic waterproofing and he had wished for his world to change, he would not have accepted as true the events that had followed since then.

He had a long way to go but incredibly he had made a start. There was only one person he could thank for this miracle and that was Sarah Preston. If he had left his den five minutes later he might have missed her. If she hadn't decided to walk as far as she did, they would never have met. It may not have been her destiny but it was certainly his from the moment he first saw her in Church Lane.

And now Wendy had given him the confirmation he wanted. She had taken his life onto a plain that was previously beyond his imagination, but at the same time she had taken away some of the glow that surrounded the miracle.

No, that was unfair.

She had only repeated what she believed she had heard. He refused to believe it, but even if it was only half the truth – an exaggerated half – it had still tainted his euphoria.

Suddenly he thought he might just have an explanation.

His mother had a very good friend she worked with. She had been to the house and he had seen them hug and kiss when she arrived and then when she left. Men didn't do things like that; they shook hands and kept their distance.

Women were different.

Looking at Wendy his mind flashed back all those years to the incident in the church graveyard. She and Sharon were doing things before he arrived on the scene. Anybody watching would have thought they were more than just close friends. He had seen photographs in his magazines of two women kissing and touching each other.

He understood what homosexuals were and he didn't think what they did together was wrong. If they were fulfilling their own dreams as he had now fulfilled his, then that was their business and no one else's; they would enter into a relationship, just the way men and women did. Sarah Preston and Elspeth Warrington hadn't done that, they were each in separate relationships with men, Sarah married to the man called Phillip, and Elspeth lived with John Davidson.

Elspeth Warrington and Sarah Preston were very close friends so of course they loved each other. And because women kiss each other that wasn't unusual either, was it? If Sarah Preston wasn't married, maybe there would be more to what Wendy had heard, maybe they could be ... well, he didn't like to use the word because she had to be wrong. It was the man Elspeth Warrington lived with who Wendy had said had been killed, so it would have been natural for Sarah Preston who was such a kind person to be comforting Elspeth Warrington when she had just lost her man.

He smiled to himself. He knew what he would do. He would go and see Elspeth Warrington and say how sorry he was for her loss. She would see that he was different now and she wouldn't treat him the way she had treated him before. Perhaps she would even talk to him.

Maybe, if he used the right words, she would talk to him about Sarah Preston. He would know then that what Wendy heard was not right. He could understand why Elspeth Warrington loved Sarah Preston because he loved Sarah Preston too.

Yes, that's what he would do.

He had the confidence now.

"What you finkin' about?" Wendy asked, the Ovaltine leaving a white moustache on her upper lip.

"You."

"What d'ya mean me?"

"I was just thinking about why you are here."

He leant across the small gap between them so that he could wipe his thumb over her lip.

"What, 'ere with you?"

"Yes and you may not have realised it but you just said *with you* rather than *wiv you*."

"You're not goin' to make me embarrassed, are you?" she said.

"Why can you say *embarrassed* so perfectly and yet you say *goin'* rather than *going*?"

She smiled. "Why is you talkin' the way you is when the last time I sees you, you couldn't put two words togevver?"

"Now you're putting it on," Michael said, also smiling.

"I'll make quicker progress that way," Wendy said in the poshest voice she could muster.

"You see, it's not that difficult."

"It is if you have to do it all the time."

They laughed. He could not remember if he had ever laughed like that before.

"So why are you here?"

She screwed up her eyes. "'Cos you fas … fasci …"

"Fascinated?"

"Yeah fascinated, you fascinated me."

"Why?"

"You're asking loads of questions."

"And you're not giving many answers."

"Well, sittin' here wiv nuffin' on, I would've fort it were bleedin' obvious."

"No, not when it's happened twice in as many days."

"What?"

"Nuffin'," he said, smiling.

"I'm 'ere cos' you treat me like a lady."

"And ladies go to bed with gentlemen on their first date, do they?"

"This one does … sometimes."

"I must remember that. And do ladies have rings through their noses and navels."

"You can leave me nose and me belly-button ou' of this. You're lucky I ain't got one down there and in me nipples."

"Am I?"

"Yeah, and anyway, you can start by learning me to speak proper. If you manage that I might take 'em out o' me nose an' belly-button an' put 'em in me ears like a proper lady."

"Your name's not Wendy, is it? Your real name is Eliza Doolittle, isn't it?"

He hadn't the faintest idea where that had come from.

"Who?"

"I don't know."

They burst out laughing again.

Mary Griffiths lay in bed next to Derek. His snoring meant she had managed to read a few more chapters of her book than she intended before she was ready to go to sleep.

She listened to the voices through the thin wall and smiled when she heard them laughing. She didn't know who the girl was but whoever she was she was working miracles. Scolding herself for having wished her son out of her house, she now rather hoped he would stay for as long as possible. Whoever the little miracle worker was she could stay as well as long as she continued to make her son as happy as he sounded now.

It really was a miracle.

"Do we talk about it?" Phillip asked.

He was sitting on the floor by the front door and Sarah was on the bottom step of the staircase.

"We'll have to at some stage – if there's going to be long enough to have another stage." She felt numb from the top of her head to the tips of her toes; it was as though she was anaesthetised.

"The spell's broken," Phillip said.

She looked at him. "What, between us?"

"No, the one that bitch cast on us both."

"She's not really a bitch, Phillip. She's one very mixed up female, but I could never agree that she's a bitch. Her emotions are all over the place. Did she really come on to you?"

"I thought we weren't going to talk about it."

"I know, but did she?"

"Yes."

"And you let her?"

She wasn't accusing him of anything. If either of them had reason to feel guilt-ridden, she did.

"At the time it didn't seem as though I had any choice."

"I know what you mean."

He nodded. "Was she the same with you?" he asked.

"Yes, but I –"

410

"How could she do it?"

"I don't know. I think if the four of us hadn't become such close friends so quickly, none of this would have happened. Losing John so soon after me disappearing up on Copper's Ridge ... I don't know, it might have disturbed her mind more than we thought. She believed she was in love –"

"*Believes*," Phillip corrected.

"All right, *believes* she is in love with me –"

"And don't forget she came on to me before she knew John was dead."

"Yes I know, Phillip. Maybe I'm just trying to find excuses for us all. We've all behaved badly, but now we must see if we can put the pieces together again ... but maybe in a different order."

"Do you think Elspeth will back off now, for all our sakes?" he said.

"If she doesn't we'll only have ourselves to blame. We're the ones in control now, not her."

"What do you think she'll do?" Phillip asked.

"I don't know. Perhaps she'll move away, maybe go back to London."

"Maybe," he said.

"But do you care?" Sarah asked.

"No, not anymore, not about her, but I would prefer it if she wasn't around as a reminder of what happened."

"Me too. If she doesn't move away perhaps we ..." She paused. "No, don't let's go there because neither of us wants that to happen."

"I agree. So what do we do now?" he said.

"Can we go to bed?"

"If that's what you want."

"What I want is for you to hold me."

"You'll be lucky if I ever let you go."

"I don't want you to let me go."

"Then I won't."

"We'll talk later, won't we?"

"We'll have to."

"Won't you get into trouble?" Michael asked as Wendy's eyes began to droop.

"Nah," she said sleepily, "I'm over eigh'een so I can do wha' I likes. But I don' want you to get the wrong idea. This is the first time I ever done this, you know, spent the night wiv somebody."

"It's the first time for me too," he told her knowing it wasn't the truth but enjoying the warmth of Wendy's body next to his.

He felt secure.

"But what we did weren't the first time for you, were it?"

He rolled his head on the pillow. "No it wasn't the first time," he said proudly.

"I didn't fink so, you was too good. You was shy but good. I'm not used to people bein' carin' and finkin' of me."

"Thank you."

"Me pleasure in more ways than one."

"What time will you have to leave in the morning?"

"I'm late shift tomorra, midnight till eight," Wendy said.

"But I'll have to catch the seven-thirty bus in the morning."

"I'm knackered."

"Then you'd better go to sleep."

Wendy draped her arm across his chest and sighed. She might come across as easy but she had her standards. When she was getting ready she never intended spending the night with Michael and she didn't intend spending the night when she crept up the stairs to his room. So why was she now pinned between him and the wall feeling warm, secure and really happy for the first time since she was a child?

It was the Ovaltine, she thought, smiling to herself: it was when his mother left the Ovaltine outside his bedroom door. She closed her eyes and drifted into what was going to be the best night's sleep for a long, long time.

Michael couldn't get to sleep.

He tried not to toss and turn because he didn't want to disturb Wendy, but every time he closed his eyes his thoughts leapt to his decision to go up to Elspeth Warrington's cottage and knock on her door. It wasn't right: he knew he was different now but Elspeth Warrington didn't know and maybe she would take one look at him and slam the door in his face before he could say anything to her.

But maybe she wouldn't.

All he wanted to do was tell her how sorry he was that her man John had been killed. Sarah had comforted her and he would like to comfort her too. He also wanted to see if he could judge for himself whether there could be any truth in Wendy's conclusions about Elspeth and Sarah.

She would have every right to slam the door in his face. What he had thought about her before had been wrong, he realised that now. What he had thought about Phillip Preston – he wouldn't call him *that man* anymore – was also wrong.

And who was responsible for that?

He sneaked his hand under Wendy's arm and cupped her breast. Sarah Preston had worked the first miracle and less than two days later Wendy had worked the second. She had ensured that the new beginning Sarah had initiated for him was now reality.

He smiled as Wendy's hand pressed his hand harder against her breast.

"You is sumfin else," she said sleepily.

Michael put the telephone back on its cradle.

He didn't like lying but it had been easy to convince Mr Foster that he wasn't feeling well and wouldn't be in this morning. It was all right to lie if good was going to come out of it … he hoped.

After a lot of thought, he didn't know exactly what he was going to do but he was sure a day, and maybe a night, would be enough. He heard his mother leave the house with

413

Derek and was certain she had listened at his bedroom door before going downstairs.

Wendy was still asleep.

He would have to wait until she left before he did anything.

Making a couple of mugs of sweet tea seemed strange but he was still smiling as he took them upstairs.

"You goin' to be late for yer bus," Wendy said, sitting up in bed and accepting the tea with a smile. "This is like bein' married ain' it?"

He sat on the edge of the bed.

"Yes, I suppose it is. I'll catch a later bus. I phoned work and told them I'll be a little late."

"What – 'cos of me?"

"I couldn't leave you here on your own."

"You really are ever so foughtful, ain't you?"

He shrugged.

Wendy took another sip of tea then handed the mug to Michael. "How long 'ave we got?" she asked.

"About an hour."

"An hour? Then we got time to make use of wha'ever that is sticking up under your dressin' gown, ain't we?"

"Yes, we have," Michael said.

After a restless night, Sarah found a freezing cold shower was little help. As the icy needles bit into her skin she wondered what today was going to bring let alone next week, next month or even next year.

If she were being honest with herself, she would admit she had seen it all coming. The ingredients for disaster had been there for a long time. By telling Elspeth most of what had really happened on Copper's Ridge, and Phillip overhearing everything, she had put their immediate let alone their long term future together in serious doubt.

Their relationship had been delicate anyway.

She did love Phillip but maybe he wasn't the right man for her. He had not excited her for years. Did she deserve to spend the rest of her life with a man who couldn't give her what she really needed?

Because she knew now exactly what that was.

So maybe their relationship wasn't just in doubt, maybe it couldn't be repaired. Maybe it was now irrecoverable. Michael and Elspeth to some extent had seen to that but in very different ways.

Did she really want to lose everything?

She was asking the same question she had asked up on Copper's Ridge, but now it was for a different reason. Why couldn't she just tell Phillip what she needed? He had thrilled and excited her when they first met and for a few years afterwards, so why couldn't he thrill and excite her again?

She had a sudden doubt: isn't an untold truth equivalent to a lie? Wouldn't their future, if there was one, be based on a lie?

Could she live with that lie even if he knew nothing about it?

When she walked up to Copper's Ridge she was totally confused. When twenty-four hours later she walked back down to Upper Slaughter she believed the confusion was no longer there.

Had she really been that wrong?

Michael had given her exactly what she wanted, what she needed, what she longed for, but her time with him had also, she realised now, brought forward what had been brewing for a very long time, even before she and Phillip moved to Upper Slaughter. She had experienced every emotion with Michael, from sheer terror to the heights of ecstasy.

Incredibly, it had all happened in the space of twenty-four hours.

Her problem was with Phillip.

It was a problem she should have accepted a lot earlier, and either done something about or simply walked away. Maybe even poor John would still be with them now if she had.

She certainly did not, and never would, regret her time with Michael, but she was disgusted by the whole episode with Elspeth. Michael was there at a time when she thought she needed direction: it was as simple as that and what came out of it was far more than she had hoped. That she had committed adultery, broken her marriage vows or simply been unfaithful were still facts, but not ones over which she would crucify herself. But with Elspeth she had initially allowed herself to be led blindly toward something she would never have wanted to do: it was no more and no less than that.

It had all been so unnecessary.

She still wondered why, if Elspeth had wanted her, did she find it necessary to make a play for Phillip? Had it all been just a game to her? If it was then it was the most dangerous game she could ever have played. It had already ruined one life and was in danger of ruining three others.

Stepping out of the shower Sarah reached for the pink towel and dried herself. She was aware that Phillip had got up while it was still dark, but whether he went out, had gone to work after all, or was waiting for her downstairs she didn't know.

After they had gone to bed he did hold her as she asked, but in silence. It was the wrong time and place to talk. They would need to talk, but it would be when they were both ready.

They were both at fault, but that was countered by the fact that they had both, in the end, averted an even worse mistake.

So would talking help?

The whole truth about Copper's Ridge would never come from Michael, of that she was absolutely sure. She would have to try to convince Phillip that nothing like that happened – if he asked, that is, and if he were willing to listen.

Maybe he had already made up his own mind.

If there was any hope for the future it would have to be on the basis of a lie, because she was afraid the whole truth would really destroy them. A new trust was something they would have to work on, something they would have to reintroduce into their relationship, but it would take time. She had already broken one promise to herself and Michael; she hoped she would not have to break any more.

She sat at her dressing table to brush her tangled hair and was shocked to see the dark shadows under her eyes, the lines at the sides of her mouth, the paleness of her skin, and her self-pitying expression.

Christ, what a mess.

Michael scraped at the loose earth with the hand trowel. Extracting the metal box from the hole in which he had buried the keys, he opened it and searched through them until he found the one he was looking for.

After pocketing the key he reburied the box.

Sarah found Phillip waiting for her in the kitchen.

After making two mugs of black coffee in silence he led the way into the living room.

"I know," he said, sitting down opposite her and clutching his mug with both hands. "I don't understand but I know."

"I'm sorry – but what do you know?"

"I heard Elspeth accuse you of something which you denied had happened, but it did happen, didn't it?"

Sarah nearly dropped her mug of coffee. She hadn't expected it to be like this. She thought she was in control, she thought she was going to find out if Phillip had any doubts about what had happened up on Copper's Ridge with Michael, and then she was going to steer him away from the truth.

Having curled up in one of the easy chairs with her dressing gown wrapped tightly round her, she thought she would be able to act normally ... well as normally as

417

circumstances allowed. But the tears came to her eyes immediately and started streaming down her face. Rather than hiding or leading him away from the truth, he had hit her with it and she wasn't prepared. The tone of his voice when he said: *I know. I don't understand but I know*, told her he *did* know. So was there any point in denying it?

But she had to make sure.

"What ... what do you know?"

"You and Michael Griffiths, up on Copper's Ridge."

"Yes, he looked after me until I could return to you."

"What do mean by *looked after*? Let's not beat around the bush. You had sex with him, didn't you?"

Sarah fiddled with the belt on her dressing gown. "I ... I ..."

"The answer is quite easy, Sarah. It's yes you did, or no you didn't."

"But ..."

"Yes or no, Sarah."

"I ..."

"Sarah, the very fact that you're crying and can't look me in the eye, tells me the answer is yes you did."

"I think we both ... we both have a lot of understanding to do," she sobbed. "I ... I didn't set out to –"

"What you set out to do and what you did are not really connected are they, Sarah?"

She was surprised to hear a softening in his tone, and guessed that inside he must be in a lot of pain. But what he had just said surely meant that he was more than half way to understanding, and she loved him for it.

She lifted her head and straightaway she saw the doubt in his eyes return. Perhaps if it had stopped at Elspeth they would have had a chance because she had tried to seduce them both, but overhearing the half-truths that were inadvertently revealed last night and now having his beliefs confirmed was too much for him – for them both.

He had drawn his own conclusions and they were right.

418

"I want to understand, believe me," he said at last. "If we're going to have a future together I need to understand, but surely you can see how difficult it is for me. If he had just helped you, I could have coped. But why him, with his reputation? Why if you needed to prove your sexuality to yourself couldn't you have come to me? Why did you need somebody else? I just can't believe that in such a short space of time our lives have been turned upside down."

"Phillip, I did not need someone else. I did not go out to find someone with whom to prove it physically. I went to think, by myself, to work it out in my mind. You must believe me ... it ... it just happened and whether you believe me or not, I *was* going to come to you. When I left here I didn't know where I was going. I needed to think first, to sort my mind out and that's the truth."

"And this was all because on Saturday evening Elspeth told you she was in love with you, and wanted your relationship to go further?"

"Yes, but ..." She wiped her eyes with her dressing gown sleeve. "I was devastated, can't you understand that? Somebody I considered a very dear friend, who I trusted completely, wanted me in a way that was totally alien to me. It was something I'd never imagined —" She didn't dare tell him about the fantasy she'd had when he made love to her and she had imagined it was Elspeth. It didn't bear thinking about now, but was proof to her of just how much she had needed to sort out the confusion in her mind.

"But that didn't stop you —"

She narrowed her eyes. "That is unfair, Phillip. I think we are equally to blame for what we both almost did with Elspeth. And if I hadn't turned up when I did there would have been no *almost* about it for you. You have admitted that. You had no idea where I was and yet you were on the point of —"

"I don't deny it, but I still didn't do it. I'm not proud of what *almost* happened but you ..."

"I believe you, Phillip. I admit I did have sex with Michael Griffiths, and you would never understand the circumstances, but that does not –"

"No, you're right. That does not explain why you did what you did."

"There *is* no explanation. What happened just happened. At the time I needed to find –"

"So why for God's sake didn't you come to me? On Saturday evening you knew I was worried sick about you –"

"You weren't up on Copper's Ridge."

"That was hours later, and you don't even sound as though you regret what happened. Do you regret it?"

It was a question she did not want to answer.

"If you and Elspeth, somebody you thought was my best friend, had finished what you started, would you have told me?"

"But I didn't do it."

"That's not the point. You may not have ... I really can't say the only word I can think of, but isn't what you did up to that point just as bad as going all the way?"

"Actually we didn't –"

"Did you touch her intimately? Did she touch you? Were you both naked?"

Phillip closed his eyes and nodded.

"Is that yes to all three questions?"

He nodded again.

Sarah took a deep breath. "And if she hadn't said anything, would you have told me?"

He looked at his hands. "I wouldn't have wanted to hurt you."

"I suppose I ought to thank you for not wanting to hurt me, but I have told you –"

"Only because I overheard," he said and stared into Sarah's eyes. "But *why?* I keep on asking myself why? The police suggested you might be having an affair ... why did you do it?"

420

"It wasn't an affair and I don't really know why, but it will never happen again."

"I'll always be looking over my shoulder wondering if he's there, looking smug about what you and he did together."

"No, that will never happen."

"How can you be so sure?"

"I just know and I think you're skating on very thin ice, don't you? You've just told me that you were in our kitchen with somebody you thought was my best friend, neither of you had any clothes on and you were seconds away from ... from doing it ..."

Phillip looked away, ignoring what Sarah had said. "I ought to go and beat the living daylights out of him."

"That won't happen either."

Phillip took a deep breath. "I've got to think."

"What about?" she asked.

"I think we both had our reasons for doing what we did. This isn't a contest to decide who has hurt the other the most. As you said, we are both at fault, we have both wronged the other. If it had just been you or just me, then one of us would be able to sit in judgement, but that's not what has happened. Between us we've created circumstances from which we will either recover or go our separate ways. I know what I want and if you want the same then that's what we should be discussing, not hurting each other more than we already have."

"Are you saying what I think you're saying?" Sarah said.

"I'm saying that I think the physical part of our marriage had become stale. I think we were both taking each other for granted and allowed complacency to creep in. I love you, Sarah, more than I think you'll ever realise and yet I've been very blind and very stupid." Kneeling down in front of her, he took her in his arms. "I'm so sorry I didn't see this coming and I'm so sorry I did what I did with Elspeth. I thought you

421

had left me but that shouldn't have given me a reason to ... well, you know what I'm trying to say."

"I do and I agree with you, Phillip. We either get through this or ... or go our separate –"

"Is that what you want?"

"*No!*"

Chapter Twenty-Four

On reaching his den Michael checked his watch. It had taken two hours. He had deliberately walked very slowly and used one of his longer but most secret routes. He didn't see anybody but more importantly he was sure nobody had seen him.

Although he had never intended returning to the den he didn't know when he left it for the last time that he would need his camouflage clothing and black cream one last time. He also needed to recover a few other items and then he really would make sure that if the den were ever discovered there would be nothing to connect it to him. Once he completed what he intended doing – although he still wasn't certain what his plan was – he would wait until his mother was out and then burn his camouflage clothing and anything else that was combustible. Other items he would put in the rubbish bin and anything he was still concerned about he would bury.

It was important that when he reached his next destination he should be flexible; it would be silly to be discovered when it was all over. When he made his original decision he didn't know how close Sarah Preston and Elspeth Warrington actually were. He still wasn't sure what he was going to say in order to find out the true relationship between them, but he did want to talk to Elspeth Warrington.

He was really sorry her man had been killed.

Watching her cottage for a few hours was a must and during that time he hoped he would work out exactly what he was trying to achieve. He had been so sure as he lay awake last night, but now he was somewhat vague about what he hoped to accomplish.

If it didn't work out he could always just walk away.

Elspeth spent the day in a grey mist.

She wandered from room to room, smoking cigarette after cigarette, and drinking. She hadn't changed her clothes since last night and she hadn't showered, washed or brushed her hair. Every reflective surface be they mirrors, windows or even shiny table tops were avoided because she didn't want to look at herself.

Her entire world had collapsed.

Everything she thought she had planned so carefully was gone forever. She had lost John. God, she really needed him to be here for her right now.

Poor, poor John.

She was going to miss him and wished ... oh, there was no point in wishing because wishes never came true.

She had lost Sarah.

Not that she ever really had Sarah. Sarah had gone to her when she needed her the most, and she had been thrilled to see her but not how Elspeth would have wanted it.

So there was no reason for her to go on.

She poured another glass of whisky but her mood became even more maudlin. She wanted to cry but the tears wouldn't come, to scream but she didn't have the energy. She was in a stupor and there was no-one to help her now.

The phone rang but she ignored it.

After a minute or so it rang again so she took the receiver off the cradle and disconnected the phone from the wall. Her mobile had already been turned off.

There was no point in plotting anymore.

There was no point in doing anything anymore.

For the umpteenth time she stopped as she reached the bottom of the stairs. She slumped to her knees, resting on the bottom step for a minute or two knowing she was only putting off the inevitable. So, with only one thought in her mind she slowly stood up and began to climb the stairs.

With each step she became reconciled to her sole purpose.

In the bathroom she opened the medicine cabinet and stared at the array of small plastic bottles, tubes and tubs.

She selected the bottles she needed.

In the bedroom she put the bottles and a full glass of whisky on the bedside table and switched on the bedside light.

She stripped off her clothes and went back into the bathroom, turned on the shower and hardly felt the hot water jets on her skin.

With her body and hair still wet, she returned to the bedroom, not even bothering to turn off the shower. Sitting on the edge of the bed, letting the water drip off her body onto the sheets and pillow, she stared at the bottles.

She understood the finality of her intentions and hoped it would be painless: she would go to sleep and never wake up.

Picking up the diary she had brought from her study, she flipped through the pages until she reached Saturday 30th September.

Picking up her pen she wrote:

Saturday 30th September:
Told Sarah I was in love with her, the biggest mistake of my life.
Sunday 1st October:
Sarah went missing.
Monday 2nd October:
Sarah safe but cautious. She acted stupidly up on Copper's Ridge but she had her reasons, and I don't think I was the only reason.

Poor John killed in a car crash – was it because of me? He never knew that Sarah was safe. I forgot to tell him. Poor sod. His loss was so unnecessary.

Sarah came to me. I still love her so much. What I tried to do was wrong, I know that now.

Tuesday 3rd October:

Mum and Dad, I'm so sorry – I love you.

Phillip, it wasn't your fault and Sarah, it was me that led him on, he was so vulnerable because of you and I had my reasons too. But now I know, as with you, it was so wrong.

Sarah, forgive me then forget me.

Carefully she replaced the top on the pen, which she put with the diary in the drawer and closed it. It felt as though everything was happening in slow motion.

Emptying the pills onto the bedside table, hoping there would be enough, she drew in her breath and put them one by one into her mouth, washing each one down with whisky.

When the last one had gone she lay down on the bed, pulled the duvet up to her chin and closed her eyes. The tears she had tried to find throughout the early morning came in a sudden rush.

Had she always known it would come to this?

Phillip had cried before but never had he cried with Sarah ... and now it was twice in one evening.

Kneeling on the living room floor with his arms wrapped around her he wished he could wave a magic wand that would whisk them away to a land where the past did not exist.

"I'm so sorry, love, I had no idea what you were going through. I am as much to blame as Elspeth, if not more so. I couldn't see what was happening to my own wife. I thought –"

"No, Phillip! I should have told you straightaway on Saturday. If I had, none of this would have happened. Elspeth was just a catalyst because I was already so mixed up with uncertainties, doubts and needs, and of course my desperate longing to have a baby."

He buried his head against her neck, crushing her to him. "It's over now. We must put it behind us and look to the future. I'll do whatever I can to make you happy and I'm so sorry that I took you, and what I thought I was doing for you, for granted."

Sarah looked up at him. "You do really want to put everything behind us so that we can move on?"

"Yes, but I have one condition."

"What?"

"That we talk about how we feel. There will be times when we'll know what the other is thinking and when those times come we'll talk. You must tell me and show me how I can make you happy – and not just in bed. I want to go back to how we were at the beginning and start all over again."

She bent forward and brushed her lips against his.

"I think there was more than one condition in there," she said, despite her tears. "But can I add a condition of my own?"

"Of course."

"Tell me you love me first thing every morning and last thing every night."

"I accept," he said, smiling through his tears. "Isn't this proof enough?"

"It'll do us both good to have a cry."

"Do you want to make sure Elspeth is all right?" he said.

"Is that my first test?"

"Of course it isn't but I just wondered."

"No, there's no need, not yet, maybe tomorrow."

"If that's what you want."

"It's what we both want."

Michael focused the binoculars on the end cottage.

The sun was setting but it was still light enough to see the windows at the back, which he knew were the kitchen and living room.

Behind Elspeth Warrington's cottage was a narrow fenced field. He smiled when he realised that over the far

427

fence was the extended church graveyard, which was about fifty yards from where he first encountered Wendy and Sharon. There was also a small copse comprising mature oak trees and bushes, and this is where he took up his position to observe the cottage. He had been here before so he knew every bump in the ground, every line of sight from the cottages where he could be totally hidden.

The sun had already dipped below the horizon and the little daylight left soon vanished in a growing bank of black clouds.

Elspeth Warrington's cottage was in darkness except for the dim glow of light in the main bedroom. Having visited the cottage before, he knew its layout.

He would wait and watch for any movement, lights going on and off, and while he waited he would think. Next to him in a waterproof bag were his jeans, sweatshirt and anorak. Before he approached the cottage, if that's what he finally ended up doing, he would change. He would go there openly because it no longer mattered to him who saw him.

Sarah relaxed in Phillip's arms, luxuriating in the knowledge that it had definitely been better than before.

It had to be, she thought.

They were fighting for survival.

He had said the right words, but words often weren't the same when they became actions. Promises were made but when the time came, they would not always be kept.

"It was rather special, wasn't it?" Sarah said.

"Any idea what the time is? I left my watch in the bathroom."

She looked over his shoulder at the alarm clock.

"Just after nine."

"We've been up here for nearly three hours."

"Is that a note of dissension I hear?"

"Not at all."

She readjusted her position so that she could see his face.

"Are we really going to get through this, Phillip?"

"I think we've just gone a hell of a long way to proving that, haven't we?"

"It'll take more than sex," she said, lowering her eyes.

"Why, that's all it took to get us into a fix in the first place? Why can't we use the same thing to get us out of it?"

"We can, but I also think we'll need to work on rebuilding trust in each other."

"That will come with time."

"But how long will it take?"

"As long as is necessary."

"We will talk, won't we?"

"We are talking."

"Can you take tomorrow off as well?"

"I've taken the whole week off. I phoned while you were in the bathroom."

"Shall we go away for a few days?"

"We're going to do just that. Do you remember that hotel we went to a year or so ago up in the Lake District?" She nodded, smiling. "We're going there. I –"

"You phoned them while I was in the bathroom."

"Something like that."

She kissed his shoulder then snuggled down next to him again. "I do love you," she whispered.

He ran his hand down her side to her hip. "I love you too."

In the three hours he had been patiently waiting, Michael saw no movement whatsoever from the cottage. No lights went on or off, no curtains were drawn and nobody appeared at any of the windows. In the other cottages in the row, he was able to track movement and even in Old Greg's cottage he had seen lights go on and off.

He thought it a little strange.

Even if she was out he was sure she would have left the hall light on and turned off all other lights. The hall light wasn't on now so he was sure she was there.

429

But to be absolutely sure he would have to get closer.

He took the bag containing his other clothes and crawled back to a large bush that screened him from view. Changing quickly, he used his camouflage trousers to wipe the cream from his face, and then put everything he didn't need in the bag which he hid in the bush to collect when whatever he was going to do was over.

Five minutes later he was standing in the back garden of Elspeth Warrington's cottage. He looked up at the bedroom window. The light was still on and the curtains drawn but there were no tell-tale shadows moving about, no sign in the dim light that there was anybody in the cottage.

Everything was perfectly still.

He glanced at the other gardens to his left, checking the windows he could see. He froze when a light was switched on next door but nobody came to the window.

He moved closer to the back door.

What should he do?

He had brought the key but didn't want to use it because he hoped he would go to the front door like anybody else. After all he was a normal person now, wasn't he?

Something was not right though. Living with the wild animals in the woods up on Copper's Ridge had sharpened his hearing and night vision, but more importantly he could sense danger before it got close to him.

He didn't know what it was but something was not as it should be.

He took the key from his pocket, slipped it into the lock and slowly turned it. The door opened a crack, then a little more. The number of back doors that didn't have security bolts had always amazed him. Most front doors were like Fort Knox but back doors were left unprotected.

Except for the faint glow from the light upstairs, the kitchen and the rest of downstairs were in complete darkness.

He stepped inside and locked the door behind him. Then he changed his mind: if he had to make a quick escape he wouldn't want to be held up unlocking the door.

430

The slow ticking of the grandmother clock he knew stood in the hall between the front door and the dining room was all he could hear – no background radio noise or television, not even from the small television set he had seen previously in the main bedroom.

He slipped off his trainers and placed them by the door. Checking his watch in the dim light he saw it was now nearly ten o'clock. He moved slowly across the hall to the bottom of the stairs. Having been in so many empty houses before he knew what it felt like to be on his own but his sixth sense was telling him there was somebody else in the cottage.

Then he heard something he hadn't detected before.

Running water.

He should leave.

If she were taking a shower and she came out of the bathroom she would scream and then all hell would break loose. What was the point of him being so careful for so long if he was going to be caught during his very last secret visit to somebody's cottage?

He looked up the stairs.

Something else was wrong.

The main bedroom door was slightly ajar because that was where the light was coming from, but the bathroom door was also open and there was no light coming from there. Why would she take a shower in the dark? If she was in the bedroom preparing to take a shower he would hear her moving about.

There was nothing.

Taking a deep breath, he mounted the first step and then the next. When he got half way up he stopped again and listened

Still nothing, except the ominous sound of running water.

Another step and he was at the top.

He listened again.

Once on the landing he checked the other doors. All were open and steam was billowing from the bathroom.

Very slowly he pushed the bathroom door fully open. He saw no one so he stepped inside. The steam took his breath away. He switched on the small torch he always carried with him.

Had he come too far already?

If he were discovered now it really would be all over.

Reaching over the bath he turned the shower off, realising straightaway it was a stupid thing to do: a noise suddenly stopping was as noticeable as one starting. But it was too late, he had done it.

He listened.

Silence.

Leaving the bathroom, he went to the main bedroom door.

Not a sound.

He looked through the crack in the door. He could see the edge of the bed, but nothing else. Putting a finger against the wooden panel on the door he applied a little pressure.

The door swung open and that is when he saw her.

His hand shot to his mouth to stifle his gasp. He had been so sure he wasn't alone in the cottage but even though she was asleep, now that he was looking at her he could not believe he had been so stupid to come upstairs. He should leave right now ... but something about the stillness made him hesitate.

Her hair almost filled the pillow and her face was towards him. She looked so innocent and peaceful and for the first time he saw how pretty she was.

He moved into the room.

If she woke now she would scream but she would think she had disturbed a burglar. She wouldn't recognise him, not after such a deep sleep.

He switched his gaze to the small bottles and empty glass on the bedside table. She hadn't moved so it would be safe to step further into the room. He picked up one of the bottles and read the label – Paracetemol. It was empty, as were the others labelled Codeine and Aspirin. He picked up the glass and smelt it – he knew what whisky smelt like.

This reminded him of a scene from one of the films he had watched – a detective picking up a bottle and looking at it before turning to his partner and saying – *overdose*.

Elspeth Warrington was not going to wake up.

He sat gingerly on the side of the bed and held his fingers against her neck to feel for a pulse. Her skin was warm and yes, there was a very faint throbbing in her neck.

She was still alive.

What should he do?

He must decide quickly.

Old Greg stood just inside the open door of his shed in the back garden, puffing on his pipe.

He hadn't been able to get to sleep. It was drizzling now. Earlier he saw young Michael Griffiths in the end garden and saw him let himself into the cottage. He guessed it was approaching eleven o'clock now but he wasn't sure. If it wasn't so overcast he would be able see the church clock in the moonlight.

Not a sound reached him.

Not until he heard the slight creak of a door being opened.

He saw Michael Griffiths locking the door and moving down the length of the garden and over the back wall.

He smiled to himself.

Gets about a bit does Michael Griffiths.

Watches a lot too.

Goes out with Wendy Fletcher and then pays Elspeth Warrington a visit.

Bit of a lad on the side is Michael Griffiths. Not the idiot people think he is. Who else could have built that den up on Copper's Ridge that Bert Jones had told him about?

Work of art, Bert had said.

Greg hadn't seen it himself but he had no reason to doubt Bert; after all he owned the woods up on Copper's Ridge.

"No harm done," Bert Jones had said. "Let the lad enjoy himself."

Michael crept stealthily back to the copse and retrieved the bag containing his other clothing. He felt inside the jacket pocket for his mobile phone. Having been so intent on what he was doing he had forgotten to take his mobile out and put it in his anorak.

He pressed the button and the light came on.

After taking a deep breath he pressed 999 but quickly cancelled the call. They would be able to trace his number. He didn't know whether it would work but he remembered being told at work that if he put 141 in front of a number he dialled, his own number would not register at the other end.

He dialled 141999 and waited.

"Emergency, which service do you require?"

"Ambulance," he said.

"What is the problem, sir?"

"A lady has taken an overdose."

"Is this lady a relative, sir?"

"No."

"What has she taken?"

"Paracetemol, codeine and ... and aspirin. Oh, and whisky."

"Is the lady conscious, sir?"

"No."

"How long ago did she take the pills?"

"Don't know."

"Are you with the lady, sir?"

"No."

"If you are not with the lady, how do you know she's taken these pills?"

Michael was getting angry. "I just know."

"I see, sir. Where are you calling from?"

"My mobile."

"Your number didn't register, sir. Will you give it to me?"

"No."

Michael thought he heard a muffled exchange.

A man's voice came on the phone. "Who is this speaking?" the voice asked.

"I can't tell you," Michael said.

"Why can't you tell me?"

"It ... it isn't important who I am but unless you send ... unless you send an ambulance now the lady will be dead." He could feel his self-control leaving him and knew he wasn't going to be able to carry on with the call.

"We will be the judge of that –"

"Number One ... St Crispin Cottages ... Upper Slaughter. Her name is Elspeth Warrington ... she ... she has taken an overdose."

Michael closed the call, breathed in deeply and walked slowly down the lane.

Chapter Twenty-Five

Old Greg stood at his gate, watching and thinking.

The week before Christmas in Upper Slaughter was never any different from previous Christmases. The tourists still came. They still walked and looked. The fir tree by the gates leading to the church was festooned in white lights, and electric lanterns lit the pathway leading to the double oak doors. The inside of the church was tastefully decorated and the visitors who sat in the pews were probably wishing they could be part of the obvious closeness that existed in this village, where time had stood still.

Nothing seemed to change, Old Greg thought. In the centre of the village green the traditional statue appeared, this year bedecked in the robes and crown of one of the wise men. Everyone in the village knew who was responsible for the six feet high effigy, but when asked by the visitors they all said the same thing: "We don't know: it appears overnight a week before Christmas every year, and each year it has a different theme. It's been happening for hundreds of years."

Welcome lights appeared on windowsills: there were gardens with decorated trees, rooms with baubles, paper streamers and tinsel. People closed their curtains later than normal so that fellow villagers and visitors could invade the privacy of the proud occupants.

Over the preceding months, Old Greg had stood and watched the steady stream of couples and families who came to view the end cottage. He wasn't surprised how quickly it had gone on the market, the quicker the better in his opinion. Waiting too long gave the ghosts time to get established, time to plot.

The *For Sale* sign with *under offer SSTC* pasted over it had been taken down after only a month, and a couple of weeks later he watched the new owners move in.

"It's a nuvver young couple," he told Grace.

"Didn't stay empty long," Grace said, looking up from her knitting.

Another bloody pullover, Old Greg thought.

"Don't think we'll be havin' any trouble wi' 'em," he said as he lit his pipe and picked up the mug of tea Grace had made.

"Wha' makes you think that?" Grace asked, swearing under her breath as usual whenever she dropped a stitch.

"Differen'," Old Greg said as he puffed on his pipe and thought about what had happened.

He congratulated himself when he had been half right after he had seen the Prestons moving into Primrose Cottage. Of course, he was sorry it ended the way it did. It was wrong that somebody should lose their life so carelessly.

When he heard the sirens about forty minutes after he witnessed Michael Griffiths leave the end cottage, he went to the front door and saw the police car and ambulance arrive. He heard the police break into the cottage and for obvious reasons he thought the worst for Elspeth Warrington ... and for Michael Griffiths. He did not want to think Michael was involved in any way but he worried about the coincidence.

When he saw the stretcher being carried to the ambulance his worry lessened just a little. The body on the stretcher wasn't completely covered. Elspeth Warrington must have been taken ill or maybe something worse.

Old Greg knew all along that Michael was what others referred to as the *Phantom Menace*, but he saw no harm in what he was doing. After all, Michael was doing no more than he did himself, but Michael chose to do it without being seen. He didn't approve of Michael going into other people's houses, although none of them had ever reported anything stolen. It was similar to the den Bert Jones had told him about. There was nothing wrong with a bit of fun as long as no harm came to anybody.

Maybe going into houses took the *fun* a bit far, but so what?

He smiled as he thought about when the police had come to see him the day after Elspeth Warrington was taken away in the ambulance. Routine enquiries they said. It was the same policeman and policewoman who had gone and told Elspeth Warrington about John Davidson's death. Upper Slaughter had never seen so many police visits in such a short time.

"Do you mind if we have a word, Mr Woolmer," the policeman asked, approaching him as he stood by the gate.

"If you must."

"Can we come in?"

"If you must."

He led the way into his cottage. Grace was cooking something that smelt like old socks.

"I'm afraid Miss Warrington at Number One has been taken into hospital. It seems she tried to take her own life, probably because she had lost her partner so tragically," PC Martin informed them.

Grace carried on stirring the pot, turning her head only to look at her husband and raise her eyebrows.

"Sorry to 'ear that," Old Greg said, "'specially so soon after her boyfriend bein' killed."

"You knew about that?"

"I knows everthin' that goes on in this village," he informed them proudly.

"Then you'll be able to tell us if you saw anybody visiting Number One in the last couple of days," PC Martin said with a smile.

"You," Old Greg volunteered without hesitation. "and the Prestons, livin' down in Primrose Cottage."

"Oh, we know about Mr and Mrs Preston," PC Gould said. "Did you see anybody else?"

438

You know nothi'," Old Greg almost said aloud but instead he looked slowly from one to the other. "Nobody else," he said, shaking his head. "I sees nobody else."

"Somebody called for an ambulance last night at about eleven o'clock, but didn't leave his name."

"Really? A man were it? I wonder who tha' could 'ave bin."

"Whoever it was saved Miss Warrington's life," PC Gould said.

"Did he? I wonder who it could 'ave bin then."

"It wasn't you was it, Mr Woolmer?"

"Nah. I would 'ave bin tucked up in bed at tha' time, but yer bloody sirens woke me."

"Did they?" PC Martin said. "Sorry about that."

"Probably woke the whole village."

"You would know, Mr Woolmer."

"Yeh, I would, wouldn' I."

The two police officers turned to leave but stopped as they got to the door. "When you see the man who made that call, please thank him, Mr Woolmer," PC Gould said. "He did save Miss Warrington's life."

"How can I if I don' know who it were?" Old Greg said as he took a puff on his pipe.

He never doubted the wisdom of not telling the police the truth. If he told them that Michael Griffiths was there and for more than just a quick visit, they might think he had something to do with the Warrington woman's attempted suicide.

He knew differently.

On the Monday afternoon he was in the back garden and he heard harsh noises coming from the Warrington woman's kitchen soon after the Preston woman arrived. Loud voices arguing then a long silence then more loud noises – a bit like someone crying. A little later he saw Phillip Preston arrive and they all left together and walked down to the hotel. He saw Elspeth Warrington come back much later in such a temper. It was dark, but he didn't watch people as closely as

439

he did without knowing when people were in a temper and when they weren't. She was temporarily mad, muttering to herself. Now she had tried to take her own life and that seemed to be the end of it.

Michael Griffiths, for whatever reason, had given her the opportunity to ask for forgiveness and maybe enjoy more years of her life than she had intended.

"Mum?"

Michael was sitting at the kitchen table with his mother, Derek and Wendy having an evening meal. "Wendy and I have something to tell you."

"Have you?" Mary Griffiths said, looking from one to the other, "and what might that be?"

She was smiling because she had a very good idea what she was about to be told. Something made her look at the calendar: she was sure it would be a day to remember.

It was the 20th December.

Wendy coughed and her embarrassment was evident in her bright red cheeks.

"Mrs Griffiths," she said, almost in a whisper. "Michael has asked me to marry 'im."

Mary had noticed that Wendy's speech had come on in leaps and bounds although understandably every now and again there was the odd lapse. She was also pleased to see the ring had disappeared from Wendy's nose.

"Has he? And what did you say?" She nudged Derek's knee under the table.

"I ... I said I would."

Mary stood up, leant across the table and drew Wendy towards her. "I'm so pleased," she said. "I really am so very pleased."

"Mum," Michael said as his mother turned to congratulate him. "There's something else."

"I know," she said, still holding onto Wendy's shoulders.

"You know?" Wendy asked, frowning.

"When is it due?"

"End ... end of June or beginning of July," Wendy told her, adding hurriedly, "but that's not why we're gettin' married."

"I hope not, young lady."

"How did you know?"

"How long have you lived with us?"

"Six weeks."

"You've hardly eaten enough to keep a mouse alive but that tummy of yours has certainly grown a bit."

"But ..."

"Mum, I love Wendy and she loves me."

"That's a good enough reason for me. Have you decided on a date for the wedding? There'll be a lot to do."

"Yes, the third Saturday in February and we have checked with the vicar. He can get the banns called in that time."

"Eight weeks," Mary said pensively. "That's plenty of time."

"Hello, love, have you had a good day now you're a lady of leisure?" Phillip asked as he walked into the kitchen.

"Yes, thank you," Sarah said, quickly drying her hands as she hurried towards him and gave him a peck on the cheek.

"Is that all I get?"

"For the moment," she said as she took his hand and dragged him to the kitchen table on which two glasses stood next to a bottle of champagne in an ice bucket.

"I see the couple who bought John and Elspeth's cottage have moved in today," Phillip said, looking quizzically at the champagne.

"Yes, they walked down the lane earlier. I was up in the front bedroom. They looked as though they were our age, maybe a bit younger."

"And?"

"And what?"

"Well maybe we ought to go and welcome them to the village. After all when we ..."

"No, Phillip, I think it might be best if we wait a while. It'll give them time to settle in."

"What you are actually saying is ... well, I know what you're saying. Anyway, what's this in aid of?" he said, looking at the champagne as he took off his coat. "I haven't forgotten our anniversary, have I?" He glanced at his watch. "Whew! It's only the 20th December and not even your birthday. Have we won the lottery?"

"Better."

"Better?"

"Yes, better. What are you planning to be doing at the end of June or maybe very early in July?"

Phillip frowned and scratched his head. "That's a bit far off. End of next June or early July, did you say?"

"Yes."

"I've no idea. Why?"

"How about becoming a daddy?"

The End

43122615R00249

Made in the USA
Charleston, SC
15 June 2015